SABRIEL

Who will guard the living when the dead arise...?

Sabriel is the daughter of the Mage Abhorsen. Ever since she was a tiny child, she has lived outside the Wall of the Old Kingdom – far away from the uncontrolled power of Free Magic, and away from the Dead who won't stay dead.

But now her father is missing and Sabriel is called upon to cross back into that world to find him. Leaving the safety of the school she has known as home, Sabriel embarks upon a quest fraught with supernatural dangers, with companions she is unsure of – for nothing is as it seems within the boundary of the Old Kingdom. There she confronts an evil that threatens much more than her life, and comes face to face with her hidden destiny...

PRAISE FOR SABRIEL

"Pacy, gripping and totally absorbing...I loved it."
Wayne Winstone, Children's and
Non-book Director, Ottakars

"An unputdownable book, completely fabulous."
Claire Nuttall, Children's Fiction Buyer, W H Smith

"This 'good versus evil' tale is raised above the rest of the fantasy genre by the quality of Garth Nix's imagination and the beauty of his writing...destined to become a classic."
Helen Davies, Books Etc

"Captured the mood of fantasy with such realism that I was enthralled from beginning to end, a really cracking story!"
Diane Sinclair, Sales Promotions Manager,
Askew's Library Services

"Every publisher thinks they have the next great children's fantasy writer. Harper Collins know they have."
Nick Hold, AML

DISCOVER MORE ABOUT GARTH NIX AND SABRIEL AT:

www.garthnix.co.uk

SABRIEL

GARTH NIX

An imprint of HarperCollins*Publishers*

to my family and friends

First published in Australia by HarperCollins*Publishers* Australia 1995
First published in Great Britain by Collins 2002
Collins is an imprint of HarperCollins*Publishers* Ltd
77-85 Fulham Palace Road, Hammersmith, London, W6 8JB

The HarperCollins website address is:
www.**fire**and**water**.com

1 3 5 7 9 8 6 4 2

Copyright © Garth Nix 1995

BOOK CLUB ISBN 0 00 767593 3

Garth Nix asserts the moral right to be identified
as the author of the work.

Printed and bound in England by
Clays Ltd, St Ives plc

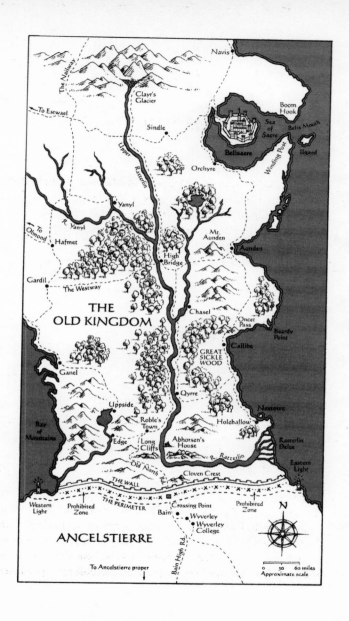

prologue

It was little more than three miles from the Wall into the Old Kingdom, but that was enough. Noonday sunshine could be seen on the other side of the Wall in Ancelstierre and not a cloud in sight. Here, there was a clouded sunset and a steady rain had just begun to fall, coming faster than the tents could be raised.

The midwife shrugged her cloak higher up against her neck and bent over the woman again, raindrops spilling from her nose on to the upturned face below. The midwife's breath blew out in a cloud of white, but there was no answering billow of air from her patient.

The midwife sighed and slowly straightened up, that single movement telling the watchers everything they needed to know. The woman who had staggered into their forest camp was dead, only holding on to life long enough to pass it on to the baby at her side. But even as the midwife picked up the pathetically small form beside the dead woman, it shuddered within its wrappings and was still.

"The child, too?" asked one of the watchers, a man who wore the mark of the Charter fresh-drawn in wood ash upon his brow. "Then there shall be no need for baptism."

His hand went up to brush the mark from his forehead then suddenly stopped, as a pale, white hand gripped his and forced it down in a single, swift motion.

"Peace!" said a calm voice. "I wish you no harm."

The white hand released its grip and the speaker stepped into the ring of firelight. The others watched him without welcome and the hands that had half sketched Charter marks, or gone to bowstrings and hilts, did not relax.

The man strode towards the bodies and looked upon them. Then he turned to face the watchers, pushing his hood back to reveal the face of someone who had taken paths far from sunlight, for his skin was a deathly white.

"I am called Abhorsen," he said and his words sent ripples through the people about him, as if he had cast a large and weighty stone into a pool of stagnant water. "And there will be a baptism tonight."

The Charter Mage looked down on the bundle in the midwife's hands and said: "The child is dead, Abhorsen. We are travellers, our life lived under the sky, and it is often harsh. We know death, lord."

"Not as I do," replied Abhorsen, smiling so his paper-white face crinkled at the corners and drew back from his equally white teeth. "And I say the child is not yet dead."

The man tried to meet Abhorsen's gaze, but faltered and looked away at his fellows. None moved, or made any sign, till a woman said, "So. It is easily done. Sign the child, Arrenil. We will make a new camp at Leovi's Ford. Join us when you are finished here."

The Charter Mage inclined his head in assent and the others drifted away to pack up their half-made camp, slow with the reluctance of having to move, but filled with a greater reluctance to remain near Abhorsen, for his name was one of secrets and unspoken fears.

When the midwife went to lay the child down and leave, Abhorsen spoke: "Wait. You will be needed."

The midwife looked down on the baby and saw that it was a girl child and, save for its stillness, could be merely sleeping. She had heard of Abhorsen, and if the girl could live... warily she picked up the child again and held her out to the Charter Mage.

"If the Charter does not—" began the man, but Abhorsen held up a pallid hand and interrupted.

"Let us see what the Charter wills."

The man looked at the child again and sighed. Then he took a small bottle from his pouch and held it aloft, crying out a chant that was the beginning of a Charter; one that listed all things that lived or grew, or once lived, or would live again, and the bonds that held them all together. As he spoke, a light came to the bottle, pulsing with the rhythm of the chant. Then the chanter was silent. He touched the bottle to the earth, then to the sign of wood ash on his forehead, and then upended it over the child.

A great flash lit the surrounding woods as the glowing liquid splashed over the child's head, and the priest cried: "By the Charter that binds all things, we name thee—"

Normally, the parents of the child would then speak the name. Here, only Abhorsen spoke and he said: "Sabriel."

As he uttered the word, the wood ash disappeared from the priest's forehead and slowly formed on the child's. The Charter had accepted the baptism.

"But... but she is dead!" exclaimed the Charter Mage, gingerly touching his forehead to make sure the ash was truly gone.

He got no answer, for the midwife was staring across the fire at Abhorsen, and Abhorsen was staring at – nothing. His eyes reflected the dancing flames, but did not see them.

Slowly, a chill mist began to rise from his body, spreading towards the man and midwife, who scuttled to the other side of the fire – wanting to get away, but now too afraid to run.

He could hear the child crying, which was good. If she had gone beyond the first gateway he could not bring her back without more stringent preparations and a subsequent dilution of her spirit.

The current was strong, but he knew this branch of the river and waded past pools and eddies that hoped to drag him under. Already, he could feel the waters leeching his spirit, but his will was strong, so they took only the colour, not the substance.

He paused to listen and, hearing the crying diminish, hastened forward. Perhaps she was already at the gateway and about to pass.

The First Gate was a veil of mist, with a single dark opening, where the river poured into the silence beyond. Abhorsen hurried towards it and then stopped. The baby had not yet passed through, but only because something had caught her and picked her up. Standing there, looming up out of the black waters, was a shadow darker than the gate.

It was several feet higher than Abhorsen and there were pale marsh-lights burning where you would expect to see eyes, and the fetid stench of carrion rolled off it – a warm stench that relieved the chill of the river.

Abhorsen advanced on the thing slowly, watching the child it held loosely in the crook of a shadowed arm. The baby was asleep, but restless, and it squirmed towards the creature, seeking a mother's breast, but it only held her away from itself, as if the child were hot or caustic.

Slowly, Abhorsen drew a small, silver handbell from the bandoleer of bells across his chest and cocked his wrist to ring it. But the shadow-thing held the baby up and spoke in a dry, slithery voice, like a snake on gravel.

"Spirit of your spirit, Abhorsen. You can't spell me while I hold her. And perhaps I shall take her beyond the gate, as her mother has already gone."

Abhorsen frowned, in recognition, and replaced the bell. "You have a new shape, Kerrigor. And you are now this side of the First Gate. Who was foolish enough to assist you so far?"

Kerrigor smiled widely and Abhorsen caught a glimpse of fires burning deep inside his mouth.

"One of the usual calling," he croaked. "But unskilled. He didn't realise it would be in the nature of an exchange. Alas, his life was not sufficient for me to pass the last portal. But now, you have come to help me."

"I, who chained you beyond the Seventh Gate?"

"Yes," whispered Kerrigor. "The irony, does not, I think, escape you. But if you want the child..."

He made as if to throw the baby into the stream and, with that jerk, woke her. Immediately, she began to cry and her little fists reached out to gather up the shadow-stuff of Kerrigor like the folds of a robe. He cried out, tried to detach her, but the tiny hands held tightly and he was forced to over-use his strength, and threw her from him. She landed, squalling, and was instantly caught up in the flow of the river, but Abhorsen lunged forward, snatching her from both the river and Kerrigor's grasping hands.

Stepping back, he drew the silver bell one-handed and swung it so it sounded twice. The sound was curiously muffled, but true, and the clear chime hung in the air, fresh and cutting, alive. Kerrigor flinched at the sound and fell backwards to the darkness that was the gate.

"Some fool will soon bring me back and then..." he cried out, as the river took him under. The waters swirled and gurgled and then resumed their steady flow.

Abhorsen stared at the gate for a time, then sighed and, placing the bell back in his belt, looked at the baby held in his arm. She stared back at him, dark eyes matching his own. Already, the colour had been drained from her skin. Nervously, Abhorsen laid a hand across the brand on her forehead and felt the glow of her spirit within. The Charter mark had kept her life contained when the river should have drained it. It was her life-spirit that had so burned Kerrigor.

She smiled up at him and gurgled a little, and Abhorsen felt a smile tilting the corner of his own mouth. Still smiling, he turned and began the long wade back up the river, to the gate that would return them both to their living flesh.

The baby wailed a scant second before Abhorsen opened his eyes, so that the midwife was already halfway around the dying fire, ready to pick her up. Frost crackled on the ground and icicles hung from Abhorsen's nose. He wiped them off with a sleeve and leaned over the child, much as any anxious father does after a birth.

"How is the babe?" he asked and the midwife stared at him wonderingly, for the dead child was now loudly alive and as deathly white as he.

"As you hear, lord," she answered. "She is very well. It is perhaps a little cold for her—"

He gestured at the fire and spoke a word, and it roared into life, the frost melting at once, the raindrops sizzling into steam.

"That will do till morning," said Abhorsen. "Then I shall take her to my house. I shall have need of a nurse. Will you come?"

The midwife hesitated and looked to the Charter Mage, who still lingered on the far side of the fire. He refused to meet her glance and she looked down once more at the little girl bawling in her arms.

"You are... you are..." whispered the midwife.

"A necromancer?" said Abhorsen. "Only of a sort. I loved the woman who lies here. She would have lived if she had loved another, but she did not. Sabriel is our child. Can you not see the kinship?"

The midwife looked at him as he leant forward and took Sabriel from her, rocking her on his chest. The baby quietened and, in a few seconds, was asleep.

"Yes," said the midwife. "I shall come with you and look after Sabriel. But you must find a wet-nurse..."

"And I daresay much else besides," mused Abhorsen. "But my house is not a place for—"

The Charter Mage cleared his throat and moved around the fire.

"If you seek a man who knows a little of the Charter," he said hesitantly, "I should wish to serve, for I have seen its work in you, lord, though I am loath to leave my fellow wanderers."

"Perhaps you will not have to," replied Abhorsen, smiling at a sudden thought. "I wonder if your leader will object to two new members joining her band. For my work means I must travel and there is no part of the Kingdom that has not felt the imprint of my feet."

"Your work?" asked the man, shivering a little, though it was no longer cold.

"Yes," said Abhorsen. "I am a necromancer, but not of the common kind. Where others of the art raise the dead, I lay them back to rest. And those that will not rest, I bind – or try to. I am Abhorsen..."

He looked at the baby again and added, almost with a note of surprise, "Father of Sabriel."

chapter one

The rabbit had been run over minutes before. Its pink eyes were glazed and blood stained its clean white fur. Unnaturally clean fur, for it had just escaped from a bath. It still smelt faintly of lavender water.

A tall, curiously pale young woman stood over the rabbit. Her night-black hair, fashionably bobbed, was hanging slightly over her face. She wore no makeup or jewellery, save for an enamelled school badge pinned to her regulation navy blazer. That, coupled with her long skirt, stockings and sensible shoes, identified her as a schoolgirl. A nameplate under the badge read 'Sabriel' and the Roman 'VI' and gilt crown proclaimed her to be both a member of the Sixth Form and a prefect.

The rabbit was, unquestionably, dead. Sabriel looked up from it and back along the bricked drive that left the road and curved up to an imposing pair of wrought-iron gates. A sign above the gate, in gilt letters of mock Gothic, announced that they were the gates to Wyverley College. Smaller letters added that the school was 'Established in 1652 for Young Ladies of Quality.'

A small figure was busy climbing over the gate, nimbly avoiding the spikes that were supposed to stop such activities. She dropped the last few feet and started running, her pigtails flying, shoes clacking on the bricks. Her head was down to gain momentum, but as cruising speed was established, she looked up, saw Sabriel and the dead rabbit, and screamed.

"Bunny!"

Sabriel flinched as the girl screamed, hesitated for a moment, then bent down by the rabbit's side and reached out with one pale hand to touch it between its long ears. Her eyes closed and her face set as if she had suddenly turned to stone. A faint whistling sound came from her slightly parted lips, like the wind heard from far away. Frost formed on her fingertips and rimed the asphalt beneath her feet and knees.

The other girl, running, saw her suddenly tip forward over the rabbit and topple towards the road, but at the last minute her hand came out and she caught herself. A second later, she had regained her balance and was using both hands to restrain the rabbit – a rabbit now inexplicably lively again, its eyes bright and shiny, as eager to be off as when it escaped from its bath.

"Bunny!" shrieked the younger girl again, as Sabriel stood up, holding the rabbit by the scruff of its neck. "Oh, thank you, Sabriel! When I heard the car skidding I thought..."

She faltered as Sabriel handed the rabbit over and blood stained her expectant hands.

"He'll be fine, Jacinth," Sabriel replied wearily. "A scratch. It's already closed up."

Jacinth examined Bunny carefully, then looked up at Sabriel, the beginnings of a wriggling fear showing at the back of her eyes.

"There isn't anything under the blood," stammered Jacinth. "What did you…"

"I didn't," snapped Sabriel. "But perhaps you can tell me what you are doing out of bounds?"

"Chasing Bunny," replied Jacinth, her eyes clearing as life reverted to a more normal situation. "You see…"

"No excuses," recited Sabriel. "Remember what Mrs Umbrade said at Assembly on Monday."

"It's not an excuse," insisted Jacinth. "It's a reason."

"You can explain it to Mrs Umbrade then."

"Oh, Sabriel! You wouldn't! You know I was only chasing Bunny. I'd never have come out—"

Sabriel held up her hands in mock defeat and gestured back to the gates.

"If you're back inside within three minutes, I won't have seen you. And open the gate this time. They won't be locked till I go back inside."

Jacinth smiled, her whole face beaming, whirled around and sped back up the drive, Bunny clutched against her neck. Sabriel watched till she had gone through the gate, then let the tremors take her till she was bent over, shaking with cold. A moment of weakness and she had broken the promise she had made both to herself and her father. It was only a rabbit and Jacinth did love it so much – but what would that lead to? It was no great step from bringing back a rabbit to bringing back a person.

Worse, it had been so easy. She had caught the spirit right at the wellspring of the river and had returned it with barely a gesture of power, patching the body with simple Charter symbols as they stepped from death to life. She hadn't even needed bells or the other apparatus of a necromancer. Only a whistle and her will.

Death and what came after death was no great mystery to Sabriel. She just wished it was.

It was Sabriel's last term at Wyverley – the last three weeks, in fact. She had graduated already, coming first in English, equal first in Music, third in Mathematics, seventh in Science, second in Fighting Arts and fourth in Etiquette. She had also been a runaway first in Magic, but that wasn't printed on the certificate. Magic only worked in those regions of Ancelstierre close to the Wall which marked the border with the Old Kingdom. Farther away, it was considered to be quite beyond the pale, if it existed at all, and persons of repute did not mention it. Wyverley College was only forty miles from the Wall, had a good all-round reputation, and taught Magic to those students who could obtain special permission from their parents.

Sabriel's father had chosen it for that reason when he had emerged from the Old Kingdom with a five-year-old girl in tow to seek a boarding school. He had paid in advance for that first year, in Old Kingdom silver deniers that stood up to surreptitious touches with cold iron. Thereafter, he had come to visit his daughter twice a year, at Midsummer and Midwinter, staying for several days on each occasion and always bringing more silver.

Understandably, the Headmistress was very fond of Sabriel. Particularly since she never seemed troubled by her father's rare visitations, as most other girls would be. Once Mrs Umbrade had asked Sabriel if she minded and had been troubled by the answer that Sabriel saw her father far more often than when he was actually there. Mrs Umbrade didn't teach Magic and didn't want to know any more about it other than the pleasant fact that some parents would pay considerable sums to have their daughters schooled in the basics of sorcery and enchantment.

Mrs Umbrade certainly didn't want to know how Sabriel saw her father. Sabriel, on the other hand, always looked forward to his unofficial visits and watched the moon, tracing its movements from the leather-bound almanac which listed the phases of the moon in both Kingdoms and gave valuable insights into the seasons, tides and other ephemerae that were never the same at any one time on both sides of the Wall. Abhorsen's sending of himself always appeared at dark of the moon.

On these nights, Sabriel would lock herself into her study (a privilege of the Sixth Form – previously she'd had to sneak into the library), put the kettle on the fire, drink tea and read a book until the characteristic wind rose up, extinguished the fire, put out the electric light and rattled the shutters – all necessary preparations, it seemed, for her father's phosphorescent sending to appear in the spare armchair.

Sabriel was particularly looking forward to her father's visit that November. It would be his last, because college was about to end and she wanted to discuss her future. Mrs Umbrade wanted her to go to university, but that meant moving further away from the Old Kingdom. Her magic would wane and parental visitations would be limited to actual physical appearances, and those might well become even less frequent. On the other hand, going to university would mean staying with some of the friends she'd had virtually all her life, girls she'd started school with at the age of five. There would also be a much greater world of social interaction, particularly with young men, of which commodity there was a distinct shortage around Wyverley College.

And the disadvantage of losing her magic could possibly be offset by a lessening of her affinity for death and the dead...

Sabriel was thinking of this as she waited, book in hand, half-drunk cup of tea balanced precariously on the arm of her chair. It was almost midnight and Abhorsen hadn't appeared. Sabriel had checked the almanac twice and had even opened the shutters to peer out through the glass at the sky. It was definitely dark of the moon, but there was no sign of him. It was the first time in her life that he hadn't appeared and she felt suddenly uneasy.

Sabriel rarely thought about what life was really like in the Old Kingdom, but now old stories came to mind and dim memories of when she'd lived there with the Travellers. Abhorsen was a powerful sorcerer, but even then...

"Sabriel! Sabriel!"

A high-pitched voice interrupted her thought, quickly followed by a hasty knock and a rattle of the doorknob. Sabriel sighed, pushed herself out of her chair, caught the teacup and unlocked the door.

A young girl stood on the other side, twisting her nightcap from side to side in trembling hands, her face white with fear.

"Olwyn!" exclaimed Sabriel. "What is it? Is Sussen sick again?"

"No," sobbed the girl. "I heard noises behind the tower door and I thought it was Rebece and Ila having a midnight feast without me, so I looked..."

"What!" exclaimed Sabriel, alarmed. No one opened outside doors in the middle of the night, not this close to the Old Kingdom.

"I'm sorry," cried Olwyn. "I didn't mean to. I don't know why I did. It wasn't Rebece and Ila – it was a black shape and it tried to get in. I slammed the door..."

Sabriel threw the teacup aside and pushed past Olwyn. She was already halfway down the corridor before she heard the porcelain smash behind her and Olwyn's horrified gasp at such cavalier treatment of good china. She ignored it and broke into a run, slapping on the light switches as she ran towards the open door of the west dormitory. As she reached it, screams broke out inside, rapidly crescendoing to an hysterical chorus. There were forty girls in the dormitory – most of the First Form, all under the age of eleven. Sabriel took a deep breath and stepped into the doorway, fingers crooked in a spell-casting stance. Even before she looked, she felt the presence of death.

The dormitory was very long and narrow, with a low roof and small windows. Beds and dressers lined each side. At the far end, a door led to the West Tower steps. It was supposed to be locked inside and out, but locks rarely prevailed against the powers of the Old Kingdom.

The door was open. An intensely dark shape stood there, as if someone had cut a man-shaped figure out of the night, carefully choosing a piece devoid of stars. It had no features at all, but the head quested from side to side, as if whatever senses it did possess worked in a narrow range. Curiously, it carried an absolutely mundane sack in one four-fingered hand, the rough-woven cloth in stark contrast to its own surreal flesh.

Sabriel's hands moved in a complicated gesture, drawing the symbols of the Charter that intimated sleep, quiet and rest. With a flourish, she indicated both sides of the dormitory and drew one of the master symbols, drawing all together. Instantly, every girl in the room stopped screaming and slowly subsided back on to her bed.

The creature's head stopped moving and Sabriel knew its attention was now centred on her. Slowly it moved, lifting one clumsy leg and swinging it forward, resting for a moment, then swinging the other a little past the first. A lumbering, rolling motion, that made an eerie, shuffling noise on the thin carpet. As it passed each bed, the electric lights above them flared once and went out.

Sabriel let her hands fall to her side and focused her eyes on the centre of the creature's torso, feeling the stuff of which it was made. She had come without any of her instruments or tools, but that led to only a moment's hesitation before she let herself slip over the border into Death, her eyes still on the intruder.

The river flowed around her legs, cold as always. The light, grey and without warmth, still stretched to an entirely flat horizon. In the distance, she could hear the roar of the First Gate. She could see the creature's true shape clearly now, not wrapped in the aura of death which it carried to the living world. It was an Old Kingdom denizen, vaguely humanoid, but more like an ape than a man and obviously only semi-intelligent. But there was more to it than that, and Sabriel felt the clutch of fear as she saw the black thread that came from the creature's back and ran into the river. Somewhere, beyond the First Gate, or even further, that umbilical rested in the hands of an Adept. As long as the thread existed the creature would be totally under the control of its master, who could use its senses and spirit as it saw fit.

Something tugged at Sabriel's physical body and she reluctantly twitched her senses back to the living world, a slight feeling of nausea rising in her as a wave of warmth rushed over her death-chilled body.

"What is it?" said a calm voice, close to Sabriel's ear. An old voice, tinged with the power of Charter Magic — Miss Greenwood, the Magistrix of the school.

"It's a Dead servant — a spirit form," replied Sabriel, her attention back on the creature. It was halfway down the dorm, still single-mindedly rolling one leg after the other. "Without free will. Something sent it back to the living world. It's controlled from beyond the First Gate."

."Why is it here?" asked the Magistrix. Her voice sounded calm, but Sabriel felt the Charter symbols gathering in her voice, forming on her tongue – symbols that would unleash lightning and flame, the destructive powers of the earth.

"It's not obviously malign, nor has it attempted any actual harm..." replied Sabriel slowly, her mind working over the possibilities. She was used to explaining purely necromantic aspects of magic to Miss Greenwood. The Magistrix had taught her Charter Magic, but necromancy was definitely not on the syllabus. Sabriel had learned more than she wanted to know about necromancy from her father... and the Dead themselves. "Don't do anything for a moment. I will attempt to speak with it."

The cold washed over her again, biting into her, as the river gushed around her legs, eager to pull her over and carry her away. Sabriel exerted her will and the cold became simply a sensation, without danger, the current merely a pleasing vibration about the feet.

The creature was close now, as it was in the living world. Sabriel held out both her hands and clapped, the sharp sound echoing for longer than it would anywhere else. Before the echo died, Sabriel whistled several notes and they echoed too, sweet sounds within the harshness of the handclap.

The thing flinched at the sound and stepped back, putting both hands to its ears. As it did so, it dropped the sack. Sabriel started in surprise. She hadn't noticed the sack before, possibly because she hadn't expected it to be there. Very few inanimate things existed in both realms, the living and the dead.

She was even more surprised as the creature suddenly bent forward and plunged into the water, hands searching for the sack. It found it almost at once, but not without losing its footing. As the sack surfaced, the current forced the creature under. Sabriel breathed a sigh of relief as she saw it slide away, then gasped as its head broke the surface and it cried out: "Sabriel! My messenger! Take the sack!" The voice was Abhorsen's.

Sabriel ran forward and an arm pushed out towards her, the neck of the sack clutched in its fingers. She reached out, missed, then tried again. The sack was secure in her grasp, as the current took the creature completely under. Sabriel looked after it, hearing the roar of the First Gate suddenly increase as it always did when someone passed its falls. She turned and started to slog back against the current to a point where she could easily return to life. The sack in her hand was heavy and there was a leaden feeling in her stomach. If the messenger was truly Abhorsen's, then he himself was unable to return to the realm of the living.

And that meant he was either dead or trapped by something that should have passed beyond the Final Gate.

Once again, a wave of nausea overcame her and Sabriel fell to her knees, shaking. She could feel the Magistrix's hand on her shoulder, but her attention was fastened on the sack she held in her hand. She didn't need to look to know that the creature was gone. Its manifestation into the living world had ceased as its spirit had gone past the First Gate. Only a pile of grave mould would remain, to be swept aside in the morning.

"What did you do?" asked the Magistrix, as Sabriel brushed her hands through her hair, ice crystals falling from her hands on to the sack that lay in front of her knees.

"It had a message for me," replied Sabriel. "So I took it."

She opened the sack and reached inside. A sword hilt met her grasp, so she drew it out, still scabbarded, and put it to one side. She didn't need to draw it to see the Charter symbols etched along its blade – the dull emerald in the pommel and the worn bronze-plated cross-guard were as familiar to her as the school's uninspired cutlery. It was Abhorsen's sword.

The leather bandoleer she drew out next was an old brown belt, a hands-breadth wide, which always smelled faintly of beeswax. Seven tubular leather pouches hung from it, starting with one the size of a small pill bottle; growing larger, till the seventh was almost the size of a jar. The bandoleer was designed to be worn across the chest, with the pouches hanging down. Sabriel opened the smallest and pulled out a tiny silver bell, with a dark, deeply-polished mahogany handle. She held it gently, but the clapper still swung slightly and the bell made a high, sweet note that somehow lingered in the mind, even after the sound was gone.

"Father's instruments," whispered Sabriel. "The tools of a necromancer."

"But there are Charter marks engraved on the bell... and the handle!" interjected the Magistrix, who was looking down with fascination. "Necromancy is Free Magic, not governed by the Charter..."

"Father's was different," replied Sabriel distantly, still staring at the bell she held in her hand, thinking of her father's brown, lined hands holding the bells. "Binding, not raising. He was a faithful servant of the Charter."

"You're going to be leaving us, aren't you?" the Magistrix said suddenly, as Sabriel replaced the bell and stood up, sword in one hand, bandoleer in the other. "I just saw it, in the reflection of the bell. You were crossing the Wall..."

"Yes. Into the Old Kingdom," said Sabriel, with sudden realisation. "Something has happened to Father... but I'll find him... so I swear by the Charter I bear."

She touched the Charter mark on her forehead, which glowed briefly and then faded so that it might never have been. The Magistrix nodded and touched a hand to her own forehead, where a glowing mark suddenly obscured all the patterns of time. As it faded, rustling noises and faint whimpers began to sound along both sides of the dormitory.

"I'll shut the door and explain to the girls," the Magistrix said firmly. "You'd better go and... prepare for tomorrow."

Sabriel nodded and left, trying to fix her mind on the practicalities of the journey, rather than on what could have happened to her father. She would take a cab as early as possible into Bain, the nearest town, and then a bus to the Ancelstierre Perimeter that faced the Wall. With luck, she would be there by early afternoon...

Behind these plans, her thoughts kept jumping back to Abhorsen. What could have happened to trap him in Death? And what could she really hope to do about it, even if she did get to the Old Kingdom?

chapter two

The Perimeter in Ancelstierre ran from coast to coast, parallel to the Wall and perhaps half a mile from it. Concertina wire lay like worms impaled on rusting steel pickets; forward defences for an interlocking network of trenches and concrete pillboxes. Many of these strong points were designed to control the ground behind them as well as in front, and almost as much barbed wire stretched behind the trenches, guarding the rear.

In fact, the Perimeter was much more successful at keeping people from Ancelstierre out of the Old Kingdom than it was at preventing things from the Old Kingdom going the other way. Anything powerful enough to cross the Wall usually retained enough magic to assume the shape of a soldier; or to become invisible and simply go where it willed, regardless of barbed wire, bullets, hand grenades and mortar bombs – which often didn't work at all, particularly when the wind was blowing from the north, out of the Old Kingdom.

Due to the unreliability of technology, the Ancelstierran

soldiers of the Perimeter garrison wore mail over their khaki battledress, had nasal and neck bars on their helmets and carried extremely old-fashioned sword-bayonets in well-worn scabbards. Shields, or more correctly, "bucklers, small, Perimeter garrison only," were carried on their backs, the factory khaki long since submerged under brightly painted regimental or personal signs. Camouflage was not considered an issue at this particular posting.

Sabriel watched a platoon of young soldiers march past the bus, while she waited for the tourists ahead of her to stampede through the front door and wondered what they thought of their strange duties. Most would have to be conscripts from far to the South, where no magic crept over the Wall and widened the cracks in what they thought of as reality. Here, she could feel magic potential brewing, lurking in the atmosphere like charged air before a thunderstorm.

The Wall itself looked normal enough, past the wasteland of wire and trenches. Just like any other medieval remnant. It was stone and old, about forty feet high and crenellated. Nothing remarkable, until the realisation set in that it was in a perfect state of preservation. And for those with the sight, the very stones crawled with Charter marks – marks in constant motion, twisting and turning, sliding and rearranging themselves under a skin of stone.

The final confirmation of strangeness lay beyond the Wall. It was clear and cool on the Ancelstierre side, and the sun was shining – but Sabriel could see snow falling steadily behind the Wall, and snow-heavy clouds clustered right up to the Wall, where they suddenly stopped, as if some mighty weather-knife had simply sheared through the sky.

Sabriel watched the snow fall and gave thanks for her almanac. Printed by letterpress, the type had left ridges in the thick, linen-rich paper, making the many handwritten annotations waver precariously between the lines. One spidery remark, written in a hand she knew wasn't her father's, gave the weather to be expected under the respective calendars for each country. Ancelstierre had "Autumn, likely to be cool". The Old Kingdom had "Winter. Bound to be snowing. Skis or snow shoes".

The last tourist left, eager to reach the observation platform. Although the Army and the Government discouraged tourists, and there was no accommodation for them within twenty miles of the Wall, one bus-load a day was allowed to come and view the Wall from a tower located well behind the lines of the Perimeter. Even this concession was often cancelled, for when the wind blew from the north, the bus would inexplicably break down a few miles short of the tower and the tourists would have to help push it back towards Bain – only to see it start again just as mysteriously as it stopped.

The authorities also made some slight allowance for the few people authorised to travel from Ancelstierre to the Old Kingdom, as Sabriel saw after she had successfully negotiated the bus's steps with her backpack, cross-country skis, stocks and sword, all threatening to go in different directions. A large sign next to the bus stop proclaimed:

PERIMETER COMMAND
NORTHERN ARMY GROUP

Unauthorised egress from the Perimeter Zone
is strictly forbidden.
Anyone attempting to cross the Perimeter Zone
will be shot without warning.
Authorised travellers must report to the
Perimeter Command HQ.

REMEMBER – NO WARNING WILL BE MADE

Sabriel read the note with interest and felt a quickening sense of excitement start within her. Her memories of the Old Kingdom were dim, from the perspective of a child, but she felt a sense of mystery and wonder kindle with the force of the Charter Magic she felt around her – a sense of something so much more alive than the bitumened parade ground, and the scarlet warning sign. And much more freedom than Wyverley College.

But that feeling of wonder and excitement came laced with a dread that she couldn't shake, a dread made up of fear for what might be happening to her father... what might have already happened...

The arrow on the sign indicating where authorised travellers should go seemed to point in the direction of a bitumen parade ground, lined with white-painted rocks, and a number of unprepossessing wooden buildings. Other than that, there were simply the beginnings of the communication trenches that sank into the ground and then zigzagged their way to the double line of trenches, blockhouses and fortifications that confronted the Wall.

Sabriel studied them for a while, and saw the flash of colour as several soldiers hopped out of one trench and went forward to the wire. They seemed to be carrying spears rather than rifles and she wondered why the Perimeter was built for modern war, but manned by people expecting something rather more medieval. Then she remembered a conversation with her father and his comment that the Perimeter had been designed far away in the south, where they refused to admit that this Perimeter was different from any other contested border. Up until a century or so ago, there had also been a wall on the Ancelstierre side. A lowish wall, made of rammed earth and peat, but a successful one.

Recalling that conversation, her eyes made out a low rise of scarred earth in the middle of the desolation of wire and she realised that was where the southern wall had been. Peering at it, she also realised that what she had taken to be loose pickets between lines of concertina wire were something different – tall constructs more like the trunks of small trees stripped of every branch. They seemed familiar to her, but she couldn't place what they were.

Sabriel was still staring at them, thinking, when a loud and not very pleasant voice erupted a little way behind her right ear.

"What do you think you're doing, miss? You can't loiter about here. On the bus or up to the Tower!"

Sabriel winced and turned as quickly as she could, skis sliding one way and stocks the other, framing her head in a St Andrew's Cross. The voice belonged to a large, but fairly young soldier, whose bristling moustaches were more evidence of martial ambition than proof of them. He had two gilded bands on his sleeve, but didn't wear the mail hauberk and helmet Sabriel had seen on the other soldiers. He smelled of shaving cream and talc, and was so clean, polished and full of himself that Sabriel immediately catalogued him as some sort of natural bureaucrat currently disguised as a soldier.

"I am a citizen of the Old Kingdom," she replied quietly, staring back into his red, flushed face and piggy eyes in the manner which Miss Prionte had taught her girls to instruct lesser domestic servants in Etiquette IV. "I am returning there."

"Papers!" demanded the soldier, after a moment's hesitation at the words, "Old Kingdom".

Sabriel gave a frosty smile (also part of Miss Prionte's curriculum) and made a ritual movement with the tips of her fingers – the symbol of disclosing, of things hidden becoming seen, of unfolding. As her fingers sketched, she formed the symbol in her mind, linking it with the papers she carried in the inner pocket of her leather tunic. Finger-sketched and mind-drawn symbol merged, and the papers were in her hand. An Ancelstierre passport, as well as the much rarer document the Ancelstierre Perimeter Command issued to people who had traffic in both countries: a hand-bound document printed by letterpress on handmade paper, with an artist's sketch instead of a photograph and prints from thumbs and toes in a purple ink.

The soldier blinked, but said nothing. Perhaps, thought Sabriel, as he took the proffered documents, the man thought it was a parlour trick. Or perhaps he just didn't notice. Maybe Charter Magic was common here, so close to the Wall.

The man looked through her documents carefully, but without real interest. Sabriel now felt certain that he was no one important from the way he pawed through her special passport. He'd obviously never seen one before. Mischievously, she started to weave the Charter mark for a snatch or catch, to flick the papers out of his hands and back into her pocket before his piggy eyes worked out what was going on.

But, in the first second of motion, she felt the flare of other Charter Magic to either side and behind her – and heard the clattering of hobnails on the bitumen. Her head snapped back from the papers and she felt her hair whisk across her forehead as she looked from side to side. Soldiers were pouring out of the huts and out of the trenches, sword-bayonets in their hands and rifles at the shoulder. Several of them wore badges that she realised marked them as Charter Mages. Their fingers were weaving warding symbols and barriers that would lock Sabriel into her footsteps, tie her to her shadow. Crude magic, but strongly cast.

Instinctively, Sabriel's mind and hands flashed into the sequence of symbols that would wipe clean these bonds, but her skis shifted and fell into the crook of her elbow, and she winced at the blow.

At the same time, a soldier ran ahead of the others, sunlight glinting on the silver stars on his helmet.

"Stop!" he shouted. "Corporal, step back from her!"

The corporal, deaf to the hum of Charter Magic, blind to the flare of half-wrought signs, looked up from her papers and gaped for a second, fear erasing his features. He dropped the passports and stumbled back.

In his face, Sabriel suddenly realised what it meant to use magic on the Perimeter and she held herself absolutely still, blanking out the partly-made signs in her mind. Her skis slipped further down her arm, the bindings catching for a moment before tearing loose and clattering on to the ground. Soldiers rushed forward and, in seconds, formed a ring around her, swords angled towards her throat. She saw streaks of silver, plated on to the blades, and crudely written Charter symbols, and understood. These weapons were made to kill things that were already dead — inferior versions of the sword she wore at her own side.

The man who'd shouted — an officer, Sabriel realised — bent down and picked up her passports. He studied them for a moment, then looked up at Sabriel. His eyes were pale blue and held a mixture of harshness and compassion that Sabriel found familiar, though she couldn't place it — till she remembered her father's eyes. Abhorsen's eyes were so dark brown they seemed black, but they held a similar feeling.

The officer closed the passport, tucked it in his belt and tilted his helmet back with two fingers, revealing a Charter mark still glowing with some residual charm of warding. Cautiously, Sabriel lifted her hand, and then, as he didn't dissuade her, reached out with two fingers to touch the mark. As she did so, he reached forward and touched her own — Sabriel felt the familiar swirl of energy and the feeling of falling into some endless galaxy of stars. But the stars here were Charter symbols, linked in some great dance that had no beginning or end, but contained and described the world in its movement. Sabriel knew only a small fraction of the symbols, but she knew what they danced and she felt the purity of the Charter wash over her.

"An unsullied Charter mark," the officer pronounced loudly, as their fingers fell back to their sides. "She is no creature or sending."

The soldiers fell back, sheathing swords and clicking on safety catches. Only the red-faced corporal didn't move, his eyes still staring at Sabriel, as if he was unsure what he was looking at.

"Show's over, Corporal," said the officer, his voice and eyes now harsh. "Get back to the pay office. You'll see stranger happenings than this in your time here – stay clear of them and you might stay alive!"

"So," he said, taking the documents from his belt and handing them back to Sabriel. "You are the daughter of Abhorsen. I am Colonel Horyse, the commander of a small part of the garrison here – a unit the Army likes to call the Northern Perimeter Reconnaissance Unit and everyone else calls the Crossing Point Scouts – a somewhat motley collection of Ancelstierrans who've managed to gain a Charter mark and some small knowledge of magic."

"Pleased to meet you, sir," popped out of Sabriel's school-trained mouth, before she could stifle it. A schoolgirl's answer, she knew, and felt a blush rise in her pale cheeks.

"Likewise," said the Colonel, bending down. "May I take your skis?"

"If you would be so kind," said Sabriel, falling back on formality.

The Colonel picked them up with ease, carefully retied the stocks to the skis, refastened the bindings that had come undone and tucked the lot under one muscular arm.

"I take it you intend to cross into the Old Kingdom?" asked Horyse, as he found the balancing point of his load and pointed at the scarlet sign on the far side of the parade ground. "We'll have to check in with Perimeter HQ — there are a few formalities, but it shouldn't take long. Is someone... Abhorsen, coming to meet you?"

His voice faltered a little as he mentioned Abhorsen, a strange stutter in so confident a man. Sabriel glanced at him and saw that his eyes flickered from the sword at her waist to the bell-bandoleer she wore across her chest. Obviously he recognised Abhorsen's sword and also the significance of the bells. Very few people ever met a necromancer, but anyone who did remembered the bells.

"Did... do you know my father?" she asked. "He used to visit me, twice a year. I guess he would have come through here."

"Yes, I saw him then," replied Horyse, as they started walking around the edge of the parade ground. "But I first met him more than twenty years ago, when I was posted here as a subaltern. It was a strange time — a very bad time, for me and everyone on the Perimeter."

He paused in mid-stride, boots crashing, and his eyes once again looked at the bells and the whiteness of Sabriel's skin, stark against the black of her hair, black as the bitumen under their feet.

"You're a necromancer," he said bluntly. "So you'll probably understand. This crossing point has seen too many battles, too many dead. Before those idiots down South took things under central command, the crossing point was moved every ten years, up to the next gate on the Wall. But forty years ago some... bureaucrat... decreed that there would be no movement. It was a waste of public money. This was, and is to be, the only crossing point. Never mind the fact that, over time, there would be such a concentration of death, mixed with Free Magic leaking over the Wall, that everything would..."

"Not stay dead," interrupted Sabriel quietly.

"Yes. When I arrived, the trouble was just beginning. Corpses wouldn't stay buried – our people or Old Kingdom creatures. Soldiers killed the day before would turn up on parade. Creatures prevented from crossing would rise up and do more damage than they did when they were alive."

"What did you do?" asked Sabriel. She knew a great deal about binding and enforcing true death, but not on such a scale. There were no Dead creatures nearby now, for she always instinctively felt the interface between life and death around her, and it was no different here than it had been forty miles away at Wyverley College.

"Our Charter Mages tried to deal with the problem, but there were no specific Charter symbols to... make them dead... only to destroy their physical shape. Sometimes that was enough and sometimes it wasn't. We had to rotate troops back to Bain or even further just for them to recover from what HQ liked to think of as bouts of mass hysteria or madness.

"I wasn't a Charter Mage then, but I was going with patrols into the Old Kingdom, beginning to learn. On one patrol, we met a man sitting by a Charter Stone, on top of a hill that overlooked both the Wall and the Perimeter.

"As he was obviously interested in the Perimeter, the officer in charge of the patrol thought we should question him and kill him if he turned out to bear a corrupted Charter or was some Free Magic thing in the shape of a man. But we didn't, of course. It was Abhorsen and he was coming to us, because he'd heard about the Dead.

"We escorted him in and he met with the General commanding the garrison. I don't know what they agreed, but I imagine it was for Abhorsen to bind the Dead and, in return, he was to be granted citizenship of Ancelstierre and freedom to cross the Wall. He certainly had the two passports after that. In any case, he spent the next few months carving the wind flutes you can see among the wire..."

"Ah!" exclaimed Sabriel. "I wondered what they were. Wind flutes. That explains a lot."

"I'm glad you understand," said the Colonel. "I still don't. For one thing, they make no sound no matter how hard the wind blows through them. They have Charter symbols on them I had never seen before he carved them, and have never seen again anywhere else. But when he started placing them... one a night... the Dead just gradually disappeared and no new ones rose."

They reached the far end of the parade ground, where another scarlet sign stood next to a communication trench, proclaiming: 'Perimeter Garrison HQ. Call and Wait for Sentry.'

A telephone handset and a bell-chain proclaimed the usual dichotomy of the Perimeter. Colonel Horyse picked up the handset, wound the handle, listened for a moment, then replaced it. Frowning, he pulled the bell-chain three times in quick succession.

"Anyway," he continued, as they waited for the sentry. "Whatever it was, it worked. So we are deeply indebted to Abhorsen and that makes his daughter an honoured guest."

"I may be less honoured and more reviled as a messenger of ill omen," said Sabriel quietly. She hesitated, for it was hard to talk about Abhorsen without tears coming to her eyes, then continued quickly, to get it over and done with. "The reason I am going into the Old Kingdom is to... to look for my father. Something has happened to him."

"I had hoped there was another reason for you to carry his sword," said Horyse. He moved the skis into the crook of his left arm, freeing his right, to return the salute of the two sentries who were running at the double up the communication trench, hobnails clacking on the wooden slats.

"There is worse, I think," added Sabriel, taking a deep breath to stop her voice breaking into sobs. "He is trapped in Death... or... or he may even be dead. And his bindings will be broken."

"The wind flutes?" asked Horyse, grounding the end of the skis, his salute dying out halfway to his head. "All the Dead here?"

"The flutes play a song only heard in Death," replied Sabriel, "continuing a binding laid down by Abhorsen. But the bound are tied to him and the flutes will have no power if... they will have no power if Abhorsen is now among the Dead. They will bind no more."

chapter three

"I am not one to blame a messenger for their tidings," said Horyse, as he handed a cup of tea over to Sabriel, who was sitting on what looked like the only comfortable chair in the dugout which was the Colonel's headquarters, "but you bring the worst news I have heard for many years."

"At least I am a living messenger... and a friendly one," Sabriel said quietly. She hadn't really thought beyond her own concern for her father. Now, she was beginning to expand her knowledge of him, to understand that he was more than just her father, that he was many different things to different people. Her simple image of him – relaxing in the armchair of her study at Wyverley College, chatting about her schoolwork, Ancelstierre technology, Charter Magic and necromancy – was a limited view, like a painting that only captured one dimension of the man.

"How long do we have until Abhorsen's bindings are broken?" asked Horyse, breaking into Sabriel's remembrance of her father. The image she had of her father reaching for a teacup in her study disappeared, banished by real tea slopping over in her enamel mug and burning her fingers.

"Oh! Excuse me. I wasn't thinking... how long till what?"

"The binding of the Dead," the Colonel reiterated, patiently. "How long till the bindings fail and the Dead are free?"

Sabriel thought back to her father's lessons and the ancient grimoire she'd spent every holiday slowly memorising. *The Book of the Dead* it was called and parts of it still made her shudder. It looked innocuous enough, bound in green leather, with tarnished silver clasps. But if you looked closely, both leather and silver were etched with Charter marks. Marks of binding and blinding, closing and imprisonment. Only a trained necromancer could open that book... and only an uncorrupted Charter Mage could close it. Her father had brought it with him on his visits and always took it away again at the end.

"It depends," she said slowly, forcing herself to consider the question objectively, without letting emotion interfere. She tried to recall the pages that showed the carving of the wind flutes, the chapters on music and the nature of sound in the binding of the Dead. "If Father... if Abhorsen is... truly dead, the wind flutes will simply fall apart under the light of the next full moon. If he is trapped before the Ninth Gate, the binding will continue until the full moon after he passes beyond or a particularly strong spirit breaks the weakened bonds."

"So the moon will tell, in time," said Horyse. "We have fourteen days till it is full."

"It is possible I could bind the Dead anew," Sabriel said

cautiously. "I mean, I haven't done it on this sort of scale. But I know how. The only thing is, if Father isn't... isn't beyond the Ninth Gate, then I need to help him as soon as I can. And before I can do that, I must get to his house and gather a few things... check some references."

"How far is this house beyond the Wall?" asked Horyse, a calculating look on his face.

"I don't know," replied Sabriel.

"What?"

"I don't know. I haven't been there since I was about four. I think it's supposed to be a secret. Father had many enemies, not just among the Dead. Petty necromancers, Free Magic sorcerers, witches—"

"You don't seem disturbed by your lack of directions," interrupted the Colonel dryly. For the first time, a hint of doubt, even fatherly condescension, had crept into his voice, as if Sabriel's youth undermined the respect due to her as both a Charter Mage and necromancer.

"Father taught me to how to call a guide who will give me directions," replied Sabriel coolly. "And I know it's less than four days' travel away."

That silenced Horyse, at least for the moment. He nodded and, standing cautiously, so his head didn't hit the exposed beams of the dugout, he walked over to a steel filing cabinet that was rusting from the dark brown mud that oozed between the pale planks of the revetment. Opening the cabinet with a practised heave of considerable force, he found a mimeographed map and rolled it out on the table.

"We've never been able to get our hands on a genuine Old

43

Kingdom map. Your father had one, but he was the only person who could see anything on it – it just looked like a square of calfskin to me. A small magic, he said, but since he couldn't teach it, perhaps not so small... Anyway, this map is a copy of the latest version of our patrol map, so it only goes out about ten miles from the crossing point. The garrison standing orders strictly forbid us to go further. Patrols tend not to come back beyond that distance. Maybe they desert, or maybe..."

His tone of voice suggested that even nastier things happened to the patrols, but Sabriel didn't question him. A small portion of the Old Kingdom lay spread out on the table and, once again, excitement stirred up within her.

"We generally go out along the Old North Road," said Horyse, tracing it with one hand, the sword calluses on his fingers rasping across the map, like the soft sandpapering of a master craftsman. "Then the patrols sweep back, either south-east or south-west, till they hit the Wall. Then they follow that back to the gate."

"What does this symbol mean?" asked Sabriel, pointing to a blacked-in square atop one of the farther hills.

"That's a Charter Stone," replied the Colonel. "Or part of one now. It was riven in two, as if struck by lightning, a month or so ago. The patrols have started to call it Cloven Crest and they avoid it if possible. Its true name is Barhedrin Hill and the stone once carried the Charter for a village of the same name. Before my time, anyway. If the village still exists it must be further north, beyond the reach of our patrols. We've never had any reports of inhabitants from it coming south to Cloven

Crest. The fact is, we have few reports of people, full stop. The Garrison Log used to show considerable interaction with Old Kingdom people – farmers, merchants, travellers and so on – but encounters have become rarer over the last hundred years and very rare in the last twenty. The patrols would be lucky to see even two or three people a year now. Real people that is, not creatures or Free Magic constructs, or the Dead. We see far too many of those."

"I don't understand," muttered Sabriel. "Father often used to talk of villages and towns... even cities, in the Old Kingdom. I remember some of them from my childhood... well, I sort of remember... I think."

"Further into the Old Kingdom, certainly," replied the Colonel. "The records mention quite a few names of towns and cities. We know that the people up there call the area around the Wall 'The Borderlands.' And they don't say it with any fondness."

Sabriel didn't answer, bending her head lower over the map, thinking about the journey that lay ahead of her. Cloven Crest might be a good waypoint. It was no more than eight miles away, so she should be able to ski there before nightfall if she left fairly soon and if it wasn't snowing too hard across the Wall. A broken Charter Stone did not bode well, but there would be some magic there and the path into Death would be easier to tread. Charter Stones were often erected where Free Magic flowed and crossroads of the Free Magic currents were often natural doorways into the realm of Death. Sabriel felt a shiver inch up her spine at the thought of what might use such a doorway and the tremor passed through to her fingers on the map.

She looked up suddenly and saw Colonel Horyse looking at her long, pale hands, the heavy paper of the map still shuddering at her touch. With an effort of will, she stilled the movement.

"I have a daughter almost your age," he said quietly. "Back in Corvere, with my wife. I would not let her cross into the Old Kingdom."

Sabriel met his gaze and her eyes were not the uncertain, flickering beacons of adolescence.

"I am only eighteen years old on the outside," she said, touching her palm against her breast with an almost wistful motion. "But I first walked in Death when I was twelve. I encountered a Fifth Gate Rester when I was fourteen and banished it beyond the Ninth Gate. When I was sixteen I stalked and banished a Mordicant that came near the school. A weakened Mordicant, but still... A year ago, I turned the final page of *The Book of the Dead*. I don't feel young any more."

"I am sorry for that," said the Colonel, then, almost as if he had surprised himself, he added, "Ah, I mean that I wish you some of the foolish joys my daughter has – some of the lightness, the lack of responsibility that goes with youth. But I don't wish it if it will weaken you in the times ahead. You have chosen a difficult path."

"Does the walker choose the path, or the path the walker?" Sabriel quoted, the words, redolent with echoes of Charter Magic, twining around her tongue like some lingering spice.

Those words were the dedication in the front of her almanac. They were also the very last words, all alone on the last page of *The Book of the Dead*.

"I've heard that before," remarked Horyse. "What does it mean?"

"I don't know," said Sabriel.

"It holds power when you say it," added the Colonel slowly. He swallowed, open-mouthed, as if the taste of the Charter marks was still in the air. "If I spoke those words, that's all they would be. Just words."

"I can't explain it," Sabriel shrugged and attempted a smile. "But I do know other sayings that are more to the point at the moment, like: 'Traveller, embrace the morning light, but do not take the hand of night'. I must be on my way."

Horyse smiled at the old rhyme, so beloved of grandmothers and nannies, but it was an empty smile. His eyes slid a little away from Sabriel's and she knew that he was thinking about refusing to let her cross the Wall. Then he sighed, the short, huffy sigh of a man who is forced into a course of action through lack of alternatives.

"Your papers are in order," he said, meeting her gaze once again. "And you are the daughter of Abhorsen. I cannot do other than let you pass. But I can't help feeling that I am thrusting you out to meet some terrible danger. I can't even send a patrol out with you, since we have five full patrols already out there."

"I expected to go alone," replied Sabriel. She had expected that, but felt a tinge of regret. A protective group of soldiers would be quite a comfort. The fear of being alone in a strange and dangerous land, even if it was her homeland, was only just below the level of her excitement. It wouldn't take much for the fear to rise over it. And always, there was the picture of her father in her mind. Her father in trouble, trapped and alone in the chill waters of Death...

"Very well," said Horyse. "Sergeant!"

A helmeted head appeared suddenly around the doorway and Sabriel realised two soldiers must have been standing on guard outside the dugout, on the steps up into the communication trench. She wondered if they'd heard.

"Prepare a crossing party," snapped Horyse. "A single person to cross. Miss Abhorsen, here. And Sergeant, if you or Private Rahise so much as talk in your sleep about what you may have heard here, then you'll be on gravedigging fatigues for the rest of your lives!"

"Yes, sir!" came the sharp reply, echoed by the unfortunate Private Rahise, who, Sabriel noted, did seem half-asleep.

"After you, please" continued Horyse, gesturing towards the door. "May I carry your skis again?"

The Army took no chances when it came to crossing the Wall. Sabriel stood alone under the great arch of the gate that pierced the Wall, but archers stood or knelt in a reverse arrowhead formation around the gate and a dozen swordsmen had gone ahead with Colonel Horyse. A hundred yards behind her, past a zigzagged lane of barbed wire, two Lewyn machine-gunners watched from a forward emplacement – though Sabriel noted they had drawn their sword-bayonets and thrust them, ready for use, in the sandbags, showing little faith in their air-cooled 45-rounds-per-minute tools of destruction.

There was no actual gate in the archway, though rusting hinges swung like mechanical hands on either side and sharp shards of oak thrust out of the ground, like teeth in a broken jaw, testimony to some explosion of modern chemistry or magical force.

It was snowing lightly on the Old Kingdom side and the wind channelled occasional snowflakes through the gate into Ancelstierre, where they melted on the warmer ground of the south. One caught in Sabriel's hair. She brushed at it lightly, till it slid down her face and was captured by her tongue.

The cold water was refreshing and, though it tasted no different from any other melted snow she'd drunk, it marked her first taste of the Old Kingdom in thirteen years. Dimly, she remembered it had been snowing then. Her father had carried her through, when he first brought her south into Ancelstierre.

A whistle alerted her and she saw a figure appear out of the snow, flanked by twelve others, who drew up in two lines leading out from the gate. They faced outwards, their swords shining, blades reflecting the light that was itself reflected from the snow. Only Horyse looked inwards, waiting for her.

With her skis over her shoulder, Sabriel picked her way among the broken timbers of the gate. Going through the arch, from mud into snow, from bright sun into the pallid luminescence of a snowfall, from her past into her future.

The stones of the Wall on either side, and above her head, seemed to call a welcome home, and rivulets of Charter marks ran through the stones like rain through dust.

"The Old Kingdom welcomes you," said Horyse, but he was watching the Charter marks run on the stones, not looking at Sabriel.

Sabriel stepped out of the shadow of the gate and pulled her cap down, so the peak shielded her face against the snow.

"I wish your mission every success, Sabriel," continued Horyse, looking back at her. "I hope... hope I see both you and your father before too long."

He saluted, turned smartly to his left and was gone, wheeling around her and marching back through the gate. His men peeled off from the line and followed. Sabriel bent down as they marched past, slid her skis back and forth in the snow, then slipped her boots into the bindings. The snow was falling steadily, but it was only a light fall and the cover was patchy. She could still easily make out the Old North Road. Fortunately, the snow had banked up in the gutters to either side of the road, and she could make good time if she kept to these narrow snow-ways. Even though it seemed to be several hours later in the Old Kingdom than it was in Ancelstierre, she expected to reach Cloven Crest before dusk.

Taking up her poles, Sabriel checked that her father's sword was easy in its scabbard and the bells hung properly from their baldric. She considered a quick Charter-spell for warmth, but decided against it. The road had a slight uphill gradient, so the skiing would be quite hard work. In her handknitted, greasy wool shirt, leather jerkin and thick, double padded skiing knickerbockers, she would probably be too warm once she got going.

With a practised motion, she pushed one ski ahead, the

opposite arm reaching forward with her pole, and slid forward, just as the last swordsman passed her on his way back through the gate. He grinned as he passed by, but she didn't notice, concentrating on building up the rhythm of her skis and poles. Within minutes, she was practically flying up the road, a slim, dark figure against the white of the ground.

chapter four

Sabriel found the first dead Ancelstierran soldier about six miles from the Wall, in the last, fading hours of the afternoon. The hill she thought was Cloven Crest was a mile or two to the north. She'd stopped to look at its dark bulk, rising rocky and treeless from the snow-covered ground, its peak temporarily hidden in one of the light, puffy clouds that occasionally let forth a shower of snow or sleet.

If she hadn't stopped, she would probably have missed the frosted-white hand that peeked out of a drift on the other side of the road. But as soon as she saw that, her attention focused and Sabriel felt the familiar pang of death.

Crossing over, her skis clacking on bare stone in the middle of the road, she bent down and gently brushed the snow away.

The hand belonged to a young man, who wore a standard-issue coat of mail over an Ancelstierran uniform of khaki serge. He was blond and grey-eyed, and Sabriel thought he had been surprised, for there was no fear in his frozen expression. She touched his forehead with one finger, closed his sightless eyes and laid two fingers against his open mouth. He had been dead twelve days, she felt. There were no obvious signs as to what had killed him. To learn more than that, she would have to follow the young man into Death. Even after twelve days, it was unlikely he had gone further than the Fourth Gate. Even so, Sabriel had a strong disinclination to enter the realm of the Dead until she absolutely had to. Whatever had trapped – or killed – her father could easily be waiting to ambush her there. This dead soldier could even be a lure.

Quashing her natural curiosity to find out exactly what had happened, Sabriel folded the man's arms across his chest, after first unclenching the grip that his right hand still had on his sword hilt – perhaps he had not been taken totally unawares after all. Then she stood and drew the Charter marks of fire, cleansing, peace and sleep in the air above the corpse, while whispering the sounds of those same marks. It was a litany that every Charter Mage knew and it had the usual effect. A glowing ember sparked up between the man's folded arms, multiplied into many stabbing, darting flames, then fire whooshed the full length of the body. Seconds later it was out and only ash remained, ash staining a corselet of blackened mail.

Sabriel took the soldier's sword from the pile of ashes and thrust it through the melted snow, into the dark earth beneath. It stuck fast, upright, the hilt casting a shadow like a cross upon the ashes. Something glinted in the shadow and, belatedly, Sabriel remembered that the soldier would have worn an identity disc or tag.

Shifting her skis again to re-balance she bent down and

hooked the chain of the identity disc on one finger, pulling it up to read the name of the man who had met his end here, alone in the snow. But both the chain and disc were machine-made in Ancelstierre and so unable to withstand the Charter Magic fire. The disc crumbled into ash as Sabriel raised it to eye level and the chain fell into its component links, pouring between Sabriel's fingers like small steel coins.

"Perhaps they'll know you from your sword," said Sabriel. Her voice sounded strange in the quiet of the snowy wilderness and, behind each word, her breath rolled out like a small, wet fog.

"Travel without regret," she added. "Do not look back."

Sabriel took her own advice as she skied away. There was an anxiety in her now that had been mostly academic before and every sense was alert, watchful. She had always been told that the Old Kingdom was dangerous and The Borderlands near the Wall particularly so. But that intellectual knowledge was tempered by her vague childhood memories of happiness, of being with her father and the band of Travellers. Now, the reality of the danger was slowly coming home...

Half a mile on she slowed and stopped to look up at Cloven Crest again, neck cricked back to watch where the sun struck between the clouds, lighting up the yellow-red granite of the bluffs. She was in cloud shadow herself, so the hill looked like an attractive destination. As she looked, it started to snow again and two snowflakes fell upon her forehead, melting into her eyes. She blinked and the melted snow traced tear trails down her cheeks. Through misted eyes, she saw a bird of prey – a hawk or kite – launch itself from the bluffs and hover, its concentration totally centred upon some small mouse or vole creeping across the snow.

The kite dropped like a cast stone, and a few seconds later, Sabriel felt some small life snuffed out. At the same time, she also felt the tug of human death. Somewhere ahead, near where the kite dined, more people lay dead.

Sabriel shivered and looked at the hill again. According to Horyse's map, the path to Cloven Crest lay in a narrow gully between two bluffs. She could see quite clearly where it must be, but the Dead lay in that direction. Whatever had killed them might also still be there.

There was sunlight on the bluffs, but the wind was driving snow clouds across the sun and Sabriel guessed it was only an hour or so till dusk. She'd lost time freeing the soldier's spirit, and now had no choice but to hurry on if she wished to reach Cloven Crest before nightfall.

She thought about what lay ahead for a moment, then chose a compromise between speed and caution. Stabbing her poles into the snow, she released her bindings, stepped out of her skis and then quickly fastened skis and poles together to be strapped diagonally across her backpack. She tied them on carefully, remembering how they'd fallen and broken her Charter-spell on the parade ground – only that morning, but it seemed like weeks ago and a world away.

That done, she started to pick her way down the centre of the road, keeping away from the gutter drifts. She'd have to leave the road fairly soon, but it looked like there was little snow on the steep, rocky slopes of Cloven Crest.

As a final precaution, she drew Abhorsen's sword, then re-sheathed it, so an inch of blade was free of the scabbard. It would draw fast and easily when she needed it.

Sabriel expected to find the bodies on the road, or near it, but they lay further on. There were many footprints and churned-up snow, leading from the road towards the path to Cloven Crest. That path ran between the bluffs, following a route gouged out by a stream falling from some deep spring higher up the hill. The path crossed the stream several times, with stepping stones or tree trunks across the water to save walkers from wet feet. Halfway up, where the bluffs almost ground together, the stream had dug itself a short gorge, about twelve feet wide, thirty feet long and deep. Here, the pathmakers had been forced to build a bridge along the stream, rather than across it.

Sabriel found the rest of the Ancelstierran patrol here, tumbled on the dark olive-black wood of the bridge, with the water murmuring beneath and the red stone arching overhead. There were seven of them along the bridge's length. Unlike the first soldier, it was quite clear what had killed them. They had been hacked apart and, as Sabriel edged closer, she realised they had been beheaded. Worse than that, whoever... whatever... had killed them had taken their heads away – almost a guarantee that their spirits would return.

Her sword did draw easily. Gingerly, her right hand almost glued to the sword hilt, Sabriel stepped around the first of the splayed-out bodies and on to the bridge. The water beneath was partly iced over, shallow and sluggish, but it was clear the soldiers had sought refuge over it. Running water was a good protection from dead creatures or things of Free Magic, but this torpid stream would not have dismayed even one of the Lesser Dead. In Spring, fed with melted snow, the stream would burst between the bluffs and the bridge would be knee-deep in clear, swift water. The soldiers would probably have survived at that time of year.

Sabriel sighed quietly, thinking of how easily seven people could be alive in one instant and then, despite everything they could do, despite their last hope, they could be dead in just another. Once again, she felt the temptation of the necromancer, to take the cards nature had dealt, to reshuffle them and deal again. She had the power to make these men live again, laugh again, love again...

But without their heads she could only bring them back as "hands", a derogatory term that Free Magic necromancers used for their lacklustre revenants, who retained little of their original intelligence and none of their initiative. They made useful servants, though, either as reanimated corpses or the more difficult Shadow Hands, where only the spirit was brought back.

Sabriel grimaced as she thought of Shadow Hands. A skilled necromancer could easily raise Shadow Hands from the heads of the newly dead. Similarly, without the heads, she couldn't give them the final rites and free their spirits. All she could do was treat the bodies with some respect and, in the process, clear the bridge. It was near to dusk, and dark already in the shadow of the gorge, but she ignored the little voice inside her that was urging her to leave the bodies and run for the open space of the hilltop.

By the time she finished dragging the bodies back down the path a way, laying them out with their swords plunged in the earth next to their headless bodies, it was dark outside the gorge too. So dark, she had to risk a faint, Charter-conjured light, that hung like a pale star above her head, showing the path before dying out.

A slight magic, but one with unexpected consequences, for, as she left the bodies behind, an answering light burned into brilliance on the upper post of the bridge. It faded into red embers almost immediately, but left three glowing Charter marks. One was strange to Sabriel, but, from the other two, she guessed its meaning. Together, they held a message.

Three of the dead soldiers had the feel of Charter Magic about them and Sabriel guessed that they were Charter Mages. They would have had the Charter mark on their foreheads. The very last body on the bridge had been one of these men and Sabriel remembered that he had been the only one not holding a weapon – his hands had been clasped around the bridge post. These marks would certainly hold his message.

Sabriel touched her own forehead Charter mark and then the bridge post. The marks flared again, then went dark. A voice came from nowhere, close to Sabriel's ear. A man's voice, husky with fear, backed by the sound of clashing weapons, screaming and total panic.

"One of the Greater Dead! It came behind us, almost from the Wall. We couldn't turn back. It has servants, hands, a Mordicant! This is Sergeant Gerren. Tell Colonel..."

Whatever he wanted to tell Colonel Horyse was lost in the moment of his own death. Sabriel stood still, listening, as if there might be more. She felt ill, nauseous, and took several deep breaths. She had forgotten that for all her familiarity with death and the Dead, she had never seen or heard anyone actually die. The aftermath she had learnt to deal with... but not the event.

She touched the bridge post again, just with one finger, and felt the Charter marks twisting through the grain of the wood. Sergeant Gerren's message would be there for ever for any Charter Mage to hear, till time did its work and bridge post and bridge rotted or were swept away by flood.

Sabriel took a few more breaths, stilled her stomach and forced herself to listen once more.

One of the Greater Dead was back in Life and that was something her father was sworn to stop. It was almost certain that this emergence and Abhorsen's disappearance were connected.

Once again, the message came and Sabriel listened. Then, brushing back her starting tears, she walked on, up the path, away from the bridge and the Dead, up towards Cloven Crest and the broken Charter Stone.

The bluffs parted and, in the sky above, stars started to twinkle, as the wind grew braver and swept the snow clouds before it into the west. The new moon unveiled itself and swelled in brightness, till it cast shadows on the snow-flecked ground.

chapter five

It was no more than a half-hour's steady climb to the flat top of Cloven Crest, though the path grew steeper and more difficult. The wind was strong now and had cleared the sky, the moonlight giving form to the landscape. But without the clouds, it had grown much colder.

Sabriel considered a Charter-spell for warmth, but she was tired and the effort of the spell might cost more than the gain in warmth. She stopped instead and shrugged on a fleece-lined oilskin that had been handed down from her father. It was a bit worn and too large, needing severe buckling-in with her sword belt and the baldric that held the bells, but it was certainly windproof.

Feeling relatively warmer, Sabriel resumed climbing up the last, winding portion of the path, where the incline was so steep the pathmakers had resorted to cutting steps out of the granite – steps now worn and crumbling, prone to sliding away underfoot.

So prone to sliding, that Sabriel reached the top without realising it. Head down, her eyes searching in the moonlight for the solid part of the next step, her foot was actually halfway up in the air before she realised that there wasn't a next step.

Cloven Crest lay before her. A narrow ridge where several slopes of the hill met to form a miniature plateau, with a slight depression in the middle. Snow lay in this depression, a fat, cigar-shaped drift, bright in the moonlight, stark white against the red granite. There were no trees, no vegetation at all, but in the very centre of the drift, a dark grey stone cast a long moonshadow. It was twice Sabriel's girth and three times her height, and looked whole till she walked closer and saw the zigzag crack that cut it down the middle.

Sabriel had never seen a true Charter Stone before, but she knew they were supposed to be like the Wall, with Charter marks running like quicksilver through the stone, forming and dissolving, only to reform again, in a never-ending story that told of the making of the world.

There were Charter marks on this stone, but they were still, as frozen as the snow. Dead marks, nothing more than meaningless inscriptions, carved into a sculptured stone.

It wasn't what Sabriel had expected, though she now realised that she hadn't thought about it properly. She'd thought of lightning or suchlike as the splitter of the stone, but forgotten lessons remembered too late told her that wasn't so. Only some terrible power of Free Magic could split a Charter Stone.

She walked closer to the stone, fear rising in her like a toothache in its first growth, signalling worse to come. The wind was stronger and colder too, out on the ridge, and the oilskin seemed less comforting, as its memories of her father brought back remembrance of certain pages of *The Book of the Dead* and tales of horror told by little girls in the darkness of their dormitory, far from the Old Kingdom. Fears came with these memories, till Sabriel wrestled them to the back of her mind, and forced herself closer to the stone.

Dark patches of... something... obscured some of the marks, but it wasn't until Sabriel pushed her face almost to the stone that she could make out what they were, so dull and black in the moonlight.

When she did see, her head snapped up and she stumbled backwards, almost overbalancing into the snow. The patches were dried blood and when she saw them Sabriel knew how the stone had been broken, and why the blood hadn't been cleaned away by rain or snow... why the stone never would be clean.

A Charter Mage had been sacrificed on the stone. Sacrificed by a necromancer to gain access to Death, or to help a Dead spirit break through into Life.

Sabriel bit her lower lip till it hurt and her hands, almost unconsciously, fidgeted, half-drawing Charter marks in nervousness and fear. The spell for that sort of sacrifice was in the last chapter of *The Book of the Dead*. She remembered it now, in sickening detail. It was one of the many things she seemed to have forgotten from that green-bound book or – had been made to forget. Only a very powerful necromancer could use that spell. Only a totally evil one would want to. And evil breeds evil, evil taints places and makes them attractive to further acts of...

"Stop it!" whispered Sabriel aloud, to still her mind of its imaginings. It was dark, windy and getting colder by the minute. She had to make a decision: to camp and call her guide, or to move on immediately in some random direction in the hope that she would be able to summon her guide from somewhere else.

The worst part of it all was that her guide was dead. Sabriel had to enter Death, albeit briefly, to call and converse with the guide. It would be easy to do so here, for the sacrifice had created a semi-permanent entry, as if a door had been wedged ajar. But who knew what might be lurking, watching, in the cold river beyond.

Sabriel stood for a minute, shivering, listening, every sense concentrated, like some small animal that knows a predator hunts nearby. Her mind ran through the pages of *The Book of the Dead*, and through the many hours she had spent learning Charter Magic from Magistrix Greenwood in the sunny North Tower of Wyverley College.

At the end of the minute, she knew that camping was out of the question. She was simply too frightened to sleep anywhere near the ruined Charter Stone. But it would be quicker to call her guide here – and the quicker she got to her father's house, the sooner she could do something to help him, so a compromise was called for. She would protect herself with Charter Magic as best she could, enter Death with all precaution, summon her guide, get directions and get out as quickly as possible. Quicker, even.

With decision came action. Sabriel dropped her skis and

pack, stuffed some dried fruit and home-made toffee in her mouth for quick energy, and adopted the meditative pose that made Charter Magic easier.

After a bit of trouble with the toffee and her teeth, she began. Symbols formed in her mind – the four cardinal Charter marks that were the poles of a diamond that would protect her from both physical harm and Free Magic. Sabriel held them in her mind, fixed them in time, and pulled them out of the flow of the never-ending Charter. Then, drawing her sword, she traced rough outlines in the snow around her, one mark at each cardinal point of the compass. As she finished each mark, she let the one in her mind run from her head to her hand, down the sword and into the snow. There, they ran like lines of golden fire and the marks became alive, burning on the ground.

The last mark was the Northmark, the one closest to the destroyed stone, and it almost failed. Sabriel had to close her eyes and use all her will to force it to leave the sword. Even then, it was only a pallid imitation of the other three, burning so weakly it hardly melted the snow.

Sabriel ignored it, quelling the nausea that had brought bile to the back of her mouth, her body reacting to the struggle with the Charter mark. She knew the Northmark was weak, but golden lines had run between all four points and the diamond was complete, if shaky. In any case, it was the best she could do. She sheathed her sword, took off her gloves, and fumbled with her bell-bandoleer, cold fingers counting the bells.

"Ranna," she said aloud, touching the first, the smallest bell. Ranna the sleepbringer, the sweet, low sound that brought silence in its wake.

"Mosrael." The second bell, a harsh, rowdy bell. Mosrael was the waker, the bell Sabriel should never use, the bell whose sound was a seesaw, throwing the ringer further into Death, as it brought the listener into Life.

"Kibeth." Kibeth the walker. A bell of several sounds, a difficult and contrary bell. It could give freedom of movement to one of the Dead or walk them through the next gate. Many a necromancer had stumbled with Kibeth and walked where they would not.

"Dyrim." A musical bell, of clear and pretty tone. Dyrim was the voice that the Dead so often lost. But Dyrim could also still a tongue that moved too freely.

"Belgaer." Another tricksome bell, that sought to ring of its own accord. Belgaer was the thinking bell, the bell most necromancers scorned to use. It could restore independent thought, memory and all the patterns of a living person. Or, slipping in a careless hand, erase them.

"Saraneth." The deepest, lowest bell. The sound of strength. Saraneth was the binder, the bell that shackled the Dead to the wielder's will.

And last, the largest bell, the one Sabriel's cold fingers found colder still, even in the leather case that kept it silent.

"Astarael, the sorrowful," whispered Sabriel. Astarael was the banisher, the final bell. Properly rung, it cast everyone who heard it far into Death. Everyone, including the ringer.

Sabriel's hand hovered, touched on Ranna, and then settled on Saraneth. Carefully, she undid the strap and withdrew the bell. Its clapper, freed of the mask, rang slightly, like the growl of a waking bear.

Sabriel stilled it, holding the clapper with her palm inside the bell, ignoring the handle. With her right hand, she drew her sword and raised it to the guard position. Charter marks along the blade caught the moonlight and flickered into life. Sabriel watched them for a moment, as portents could sometimes be seen in such things. Strange marks raced across the blade, before transmuting into the more usual inscription, one that Sabriel knew well. She bowed her head and prepared to enter into Death.

Unseen by Sabriel, the inscription began again, but parts of it were not the same. "I was made for Abhorsen, to slay those already Dead," was what it usually said. Now it continued, "The Clayr saw me, the Wallmaker made me, the King quenched me, Abhorsen wields me."

Sabriel, eyes closed now, felt the boundary between Life and Death appear. On her back, she felt the wind, now curiously warm, and the moonlight, bright and hot like sunshine. On her face, she felt the ultimate cold and, opening her eyes, saw the grey light of Death.

With an effort of will, her spirit stepped through, sword and bell prepared. Inside the diamond her body stiffened and fog blew up in eddies around her feet, twining up her legs. Frost rimed her face and hands and the Charter marks flared at each apex of the diamond. Three steadied again, but the Northmark blazed brighter still – and went out.

The river ran swiftly, but Sabriel set her feet against the current and ignored both it and the cold, concentrating on looking around, alert for a trap or ambush. It was quiet at this particular entry point to Death. She could hear the water tumbling through the Second Gate, but nothing else. No splashing, or gurgling, or strange mewlings. No dark, formless shapes or grim silhouettes, shadowy in this grey light.

Carefully holding her position, Sabriel looked all around her again, before sheathing her sword and reaching into one of the thigh pockets in her woollen knickerbockers. The bell, Saraneth, stayed ready in her left hand. With her right, she drew out a paper boat and, still one-handed, opened it out to its proper shape. Beautifully white, almost luminous in this light, it had one small, perfectly round stain at its bow, where Sabriel had carefully blotted a drop of blood from her finger.

Sabriel laid it flat on her hand, lifted it to her lips and blew on it as if she were launching a feather. Like a glider, it flew from her hand into the river. Sabriel held that launching breath as the boat was almost swamped, only to breathe in with relief as it breasted a ripple, righted itself and surged away with the current. In a few seconds it was out of sight, heading for the Second Gate.

It was the second time in her life that Sabriel had launched just such a paper boat. Her father had shown her how to make them, but had impressed on her to use them sparingly. No more than thrice every seven years, he had said, or a price would have to be paid, a price much greater than a drop of blood.

As events should follow as they had the first time, Sabriel knew what to expect. Still, when the noise of the Second Gate

stilled for a moment some ten or twenty, or forty, minutes later
– time being slippery in Death – she drew her sword and
Saraneth hung down in her hand, its clapper free, waiting to be
heard. The Gate had stilled because someone... something...
was coming back from the deeper realms of Death.

Sabriel hoped it was the one she had invited with the
paper boat.

chapter six

Charter Magic on Cloven Crest. It was like a scent on the wind to the thing that lurked in the caves below the hill, some mile or more to the west of the broken Charter Stone.

It had been human once, or human-like at least, in the years it had lived under the sun. That humanity had been lost in the centuries the thing spent in the chill waters of Death, ferociously holding its own against the current, demonstrating an incredible will to live again. A will it didn't know it possessed before a badly-cast hunting spear bounced from a rock and clipped its throat, just enough for a last few minutes of frantic life.

By sheer effort of will, it had held itself on the life side of the Fourth Gate for three hundred years, growing in power, learning the ways of Death. It preyed on lesser spirits and served or avoided greater ones. Always, the thing held on to life. Its chance finally came when a mighty spirit erupted from beyond the Seventh Gate, smashing through each of the Upper Gates in turn, till it went ravening into Life. Hundreds of the Dead had followed and this particular spirit had joined the throng. There had been terrible confusion and a mighty enemy at the very border between Life and Death, but, in the melee, it had managed to sneak around the edges and squirm triumphantly into Life.

There were plenty of recently-vacated bodies where it emerged, so the thing occupied one, animated it and ran away. Soon after, it found the caves it now inhabited. It even decided to give itself a name. Thralk. A simple name, not too difficult for a partially-decomposed mouth to voice. A male name. Thralk could not remember what its original sex had been, those centuries before, but its new body was male.

It was a name to instil fear in the few small settlements that still existed in this area of The Borderlands, settlements Thralk preyed upon, capturing and consuming the human life he needed to keep himself on the living side of Death.

Charter Magic flared on Cloven Crest again and Thralk sensed that it was strong, pure Charter lore – but weakly cast. The strength of the magic scared him, but the lack of skill behind it was reassuring and strong magic meant a strong life. Thralk needed that life, needed it to shore up the body he used, needed it to replenish the leakage of his spirit back into Death. Greed won over fear. The Dead thing left the mouth of the cave and started climbing the hill, his lidless, rotting eyes fixed on the distant crest.

Sabriel saw her guide, first as a tall, pale light drifting over the swirling water towards her, and then, as it stopped several yards away, as a blurred, glowing, human shape, its arms outstretched in welcome.

"Sabriel."

The words were fuzzy and seemed to come from much farther away than where the shining figure stood, but Sabriel smiled as she felt the warmth in the greeting. Abhorsen had never explained who or what this luminous person was, but Sabriel thought she knew. She'd summoned this advisor only once before – when she'd first menstruated.

There was minimal sex education at Wyverley College – none at all till you were fifteen. The older girls' stories about menstruation were many, varied and often meant to scare. None of Sabriel's friends had reached puberty before her, so in fear and desperation she had entered Death. Her father had told her that the one the paper boat summoned would answer any question and would protect her – and so it had. The glowing spirit answered all her questions and many more besides, till Sabriel was forced to return to Life.

"Hello, Mother," said Sabriel, sheathing her sword and carefully muffling Saraneth with her fingers inside the bell.

The shining shape didn't answer, but that wasn't unexpected. Apart from her one-word greeting, she could only answer questions. Sabriel wasn't really sure if the manifestation was the very unusual dead spirit of her mother, which was unlikely, or some residual protective magic left by her.

"I don't have much time," Sabriel continued. "I'd love to ask about… oh, everything, I guess… but at the moment, I need to know how to get to father's house from Cloven Crest… I mean Barhedrin Ridge."

The sending nodded and spoke. As Sabriel listened, she also saw pictures in her head of what the woman was describing; vivid images, like memories of a journey she'd taken herself.

"Go to the northern side of the ridge. Follow the spur that begins there down till it reaches the valley floor. Look at the sky... there won't be any cloud. Look to the bright red star, Uallus, near the horizon, three fingers east of north. Follow that star till you come to a road that runs from south-west to north-east. Take that road for a mile to the north-east, till you reach a mile marker and the Charter Stone behind it. A path behind the stone leads to the Long Cliffs immediately north. Take the path. It ends in a door in the Cliffs. The door will answer to Mosrael. Beyond the door is a tunnel, sloping sharply upwards. Beyond the tunnel lies Abhorsen's Bridge. The house is over the bridge. Go with love – and do not tarry, do not stop, no matter what happens."

"Thank you," Sabriel began, carefully filing the words away with the accompanying thoughts. "Could you also..."

She stopped as the mother-sending in front of her suddenly raised both arms as if shocked and shouted "Go!"

At the same time, Sabriel felt the diamond of protection around her physical body twinge in warning and she became aware that the Northmark had failed. Instantly, she turned on her left heel and began racing back to the border with Life, drawing her sword. The current almost seemed to strengthen against her, twining around her legs, but then fell away before her urgency. Sabriel reached the border and, with a furious thrust of will, her spirit emerged back into Life.

For a second, she was disoriented, suddenly freezing again and thick-witted. A grinning, corpse-like creature was just stepping through the failed Northmark, its arms reaching to embrace her, carrion-breath misting out of a mouth unnaturally wide.

Thralk had been pleased to find the Charter Mage's spirit wandering and a broken diamond of protection. The sword had worried him a little, but it was frosted over and his shrivelled eyes couldn't see the Charter marks that danced beneath the rime. Similarly, the bell in Sabriel's left hand looked like a lump of ice or snow, as if she'd caught a snowball. All in all, Thralk felt very fortunate, particularly as the life that blazed within this still victim was particularly young and strong. Thralk sidled closer still and his double-jointed arms reached to embrace Sabriel's neck.

Just as his slimy, corrupted fingers stretched forward, Sabriel opened her eyes and demonstrated the stop-thrust that had earned her second place in Fighting Arts and, later, lost her the First. Her arm and sword straightened like one limb to their full extent and the sword point ripped through Thralk's neck, and into eight inches of air beyond.

Thralk screamed, his reaching fingers gripping the sword to push himself free – only to scream again as Charter marks flared on the blade. White-hot sparks plumed between his knuckles and Thralk suddenly knew what he'd encountered.

"Abhorsen!" he croaked, falling backwards as Sabriel twisted the blade free with one explosive jerk.

Already, the sword was affecting the dead flesh Thralk inhabited, Charter Magic burning through reanimated nerves, freezing those all-too-fluid joints. Fire rose in Thralk's throat, but he spoke, to distract this terrible opponent while his spirit tried to shuck the body, like a snake its skin, and retreat into the night.

"Abhorsen! I will serve you, praise you, be your Hand... I know things, alive and dead... I will help lure others to you..."

The clear, deep sound of Saraneth cut through the whining, broken voice like a foghorn booming above the shriek of seagulls. The chime vibrated on and on, echoing into the night, and Thralk felt it bind him even as his spirit leaked out of the body and made for flight. The bell bound him to paralysed flesh, bound him to the will of the bell-ringer. Fury seethed in him, anger and fear fuelling his struggle, but the sound was everywhere, all around him, all through him. He would never be free of it.

Sabriel watched the misshapen shadow writhing, half out of the corpse, half in it, the body bleeding a pool of darkness. It was still trying to use the corpse's mouth, but without success. She considered going with it into Death, where it would have a shape and she could make it answer with Dyrim. But the broken Charter Stone loomed nearby and she felt it as an ever-present fear, like a cold jewel upon her breast. In her mind, she heard her mother-sending's words, "Do not tarry, do not stop, no matter what happens."

Sabriel thrust her sword point-first into the snow, put Saraneth away and drew Kibeth from the bandoleer, using both hands. Thralk sensed it and his fury gave way to pure, unadulterated fear. After all the centuries of struggle, he knew true death had come for him at last.

Sabriel took up a careful stance, with the bell held in a curious two-handed grip. Kibeth seemed almost to twitch in her hands, but she controlled it, swinging it backwards, forwards, and then in a sort of odd figure eight. The sounds, all from the one bell, were very different to each other, but they made a little marching tune, a dancing song, a parade.

Thralk heard them and felt forces grip him. Strange, inexorable powers that made him find the border, made him return to Death. Vainly, almost pathetically, he struggled against them, knowing he couldn't break free. He knew that he would walk through every Gate, to fall at last through the Ninth. He gave up the struggle and used the last of his strength to form a semblance of a mouth in the middle of his shadow-stuff, a mouth with a writhing tongue of darkness.

"Curse you!" he gurgled. "I will tell the Servants of Kerrigor! I will be revenged..."

His grotesque, gulping voice was chopped off in mid-sentence, as Thralk lost free will. Saraneth had bound him, but Kibeth gripped him and Kibeth walked him, walked him so Thralk would be no more. The twisting shadow simply disappeared and there was only snow under a long-dead corpse.

Even though the revenant was gone, his last words troubled Sabriel. The name Kerrigor, while not exactly familiar, touched some basic fear in her, some memory. Perhaps Abhorsen had spoken this name, which undoubtedly belonged to one of the Greater Dead. The name scared her in the same way the broken stone did, as if they were tangible symbols of a world gone wrong, a world where her father was lost, where she herself was terribly threatened.

Sabriel coughed, feeling the cold in her lungs, and very carefully replaced Kibeth in the bandoleer. Her sword seemed to have burned itself clean, but she ran a cloth over the blade before returning it to the scabbard. She felt very tired as she swung her pack back on, but there was no doubt in her mind that she must move on immediately. Her mother-spirit's words kept echoing in her mind and her own senses told her something was happening in Death, something powerful was moving towards Life, moving towards emergence at the broken stone.

There had been too much death and too much Charter Magic on this hill, and the night was yet to reach its blackest. The wind was swinging around, the clouds regaining their superiority over sky. Soon, the stars would disappear and the young moon would be wrapped in white.

Quickly, Sabriel scanned the heavens, looking for the three bright stars that marked the Buckle of the North Giant's Belt. She found them, but then had to check the star map in her almanac, a handmade match stinking as it cast a yellow flicker on the pages, for she didn't dare use any more Charter Magic till she was away from the broken stone. The almanac showed that she had remembered correctly: the Buckle was due north in the Old Kingdom; its other name was Mariner's Cheat. In Ancelstierre, the Buckle was easily ten degrees west of north.

North located, Sabriel started to make her way to that side of the crest, looking for the spur that slanted down to the valley lost in darkness below. The clouds were thickening and she wanted to reach level ground before the moonlight disappeared. At least the spur, when found, looked like easier going than the broken steps to the south, though its gentle slope proclaimed a long descent to the valley.

In fact, it took several hours before Sabriel reached the valley floor, stumbling and shivering, a very pale Charter flame dancing a little ways in front of her. Too insubstantial to really ease her path, it had helped her avoid major disaster, and she hoped it was pallid enough to be taken for marsh-gas or chance reflection. In any case, it had proved essential when clouds closed the last remaining gap in the sky.

So much for no cloud, Sabriel thought, as she looked towards what she guessed was still north, searching for the red star, Uallus. Her teeth were chattering and would not be stilled, and a shiver that had started with her ice-cold feet was repeating itself through every limb. If she didn't keep moving, she'd simply freeze where she stood – particularly as the wind was rising once more...

Sabriel laughed quietly, almost hysterically, and turned her face to feel the breeze. It was an easterly, gaining strength with the minute. Colder, yes, but it also cleared the cloud, sweeping it to the west – and there, in the first cleared broom-stroke of the wind, was Uallus gleaming red. Sabriel smiled, stared at it, took stock of the little she could see around her, and started off again, following the star, a whispering voice constant in the back of her mind.

Do not tarry, do not stop, no matter what happens.

The smile lasted as Sabriel found the road and, with a good cover of snow in each gutter, she skied, making good time.

By the time Sabriel found the mile marker and the Charter Stone behind it, no trace of the smile could be seen on her pale face. It was snowing again, snowing sideways as the wind grew more frenzied, taking the snowflakes and whipping them into her eyes, now the only exposed portion of her entire body. Her boots were soaked too, despite the mutton fat she'd rubbed into them. Her feet, face and hands were freezing and she was exhausted. She'd dutifully eaten a little every hour, but now, simply couldn't open her frozen jaws.

For a short time, at the intact Charter Stone that rose proudly behind the smaller mile-marker, Sabriel had made herself warm, invoking a Charter-spell for heat. But she'd grown too tired to maintain it without the assistance of the stone and the spell dissipated almost as soon as she walked on. Only the mother-spirit's warning kept her going. That, and the sensation that she was being followed.

It was only a feeling and in her tired, chilled state, Sabriel wondered if it was just imagination. But she wasn't in any state to face up to anything that might not be imagined, so she forced herself to go on.

Do not tarry, do not stop, no matter what happens.

The path from the Charter Stone was better made than the one that climbed Cloven Crest, but steeper. The pathmakers here had to cut through a dense, greyish rock, which did not erode like granite, and they had built hundreds of wide, low steps, carved with intricate patterns. Whether these meant something, Sabriel didn't know. They weren't Charter marks or symbols of any language that she knew, and she was too tired to speculate. She concentrated on one step at a time, using her hands to push down on her aching thighs, coughing and gasping, head down to avoid the flying snow.

The path grew steeper still and Sabriel could see the cliff-face ahead, a huge, black, vertical mass, a much darker backdrop to the swirling snow than the clouded sky, palely backlit by the moon. But she didn't seem to get any closer as the path switchbacked to and fro, rising further and further up from the valley below.

Then, suddenly, Sabriel was there. The path turned again and her little will-o'-the-wisp light reflected back from a wall, a wall that stretched for miles to either side and for hundreds of yards upwards. Clearly, these were the Long Cliffs and the path had ended.

Almost sobbing with relief, Sabriel pushed herself forward to the very base of the cliff and the little light rose above her head to disclose grey, lichen-veined rock. But even with that light, there was no sign of a door – nothing but jagged, impervious rock, going up and out of her tiny circle of illumination. There was no path and nowhere else to go.

Wearily, Sabriel knelt in a patch of snow and rubbed her hands together vigorously, trying to restore circulation, before drawing Mosrael from the bandoleer. Mosrael, the waker. Sabriel stilled it carefully and concentrated her senses, feeling for anything Dead that might be near and should not be woken. There was nothing close, but once again Sabriel felt something behind her, something following her, far down on the path. Something Dead, something reeking of power. She tried to judge how distant the thing was, before forcing it from her thoughts. Whatever it might be, it was too far away to hear even Mosrael's raucous voice. Sabriel stood up and rang the bell.

It made a sound like tens of parrots screeching, a noise that burst into the air and wove itself into the wind, echoing from the cliffs, multiplying into the scream of a thousand birds.

Sabriel stilled the bell at once and put it away, but the echoes raced across the valley and she knew the thing behind her had heard. She felt it fix its attention on where she was and she felt it quicken its pace, like watching the muscles on a racehorse going from the walk to a gallop. It was coming up the steps at least four or five at a time. She felt the rush of it in her head and the fear rising in her at equal pace, but she still went to the path and looked down, drawing her sword as she did so.

There, between gusts of snow, she saw a figure leaping from step to step; impossible leaps, that ate up the distance between them with horrible appetite. It was manlike, more than man-high, and flames ran like burning oil on water where it trod. Sabriel cried out as she saw it, and felt the Dead spirit within. *The Book of the Dead* opened to fearful pages in her memory and descriptions of evil poured into her head. It was a Mordicant that hunted her – a thing that could pass at will through Life and Death, its body of bog-clay and human blood moulded and infused with Free Magic by a necromancer, and a Dead spirit placed inside as its guiding force.

Sabriel had banished a Mordicant once, but that had been forty miles from the Wall, in Ancelstierre, and it had been weak, already fading. This one was strong, fiery, new-born. It would kill her, she suddenly knew, and subjugate her spirit. All her plans and dreams, her hopes and courage, fell out of her to be replaced by pure, unthinking panic. She turned to one side, then the other, like a rabbit running from a dog, but the only way down was the path and the Mordicant was only a hundred yards below, closing with every blink, with every falling snowflake. Flames were spewing from its mouth and it thrust its pointed head back and howled as it ran, a howl like the last shout of someone falling to their death, underlaid with the squeal of fingernails on glass.

Sabriel, a scream somehow stuck and choking in her throat, turned to the cliff, hammering on it with the pommel of her sword.

"Open! Open!" she screamed, as Charter marks raced through her brain – but not the right ones for forcing a door, a spell she'd learned in the Second Form. She knew it like she knew her times tables, but the Charter marks just wouldn't come, and why was twelve times twelve sticking in her head when she wanted Charter marks...

The echoes from Mosrael faded and in that silence the pommel struck on something that thudded hollowly, rather than throwing sparks and jarring her hand. Something wooden, something that hadn't been there before. A door, tall and strangely narrow, its dark oak lined with silver Charter marks dancing through the grain. An iron ring, exactly at hand height, touched Sabriel's hip.

Sabriel dropped her sword with a gasp, grabbed the ring, and pulled. Nothing happened. Sabriel tugged again, half-turning to look over her shoulder, almost cringing at what she would see.

The Mordicant turned the last corner and its eyes met hers. Sabriel shut them, unable to bear the hatred and bloodlust glowing in its gaze like a poker left too long in the forge. It howled again and almost flowed up the remaining steps, flames dripping from its mouth, claws and feet.

Sabriel, eyes still closed, pushed on the ring. The door flew open and she fell in, crashing to the ground in a flurry of snow, eyes snapping open. Desperately, she twisted herself around on the ground, ignoring the pain in her knees and hands. Reaching back outside, she snagged the hilt of her sword and snatched it in.

As the blade cleared the doorway, the Mordicant reached it, and twisting itself sideways to pass the narrow portal, thrust an arm inside. Flames boiled from its grey-green flesh, like beads of sweat, and small plumes of black smoke spiralled from the flames, bringing with them a stench like burning hair.

Sabriel, sprawled defenceless on the floor, could only stare in terror as the thing's four-taloned hand slowly opened and reached out for her.

chapter seven

But the hand didn't close; the talons failed to rend defenceless flesh.

Instead, Sabriel felt a sudden surge of Charter Magic and Charter marks flared around the door, blazing so brightly that they left red after-images at the back of her eyes, black dots dancing across her vision.

Blinking, she saw a man step out from the stones of the wall, a tall and obviously strong man, with a longsword the twin of Sabriel's own. This sword came whistling down on the Mordicant's arm, biting out a chunk of burning, marsh-rotten flesh. Rebounding, the sword flicked back again and hewed another slice, like an axeman sending chips flying from a tree.

The Mordicant howled, more in anger than in pain – but it withdrew the arm and the stranger threw himself against the door, slamming it shut with the full weight of his mail-clad body. Curiously for mail, it made no sound, no jangling from the flow of hundreds of steel links. A strange body under it too, Sabriel saw, as the black dots and the red wash faded, revealing that her rescuer wasn't human at all. He had seemed solid enough, but every square inch of him was defined by tiny, constantly moving Charter marks and Sabriel could see nothing between them but empty air.

He... it was a Charter-ghost, a sending.

Outside, the Mordicant howled again, like a steam train venting pressure, then the whole corridor shook and hinges screeched in protest as the thing threw itself against the door. Wood splintered and clouds of thick grey dust fell from the ceiling, mocking the falling snow outside.

The sending turned to face Sabriel and offered its hand to help her up. Sabriel took it, looking up at it as her tired, frozen legs struggled to make a tenth-round comeback. Close to, the illusion of flesh was imperfect, fluid and unsettling. Its face wouldn't stay fixed, migrating between scores of possibilities. Some were women, some were men — but all bore tough, competent visages. Its body and clothing changed slightly too, with every face, but two details always remained the same: a black surcoat with the blazon of a silver key, and a longsword redolent with Charter Magic.

"Thank you," Sabriel said nervously, flinching as the Mordicant pounded the door again. "Can... do you think that... will it get through?"

The sending nodded grimly and let go her hand to point up the long corridor, but it did not speak. Sabriel turned her head to follow its pointing hand and saw a dark passage that rose up into darkness. Charter marks illuminated where they stood, but faded only a little way on. Despite this, the darkness seemed friendly and she could almost taste the Charter-spells that rode on the corridor's dusty air.

"I must go on?" asked Sabriel, as it pointed again, more urgently. The sending nodded and flapped its hand backwards and forwards, indicating haste. Behind him, another crashing blow caused another great billow of dust and the door sounded as if it was weakening. Once again, the vile, burnt smell of the Mordicant wafted through the air.

The doorkeeper wrinkled its nose and gave Sabriel a bit of a push in the right direction, like a parent urging a reluctant child to press on. But Sabriel needed no urging. Her fear was still burning in her. Momentarily extinguished by the rescue, the smell of the Mordicant was all it needed to blaze again. She set her face upwards and started to walk quickly, into the passage.

She looked back after a few yards, to see the doorkeeper waiting near the door, its sword at the guard position. Beyond it, the door was bulging in, iron-bound planks bursting, breaking around a hole as big as a dinner plate.

The Mordicant reached in and broke off more planks, as easily as it might snap toothpicks. It was obviously furious that its prey was getting away, for it burned all over now. Yellow-red flames vomited from its mouth in a vile torrent and black smoke rose like a second shadow around it, eddying in crazy circles as it howled.

Sabriel looked away, setting off at a fast walk, but the walk grew faster and faster, became a jog and then a run. Her feet pounded on the stone, but it wasn't until she was almost sprinting, that she realised why she could – her pack and skis were still back at the lower door. For a moment, she was struck with a nervous inclination to go back, but it passed before it even became conscious thought. Even so, her hands checked scabbard and bandoleer, and gained reassurance from the cool metal of sword hilt and the hand-smoothed wood of the bell handles.

It was light too, she realised as she ran. Charter marks ran in the stone, keeping pace with her. Charter marks for light and for fleetness, and for many other things she didn't know. Strange marks and many of them – so many that Sabriel wondered how she could have ever thought that a First in magic from an Ancelstierran school would make her a great mage in the Old Kingdom. Fear and realisation of ignorance were strong medicines against stupid pride.

Another howl came racing up the passage and echoed onwards, accompanied by many crashes, and thuds or clangs of steel striking supernatural flesh or ricocheting off stone. Sabriel didn't need to look back to know the Mordicant had broken through the door and was now fighting the doorkeeper – or pushing past him. Sabriel knew little of such sendings, but a common failing with the sentinel variety was an inability to leave their post. Once the creature got a few feet past the doorkeeper, the sending would be useless – and one great charge would soon get the Mordicant past.

That thought gave her another burst of speed, but Sabriel knew that it was the last. Her body, pushed by fear and weakened by cold and exertion, was on the edge of failure. Her legs felt stiff, muscles ready to cramp, and her lungs seemed to bubble with fluid rather than air.

Ahead, the corridor seemed to go on and on, sloping ever upwards. But the light only shone where Sabriel ran, so perhaps the exit might not be too far ahead, perhaps just past the next little patch of darkness...

Even as this thought passed through her mind, Sabriel saw a glow that sharpened into the bright tracing of a doorway. She half gasped, half cried out, both slight human noises drowned out by the unholy, inhuman screech of the Mordicant. It was past the doorkeeper.

At the same time, Sabriel became aware of a new sound ahead, a sound she had initially thought was the throb of blood in her ears, the pounding of a racing heart. But it was outside, beyond the upper door. A deep, roaring noise, so low it was almost a vibration, a shudder that she felt through the floor, rather than heard.

Heavy trucks passing on a road above, Sabriel thought, before remembering where she was. In that same instant, she recognised the sound. Somewhere ahead, out of these encircling cliffs, a great waterfall was crashing down. And a waterfall that made so great a sound must be fed by an equally great river.

Running water! The prospect of it fuelled Sabriel with sudden hope and with that hope came the strength she thought beyond her. In a wild spurt of speed, she almost hit the door, hands slapping against the wood, slowing for the instant she needed to find the handle or ring.

But another hand was already on the ring when she touched it, though none had been there a second before. Again, Charter marks defined this hand, and Sabriel could see the grain of the wood and the blueing of the steel through the palm of another sending.

This one was smaller, of indeterminate sex, for it was wearing a habit like a monk's, with the hood drawn across its head. The habit was black and bore the emblem of the silver key front and back.

It bowed and turned the ring. The door swung open, to reveal bright starlight shining down between clouds fleeing the newly-risen wind. The noise of the waterfall roared through the open doorway, accompanied by flecks of flying spray. Without thinking, Sabriel stepped out.

The cowled doorkeeper came with her and shut the door behind it, before dragging a delicate, silver portcullis down across the door and locking it with an iron padlock. Both defences apparently came out of thin air. Sabriel looked at them and felt power in them, for both were also Charter sendings. But door, portcullis and lock would only slow the Mordicant, not stop it. The only possible escape lay across the swiftest of running water, or the untimely glare of a noonday sun.

The first lay at her feet and the second was still many hours away. Sabriel stood on a narrow ledge that projected out from the bank of a river at least four hundred yards wide. A little to her right, a scant few paces away, this mighty river hurled itself over the cliff, to make a truly glorious waterfall. Sabriel leaned forward a little, to look at the waters crashing below, creating huge white wings of spray that could easily swallow her entire school, new wing and all, like a rubber duck swamped in an unruly bath.

It was a very long fall and the height, coupled with the sheer power of the water, made her quickly look back to the river. Straight ahead, halfway across, Sabriel could just make out an island, an island perched on the very lip of the waterfall, dividing the river into two streams. It wasn't a very big island, about the size of a football field, but it rose like a ship of jagged rock from the turbulent waters.

Limestone-white walls circled the island, the height of six men. Behind those walls was a house. It was too dark to see clearly, but there was a tower, a thrusting, pencil silhouette, with red tiles that were just beginning to catch the dawning sun. Below the tower, a dark bulk hinted at the existence of a hall, a kitchen, bedrooms, armoury, buttery and cellar. The study, Sabriel suddenly remembered, occupied the second to top floor of the tower. The top floor was an observatory, both of stars and the surrounding territory.

It was Abhorsen's House. Home, although Sabriel had only visited it twice or maybe three times, all when she was too young to remember much. That period of her life was hazy and mostly filled with recollections of the Travellers, the interiors of their wagons, and many different campsites that all blurred together. She didn't even remember the waterfall, though the sound of it did stir some recognition – something had lodged in the mind of a four-year-old girl.

Unfortunately, she didn't remember how to get to the house. Only the words her mother-sending had given her – Abhorsen's Bridge.

She hadn't realised she'd spoken these words aloud, till the little gate warden tugged at her sleeve and pointed down. Sabriel looked and saw steps carved into the bank, steps leading right down to the river.

This time, Sabriel didn't hesitate. She nodded to the Charter sending and whispered, "Thank you," before taking the steps. The Mordicant's presence was pressing at her again, like a stranger's rank breath behind her ear. She knew it had reached the upper gate, though the sound of its battering and destruction was drowned in the greater roar of the waters.

The steps led to the river, but did not end there. Though invisible from the ledge, there were stepping stones leading out to the island. Sabriel eyed them nervously and looked at the water. It was clearly very deep and rushing past at an alarming speed. The stepping stones were barely above its boisterous wavelets and, even though they were wide and cross-hatched for grip, they were also wet with spray and the slushy remnants of snow and ice.

Sabriel watched a small piece of ice from upstream hurtle by, and pictured its slingshot ride over the falls, to be smashed apart so far below. She imagined herself in its place, and then thought of the Mordicant behind her, of the Dead spirit that was at its heart, of the death it would bring, and the imprisonment she would suffer beyond death.

She jumped. Her boots skidded a little and her arms flailed for balance, but she ended up steady, bent over in a half-crouch.

Hardly waiting to re-balance, she jumped to the next stone and then the one after that, and again, in a mad leapfrog through the spray and thunder of the river. When she was halfway out, with a hundred yards of pure, ferocious water behind her, she stopped and looked back.

The Mordicant was on the ledge, the silvery portcullis broken and mangled in its grip. There was no sign of the gate warden, but that was not surprising. Defeated, it would merely fade until the Charter-spell renewed itself – hours, days or even years later.

The Dead thing was curiously still, but it was clearly watching Sabriel. Even so powerful a creature couldn't cross this river and it made no attempt to do so. In fact, the longer Sabriel stared at it, the more it seemed to her that the Mordicant was content to wait. It was a sentry, guarding what might be the only exit from the island. Or perhaps it was waiting for something to happen, or for someone to arrive...

Sabriel suppressed a shudder and jumped on. There was more light now, heralding the advent of the sun, and she could see a sort of wooden landing stage leading up to a gate in the white wall. Treetops were also visible behind the walls, winter trees, their branches bare of green raiment. Birds flew between trees and tower, little birds launching themselves for their morning forage. It was a vision of normality, of a haven. But Sabriel could not forget the tall, flame-etched silhouette of the Mordicant, brooding on the ledge.

Wearily, she made the jump to the last stone and collapsed on the steps of the landing stage. Even her eyelids could barely move and her field of vision had narrowed to a little slit directly to her front. The grain of the planks of the landing stage loomed close, as she crawled up to the gate and half-heartedly fell against it.

The gate swung open, pitching her on to a paved courtyard, the beginning of a red-brick path, the bricks ancient, their redness the colour of dusty apples. The path wound up to the front door of the house, a cheerful sky-blue door, bright against whitewashed stone. A bronze doorknocker in the shape of a lion's head holding a ring in its mouth gleamed in counterpoint to the white cat that lay coiled on the rush mat before the door.

Sabriel lay on the bricks and smiled up at the cat, blinking back tears. The cat twitched and turned its head ever so slightly to look at her, revealing bright, green eyes.

"Hello, puss," croaked Sabriel, coughing as she staggered once more to her feet and walked forward, groaning and creaking with every step. She reached down to pat the cat and froze – for, as the cat thrust its head up, she saw the collar around its neck and the tiny bell that hung there. The collar was only red leather, but the Charter-spell on it was the strongest, most enduring binding that Sabriel had ever seen or felt – and the bell was a miniature Saraneth. The cat was no cat, but a Free Magic creature of ancient power.

"Abhorsen," mewed the cat, its little pink tongue darting. "About time you got here."

Sabriel stared at it for a moment, gave a little sort of moan and fell forward in a faint of exhaustion and dismay.

chapter eight

S abriel awoke to soft candlelight, the warmth of a feather bed and silken sheets, delightfully smooth under heavy blankets. A fire burned briskly in a red-brick fireplace and wood-panelled walls gleamed with the dark mystery of well-polished mahogany. A blue-papered ceiling with silver stars dusted across it, faced her newly opened eyes. Two windows confronted each other across the room, but they were shuttered, so Sabriel had no idea what time it was, no more than she had any remembrance of how she'd got there. It was definitely Abhorsen's House, but her last memory was of fainting on the doorstep.

Gingerly – for even her neck ached from her day and night of travel, fear and flight – Sabriel lifted her head to look around and once again met the green eyes of the cat that wasn't a cat. The creature was lying near her feet, at the end of the bed.

"Who... what are you?" Sabriel asked nervously, suddenly all too aware that she was naked under the soft sheets. A sensuous delight, but a defenceless one. Her eyes flickered to her sword-belt and bell-bandoleer, carefully draped on a clothes-horse near the door.

"I have a variety of names," replied the cat. It had a strange voice, half-mew, half-purr, with hissing on the vowels. "You may call me Mogget. As to what I am, I was once many things, but now I am only several. Primarily, I am a servant of Abhorsen. Unless you would be kind enough to remove my collar?"

Sabriel gave an uneasy smile and shook her head firmly. Whatever Mogget was, that collar was the only thing that kept it as a servant of Abhorsen... or anybody else. The Charter marks on the collar were quite explicit about that. As far as Sabriel could tell, the binding spell was over a thousand years old. It was quite possible that Mogget was some Free Magic spirit as old as the Wall or even older. She wondered why her father hadn't mentioned it, and with a pang, wished that she had awoken to find her father here, in his house, both their troubles over.

"I thought not," said Mogget, combining a careless shrug with a limbering stretch. It... or he, for Sabriel felt the cat was definitely masculine, jumped to the parquet floor and sauntered over to the fire. Sabriel watched, her trained eye noting that Mogget's shadow was not always that of a cat.

A knock at the door interrupted her study of the cat, the sharp sound making Sabriel jump nervously, the hair on the back of her neck frizzing to attention.

"It's only one of the servants," Mogget said, in a patronising tone. "Charter sendings, and pretty low-grade ones at that. They always burn the milk."

Sabriel ignored him and said, "Come in." Her voice shook and she realised that shaky nerves and weakness would be with her for a while.

The door swung open silently and a short, robed figure drifted in. It was similar to the upper gatewarden, being cowled and so without a visible face, but this one's habit was of light cream rather than black. It had a simple cotton underdress draped over one arm, a thick towel over the other and its Charter-woven hands held a long woollen surcoat and a pair of slippers. Without a word, it went to the end of the bed and put the garments on Sabriel's feet. Then it crossed to a porcelain basin that sat in a silver filigree stand, above a tiled area of the floor to the left of the fire. There, it twisted a bronze wheel and steaming hot water splashed and gurgled from a pipe in the wall, bringing with it the stench of something sulphurous and unpleasant. Sabriel wrinkled her nose.

"Hot springs," commented Mogget. "You won't smell it after a while. Your father always said that having permanent hot water was worth bearing the smell. Or was it your grandfather who said that? Or great-great-aunt? Ah, memory…"

The servant stood immobile while the basin filled, then twisted the wheel to cut the flow as water slopped over the rim to the floor, close to Mogget – who leapt to his feet and padded away, keeping a cautious distance from the Charter sending. Just like a real cat, Sabriel thought. Perhaps the imposed shape impressed behaviour too, over the years – or centuries. She liked cats. The school had a cat, a plump marmalade feline, who went by the name of Biscuits. Sabriel thought about the way it slept on the windowsill of the Prefect's Room and then found herself thinking about the school in general, and what her friends would be doing. Her eyelids drooped as she imagined an Etiquette class and the Mistress droning on about silver salvers...

A sharp clang woke her with yet another start, sending further stabs of pain through tired muscles. The Charter sending had tapped the bronze wheel with the poker from the fireplace. It was obviously impatient for Sabriel to have her wash.

"Water's getting cold," explained Mogget, leaping up to the bed again. "And they'll be serving dinner in half an hour."

"They?" asked Sabriel, sitting up and reaching forward to grab slippers and towel, preparatory to sidling out of bed and into them.

"Them," said Mogget, butting his head in the direction of the sending, who had stepped back from the basin and was now holding out a bar of soap.

Sabriel shuffled over to the basin, the towel wrapped firmly around her, and gingerly touched the water. It was delightfully hot, but before she could do anything with it, the sending stepped forward, whisked the towel off her and upended the whole basin over her head.

Sabriel shrieked, but again before she could do anything else, the sending had put back the basin, turned the wheel for more hot water and was soaping her down, paying particular attention to her head, as if it wanted to get soap in Sabriel's eyes, or suspected an infestation of nits.

"What are you doing!" Sabriel protested, as the strangely cool hands of the sending scrubbed at her back and then, quite without interest, at her breasts and stomach. "Stop it! I'm quite old enough to wash myself, thank you!"

But Miss Prionte's techniques for dealing with domestic servants didn't seem to work on domestic sendings. It kept scrubbing, occasionally tipping hot water over Sabriel.

"How do I stop it?" she spluttered to Mogget, as still more water cascaded over her head and the sending started to scrub lower regions.

"You can't," replied Mogget, who seemed quite amused by the spectacle. "This one's particularly recalcitrant."

"What do you... ow!... stop that! What do you mean, this one?"

"There's lots about the place," said Mogget. "Every Abhorsen seems to have made their own. Probably because they get like this one after a few hundred years. Privileged family retainers, who always think they know best. Practically human, in the worst possible way."

The sending paused in its scrubbing just long enough to flick some water at Mogget, who jumped the wrong way and yowled as it hit him. Just before another great basin-load of water hit Sabriel, she saw the cat shoot under the bed, his tail dividing the bedspread.

"That's enough, thank you!" she pronounced, as the last drench of water drained out through a grille in the tiled area. The sending had probably finished anyway, thought Sabriel, as it stopped washing and started to towel her dry. She snatched the towel back from it and tried to finish the job herself, but the sending counterattacked by combing her hair, causing another minor tussle. Eventually, between the two of them, Sabriel shrugged on the underdress and surcoat, and submitted to a manicure and vigorous hair-brushing.

She was admiring the tiny, repeated silver key motif on the black surcoat in the mirror that backed one of the window-shutters, when a gong sounded somewhere else in the house and the servant-sending opened the door. A split second later, Mogget raced through, with a cry that Sabriel thought was "Dinner!" She followed, rather more sedately, the sending closing the door behind her.

Dinner was in the main hall of the house. A long, stately room that took up half the ground floor, it was dominated by the floor to ceiling stained-glass window at the western end. The window showed a scene from the building of the Wall and, like many other things around the house, was heavily laden with Charter Magic. Perhaps there was no real glass in it at all, Sabriel mused, as she watched the light of the evening sun play in and around the toiling figures that were building the Wall. As with the sendings, if you looked closely enough you could see tiny Charter marks making up the patterns. It was hard to see through the window, but judging from the sun, it was almost dusk. Sabriel realised she must have slept for a full day, or possibly even two.

A table nearly as long as the hall stretched away from her – a brightly polished table of some light and lustrous timber, heavily laden with silver salt cellars, candelabra and rather fantastic-looking decanters and covered dishes. But only two places were fully set, with a plethora of knives, forks, spoons and other instruments, which Sabriel only recognised from obscure drawings in her Etiquette textbook. She'd never seen a real golden straw for sucking the innards out of a pomegranate before, for example.

One place was before a high-backed chair at the head of the table and the other was to the left of this, in front of a cushioned stool. Sabriel wondered which was hers, till Mogget jumped up on the stool and said, "Come on! They won't serve till you're seated."

"They" were more sendings. Half a dozen in all, including the cream-dressed tyrant of the bedroom. They were all basically the same; human in shape, but cowled or veiled. Only their hands were visible and these were almost transparent, as if Charter marks had been lightly etched on prosthetic hands carved from moonstone. The sendings stood grouped around a door – the kitchen door, for Sabriel saw fires beyond them and smelled the tang of cooking – and stared at her. It was rather unnerving, not to meet any eyes.

"Yes, that's her," Mogget said caustically. "Your new mistress. Now let's have dinner."

None of the sendings moved, till Sabriel stepped forward. They stepped forward too, and all dropped to one knee or whatever supported them beneath the floor-length robes. Each held out their pale right hand, Charter marks running bright trails around their palms and fingers.

Sabriel stared for a moment, but it was clear they offered their services, or loyalty, and expected her to do something in return. She walked to them and gently pressed each upthrust hand in turn, feeling the Charter-spells that made them whole. Mogget had spoken truly, for some of the spells were old, far older than Sabriel could guess.

"I thank you," she said slowly. "On behalf of my father, and for the kindness you have shown me."

This seemed to be appropriate or enough to be going on with. The sendings stood, bowed, and went about their business. The one in the cream habit pulled out Sabriel's chair and placed her napkin as she sat. It was of crisp black linen, dusted with tiny silver keys, a miracle of needlework. Mogget, Sabriel noticed, had a plain white napkin, with evidence of old stains.

"I've had to eat in the kitchen for the last two weeks," Mogget said sourly, as two sendings approached from the kitchen, bearing plates that signalled their arrival with a tantalising odour of spices and hot food.

"I expect it was good for you," Sabriel replied brightly, taking a mouthful of wine. It was a fruity, dry white wine, though Sabriel hadn't developed a palate to know whether it was good or merely indifferent. It was certainly drinkable. Her first major experiments with alcohol lay several years behind her, enshrined in memory as significant occasions shared with two of her closest friends. None of the three could ever drink brandy again, but Sabriel had started to enjoy wine with her meals.

"Anyway, how did you know I was coming?" Sabriel asked. "I didn't know myself, till... till father sent his message."

The cat didn't answer at once, his attention focused on the plate of fish the sending had just put down – small, almost circular fish, with the bright eyes and shiny scales of the freshly caught. Sabriel had them too, but hers were grilled, with a tomato, garlic and basil sauce.

"I have served ten times as many of your forebears as you have years," Mogget replied at last. "And though my powers wane with the ebb of time, I always know when one Abhorsen falls and another takes their place."

Sabriel swallowed her last mouthful, all taste gone, and put down her fork. She took a mouthful of wine to clear her throat, but it seemed to have become vinegar, making her cough.

"What do you mean by fall? What do you know? What has happened to Father?"

Mogget looked up at Sabriel, eyes half-lidded, meeting her gaze steadily, as no normal cat could.

"He is dead, Sabriel. Even if he hasn't passed the Final Gate, he will walk in life no more. That is—"

"No," interrupted Sabriel. "He can't be! He cannot be. He is a necromancer... he can't be dead..."

"That is why he sent the sword and bells to you, as his aunt sent them to him, in her time," Mogget continued, ignoring Sabriel's outburst. "And he was not a necromancer, he was Abhorsen."

"I don't understand," Sabriel whispered. She couldn't face Mogget's eyes any more. "I don't know... I don't know enough. About anything. The Old Kingdom, Charter Magic, even my own father. Why do you say his name as if it were a title?"

"It is. He was the Abhorsen. Now you are."

Sabriel digested this in silence, staring at the swirls of fish and sauce on her plate, silver scales and red tomato blurring into a pattern of swords and fire. The table blurred too, and the room beyond, and she felt herself reaching for the border with Death. But try as she might, she couldn't cross it. She sensed it, but there was no way to cross, in either direction – Abhorsen's House was too well protected. But she did feel something at the border. Inimical things lurked there, waiting for her to cross, but there was also the faintest thread of something familiar, like the scent of a woman's perfume after she has left the room, or the waft of a particular pipe tobacco around a corner. Sabriel focused on it and threw herself once more at the barrier that separated her from Death.

Only to ricochet back to Life, as sharp claws pricked her arm. Her eyes snapped open, blinking off flakes of frost, to see Mogget, fur bristling, one paw ready to strike again.

"Fool!" he hissed. "You are the only one who can break the wards of this House and they wait for you to do so!"

Sabriel stared at the angry cat, unseeing, biting back a sharp and proud retort as she realised the truth in Mogget's words. There were Dead spirits waiting and probably the Mordicant would cross as well – and she would have faced them alone and weaponless.

"I'm sorry," she muttered, bowing her head into two frosted hands. She hadn't felt this stupidly awful since she'd burned one of the Headmistress's rose bushes with an uncontrolled Charter-spell, narrowly missing the school's ancient and much-loved gardener. She had cried then, but she was older now, and could keep the tears at bay.

"Father is not yet truly dead," she said, after a moment. "I felt his presence, though he is trapped beyond many gates. I could bring him back."

"You must not," said Mogget firmly and his voice now seemed to carry all the weight of centuries. "You are Abhorsen and must put the Dead to rest. Your path is chosen."

"I can walk a different path," Sabriel replied firmly, raising her head.

Mogget seemed about to protest again, then he laughed – a sardonic laugh – and jumped back to his stool.

"Do as you will," he said. "Why should I gainsay you? I am but a slave, bound to service. Why would I weep if Abhorsen falls to evil? It is your father who would curse you, and your mother too – and the Dead who will be merry."

"I don't think he's dead," Sabriel said, bright blushes of withheld emotion in her pallid cheeks, frost melting, trickling down around her face. "His spirit felt alive. He is trapped in Death, I think, but his body lives. Would I still be reviled if I brought him back then?"

"No," said Mogget, calm again. "But he has sent the sword and bells. You are only wishing that he lives."

"I feel it," Sabriel said simply. "And I must find out if my feeling is true."

"Perhaps it is so – though strange." Mogget seemed to be musing to himself, his voice a soft half-purr. "I have grown dull. This collar strangles me, chokes my wits..."

"Help me, Mogget," Sabriel suddenly pleaded, reaching over to touch her hand to the cat's head, scratching under the collar. "I need to know – I need to know so much!"

Mogget purred under the scratching, but as Sabriel leaned close, she could hear the faint peal of the tiny Saraneth bell cut through the purr and she was reminded that Mogget was no cat, but a Free Magic creature. For a moment, Sabriel wondered what Mogget's true shape was and his true nature.

"I am the servant of Abhorsen," Mogget said at last. "And you are Abhorsen, so I must help you. But you must promise me that you will not raise your father, if his body is dead. Truly, he would not wish it."

"I cannot promise. But I will not act without much thought. And I will listen to you, if you are by me."

"I guessed as much," Mogget said, twisting his head away from Sabriel's hand. "It is true that you are sadly ignorant or you would promise with a will. Your father should never have sent you beyond the Wall."

"Why did he?" asked Sabriel, her heart suddenly leaping with the question that had been with her all her schooldays, a question Abhorsen had always smiled away with the one word, "Necessity."

"He was afraid," replied Mogget, turning his attention back to the fish. "You were safer in Ancelstierre."

"What was he afraid of?"

"Eat your fish," replied Mogget, as two sendings appeared from the kitchen, bearing what was obviously the next course. "We'll talk later. In the study."

chapter nine

anterns lit the study, old brass lanterns that burned with Charter Magic in place of oil. Smokeless, silent and eternal, they provided as good a light as the electric bulbs of Ancelstierre.

Books lined the walls, following the curves of the tower around, save for where the stair rose from below, and the ladder climbed to the observatory above.

A redwood table sat in the middle of the room, its legs scaled and beady-eyed, ornamental flames licking from the mouths of the dragon-heads that gripped each corner of the tabletop. An inkwell, pens, papers and a pair of bronze map dividers lay upon the table. Chairs of the same red wood surrounded it, their upholstery black with a variation on the silver key motif.

The table was one of the few things Sabriel remembered from her childhood visits. "Dragon desk" her father had called it, and she'd wrapped herself around one of those dragon legs, her head not even reaching the underside of the table.

Sabriel ran her hand over the smooth, cool wood, feeling both her memory of it and the current sensation, then she sighed, pulled up a chair and put down the three books she'd tucked under her arm. Two, she put together close to her, the other she pushed to the centre of the table. This third book came from the single glassed-in cabinet among the bookshelves and now lay like some quiescent predator, possibly asleep, possibly waiting to spring. Its binding was of pale green leather and Charter marks burned in the silver clasps that held it closed. *The Book of the Dead*.

The other two books were normal enough by comparison. Both were Charter Magic spell books, listing mark after mark and how they could be used. Sabriel didn't even recognise most of the marks after chapter four in the first book. There were twenty chapters in each volume.

Doubtless there were many other books that would be useful, Sabriel thought, but she still felt too tired and shaky to get more down. She planned to talk to Mogget, then study for an hour or two, before going back to bed. Even four or five waking hours seemed too much after her ordeal, and the loss of consciousness involved in sleep suddenly seemed very appealing.

Mogget, as if he had heard Sabriel thinking of him, appeared at the top of the steps and sauntered over to sprawl on a well-upholstered footstand.

"I see you have found *that* book," he said, tail flicking backwards and forwards as he spoke. "Take care you do not read too much."

"I've already read it all, anyway," replied Sabriel, shortly.

"Perhaps," remarked the cat. "But it isn't always the same book. Like me, it is several things, not one."

Sabriel shrugged, as if to show that she knew all about the book. But that was just bravado – the inner Sabriel was afraid of *The Book of the Dead*. She had worked her way through every chapter, under her father's direction, but her normally excellent memory held only selected pages of this tome. If it changed its contents as well – she suppressed a shiver, and told herself that she knew all that was necessary.

"My first step must be to find my father's body," she said. "Which is where I need your help, Mogget."

"I have no knowledge of where he met his end," Mogget stated, with finality. He yawned and started licking his paws.

Sabriel frowned and found herself pulling in her lips, a characteristic she had deplored in the unpopular history teacher at school, who often went "thin-lipped" in anger or exasperation.

"Just tell me when you last saw him and what his plans were."

"Why don't you read his diary," suggested Mogget, in a momentary break from cleaning himself.

"Where is it?" asked Sabriel, excited. A diary would be tremendously helpful.

"He probably took it with him," replied Mogget. "I haven't seen it."

"I thought you had to help me!" Sabriel said, another frown wrinkling across her forehead, reinforcing the thin lips. "Please answer my question."

"Three weeks ago," Mogget mumbled, mouth half muffled in the fur of his stomach, pink tongue alternating between words and cleansing. "A messenger came from Belisaere, begging for his help. Something Dead, something that could pass the wards, was preying on them. Abhorsen – I mean the previous Abhorsen, ma'am – suspected that there was more to it than that, Belisaere being Belisaere. But he went."

"Belisaere. The name's familiar – it's a town?"

"A city. The capital. At least it was, when there was still a Kingdom."

"Was?"

Mogget stopped washing and looked across, eyes narrowing to frowning slits. "What did they teach you in that school? There hasn't been a King or Queen for two hundred years, and not even a Regent for twenty. That's why the Kingdom sinks day by day, into a darkness from which no one will rise..."

"The Charter—" Sabriel began, but Mogget interrupted with a yowl of derision.

"The Charter crumbles too," he mewed. "Without a ruler, Charter Stones broken one by one with blood, one of the Great Charters twi... twis... twisted—"

"What do you mean, one of the Great Charters?" Sabriel interrupted in turn. She had never heard of such a thing. Not for the first time, she also wondered what she'd been taught in school, and why her father had kept so quiet about the state of the Old Kingdom.

But Mogget was silent, as if the things he'd already said had stopped his mouth. For a moment, he seemed to be trying to form words, but nothing came from his small red mouth. Finally, he gave up. "I cannot tell you. It's part of my binding, curse it! Suffice to say that the whole world slides into evil and many are helping the slide."

"And others resist it," said Sabriel. "Like my father. Like me."

"It depends what you do," Mogget said, as if he doubted that someone as patently useless as Sabriel would make much difference. "Not that I care—"

The sound of the trapdoor opening above their heads stopped the cat in mid-speech. Sabriel tensed, looking up to see what was coming down the ladder, then started breathing again as she realised that it was only another Charter sending, its black habit flopping over the rungs of the ladder as it came down. This one, like the guards on the cliff corridor – but unlike the other House servants – had the silver key emblazoned on its chest and back. It bowed to Sabriel and pointed up.

With a feeling of foreboding, Sabriel knew that it wanted her to look at something from the observatory. Reluctantly, she pushed her chair back and went over to the ladder. A cold draught was blowing in through the open trapdoor, carrying with it the chill of ice from further up the river. Sabriel shivered, as her hands touched the cold metal rungs.

Emerging into the observatory, the chill passed, for the room was still lit by the last, red light of the setting sun, giving an illusion of warmth and making Sabriel squint. She had no memory of this room, so it was with delight that she saw that it was totally walled in glass, or something like it. The bare beams of the red-tiled roof rested on transparent walls, so cleverly mortised together that the roof was like a work of art, complete with the slight draught that reduced its perfection to a more human level.

A large telescope of gleaming glass and bronze dominated the observatory, standing triumphant on a tripod of dark wood and darker iron. A tall observer's stool stood next to it and a lectern, a star chart still spilled across it. A thick, toe wriggle-inviting carpet lay under all, a carpet that was also a map of the heavens, showing many different, colourful constellations and whirling planets, woven in thick, richly-dyed wool.

The sending, who had followed Sabriel, went to the south wall and pointed out towards the southern river bank, its pallid, Charter-drawn hand pointing directly at the spot where Sabriel had emerged after her underground flight from the Mordicant.

Sabriel looked where it pointed, shielding her right eye from the west-falling sun. Her gaze crossed the white tops of the river and was drawn to the ledge, despite an inner quailing about what she would see.

As she feared, the Mordicant was still there. But with what she had come to think of as her Death sight, Sabriel sensed it was quiescent, temporarily just an unpleasant statue, a foreground to other, more active shapes that bustled about in some activity behind.

Sabriel stared a little longer, then went to the telescope, narrowly avoiding Mogget, who had somehow appeared underfoot. Sabriel wondered how he had got up the ladder, then dismissed the thought as she concentrated on what was happening outside.

Unaided, she hadn't been certain what the shapes around the Mordicant were, but they sprang sharply at her through the telescope, drawn so close she felt she could somehow lean forward and snatch them away.

They were men and women – living, breathing people. Each was shackled to a partner's leg by an iron chain and they shuffled about in these pairs under the dominating presence of the Mordicant. There were scores of them, coming out of the corridor, carrying heavily-laden leather buckets or lengths of timber, taking them across the ledge and down the steps to the river. Then they filed back again, buckets empty, timber left behind.

Sabriel depressed the telescope a little and almost growled in exasperation and anger as she saw the scene by the river. More living slaves were hammering long boxes together from the timber, and these boxes were being filled with earth from the buckets. As each box was filled, it was pushed out to bridge the gap from shore to stepping stone and locked in place by slaves hammering iron spikes into the stone.

This particular part of the operation was being directed by something that lurked well back from the river, halfway up the steps. A man-shaped blot of blackest night, a moving silhouette. A necromancer's Shadow Hand, or some free-willed Dead spirit that scorned the use of a body.

As Sabriel watched, the last of four boxes was thrust out to the first stepping stone, spiked in place, and then chained to its three adjacent fellows. One slave, fastening the chain, overbalanced and went headfirst into the water, his shacklemate following a second later. Their screams, if any, were drowned by the roar of the waterfall as effectively as its waters took their bodies. A few seconds later, Sabriel felt their lives snuffed out.

The other slaves at the river's edge stopped working for a moment, either shocked at the sudden loss, or momentarily made more afraid of the river than their masters. But the Shadow Hand on the steps moved towards them, its legs like treacle, pouring down the slope, lapping over each step in turn. It gestured for some of the nearer slaves to walk across the earth-filled boxes to the stepping stone. They did so, to cluster unhappily amid the spray.

The Shadow Hand hesitated then, but the Mordicant on the ledge above seemed to stir and rock forward a little, so the shadowy abomination gingerly trod on the boxes – and walked across to the stepping stone, taking no scathe from the running water.

"Grave dirt," commented Mogget, who obviously didn't need the telescope. "Carted up by the villagers from Qyrre and Roble's Town. I wonder if they've got enough to cross all the stones."

"Grave dirt," commented Sabriel bleakly, watching a fresh round of slaves arriving with buckets and more timber. "I had forgotten it could negate the running water. I thought... I thought I would be safe here, for a time."

"Well, you are," said Mogget. "It'll take at least until

tomorrow evening before their bridge is complete, particularly allowing for a couple of hours off around noon, when the Dead will have to hide if it isn't overcast. But this shows planning and that means a leader. Still, every Abhorsen has enemies. It may just be a petty necromancer with a better brain for strategy than most."

"I slew a Dead thing at Cloven Crest," Sabriel said slowly, thinking aloud. "It said it would have its revenge and spoke of telling the Servants of Kerrigor. Do you know that name?"

"I know it," spat Mogget, tail quivering straight out behind him. "But I cannot speak of it, except to say it is one of the Greater Dead and your father's most terrible enemy. Do not say it lives again!"

"I don't know," replied Sabriel, looking down at the cat, whose body seemed twisted, as if in turmoil between command and resistance. "Why can't you tell me more? The binding?"

"A... a perversion of... the g... g... yes," Mogget croaked out with effort. Though his green eyes seemed to grow luminous and fiery with anger at his own feeble explanation, he could say no more.

"Coils within coils," remarked Sabriel thoughtfully. There seemed little doubt that some evil power was working against her, from the moment she'd crossed the Wall – or even before that, if her father's disappearance was anything to go by.

She looked back through the telescope again and took some heart in the slowing of the work as the last light faded, though at the same time she felt a pang of sympathy for the poor people the Dead had enslaved. Many would probably freeze to death or die of exhaustion, only to be brought back as dull-witted Hands. Only those who went over the waterfall would escape that fate. Truly, the Old Kingdom was a terrible place, when even death did not mean an end to slavery and despair.

"Is there another way out?" she asked, swivelling the telescope around 180 degrees to look at the northern bank. There were stepping stones going there, too, and another door high on the riverbank, but there were also dark shapes clustered on the ledge by the door. Four or five Shadow Hands, too many for Sabriel to fight through alone.

"It seems not," she answered herself grimly. "What of defences, then? Can the sendings fight?"

"The sendings don't need to fight," replied Mogget. "For there is another defence, though it is a rather constrictive one. And there is one other way out, though you probably won't like it."

The sending next to her nodded and pantomimed something with its arm that looked like a snake wiggling through grass.

"What's that?" asked Sabriel, fighting back a sudden urge to break into hysterical laughter. "The defence or the way out?"

"The defence," replied Mogget. "The river itself. It can be invoked to rise almost to the height of the island walls – four times your height above the stepping stones. Nothing can pass such a flood, in or out, till it subsides, in a matter of weeks."

"So how would I get out?" asked Sabriel. "I can't wait weeks!"

"One of your ancestors built a flying device. A Paperwing, she called it. You can use that, launched out over the waterfall."

"Oh," said Sabriel, in a little voice.

"If you do wish to raise the river," Mogget continued, as if he hadn't noticed Sabriel's sudden silence, "then we must begin the ritual immediately. The flood comes from meltwater and the mountains are many leagues upstream. If we call the waters now, the flood will be on us by dusk tomorrow."

chapter ten

The arrival of the floodwaters was heralded by great chunks of ice that came battering against the wooden bridge of grave dirt boxes like storm-borne icebergs ramming anchored ships. Ice shattered, wood splintered; a regular drumming that beat out a warning, announcing the great wave that followed the outriding ice.

Dead Hands and living slaves scurried back along the coffin bridge, the Dead's shadowy bodies losing shape as they ran, so they became like long, thick worms of black crepe, squirming and sliding over rocks and boxes, throwing human slaves aside without mercy, desperate to escape the destruction that came roaring down the river.

Sabriel, watching from the tower, felt the people die, convulsively swallowing as she sensed their last breaths gurgling, sucking water instead of air. Some of them, at least two pairs, had deliberately thrown themselves into the river, choosing a final death, rather than risk eternal bondage. Most had been knocked, pushed or simply scared aside by the Dead.

The wavefront of the flood came swiftly after the ice, shouting as it came, a higher, fiercer roar than the deep bellow of the waterfall. Sabriel heard it for several seconds before it rounded the last bend of the river, then suddenly, it was almost upon her. A huge, vertical wall of water, with chunks of ice on its crest like marble battlements and all the debris of four hundred miles swilling about in its muddy body. It looked enormous, far taller than the island's walls, taller even than the tower where Sabriel stared, shocked at the power she had unleashed, a power she had hardly dreamed possible when she'd summoned it the night before.

It had been a simple enough summoning. Mogget had taken her to the cellar and then down a winding, narrow stair, that grew colder and colder as they descended. Finally, they reached a strange grotto, where icicles hung and Sabriel's breath blew clouds of white, but it was no longer cold, or perhaps so cold she no longer felt it. A block of pure, blue-white ice stood upon a stone pedestal, both limned with Charter marks, marks strange and beautiful. Then, following Mogget's instruction, she'd simply placed her hand on the ice and said, "Abhorsen pays her respects to the Clayr and requests the gift of water." That was all. They'd gone back up the stairs, a sending locked the cellar door behind them, and another brought Sabriel a nightshirt and a cup of hot chocolate.

But that simple ceremony had summoned something that seemed totally out of control. Sabriel watched the wave racing towards them, trying to calm herself, but her breath raced in and out as quickly as her stomach flipped over. Just as the wave hit, she screamed and ducked under the telescope.

The whole tower shook, stones screeching as they moved, and for a moment, even the sound of the waterfall was lost in a crack that sounded as if the island had been levelled by the first shock of the wave.

But, after a few seconds, the floor stopped shaking and the crash of the flood subsided to a controlled roar, like a shouting drunk made aware of company. Sabriel hauled herself up the tripod and opened her eyes.

The walls had held, and though now the wave was past, the river still raged a mere handspan below the island's defences and was almost up to the tunnel doors on either bank. There was no sign of the stepping stones, the coffin bridge, the Dead, or any people – just a wide, brown rushing torrent, carrying debris of all descriptions. Trees, bushes, parts of buildings, livestock, chunks of ice – the flood had claimed its tribute from every riverbank for hundreds of miles.

Sabriel looked at this evidence of destruction and inwardly counted the number of villagers who had died on the grave boxes. Who knew how many other lives had been lost, or livelihoods threatened, upstream? Part of her tried to rationalise her use of the flood, telling her that she had to do it in order to fight on against the Dead. Another part said she had simply summoned the flood to save herself.

Mogget had no time for such introspection, mourning or pangs of responsibility. He left her watching, blank-eyed, for no more than a minute, before padding forward and delicately inserting his claws in Sabriel's slippered foot.

"Ow! What did you—"

"There's no time to waste sightseeing" Mogget said. "The sendings are readying the Paperwing on the eastern wall. And your clothing and gear has been ready for at least half an hour."

"I've got all..." Sabriel began, then she remembered that her pack and skis lay at the bottom end of the entrance tunnel, probably as a pile of Mordicant-burned ash.

"The sendings have got everything you'll need and a few things you won't, knowing them. You can get dressed, pack up and head off for Belisaere. I take it you intend to go to Belisaere?"

"Yes," replied Sabriel shortly. She could detect a tone of smugness in Mogget's voice.

"Do you know how to get there?"

Sabriel was silent. Mogget already knew the answer was "no." Hence the smugness.

"Do you have a... er... map?"

Sabriel shook her head, clenching her fists as she did so, resisting the urge to lean forward and spank Mogget, or perhaps give his tail a judicious tug. She had searched the study and asked several of the sendings, but the only map in the house seemed to be the starmap in the tower. The map Colonel Horyse had told her about must still be with Abhorsen. With Father, Sabriel thought, suddenly confused about their identities. If she was now Abhorsen, who was her father? Had he too once had a name that was lost in the responsibility of being Abhorsen? Everything that had seemed so certain and solid in her life a few days ago was crumbling. She didn't even know who she was really, and trouble seemed to beset her from all sides – even a supposed servant of Abhorsen like Mogget seemed to provide more trouble than service.

"Do you have anything positive to say – anything that might actually help?" she snapped.

Mogget yawned, showing a pink tongue that seemed to contain the very essence of scorn.

"Well, yes. Of course. I know the way, so I'd better come with you."

"Come with me?" Sabriel asked, genuinely surprised. She unclenched her fists, bent down, and scratched between the cat's ears, till he ducked away.

"Someone has to look after you," Mogget added. "At least till you've grown into a real Abhorsen."

"Thank you," said Sabriel. "I think. But I would still like a map. Since you know the country so well, would it be possible for you to – I don't know – describe it, so I can make a sketch map or something?"

Mogget coughed, as if a hairball had suddenly lodged in his throat, and thrust his head back a little. "You! Draw a sketch map? If you must have one, I think it would be better if I undertook the cartography myself. Come down to the study and put out an inkwell and paper."

"As long as I get a usable map I don't care who draws it," Sabriel remarked, as she went backwards down the ladder. She tilted her head to watch how Mogget came down, but there was only the open trapdoor. A sarcastic meow under her feet announced that Mogget had once again managed to get between rooms without visible means of support.

"Ink and paper," the cat reminded her, jumping up on to the dragon desk. "The thick paper. Smooth side up. Don't bother with a quill."

Sabriel followed Mogget's instructions, then watched with a resigned condescension that rapidly changed to surprise as the cat crouched by the square of paper, his strange shadow falling on it like a dark cloak thrown across sand, pink tongue out in concentration. Mogget seemed to think for a moment, then one bright ivory claw shot out from a white pad – he delicately inked the claw in the inkwell and began to draw. First, a rough outline, in swift, bold strokes; the penning in of the major geographical features; then the delicate process of adding important sites, each named in fine, spidery writing. Last of all, Mogget marked Abhorsen's House with a small illustration, before leaning back to admire his handiwork and lick the ink from his paw. Sabriel waited a few seconds to be sure he was done, then cast drying sand over the paper, her eyes trying to absorb every detail, intent on learning the physical face of the Old Kingdom.

"You can look at it later," Mogget said after a few minutes, when his paw was clean, but Sabriel was still bent over the table, nose inches from the map. "We're still in a hurry. You'd better go and get dressed, for a start. Do try to be quick."

"I will," smiled Sabriel, still looking at the map. "Thank you, Mogget."

The sendings had laid out a great pile of clothes and equipment in Sabriel's room, and four of them were in attendance to help her get everything on and organised. She had hardly stepped inside before they'd stripped her indoor dress and slippers off and she'd only just managed to remove her own underclothes before ghostly Charter traced hands tickled her sides. A few seconds later, she was suffering them anyway, as they pulled a thin, cotton-like undergarment over her head and a pair of baggy drawers up her legs. Next came a linen shirt, then a tunic of doeskin and breeches of supple leather, reinforced with some sort of hard, segmented plates at thighs, knees and shins, not to mention a heavily padded bottom, no doubt designed for riding.

A brief respite followed, lulling Sabriel into thinking that might be it, but the sendings had merely been arranging the next layer for immediate fitting. Two of them pushed her arms into a long, armoured coat that buckled up at the sides, while the other two unlaced a pair of hobnailed boots and waited.

The coat wasn't like anything Sabriel had ever worn before, including the mail hauberk she'd worn in Fighting Arts lessons at school. It was as long as a hauberk, with split skirts coming down to her knees and sleeves swallow-tailed at her wrists, but it seemed to be entirely made of tiny overlapping plates, much like a fish's scales. They weren't metal, either, but some sort of ceramic, or even stone. Much lighter than steel, but clearly very strong, as one sending demonstrated, by cutting down it with a dagger, striking sparks without leaving a scratch.

Sabriel thought the boots completed the ensemble, but as the laces were done up by one pair of sendings, the other pair were back in action. One raised what appeared to be a blue and silver striped turban, but Sabriel, pulling it down to just above her eyebrows, found it to be a cloth-wrapped helmet, made from the same material as the armour.

The other sending waved out a gleaming, deep blue surcoat, dusted with embroidered silver keys that reflected the light in all directions. It waved the coat to and fro for a moment, then whipped it over Sabriel's head and adjusted the drape with a practised motion. Sabriel ran her hand over its silken expanse and discreetly tried to rip it in one corner, but, for all its apparent fragility, it wouldn't tear.

Last of all came sword belt and bell bandoleer. The sendings brought them to her, but made no attempt to put them on. Sabriel adjusted them herself, carefully arranging bells and scabbard, feeling the familiar weight – bells across her breast and sword balanced on her hip. She turned to the mirror and looked at her reflection, both pleased and troubled by what she saw. She looked competent, professional, a traveller who could look after herself. At the same time, she looked less like someone called Sabriel and more like the Abhorsen, capital letter and all.

She would have looked longer, but the sendings tugged at her sleeves and directed her attention to the bed. A leather backpack lay open on it and, as Sabriel watched, the sendings packed it with her remaining old clothes, including her father's oilskin, spare undergarments, tunic and trousers, dried beef and biscuits, a water bottle and several small leather pouches full of useful things, each of which were painstakingly opened and shown to her: telescope, sulphur matches, clockwork firestarter, medicinal herbs, fishing hooks and line, a sewing kit and a host of other small essentials. The three books from the library and the map went into oilskin pouches, and then into an outside pocket.

Backpack on, Sabriel tried a few basic exercises and was relieved to find that the armour didn't restrict her too much – hardly at all in fact, though the pack was not something she'd like to have on in a fight. She could even touch her toes, so she did, several times, before straightening up to thank the sendings.

They were gone. Instead, there was Mogget, stalking mysteriously towards her from the middle of the room.

"Well, I'm ready," Sabriel said.

Mogget didn't answer, but sat at her feet and made a movement that looked very much like he was going to be sick. Sabriel recoiled, disgusted, then halted, as a small metallic object fell from Mogget's mouth and bounced on the floor.

"Almost forgot," said Mogget. "You'll need this if I'm to come with you."

"What is it?" asked Sabriel, bending down to pick up a ring; a small silver ring, with a ruby gripped between two silver claws that grew out of the band.

"Old," replied Mogget enigmatically. "You'll know if you need to use it. Put it on."

Sabriel looked at it closely, holding it between two fingers as she slanted it towards the light. It felt, and looked, quite ordinary. There were no Charter marks on the stone or band; it seemed to have no emanations or aura. She put it on.

It felt cold as it slipped down her finger, then hot, and

suddenly she was falling, falling into infinity, into a void that had no end and no beginning. Everything was gone, all light, all substance. Then Charter marks suddenly exploded all around her and she felt gripped by them, halting her headlong fall into nothing, accelerating her back up, back into her body, back to the world of Life and Death.

"Free Magic," Sabriel said, looking down at the ring gleaming on her finger. "Free Magic, connected to the Charter. I don't understand."

"You'll know if you need to use it," Mogget repeated, almost as if it were some lesson to be learned by rote. Then, in his normal voice: "Don't worry about it till then. Come – the Paperwing is ready."

chapter eleven

The Paperwing sat on a jury-rigged platform of freshly-sawn pine planks, teetering out over the eastern wall. Six sendings clustered around the craft, readying it for flight. Sabriel looked up at it as she climbed the stairs, an unpleasant feeling rising with her. She had been expecting something similar to the aircraft that had begun to be common in Ancelstierre, like the biplane that had performed aerobatics at the last Wyverley College Open Day. Something with two wings, rigging and a propeller – though she had assumed a magical engine rather than a mechanical one.

But the Paperwing didn't look anything like an Ancelstierran aeroplane. It most closely resembled a canoe with hawk-wings and a tail. On closer inspection, Sabriel saw that the central fuselage was probably based on a canoe. It was tapered at each end and had a central hole for a cockpit. Wings sprouted on each side of this canoe shape – long, swept-back wings that looked very flimsy. The wedge-shaped tail didn't look much better.

Sabriel climbed the last few steps with sinking expectations. The construction material was now clear and so was the craft's name – the whole thing was made up from many sheets of paper, bonded together with some sort of laminate. Painted powder-blue, with silver bands around the fuselage and silver stripes along the wings and tail, it looked pretty, decorative and not at all airworthy. Only the yellow falcon eyes painted on its pointed prow hinted at its capacity for flight.

Sabriel looked at the Paperwing again and then out at the waterfall beyond. Now, fed by floodwaters, it looked even more frightening than usual. Spray exploded for tens of yards above its lip – a roaring mist the Paperwing would have to fly through before it reached the open sky beyond. Sabriel didn't even know if it was waterproof.

"How often has this... thing... flown before?" she asked, nervously. Intellectually, she accepted that she would soon be sitting in this craft, to be launched out towards the crashing waters – but her subconscious, and her stomach, seemed very keen to stay firmly on the ground.

"Many times," replied Mogget, easily jumping from the platform to the cockpit. His voice echoed there for a moment, till he climbed back up, furry cat-face propped on the rim. "The Abhorsen who made it once flew it to the sea and back in a single afternoon. But she was a great weather-witch and could work the winds. I don't suppose—"

"No," said Sabriel, made aware of another gap in her education. She knew that wind-magic was largely whistled Charter marks, but that was all. "No. I can't."

"Well," continued Mogget, after a thoughtful pause, "the Paperwing does have some elementary charms to ride the wind. You'll have to whistle them, though. You can whistle, I trust?"

Sabriel ignored him. All necromancers had to be musical, had to be able to whistle, to hum, to sing. If they were caught in Death without bells, or other magical instruments, their vocal skills were a weapon of last recourse.

A sending came and took her pack, helping her to wrestle it off, then stowing it at the rear of the cockpit. Another took Sabriel's arm and directed her to what appeared to be a leather half-hammock strung across the cockpit – obviously the pilot's seat. It didn't look terribly safe either, but Sabriel forced herself to climb in, after giving her scabbarded sword into the hands of yet another sending.

Surprisingly, her feet didn't go through the paper-laminated floor. The material even felt reassuringly solid and, after a minute of squirming, swaying and adjustment, the hammock-seat was very comfortable. Sword and scabbard were slid into a receptacle at her side and Mogget took up a position on top of the straps holding down her pack, just behind her shoulders, for the seat made her recline so far she was almost lying down.

From her new eye level, Sabriel saw a small, oval mirror of silvered glass, fixed just below the cockpit rim. It glittered in the late afternoon sun and she felt it resonate with Charter Magic. Something about it prompted her to breathe upon it, her hot breath clouding the glass. It stayed misted for a moment, then a Charter mark slowly appeared, as if a ghostly finger was drawn across the clouded mirror.

Sabriel studied it carefully, absorbing its purpose and effect. It told her of the marks that would follow: marks to raise the lifting winds, marks for descending in haste, marks to call the wind from every corner of the compass rose. There were other marks for the Paperwing and, as Sabriel absorbed them, she saw that the whole craft was lined with Charter Magic, infused with spells. The Abhorsen who made it had laboured long, and with love, to create something that was more like a magical bird than an aircraft.

Time passed and the last mark faded. The mirror cleared to be only a plate of silver glass shining in the sun. Sabriel sat, silent, fixing the Charter marks in her memory, marvelling at the power and the skill that had made the Paperwing and had thought of this method of instruction. Perhaps one day, she too would have the mastery to create such a thing.

"The Abhorsen who made this," Sabriel asked. "Who was she? I mean, in relation to me?"

"A cousin," purred Mogget, close to her ear. "Your great-great-great-great-grandmother's cousin. The last of that line. She had no children."

Maybe the Paperwing was her child, Sabriel thought, running her hand along the sleek surface of the fuselage, feeling the Charter marks quiescent in the fabric. She felt a lot better about their forthcoming flight.

"We'd best hurry," Mogget continued. "It will be dark all too soon. Do you have the marks remembered?"

"Yes," replied Sabriel firmly. She turned to the sendings, who were now lined up behind the wings, anchoring the Paperwing till it was time for it to be unleashed upon the sky. Sabriel wondered how many times they'd performed this task and for how many Abhorsens.

"Thank you," she said to them. "For all your care and kindness. Goodbye."

With that last word, she settled back in the hammock-seat, gripped the rim of the cockpit with both hands and whistled the notes of the lifting wind, visualising the requisite string of Charter marks in her mind, letting them drip down into her throat and lips, and out into the air.

Her whistle sounded clear and true, and a wind rose behind to match it, growing stronger as Sabriel exhaled. Then, with a new breath, she changed to a merry, joyous trill. Like a bird revelling in flight, the Charter marks flowing from pursed lips out into the Paperwing itself. With this whistling, the blue and silver paint seemed to come alive, dancing down the fuselage, sweeping across the wings, a gleaming, lustrous plumage. The whole craft shook and shivered, suddenly flexible and eager to begin.

The joyous trill ended with one single, long, clear note and a Charter mark that shone like the sun. It danced to the Paperwing's prow and sank into the laminate. A second later, the yellow eyes blinked, grew fierce and proud, looking up to the sky ahead.

The sendings were struggling now, barely able to hold the Paperwing back. The lifting wind grew stronger still, plucking at the silver-blue plumage, thrusting it forward. Sabriel felt the Paperwing's tension, the contained power in its wings, the exhilaration of that last moment when freedom is assured.

"Let go!" she cried, and the sendings complied, the Paperwing leaping up into the arms of the wind, out and upward, splashing through the spray of the waterfall as if it were no more than a spring shower, flying out into the sky and the broad valley beyond.

It was quiet and cold, a thousand feet or more above the valley. The Paperwing soared easily, the wind firm behind it, the sky clear above, save for the faintest wisps of cloud. Sabriel reclined in her hammock-seat, relaxing, running the Charter marks she'd learned over and over in her mind, making sure she had them properly pigeonholed. She felt free and somehow clean, as if the dangers of the last few days were dirt, washed away by the following wind.

"Turn more to the north," Mogget's voice suddenly said behind her, disturbing her carefree mood. "Do you recall the map?"

"Yes," replied Sabriel. "Shall we follow the river? The Ratterlin, it's called, isn't it? It runs nor-nor-east most of the time."

Mogget didn't reply at once, though Sabriel heard his purring breath close by. He seemed to be thinking. Finally, he said, "Why not? We may as well follow it to the sea. It branches into a delta there, so we can find an island to camp on tonight."

"Why not just fly on?" asked Sabriel cheerily. "We could be in Belisaere by tomorrow night, if I summon the strongest winds."

"The Paperwing doesn't like to fly at night," Mogget said, shortly. "Not to mention that you would almost certainly lose control of the stronger winds – it is much more difficult than it seems at first. And the Paperwing is much too conspicuous, anyway. Have you no common sense, Abhorsen?"

"Call me Sabriel," Sabriel replied, equally shortly. "My father is Abhorsen."

"As you wish, mistress," said Mogget. The "mistress" sounded extremely sarcastic.

The next hour passed in belligerent silence, but Sabriel, for her part, soon lost her anger in the novelty of flight. She loved the scale of it all, to see the tiny patchworked fields and forests below, the dark strip of the river, the occasional tiny building. Everything was so small and seemed so perfect, seen from afar.

Then the sun began to sink and though the red wash of its fading light made the aerial perspective even prettier, Sabriel felt the Paperwing's desire to descend, felt the yellow eyes focusing on green earth, rather than blue sky. As the shadows lengthened, Sabriel felt that same desire and began to look as well.

The river was already breaking up into the myriad streams and rivulets that would form the swampy Ratterlin delta, and far off, Sabriel could see the dark bulk of the sea. There were many islands in the delta, some as large as football fields covered with trees and shrubs, others no bigger than two armspans of mud. Sabriel picked out one of the medium-sized ones, a flattish diamond with low, yellow grass, a few leagues ahead, and whistled down the wind.

It faded gradually with her whistle and the Paperwing began to descend, occasionally nudged this way or that by Sabriel's control of the wind or its own tilt of a wing. Its yellow eyes, and Sabriel's deep-brown eyes, were fixed on the ground below. Only Mogget, being Mogget, looked behind them and above.

Even so, he didn't see their pursuers until they came wheeling out of the sun, so his yowling cry gave only a few seconds' warning, just long enough for Sabriel to turn and see the hundreds of fast-moving shapes diving down upon them. Instinctively, she conjured Charter marks in her mind, mouth pursed, whistling the wind back up, turning them to the north.

"Gore crows!" hissed Mogget, as the flapping shapes checked their dive and wheeled to pursue their suddenly enlivened prey.

"Yes," shouted Sabriel, though she wasn't sure why she answered. Her attention was all on the gore crows, trying to gauge whether they'd intercept or not. She could already feel the wind testing the edges of her control, as Mogget had prophesied, and to whip it up further might have unpleasant results. But she could also feel the presence of the gore crows, feel the admixture of Death and Free Magic that gave life to their rotten, skeletal forms.

Gore crows didn't last very long in sun and wind – these must have been made the previous night. A necromancer had trapped quite ordinary crows, killing them with ritual and ceremony, before infusing the bodies with the broken, fragmented spirit of a single dead man or woman. Now, they were truly carrion birds, birds guided by a single, if stupid, intelligence. They flew by force of Free Magic and killed by force of numbers.

Despite her quickness in calling the wind, the flock was still closing rapidly. They'd dived from high above and kept their speed, the wind stripping feathers and putrid flesh from their spell-woven bones.

For a moment, Sabriel considered turning the Paperwing back into the very centre of this great murder of crows, like an avenging angel, armed with sword and bells. But there were simply too many gore crows to fight, particularly from an aircraft speeding along several hundred feet above the ground. One over-eager sword thrust would mean a fatal fall – if the gore crows didn't kill her on the way down.

"I'll have to summon a greater wind!" she yelled at Mogget, who was now sitting right up on her pack, fur bristling, yowling challenges at the crows. They were very close now, flying in an eerily exact formation – two long lines, like arms outstretched to snatch the fleeing Paperwing from the sky. Very little of their once-black plumage had survived their rushing dive, white bone shining through in the last light of the sun. But their beaks were still glossily black and gleaming sharp, and Sabriel could now see the red glints of the fragmented Dead spirit in the empty sockets of their eyes.

Mogget didn't reply. Possibly, he hadn't even heard her above his yowling and the gore crows' cawing as they closed the last few yards to attack, a strange, hollow sound, as dead as their flesh.

For a second of panic, Sabriel felt her dry lips unable to purse, then she wet them and the whistle came, slow and erratic. The Charter marks felt clumsy and difficult in her head, as if she were trying to push a heavy weight on badly-made rollers – then, with a last effort, they came easily, flowing into her whistled notes.

Unlike her earlier, gradual summonings, this wind came with the speed of a slamming door, howling up behind them with frightening violence, picking up the Paperwing and shunting it forward like a giant wave lifting up a slender boat. Suddenly, they were going so fast that Sabriel could barely make out the ground below and the individual islands of the delta merged into one continuous blur of motion.

Eyes closed to protective slits, she craned her head around, the wind striking her face like a vicious slap. The pursuing gore crows were all over the sky now, formation lost, like small black stains against the red and purple sunset. They were flapping uselessly, trying to come back together, but the Paperwing was already a league or more away. There was no chance they could catch up.

Sabriel let out a sigh of relief, but it was a sigh tempered with new anxieties. The wind was carrying them at a fearful pace, and it was starting to veer northwards, which it wasn't supposed to do. Sabriel could see the first stars twinkling now, and they were definitely turning towards the Buckle.

It was an effort to call up the Charter marks again and whistle the spell to ease the wind, and turn it back to the east, but Sabriel managed to cast it. But the spell failed to work – the wind grew stronger, and shifted more, till they were careening straight towards the Buckle, directly north.

Sabriel, hunkered down in the cockpit, eyes and nose streaming and face frozen, tried again, using all her willpower to force the Charter marks into the wind. Even to her, her whistle sounded feeble, and the Charter marks once again vanished into what had now become a gale. Sabriel realised she had totally lost control.

In fact, it was almost as if the spell had the opposite effect, for the wind grew wilder, snatching the Paperwing up in a great spiral, like a ball thrown between a ring of giants, each one taller than the last. Sabriel grew dizzy, and even colder, and her breath came fast and shallow, trying to salvage enough air to keep her alive. She tried to calm the winds again, but couldn't gain the breath to whistle and the Charter marks slipped from her mind, till all she could do was desperately hang on to the straps in the hammock-seat as the Paperwing tried its best to ride the storm.

Then, without warning, the wind ceased its upward dance. It just dropped, and with it went the Paperwing. Sabriel fell upwards, straps suddenly tight, and Mogget almost clawed through the pack in his efforts to stay connected with the aircraft. Jolted by this new development, Sabriel felt her exhaustion burn away. She tried to whistle the lifting wind, but it too was beyond her power. The Paperwing seemed unable to halt its headlong descent. It fell, nose tilting further and further forward till they were diving almost vertically, like a hammer rushing to the anvil of the ground below.

It was a long way down. Sabriel screamed once, then tried to put some of her fear-found strength into the Paperwing. But the marks flowed into her whistle without effect, save for a golden sparkle that briefly illuminated her white, wind-frozen face. The sun had completely set and the dark mass of the ground below looked all too much like the grey river of Death – the river their spirits would cross into in a few short minutes, never to return to the warm light of Life.

"Loose my collar," mewed a voice at Sabriel's ear, followed by the curious sensation of Mogget digging his claws into her armour as he clambered into her lap. "Loose my collar!"

Sabriel looked at him, at the ground, at the collar. She felt stupid, starved of oxygen, unable to decide. The collar was part of an ancient binding, a terrible guardian of tremendous power. It would only be used to contain an inexpressible evil or uncontrollable force.

"Trust me!" howled Mogget. "Loose my collar and remember the ring!"

Sabriel swallowed, closed her eyes, fumbled with the collar and prayed that she was doing the right thing. "Father, forgive me," she thought, but it was not just to her father that she spoke, but to all the Abhorsens who had come before her – especially the one who had made the collar so long ago.

Surprisingly for such an ancient spell, she felt little more than pins and needles as the collar came free. Then it was open and suddenly heavy, like a lead rope or a ball and chain. Sabriel almost dropped it, but it became light again, then insubstantial. When Sabriel opened her eyes, the collar had simply ceased to exist.

Mogget sat still, on her lap, and seemed unchanged – then he seemed to glow with an internal light and expand, till he became frayed at the edges and the light grew and grew.

Within a few seconds, there was no cat-shape left, just a shining blur too bright to look at. It seemed to hesitate for a moment and Sabriel felt its attention flicker between aggression towards her and some inner struggle. It almost formed back into the cat-shape again, then suddenly split into four shafts of brilliant white. One shot forward, one aft, and two seemed to slide into the wings.

Then the whole Paperwing shone with fierce white brilliance, and it abruptly stopped its headlong dive and levelled out. Sabriel was flung violently forward, body checked by straps, but her nose almost hit the silver mirror, neck muscles cording out with an impossible effort to keep her head still.

Despite this sudden improvement, they were still falling. Sabriel, hands now clasped behind her savagely aching neck, saw the ground rushing up to fill the horizon. Treetops suddenly appeared below, the Paperwing, imbued with the strange light, just clipping through the upper branches with a sound like hail on a tin roof. Then, they dropped again, skimming scant yards above what looked like a cleared field, but still too fast to land without total destruction.

Mogget, or whatever Mogget had become, braked the Paperwing again, in a series of shuddering halts that added bruises on top of bruises. For the first time, Sabriel felt the incredible relief of knowing that they would survive. One more braking effort and the Paperwing would be safely down, to skid a little in the long, soft grass of the field.

Mogget braked and Sabriel cheered as the Paperwing gently lay its belly on the grass and slid to what should have been a perfect landing. But the cheer suddenly became a shriek of alarm, as the grass parted to reveal the lip of an enormous dark hole directly in their path.

Too low to rise, and now too slow to glide over a hole at least fifty yards across, the Paperwing reached the edge, flipped over and spiralled towards the bottom of the hole, hundreds of feet below.

chapter twelve

Sabriel regained consciousness slowly, her brain fumbling
for connections to her senses. Hearing came first, but that
only caught her own laboured breathing and the creak of
her armoured coat as she struggled to sit up. For the moment,
sight eluded her and she was panicked, afraid of blindness, till
memory came. It was night and she was at the bottom of a
sinkhole – a great, circular shaft bored into the ground, by either
nature or artifice. From her brief glimpse of it as they'd fallen,
she guessed it was easily fifty yards in diameter and a hundred
deep. Daylight would probably illuminate its murky depths, but
starlight was insufficient.

Pain came next, hard on the heels of memory. A thousand
aches and bruises, but no serious injury. Sabriel wiggled her
toes and fingers, flexed muscles in arms, back and legs. They all
hurt, but everything seemed to work.

She vaguely recalled the last few seconds before impact –
Mogget, or the white force, slowing them just before they hit –
but the actual instant of the crash might never have been, for

she couldn't remember it. Shock, she thought to herself, in an abstract way, almost like she was diagnosing someone else.

Her next thought came some time later and with it the realisation that she must have passed out again. With this awakening, she felt a little sharper, her mind catching some slight breeze to carry her out of the mental doldrums. Working by touch, she unstrapped herself and felt behind her for the pack. In her current state, even a simple Charter-spell for light was out of the question, but there were candles there, and matches, or the clockwork igniter.

As the match flared, Sabriel's heart sank. In the small, flickering globe of yellow light, she saw that only the central cockpit portion of the Paperwing survived – the sad blue and silver corpse of a once marvellous creation. Its wings lay torn and crumpled underneath it, and the entire nose section lay some yards away, shorn off completely. One eye stared up at the circular patch of sky above, but it was no longer fierce and alive. Just yellow paint and laminated paper.

Sabriel stared at the wreckage, regret and sorrow coursing like influenza in her bones, till the match burnt her fingers. She lit another, and then a candle, expanding both her light and field of vision.

More small pieces of the Paperwing were strewn over a large, open, flat area. Groaning with the effort of motivating bruised muscles, Sabriel levered herself out of the cockpit to have a closer look at the ground.

This revealed the flat area to be man-made: flagstones, carefully laid. Grass had long grown between the stones and lichen upon them, so it was clearly not recent work. Sabriel sat on the cool stones and wondered why anyone would do such work at the bottom of a sinkhole.

Thinking about that seemed to kickstart her befuddled wits and she started to wonder about a few other things. Where, for instance, was the force that had once been Mogget? And what was it? That reminded her to fetch her sword and check the bells.

Her turbaned helmet had rotated around on her head and was almost back-to-front. Slowly, she slid it around, feeling every slight movement all the way down her now very stiff neck.

Balancing her first candle on the paving in a pool of cooling wax, she dragged her pack and weapons out of the wreckage and lit another two candles. She put one down near the first and took the other to light her way, walking around the destroyed Paperwing, searching for any sign of Mogget. At the dismembered prow of the craft, she gently touched the eyes, wishing she could close them.

"I am sorry," she whispered. "Perhaps I will be able to make a new Paperwing one day. There should be another, to carry on your name."

"Sentiment, Abhorsen?" said a voice somewhere behind her, a voice that managed to sound like Mogget and not at all like him at the same time. It was louder, harsher, less human, and every word seemed to crackle, like the electric generators she'd used in Wyverley College Science classes.

"Where are you?" asked Sabriel, swiftly turning. The voice had sounded close, but there was nothing visible within the sphere of candlelight. She held her own candle higher and transferred it to her left hand.

"Here," snickered the voice and Sabriel saw lines of white fire run out from under the ruined fuselage, lines that lit the paper laminate as they ran, so that, within a second, the Paperwing was burning fiercely, yellow-red flames dancing under thick white smoke, totally obscuring whatever had emerged from under the stricken craft.

No Death sense twitched, but Sabriel could almost smell the Free Magic: tangy, unnatural, nerve-jangling, tainting the thick odour of natural smoke. Then she saw the white fire-lines again, streaming out, converging, roiling, coming together – and a blazing, blue-white creature stepped out from the funeral pyre of the Paperwing.

Sabriel couldn't look at it directly, but from the corners of her arm-shielded eyes, she saw something human in shape, taller than her and thin, almost starved. It had no legs, the torso and head balanced upon a column of twisting, whirling force.

"Free, save for the blood price," it said, advancing. All trace of Mogget's voice was lost now, submerged in zapping, crackling menace.

Sabriel had no doubt about the meaning of a blood price and who would pay it. Summoning all her remaining energies, she called three Charter marks to the forefront of her mind, and hurled them towards the thing, shouting their names.

"Anet! Calew! Ferhan!"

The marks became silver blades as they left her hand, mind and voice, flashing through the air swifter than any thrown dagger – and went straight through the shining figure, apparently without effect.

It laughed, a series of rises and falls like a dog screaming in pain, and lazily slid forward. Its languid motion seemed to declare it would have no more trouble disposing of Sabriel than it had in burning the Paperwing.

Sabriel drew her sword and backed away, determined not to panic as she had done when faced by the Mordicant. Her head flicked backwards and forwards, neck pain forgotten, checking the ground behind her and marking her opponent. Her mind raced, considering options. Perhaps one of the bells – but that would mean dropping a candle. Could she count on the creature's blazing presence to light her way?

Almost as if it could read her mind, the creature suddenly started to lose its brilliance, sucking darkness into its swirling body like a sponge soaking up ink. Within a few seconds, Sabriel could barely make it out – a fearful silhouette, back-lit by the orange glow of the burning Paperwing.

Desperately, Sabriel tried to remember what she knew of Free Magic elementals and constructs. Her father had rarely mentioned them and Magistrix Greenwood had only lightly delved into the subject. Sabriel knew the binding spells for two of the lesser kindred of Free Magic beings, but the creature before her was neither Margrue nor Stilken.

"Keep thinking, Abhorsen," laughed the creature, advancing again. "Such a pity your head doesn't work too well."

"You saved it from not working for ever," Sabriel replied warily. It had braked the Paperwing, after all, so perhaps there was some good in it somewhere, some remnant of Mogget, if only it could be brought out.

"Sentiment," the thing replied, still silently sliding forward. It laughed again and a dark, tendril-like arm suddenly unleashed itself, snapping across the intervening space to strike Sabriel across the face.

"A memory, now purged," it added, as Sabriel staggered back from a second attack, sword flashing across to parry. Unlike the silver spell darts, the Charter-etched blade did connect with the unnatural flesh of the creature, but had no effect apart from jarring Sabriel's arm.

Her nose was bleeding too, a warm and salty flow, stinging her wind-chafed lips. She tried to ignore it, tried to use the pain of what was probably a broken nose to get her mind back to full operational speed.

"Memories, yes, many memories," continued the creature. It was circling around her now, pushing her back the way they'd come, back towards the fading fire of the Paperwing. That would burn out soon and then there would only be darkness, for Sabriel's candle was now a lump of blown-out wax, falling forgotten from her hand.

"Millennia of servitude, Abhorsen. Chained by trickery, treachery... captive in a repulsive, fixed-flesh shape... but there will be payment, slow payment – not quick, not quick at all!"

A tendril lashed out, low this time, trying to trip her. Sabriel leapt over it, blade extended, lunging for the creature's chest. But it shimmied aside, extruding extra arms as she tried to jump back, catching her in mid-leap, drawing her close.

Sword-arm pinioned at her side, it tightened its grip, till she was close against its chest, her face a finger-width from its boiling, constantly moving flesh, as if a billion tiny insects buzzed behind a membrane of utter darkness.

Another arm gripped the back of her helmet, forcing her to look up, till she saw its head, directly above her. A thing of most basic anatomy, its eyes were like the sinkhole, deep pits without apparent bottom. It had no nose, but a mouth that split the horrid face in two, a mouth slightly parted to reveal the burning blue-white glare that it had first used as flesh.

All Charter Magic had fled from Sabriel's mind. Her sword was trapped, the bells likewise, and even if they weren't, she didn't know how to use them properly against things not Dead. She ran over them mentally anyway, in a frantic, lightning inventory of anything that might help.

It was then her tired, concussed mind remembered the ring. It was on her left hand, her free hand, cool silver on the index finger.

But she didn't know what to do with it – and the creature's head was bowing down towards her own, its neck stretching impossibly long, till it was like a snake's head rearing above her, the mouth opening wider, growing brighter, fizzing with white-hot sparks that fell upon her helmet and face, burning cloth and skin, leaving tiny, tattoo-like scars. The ring felt loose on her finger. Sabriel instinctively curled her hand and the ring felt looser still, slipping down her finger, expanding, growing, till without looking, Sabriel knew she held a silver hoop as wide or wider than the creature's slender head. And she suddenly knew what to do.

"First, the plucking of an eye," said the thing, breath as hot as the falling sparks, scorching her face with instant sunburn. It tilted its head sideways and opened its mouth still wider, lower jaw dislocating out.

Sabriel took one last, careful look, screwed her eyes tight against the terrible glare, and flipped the silver hoop up, and she hoped, over the thing's neck.

For a second, as the heat increased and she felt a terrible burning pain against her eye, Sabriel thought she'd missed. Then the hoop was wrenched from her hand and she was thrown away, hurled out like an angry fisherman's rejected minnow.

On the cool flagstones again, she opened her eyes, the left one blurry, sore and swimming with tears – but still there and still working.

She had put the silver hoop over the thing's head and it was slowly sliding down that long, sinuous neck. The ring was shrinking again as it slid, impervious to the creature's desperate attempts to get it off. It had six or seven hands now, formed directly from its shoulders, all squirming about, trying to force fingers under the ring. But the metal seemed inimical to the creature's substance, like a hot pan to human fingers, for the fingers flinched and danced around it, but could not take hold for longer than a second.

The darkness that stained it was ebbing too, draining down through its thrashing, twisting support, leaving glowing whiteness behind. Still the creature fought with the ring, blazing hands forming and reforming, body twisting and turning, even bucking, as if it could throw the ring like a rider from a horse.

Finally, it gave up and turned towards Sabriel, screaming and crackling. Two long arms sprang out from it, reaching towards Sabriel's sprawling body, talons growing from the hands, raking the stone with deep gouges as they scrabbled towards her, like spiders scuttling to their prey – only to fall short by a yard or more.

"No!" howled the thing and its whole, twisting, coiling body lurched forward, killing arms outstretched. Again, the talons fell short, as Sabriel crawled, rolled and pushed herself away.

Then the silver ring contracted once more and a terrible shout of anguish, rage and despair came from the very centre of the white-flaming thing. Its arms suddenly shrank back to its torso; the head fell into the shoulders and the whole body sank into an amorphous blob of shimmering white, with a single, still-large silver band around the middle, the ruby glittering like a drop of blood.

Sabriel stared at it, unable to look aside, or do anything else, even quell the flow from her bleeding nose, which now covered half her face and chin, her mouth glued shut with dried and clotting blood. It seemed to her that something was left undone, something that she had to provide.

Nervously crawling closer, she saw that there were now marks on the ring. Charter marks that told her what she must do. Wearily, she got up on her knees and fumbled with the bell bandoleer. Saraneth was heavy, almost beyond her strength, but she managed to draw it out and the deep, compelling voice rang through the sinkhole, seeming to pierce the glowing, silver-bound mass.

The ring hummed in answer to the bell and exuded a pear-shaped drop of its own metal, which cooled to become a miniature Saraneth. At the same time, the ring changed colour and consistency. The ruby's colour seemed to run and a red wash spread through the silver. It was now dull and ordinary, no longer a silver band, but a red leather collar, with a miniature silver bell.

With this change, the white mass quivered and shone bright again, till Sabriel had to shield her eyes once more. When the shadows grew together again, she looked back, and there was Mogget, collared in red leather, sitting up and looking like he was about to throw up a hairball.

It wasn't a hairball, but a silver ring, the ruby reflecting Mogget's internal light. It rolled to Sabriel, tinkling across the stone. She picked it up and slid it back on her finger.

Mogget's glow faded and the burning Paperwing was now only faint embers, sad memories and ash. Darkness returned, cloaking Sabriel, wrapping her up with all her hurts and fears. She sat, silent, not even thinking.

A little later, she felt a soft cat nose against her folded hands, and a candle, damp from Mogget's mouth.

"Your nose is still bleeding," said a familiar, didactic voice. "Light the candle, pinch your nose and get some blankets out for us to sleep. It's getting cold."

"Welcome back, Mogget," whispered Sabriel.

chapter thirteen

Neither Sabriel nor Mogget mentioned the happenings of the previous night when they awoke. Sabriel, bathing her seriously swollen nose in an inch of water from her canteen, found that she didn't particularly want to remember a waking nightmare, and Mogget was quiet, in an apologetic way. Despite what happened later, freeing Mogget's alter ego, or whatever it was, had saved them from certain destruction by the wind.

As she'd expected, dawn had brought some light to the sinkhole, and as the day progressed, this had grown to a level approximating twilight. Sabriel could read and see things close by quite clearly, but they merged into indistinct gloom twenty or thirty yards away.

Not that the sinkhole was much larger than that – perhaps a hundred yards in diameter, not the fifty she'd guessed at when she was coming down. The entire floor of it was paved, with a circular drain in the middle, and there were several tunnel entrances into the sheer rock walls – tunnels which Sabriel knew she would eventually have to take, as there was no water in the sinkhole. There seemed little chance of rain, either. It was cool, but nowhere near as cold as the plateau near Abhorsen's House. The climate was mitigated by proximity to the ocean and an altitude that could easily be sea-level or below, for in daylight Sabriel could see that the sinkhole was at least a hundred yards deep.

Still, with a half-full canteen of water gurgling by her side, Sabriel was quite content to slouch upon her slightly scorched pack and apply herbal creams to her bruises, and a poultice of evil-smelling tanmaril leaves to her strange sunburn. Her nose was a different matter when it came to treatment. It wasn't broken – merely hideous, swollen and encrusted with dried blood, which hurt too much to clean off completely.

Mogget, after an hour or so of sheepish silence, sauntered off to explore, refusing Sabriel's offer of hard cakes and dried meat for breakfast. She expected he'd find a rat or something equally appetising, instead. In a way, she was quite pleased he was gone. The memory of the Free Magic beast that lay within the little white cat was still disturbing.

Even so, when the sun had risen to become a little disc surrounded by the greater circumference of the sinkhole's rim, she started to wonder why he hadn't come back. Levering herself up, she limped over to the tunnel he'd chosen, using her sword as a walking stick and complaining quietly as every bruise reminded her of its location.

Of course, just as she was lighting a candle at the tunnel entrance Mogget reappeared behind her.

"Looking for me?" he mewed innocently.

"Who else?" replied Sabriel. "Have you found anything? Anything useful, I mean. Water, for instance."

"Useful?" mused Mogget, rubbing his chin back along his two outstretched front legs. "Perhaps. Interesting, certainly. Water? Yes."

"How far away?" asked Sabriel, all too aware of her bruise-limited mobility. "And what does interesting mean? Dangerous?"

"Not far, by this tunnel," replied Mogget. "There is a little danger getting there – a trap and a few other oddments, but nothing that will harm you. As to the interesting part, you will have to see for yourself, Abhorsen."

"Sabriel," said Sabriel automatically, as she tried to think ahead. She needed at least two days' rest, but no more than that. Every day lost before she found her father's corporeal body might mean disaster. She simply had to find him soon. A Mordicant, Shadow Hands, gore crows – it was now all too clear that some terrible enemy was arrayed against both father and daughter. That enemy had already trapped her father, so it had to be a very powerful necromancer, or some Greater Dead creature. Perhaps this Kerrigor...

"I'll get my pack," she decided, trudging back, Mogget slipping backwards and forwards across her path like a kitten, almost tripping her over, but always just getting out of the way. Sabriel put this down to inexplicable catness and didn't comment.

As Mogget had promised, the tunnel wasn't long, and its well-made steps and cross-hatched floor made passage easy, save for the part where Sabriel had to follow the little cat exactly across the stones, to avoid a cleverly concealed pit. Without Mogget's guidance, Sabriel knew she would have fallen in.

There were magical wardings too. Old, inimical spells lay like moths in the corners of the tunnel, waiting to fly up at her, to surround and choke her with power – but something checked their first reaction and they settled again. A few times, Sabriel experienced a ghostly touch, like a hand reaching out to brush the Charter mark on her forehead, and almost at the end of the tunnel, she saw two guard sendings melting into the rock, the tips of their halberds glinting in her candlelight before they too merged into stone.

"Where are we going?" she whispered, nervously, as the door in front of them slowly creaked open – without visible means of propulsion.

"Another sinkhole," Mogget said, matter-of-factly. "It is where the First blood... ach..."

He choked, hissed and then rephrased his sentence rather drably with, "It is interesting."

"What do you mean—" Sabriel began, but she fell silent as they passed the doorway, magical force suddenly tugging at her hair, her hands, her surcoat, the hilt of her sword. Mogget's fur stood on end and his collar rotated halfway around of its own accord, till the Charter marks of binding were uppermost and clearly readable, bright against the leather.

Then they were out, standing at the bottom of another sinkhole, in a premature twilight, for the sun was already slipping over the circumscribed horizon of the sinkhole rim.

This sinkhole was much wider than the first – perhaps a mile across and deeper, say six or seven hundred feet. Despite its size, the entire vast pit was sealed off from the upper air by a gleaming, web-thin net, which seemed to merge into the rim wall about a quarter of the way down from the surface. Sunlight had given it away, but even so, Sabriel had to use her telescope to see the delicate diamond-pattern weave clearly. It looked flimsy, but the presence of several desiccated bird-corpses indicated considerable strength. Sabriel guessed the unfortunate birds had dived into the net, eyes greedily intent on food below.

In the sinkhole itself, there was considerable, if uninspiring vegetation – mostly stunted trees and malformed bushes. But Sabriel had little attention to spare for the trees, for in between each of these straggling patches of greenery, there were paved areas – and on each of these paved areas rested a ship.

Fourteen open-decked, single-masted longboats, their black sails set to catch a non-existent wind, oars out to battle an imaginary tide. They flew many flags and standards, all limp against mast and rigging, but Sabriel didn't need to see them unfurled to know what strange cargo these ships might bear. She'd heard of this place, as had every child in the northern parts of Ancelstierre, close to the Old Kingdom. Hundreds of tales of treasure, adventure and romance were woven around this strange harbour.

"Funerary ships," said Sabriel. "Royal ships."

She had further confirmation that this was so, for there were binding spells woven into the very dirt her feet scuffed at the tunnel entrance, spells of final death that could only have been laid by an Abhorsen. No necromancer would ever raise any of the ancient rulers of the Old Kingdom.

"The famous burial ground of the First... ckkk... the Kings and Queens of the Old Kingdom," pronounced Mogget, after some difficulty. He danced around Sabriel's feet, then stood on his hind legs and made expansive gestures, like a circus impresario in white fur. Finally, he shot off into the trees.

"Come on – there's a spring, spring, spring!" he carolled, as he leaped up and down in time with his words.

Sabriel followed at a slower pace, shaking her head and wondering what had happened to make Mogget so cheerful. She felt bruised, tired and depressed, shaken by the Free Magic monster and sad about the Paperwing.

They passed close by two of the ships on their way to the spring. Mogget led her a merry dance around both of them, in a mad circumnavigation of twists, leaps and bounds, but the sides were too high to look in and she didn't feel like shinning up an oar. She did pause to look at the figureheads – imposing men, one in his forties, the other somewhat older. Both were bearded, had the same imperious eyes, and wore armour similar to Sabriel's, heavily festooned with medallions, chains and other decorations. Each held a sword in his right hand and an unfurling scroll that turned back on itself in their left – the heraldic representation of the Charter.

The third ship was different. It seemed shorter and less ornate, with a bare mast devoid of black sails. No oars sprang from its sides, and as Sabriel reached the spring that lay under its stern, she saw uncaulked seams between the planking and realised that it was incomplete.

Curious, she dropped her pack by the little pool of bubbling water and walked around to the bow. This was different too, for the figurehead was a young man – a naked young man, carved in perfect detail.

Sabriel blushed a little, for it was an exact likeness, as if a young man had been transformed from flesh to wood, and her only prior experience of naked men was in clinical cross-sections from biology textbooks. His muscles were lean and well-formed, his hair short and tightly curled against his head. His hands, well-shaped and elegant, were partly raised, as if to ward off some evil.

The detail even extended to a circumcised penis, which Sabriel glanced at in an embarrassed way, before looking back at his face. He was not exactly handsome, but not displeasing. It was a responsible visage, with the shocked expression of someone who has been betrayed and only just realised it. There was fear there too, and something like hatred. He looked more than a little mad. His expression troubled her, for it seemed too human to be the result of a woodcarver's skill, no matter how talented.

"Too life-like," Sabriel muttered, stepping back from the figurehead, hand falling to the hilt of her sword, her magical senses reaching out, seeking some trap or deception.

There was no trap, but Sabriel did feel something in or around the figurehead. A feeling similar to that of a Dead revenant, but not the same – a niggling sensation that she couldn't place.

Sabriel tried to identify it, while she looked over the figurehead again, carefully examining him from every angle. The man's body was an intellectual problem now, so she looked without embarrassment, studying his fingers, fingernails and skin, noting how perfectly they were carved, right down to the tiny scars on his hands, the product of sword and dagger practice. There was also the faint sign of a baptismal Charter mark on his forehead and the pale trace of veins on his eyelids.

That inspection led her to certainty about what she'd detected, but she hesitated about the action that should be taken and went in search of Mogget. Not that she put a lot of faith in advice or answers from that quarter, given his present propensity towards behaving as a fairly silly cat – though perhaps this was a reaction to his brief experience of being a Free Magic beast again, something that might not have happened for millennia. The cat form was probably a welcome relief.

In fact, no advice at all could be had from Mogget. Sabriel found him asleep in a field of flowers near the spring, his tail and paddy-paws twitching to a dream of dancing mice. Sabriel looked at the straw-yellow flowers, sniffed one, scratched Mogget behind the ears, then went back to the figurehead. The flowers were catbalm, explaining both Mogget's previous mood and his current somnolence. She would have to make up her own mind.

"So," she said, addressing the figurehead like a lawyer before a court. "You are the victim of some Free Magic spell and necromantic trickery. Your spirit lies neither in Life nor Death, but somewhere in between. I could cross into Death and find you near the border, I'm sure – but I could find a lot of trouble as well. Trouble I can't deal with in my current pathetic state. So what can I do? What would Father – Abhorsen... or any Abhorsen – do in my place?"

She thought about it for a while, pacing backwards and forwards, bruises temporarily forgotten. That last question seemed to make her duty clear. Sabriel felt sure her father would free the man. That's what he did, that was what he lived for. The duty of an Abhorsen was to remedy unnatural necromancy and Free Magic sorcery.

She didn't think further than that, perhaps due to the injudicious sniffing of the catbalm. She didn't even consider that her father would probably have waited until he was fitter – perhaps till the next day. After all, this young man must have been incarcerated for many years, his physical body transformed into wood, and his spirit somehow trapped in Death. A few days would make no difference to him. An Abhorsen didn't have to immediately take on any duty that presented itself...

But for the first time since she'd crossed the Wall, Sabriel felt there was a clear-cut problem for her to solve. An injustice to be righted and one that should involve little more than a few minutes on the very border of Death.

Some slight sense of caution remained with her, so she went and picked up Mogget, placing the dozing cat near the feet of the figurehead. Hopefully, he would wake up if any physical danger threatened – not that this was likely, given the wards and guards on the sinkhole. There were even barriers that would make it difficult to cross into Death and more than difficult for something Dead to follow her back. All in all, it seemed like the perfect place to undertake a minor rescue.

Once more, she checked the bells, running her hands over the smooth wood of the handles, feeling their voices within, eagerly awaiting release. This time, it was Ranna she freed from its leather case. It was the least noticeable of the bells, its very nature lulling listeners, beguiling them to sleep or inattention.

Second thoughts brushed at her like doubting fingers, but she ignored them. She felt confident, ready for what would only be a minor stroll in Death, amply safeguarded by the protections of this royal necropolis. Sword in one hand, bell in the other, she crossed into Death.

Cold hit her, and the relentless current, but she stood where she was, still feeling the warmth of Life on her back. This was the very interface between the two realms, where she would normally plunge ahead. This time, she planted her feet against the current and used her continuing slight contact with Life as an anchor to hold her own against the waters of Death.

Everything seemed quiet, save for the constant gurgling of the water about her feet and the far-off crash of the First Gate. Nothing stirred, no shapes loomed up in the grey light. Cautiously, Sabriel used her sense of the Dead to feel out anything that might be lurking, to feel the slight spark of the trapped, but living, spirit of the young man. Back in

Life, she was physically close to him, so she should be near his spirit here.

There was something, but it seemed further into Death than Sabriel expected. She tried to see it, squinting into the curious greyness that made distance impossible to judge, but nothing was visible. Whatever was there lurked beneath the surface of the water.

Sabriel hesitated, then walked towards it, carefully feeling her way, making sure of every footfall, guarding against the gripping current. There was definitely something odd out there. She could feel it quite strongly – it had to be the trapped spirit. She ignored the little voice at the back of her mind that suggested it was a fiercely devious Dead creature, strong enough to hold its own against the race of the river...

Nevertheless, when she was a few paces back from whatever it was, Sabriel let Ranna sound – a muffled, sleepy peal that carried the sensation of a yawn, a sigh, a head falling forward, eyes heavy – a call to sleep.

If there was a Dead thing there, Sabriel reasoned, it would now be quiescent. She put her sword and bell away, edged forward to a good position, and reached down into the water.

Her hands touched something as cold and hard as ice, something totally unidentifiable. She flinched back, then reached down again, till her hands found something that was clearly a shoulder. She followed this up to a head and traced the features. Sometimes a spirit bore little relation to the physical body, and sometimes living spirits became warped if they spent too long in Death, but this one was clearly the counterpart of the figurehead. It lived too, somehow encased and protected from Death, as the living body was preserved in wood.

Sabriel gripped the spirit-form under the arms and pulled. It rose up out of the water like a killer whale, pallid white and rigid as a statue. Sabriel staggered backwards and the river, ever-eager, wrapped her legs with tricksome eddies – but she steadied herself before it could drag her down.

Changing her hold a little, Sabriel began to drag the spirit-form back towards Life. It was hard going, much harder than she'd expected. The current seemed far too strong for this side of the First Gate and the crystallised spirit – or whatever it was – was much, much heavier than any spirit should be.

With nearly all her concentration bent on staying upright and heading in the right direction, Sabriel almost didn't notice the sudden cessation of noise that marked the passage of something through the First Gate. But she'd learned to be wary over the last few days and her conscious fears had become enshrined in subconscious caution.

She heard, and listening carefully, caught the soft slosh-slosh of something half-wading, half-creeping, moving as quietly as it could against the current. Moving towards her. Something Dead was hoping to catch her unawares.

Obviously, some alarm or summons had gone out beyond the First Gate and whatever was stalking towards her had come in answer to it. Inwardly cursing herself for stupidity, Sabriel looked down at her spirit burden. Sure enough, she could just make out a very thin black line, fine as cotton thread, running from his arm into the water – and thence to the deeper, darker regions of Death. Not a controlling thread, but one that would let some distant adept know the spirit had been moved. Fortunately, sounding Ranna would have slowed the message, but was she close enough to Life...

She increased her speed a little, but not too much, pretending she hadn't noticed the hunter. Whatever it was, it seemed quite reluctant to close in on her.

Sabriel quickened her pace a little more, adrenaline and suspense feeding her strength. If it rushed her, she would have to drop the spirit – and he would be carried away, lost for ever. Whatever magic had preserved his living spirit here on the boundary couldn't possibly prevail if he went past the First Gate. If that happened, Sabriel thought, she would have precipitated a murder rather than a rescue.

Four steps to Life – then three. The thing was closing now – Sabriel could see it, low in the water, still creeping, but faster now. It was obviously a denizen of the Third or even some later Gate, for she couldn't identify what it once had been. Now it looked like a cross between a hog and a segmented worm and it moved in a series of scuttles and sinuous wriggles.

Two steps. Sabriel shifted her grip again, wrapping her left arm completely around the spirit's chest and balancing the weight on her hip, freeing her right arm, but she still couldn't draw her sword, or clear the bells.

The hog-thing began to grunt and hiss, breaking into a diving, rushing gallop, its long, yellow-crusted tusks surfing through the water, its long body undulating along behind.

Sabriel stepped back, turned, and threw herself and her precious cargo headfirst into Life, using all her will to force them through the wards on the sinkhole. For an instant, it seemed that they would be repulsed, then, like a pin pushing through a rubber band, they were through.

Shrill squealing followed her, but nothing else. Sabriel found herself face-down on the ground, hands empty, ice crystals crunching as they fell from her frosted body. Turning her head, she met the gaze of Mogget. He stared at her, then closed his eyes and went back to sleep.

Sabriel rolled over and got to her feet, very, very slowly. She felt all her pains come back and wondered why she'd been so hasty to perform deeds of derring-do and rescue. Still, she had managed it. The man's spirit was back where it belonged, back in Life.

Or so she thought, till she saw the figurehead. It hadn't changed at all to outward sight, though Sabriel could now feel the living spirit in it. Puzzled, she touched his immobile face, fingers tracing the grain of the wood.

"A kiss," said Mogget sleepily. "Actually, just a breath would do. But you have to start kissing someone sometime, I suppose."

Sabriel looked at the cat, wondering if this was the latest symptom of catbalm-induced lunacy. But he seemed sober enough, and serious.

"A breath?" she asked. She didn't want to kiss just any wooden man. He looked nice enough, but he might not be like his looks. A kiss seemed very forward. He might remember it and make assumptions.

"Like this?" She took a deep breath, leaned forward, exhaled a few inches from his nose and mouth, then stepped back to see what would happen – if anything.

Nothing did.

"Catbalm!" exclaimed Sabriel, looking at Mogget. "You shouldn't—"

A small sound interrupted her. A small, wheezing sound that didn't come from her or Mogget. The figurehead was breathing, air whistling between carved wooden lips like the issue from an aged, underworked bellows.

The breathing grew stronger, and with it, colour began to flow through the carving, dull wood giving way to the lustre of flesh. He coughed and the carven chest became flexible, suddenly rising and falling as he began to pant like a recovering sprinter.

His eyes opened and met Sabriel's. Fine grey eyes, but muzzy and unfocused. He didn't seem to see her. His fingers clenched and unclenched, and his feet shuffled, as if he were running in place. Finally, his back peeled away from the ship's hull. He took one step forward and fell into Sabriel's arms.

She lowered him hastily to the ground, all too aware that she was embracing a naked young man – in circumstances considerably different than the various scenarios she'd imagined with her friends at school or heard about from the earthier and more privileged day-girls.

"Thank you," he said, almost drunkenly, the words terribly slurred. He seemed to focus on her – or her surcoat – for the first time, and added, "Abhorsen."

Then he went to sleep, mouth curling up at the corners, frown dissolving. He looked younger than he did as a fixed-expression figurehead.

Sabriel looked down at him, trying to ignore curiously fond feelings that had appeared from somewhere. Feelings similar to those that had made her bring back Jacinth's rabbit.

"I suppose I'd better get him a blanket," she said reluctantly, as she wondered what on earth had possessed her to add this complication to her already confusing and difficult circumstances. She supposed she would have to get him to safety and civilisation, at the very least – if there was any to be found.

"I can get a blanket if you want to keep staring at him," Mogget said slyly, twining himself around her ankles in a sensuous pavane.

Sabriel realised she really was staring and looked away.

"No. I'll get it. And my spare shirt, I suppose. The breeches might fit him with a bit of work, I guess – we'd be much the same height. Keep watch, Mogget. I'll be back in a minute."

Mogget watched her hobble off, then turned back to the sleeping man. Silently, the cat padded over and touched his pink tongue to the Charter mark on the man's forehead. The mark flared, but Mogget didn't flinch, till it grew dull again.

"So," muttered Mogget, tasting his own tongue by curling it back on itself. He seemed somewhat surprised and more than a little angry. He tasted the mark again and then shook his head in distaste, the miniature Saraneth on his collar ringing a little peal that was not of celebration.

chapter fourteen

Grey mist coiling upwards, twining around him like a clinging vine, gripping arms and legs, immobilising, strangling, merciless. So firmly grown about his body there was no possibility of escape, so tight his muscles couldn't even flex under skin, his eyelids couldn't blink. And nothing to see but patches of darker grey, crisscrossing his vision like wind-blown scum upon a fetid pool.

Then, suddenly, fierce red light, pain exploding everywhere, rocketing from toes to brain and back again. The grey mist clearing, mobility returning. No more grey patches, but blurry colours, slowly twisting into focus. A woman, looking down at him, a young woman, armed and armoured, her face... battered. No, not a woman. The Abhorsen, for she wore the blazon and the bells. But she was too young, not the Abhorsen he knew or any of the family...

"Thank you," he said, the words coming out like a mouse creeping from a dusty larder. "Abhorsen."

Then he fainted, his body rushing gladly to welcome real sleep, true unconsciousness and sanity-restoring rest.

He awoke under a blanket and felt a moment's panic when the thick grey wool pressed upon his mouth and eyes. He struggled with it, threw it back with a gasp, and relaxed as he felt fresh air on his face and dim sunlight filtering down from above. He looked up and saw from the reddish hue that it must be soon after dawn. The sinkhole puzzled him for a few seconds – disoriented, he felt dizzy and stupid, till he looked at the tall masts all around, the black sails and the unfinished ship nearby.

"Holehallow," he muttered to himself, frowning. He remembered it now. But what was he doing here? Completely naked under a rough camping blanket?

He sat up and shook his head. It was sore and his temples were throbbing, seemingly from the battering-ram effect of a severe hangover. But he felt certain he hadn't been drinking. The last thing he remembered was going down the steps. Rogir had asked him... no... the last thing was the fleeting image of a pale, concerned face, bloodied and bruised, black hair hanging out in a fringe under her helmet. A deep blue surcoat, with the blazon of silver keys. The Abhorsen.

"She's washing at the spring," said a soft voice, interrupting his faltering recollection. "She got up before the sun. Cleanliness is a wonderful thing."

The voice did not seem to belong to anything visible, till the man looked up at the nearby ship. There was a large, irregular hole in the bow, where the figurehead should have been and a white cat was curled up in the hole, watching him with an unnaturally sharp, green-eyed gaze.

"What are you?" said the man, his eyes cautiously flickering from side to side, looking for a weapon. A pile of clothes was the only thing nearby, containing a shirt, trousers and some underwear, but it was weighted down with a largish rock. His hand sidled out towards the rock.

"Don't be alarmed," said the cat. "I'm but a faithful retainer of the Abhorsen. Name of Mogget. For the moment."

The man's hand closed on the rock, but he didn't lift it. Memories were slowly sidling back to his benumbed mind, drawn like grains of iron to a magnet. There were memories of various Abhorsens among them – memories that gave him an inkling of what this cat-creature was.

"You were bigger when we last met," he hazarded, testing his guess.

"Have we met?" replied Mogget, yawning. "Dear me. I can't recall it. What was the name?"

A good question, thought the man. He couldn't remember. He knew who he was, in general terms, but his name eluded him. Other names came easily though and some flashes of memory concerning what he thought of as his immediate past. He growled and grimaced as they came to him, and clenched his fists in pain and anger.

"Unusual name," commented Mogget. "More of a bear's name, that growl. Do you mind if I call you Touchstone?"

"What!" the man exclaimed, affronted. "That's a fool's name! How dare—"

"Is it unfitting?" interrupted Mogget coolly. "You do remember what you've done?"

The man was silent then, for he suddenly did remember, though he didn't know why he'd done it or what the consequences had been. He also remembered that since this was the case, there was no point trying to remember his name. He was no longer fit to bear it.

"Yes, I remember," he whispered. "You may call me Touchstone. But I shall call you—"

He choked, looked surprised, then tried again.

"You can't say it," Mogget said. "A spell tied to the corruption of – but I can't say it, nor tell anyone the nature of it or how to fix it. You won't be able to talk about it either and there may be other effects. Certainly, it has affected me."

"I see," replied Touchstone, sombrely. He didn't try the name again. "Tell me, who rules the Kingdom?"

"No one," said Mogget.

"A regency, then. That is perhaps—"

"No. No regency. No one reigns. No one rules. There was a regency at first, but it declined... with help."

"What do you mean at first?" asked Touchstone. "What exactly has happened? Where have I been?"

"The regency lasted for one hundred and eighty years," Mogget announced callously. "Anarchy has held sway for the last twenty, tempered by what a few remaining loyalists could do. And you, my boy, have been adorning the front of this ship as a lump of wood for the last two hundred years."

"The family?"

"All dead and past the Final Gate, save one, who should be. You know who I mean."

For a moment, this news seemed to return Touchstone to his wooden state. He sat frozen, only the slight movement of his chest showing continued life. Then tears started in his eyes and his head slowly fell to meet his upturned hands.

Mogget watched without sympathy, till the young man's back ceased its heaving and the harsh in-drawn gasps between sobs became calmer.

"There's no point crying over it," the cat said harshly. "Plenty of people have died trying to put the matter to rights. Four Abhorsens have fallen in this century alone, trying to deal with the Dead, the broken stones and the – the original problem. My current Abhorsen certainly isn't lying around crying her eyes out. Make yourself useful and help her."

"Can I?" asked Touchstone bleakly, wiping his face with the blanket.

"Why not?" snorted Mogget. "Get dressed, for a start. There are some things aboard here for you as well. Swords and suchlike."

"But I'm not fit to wield royal—"

"Just do as you're told," Mogget said firmly. "Think of yourself as Abhorsen's sworn sword-hand, if it makes you feel better, though in this present era, you'll find common sense is more important than honour."

"Very well," Touchstone muttered, humbly. He stood up and put on the underclothes and shirt, but couldn't get the trousers past his heavily muscled thighs.

"There's a kilt and leggings in one of the chests back here," Mogget said, after watching Touchstone hopping around on one leg, the other trapped in too-tight leather.

Touchstone nodded, divested himself of the trousers and clambered up through the hole, taking care to keep as far away from Mogget as possible. Halfway up, he paused, arms braced on either side of the gap.

"You won't tell her?" he asked.

"Tell who? Tell what?"

"Abhorsen. Please, I'll do all I can to help. But it wasn't intentional. My part, I mean. Please, don't tell her—"

"Spare me the pleadings," said Mogget, in a disgusted tone. "I can't tell her. You can't tell her. The corruption is wide and the spell rather indiscriminate. Hurry up – she'll be back soon. I'll tell you the rest of our current saga while you dress."

Sabriel returned from the spring feeling healthier, cleaner and happier. She'd slept well and the morning's ablutions had cleared off the blood. The bruises, swellings and sunburn had all responded well to her herbal treatments. All in all, she felt about eighty per cent normal, rather than ten per cent functional, and she was looking forward to having some company at breakfast other than the sardonic Mogget. Not that he didn't have his uses, such as guarding unconscious or sleeping humans. He'd also assured her that he had tested the Charter mark on the figurehead-man, finding him to be unsullied by Free Magic or necromancy.

She'd expected the man to still be asleep, so she felt a faint frisson of surprise and suspense when she saw a figure standing by the ship's bow, facing the other way. For a second, her hand twitched to her sword, then she saw Mogget nearby, precariously draped on the ship's rail.

She approached nervously, her curiosity tempered by the need to be wary of strangers. He looked different dressed. Older and somewhat intimidating, particularly since he seemed to have scorned her plain clothing for a kilt of gold-striped red, with matching leggings of red-striped gold, disappearing into turned-down thigh boots of russet doeskin. He was wearing her shirt, though, and preparing to put on a red leather jerkin. It had detachable, lace-up sleeves, which seemed to be giving him some problems. Two swords lay in three-quarter scabbards near his feet, stabbing points shining four inches out of the leather. A wide belt with the appropriate hooks already encircled his waist.

"Curse these laces," he said, when she was about ten paces away. A nice voice, quite deep, but currently frustrated and peaking with temper.

"Good morning," said Sabriel.

He whirled around, dropping the sleeves, almost ducking to his swords, before recovering to transform the motion into a bow, culminating in a descent to one knee.

"Good morning, milady," he said huskily, head bowed, carefully not meeting her gaze. She saw that he'd found some earrings, large gold hoops clumsily pushed through pierced lobes, for they were bloodied. Apart from them, all she could see was the top of his curly-haired head.

"I'm not 'milady'," said Sabriel, wondering which of Miss Prionte's etiquette principles applied to this situation. "My name is Sabriel."

"Sabriel? But you are the Abhorsen," the man said slowly. He didn't sound overly bright, Sabriel thought, with sinking expectations. Perhaps there would be very little conversation at breakfast after all.

"No, my father is the Abhorsen," she said, with a stern look at Mogget, warning him not to interfere. "I'm a sort of stand-in. It's a bit complicated, so I'll explain later. What's your name?"

He hesitated, then mumbled, "I can't remember, milady. Please, call me... call me Touchstone."

"Touchstone?" asked Sabriel. That sounded familiar, but she couldn't place it for a moment. "Touchstone? But that's a jester's name, a fool's name. Why call you that?"

"That's what I am," he said dully, without inflection.

"Well, I have to call you something," Sabriel continued. "Touchstone. You know, there is the tradition of a wise fool, so perhaps it's not so bad. I guess you think you're a fool because you've been imprisoned as a figurehead – and in Death, of course."

"In Death!" exclaimed Touchstone. He looked up and his grey eyes met Sabriel's. Surprisingly, he had a clear, intelligent gaze. Perhaps there is some hope for him after all, she thought, as she explained: "Your spirit was somehow preserved just beyond the border of Death and your body preserved as the wooden figurehead. Both necromantic and Free Magic would have been involved. Very powerful magic, on both counts. I am curious as to why it was used on you."

Touchstone looked away again and Sabriel sensed a certain shiftiness or embarrassment. She guessed that the forthcoming explanation would be a half-truth, at best.

"I don't remember very well," he said, slowly. "Though things are coming back. I am... I was... a guardsman. The Royal

Guard. There was some sort of attack upon the Queen... an ambush in the – at the bottom of the stairs. I remember fighting, with blade and Charter Magic – we were all Charter Mages, all the guard. I thought we were safe, but there was treachery... then... I was here. I don't know how."

Sabriel listened carefully, wondering how much of what he said was true. It was likely that his memory was impaired, but he possibly was a royal guard. Perhaps he had cast a diamond of protection... that could have been why his enemies could only imprison him, rather than kill. But, surely they could have waited till it failed. Why the bizarre method of imprisonment? And, most importantly, how did the figurehead manage to get placed in this most protected of places?

She filed all these questions for later investigation, for another thought had struck her. If he really was a royal guard, the Queen he had guarded must have been dead and gone for at least two hundred years and, with her, everyone and everything he knew.

"You have been a prisoner for a long time," she said gently, uncertain about how to break the news. "Have you... I mean did you... well, what I mean is it's been a very long time—"

"Two hundred years," whispered Touchstone. "Your minion told me."

"Your family..."

"I have none," he said. His expression was set, as immobile as the carved wood of the previous day. Carefully, he reached over and drew one of his swords, offering it to Sabriel hilt-first.

"I would serve you, milady, to fight against the enemies of the Kingdom."

Sabriel didn't take the sword, though his plea made her reflexively reach out. But a moment's thought closed her open palm and her arm fell back to her side. She looked at Mogget, who was watching the proceedings with unabashed interest.

"What have you told him, Mogget?" she asked, suspicion wreathing her words.

"The state of the Kingdom, generally speaking," replied the cat. "Recent events. Our descent here, more or less. Your duty as Abhorsen to remedy the situation."

"The Mordicant? Shadow Hands? Gore crows? The Dead adept, whoever it may be?"

"Not specifically," said Mogget, cheerfully. "I thought he could presume as much."

"As you see," Sabriel said, rather angrily, "my 'minion' has not been totally honest with you. I was raised across the Wall, in Ancelstierre, so I have very little idea about what is going on. I have huge gaps in my knowledge of the Old Kingdom, including everything from geography to history to Charter Magic. I face some dire enemies, probably under the overall direction of one of the Greater Dead, a necromantic adept. And I'm not out to save the Kingdom, just to find my father, the real Abhorsen. So I don't want to take your oath or service or anything like that, particularly as we've only just met. I am happy for you to accompany us to the nearest approximation of civilisation, but I have no idea what I will be doing after that. And please remember that my name is Sabriel. Not milady. Not Abhorsen. Now, I think it's time for breakfast."

With that, she stalked over to her pack, and started getting out some oatmeal and a small cooking pot. Touchstone stared after her for a moment, then picked himself up, attached his swords, put on the sleeveless jerkin, tied the sleeves to his belt and wandered off to the nearest clump of trees.

Mogget followed him there and watched him pick up dead branches and sticks for a fire.

"She really did grow up in Ancelstierre," said the cat. "She doesn't realise refusing your oath is an insult. And it's true enough about her ignorance. That's one of the reasons she needs your help."

"I can't remember much," said Touchstone, snapping a branch in half with considerable ferocity. "Except my most recent past. Everything else is like a dream. I'm not sure if it's real or not, learned or imagined. And I wasn't insulted. My oath isn't worth much."

"But you'll help her," said Mogget. It wasn't a question.

"No," said Touchstone. "Help is for equals. I'll serve her. That's all I'm good for."

As Sabriel feared, there was little conversation over breakfast. Mogget went off in search of his own, and Sabriel and Touchstone were hindered by the sole cooking pot and single spoon, so they took it in turns to eat half the porridge. Even allowing for this difficulty, Touchstone was uncommunicative. Sabriel started asking a lot of questions, but as his standard response was, "I'm sorry, I can't remember," she soon gave up.

"I don't suppose you can remember how to get out of this sinkhole, either," she asked in exasperation, after a particularly long stretch of silence. Even to her, this sounded like a prefect addressing a miscreant twelve-year-old.

"No, I'm sorry..." Touchstone began automatically, then he paused, and the corner of his mouth quirked up with a momentary spasm of pleasure. "Wait! Yes – I do remember! There's a hidden stair, to the north of King Janeurl's ship... oh, I can't remember which one that is..."

"There's only four ships near the northern rim," Sabriel mused. "It won't be too hard to find. How's your memory for other geography. The Kingdom, for instance?"

"I'm not sure," replied Touchstone, guardedly, bowing his head again. Sabriel looked at him and took a deep breath to calm the eel-like writhings of anger that were slowly getting bigger and bigger inside her. She could excuse his faulty memory – after all, that was due to magical incarceration. But the servile manner that went with it seemed to be an affectation. He was like a bad actor playing the butler – or rather, a non-actor trying to impersonate a butler as best he could. But why?

"Mogget drew me a map," she said, talking as much to calm herself as for any real communication. "But, as he apparently has only left Abhorsen's House for a few weekends over the last thousand years, even two-hundred-year-old memories..."

Sabriel paused and bit her lip, suddenly aware that her annoyance with him had made her spiteful. He looked up as she stopped speaking, but no reaction showed on his face. He might as well still be carved from wood.

"What I mean is," Sabriel continued carefully, "it would be very helpful if you could advise me on the best route to Belisaere, and the important landmarks and locations on the way."

She got the map out of the special pocket in the pack and removed the protective oilskin. Touchstone took one end as she unrolled it and weighted his two corners with stones, while Sabriel secured hers with the telescope case.

"I think we're about here," she said, tracing her finger from Abhorsen's House, following the Paperwing's flight from there to a point a little north of the Ratterlin river delta.

"No," said Touchstone, sounding decisive for the first time, his finger stabbing the map an inch to the north of Sabriel's own. "This is Holehallow, here. It's only ten leagues from the coast and at the same latitude as Mount Anarson."

"Good!" exclaimed Sabriel, smiling, her anger slipping from her. "You do remember. Now, what's the best route to Belisaere and how long will it take?"

"I don't know the current conditions, mi... Sabriel," Touchstone replied. His voice grew softer, more subdued. "From what Mogget says, the Kingdom is in a state of anarchy. Towns and villages may no longer exist. There will be bandits, the Dead, Free Magic unbound, fell creatures..."

"Ignoring all that," Sabriel asked, "which way did you normally go?"

"From Nestowe, the fishing village here," Touchstone said, pointing at the coast to the east of Holehallow. "We'd ride north along the Shoreway, changing horses at post houses. Four days to Callibe, a rest day there. Then the interior road up through

Oncet Pass, six days all told to Aunden. A rest day in Aunden, then four days to Orchyre. From there, it would be a day's ferry passage, or two days' riding, to the Westgate of Belisaere."

"Even without the rest days, that'd be eighteen days' riding, at least six weeks' walking. That's too long. Is there any other way?"

"A ship, or boat, from Nestowe," interrupted Mogget, stalking up behind Sabriel, to place his paw firmly on the map. "If we can find one and if either of you can sail it."

chapter fifteen

The stair was to the north of the middle ship of the four. Concealed by both magic and artifice, it seemed to be little more than a particularly wet patch of the damp limestone that formed the sinkhole wall, but you could walk right through it, for it was really an open door with steps winding up behind.

They decided to take these steps the next morning, after another day of rest. Sabriel was eager to move on, for she felt that her father's peril could only be increasing, but she was realistic enough to assess her own need for recovery time. Touchstone too probably needed a rest, she thought. She'd tried to coax more information out of him while they'd searched for the steps, but he was clearly reluctant to even open his mouth, and when he did, Sabriel found his humble apologies ever more irritating. After the door was found she gave up altogether and sat in the grass near the spring, reading her father's books on Charter Magic. *The Book of the Dead* stayed wrapped in oilskin. Even then, she felt its presence, brooding in her pack...

Touchstone stayed at the opposite end of the ship, near the bow, performing a series of fencing exercises with his twin swords, and some stretches and minor acrobatics. Mogget watched him from the undergrowth, green eyes glittering, as if intent on a mouse.

Lunch was a culinary and conversational failure. Dried beef strips, garnished with watercress from the fringes of the spring, and monosyllabic responses from Touchstone. He even went back to "milady," despite Sabriel's repeated requests to use her name. Mogget didn't help by calling her Abhorsen. After lunch, everyone went back to their respective activities. Sabriel to her book, Touchstone to his exercises and Mogget to his watching.

Dinner was not something anyone had looked forward to. Sabriel tried talking to Mogget, but he seemed to be infected with Touchstone's reticence, though not with his servility. As soon as they'd eaten, everyone left the raked-together coals of the campfire – Touchstone to the west, Mogget north and Sabriel east – and went to sleep on as comfortable a stretch of ground as could be discovered.

Sabriel woke once in the night. Without getting up, she saw that the fire had been rekindled and Touchstone sat beside it, staring into the flames, his eyes reflecting the capering, gold-red light. His face looked drawn, almost ill.

"Are you all right?" Sabriel asked quietly, propping herself up on one elbow.

Touchstone started, rocked back on his heels, and almost fell over. For once, he didn't sound like a sulky servant.

"Not really. I remember what I would not and forget what I should not. Forgive me."

Sabriel didn't answer. He had spoken the last two words to the fire, not to her.

"Please, go back to sleep, milady," Touchstone continued, slipping back to his servile role. "I will wake you in the morning."

Sabriel opened her mouth to say something scathing about the arrogance of pretended humility, then shut it and subsided back under her blanket. Just concentrate on rescuing Father, she told herself. That is the one important thing. Rescue Abhorsen. Don't worry about Touchstone's problems or Mogget's curious nature. Rescue Abhorsen. Rescue Abhorsen. Rescue Abhors... rescue...

"Wake up!" Mogget said, right in her ear. She rolled over, ignoring him, but he leapt across her head and repeated it in her other ear. "Wake up!"

"I'm awake," grumbled Sabriel. She sat up with the blanket wrapped around her, feeling the pre-dawn chill on her face and hands. It was still extremely dark, save for the uneven light of the fire and the faintest brushings of dawn light above the sinkhole. Touchstone was already making the porridge. He'd also washed and shaved – using a dagger from the look of the nicks and cuts on his chin and neck.

"Good morning," he said. "This will be ready in five minutes, milady."

Sabriel groaned at that word again, picked up her shirt and trousers, and staggered off to find a suitable bush en route to the spring, a shambling, blanket-shrouded excuse for a human being.

The icy water of the spring completed the waking up process without kindness, Sabriel exposing herself to it and the marginally warmer air for no more than the ten seconds it took to shed undershirt, wash and get dressed again. Clean, awake and clothed, she returned to the campfire and ate her share of the porridge. Then Touchstone ate, while Sabriel buckled on armour, sword and bells. Mogget lay near the fire, warming his white-furred belly. Not for the first time, Sabriel wondered if he needed to eat at all. He obviously liked food, but he seemed to eat for amusement, rather than sustenance.

Touchstone continued being a servant after breakfast, cleaning pot and spoon, quenching the fire and putting everything away. But when he was about to swing the pack on his back, Sabriel stopped him.

"No, Touchstone. It's my pack. I'll carry it, thank you."

He hesitated, then passed it to her and would have helped her put it on, but she had her arms through the straps and the pack swung on before he could take the weight.

Half an hour later, perhaps a third of the way up the narrow, stone-carved stair, Sabriel regretted her decision to take the pack. She still wasn't totally recovered from the Paperwing crash and the stair was very steep, and so narrow that she had difficulty negotiating the spiralling turns. The pack always seemed to jam against the outside or inside wall, no matter which way she turned.

"Perhaps we should take it in turns to carry the pack," she said reluctantly, when they stopped at a sort of alcove to catch their breath. Touchstone, who had been leading, nodded and came back down a few steps to take the pack.

"I'll lead, then," Sabriel added, flexing her back and shoulders, shuddering slightly at the pack-induced layer of sweat on her back, greasy under armour, tunic, shirt and undershirt. She picked up her candle from the bench and stepped up.

"No," said Touchstone, stepping in her way. "There are guards – and guardians – on this stair. I know the words and signs to pass them. You are the Abhorsen, so they might let you past, but I am not sure."

"Your memory must be coming back," Sabriel commented, slightly peeved at being thwarted. "Tell me, is this stair the one you mentioned when you said the Queen was ambushed?"

"No," Touchstone replied flatly. He hesitated, then added, "That stair was in Belisaere."

With that, he turned and continued up the stairs. Sabriel followed, Mogget at her heels. Now that she wasn't lumbered by her pack, she felt more alert. Watching Touchstone, she saw him pause occasionally and mutter some words under his breath. Each time, there was the faint, feather-light touch of Charter Magic. Subtle magic, much cleverer than in the tunnel below. Harder to detect and probably much more deadly, Sabriel thought. Now she knew it was there, she also picked up the faint sensation of Death. This stair had seen killings, a long, long, time ago.

Finally, they came to a large chamber, with a set of double doors to one side. Light leaked in from a large number of small, circular holes in the roof, or as Sabriel soon saw, through an overgrown lattice that had once been open to air and sky.

"That's the outside door," Touchstone said, unnecessarily. He snuffed out his candle, took Sabriel's, now little more than a stub of wax, and put both in a pocket stitched to the front of his kilt. Sabriel thought of joking about the hot wax and the potential for damage, but thought better of it. Touchstone was not the lighthearted type.

"How does it open?" asked Sabriel, indicating the door. She couldn't see any handle, lock or key. Or any hinges, for that matter.

Touchstone was silent, eyes unfocused and staring, then he laughed, a bitter little chuckle.

"I don't remember! All the way up the stair, all the words and signals... and now useless! Useless!"

"At least you got us up the steps," Sabriel pointed out, alarmed by the violence of his self-loathing. "I'd still be sitting by the spring, watching it bubble, if you hadn't come along."

"You would have found the way out," Touchstone muttered. "Or Mogget would. Wood! Yes, that's what I deserve to be—"

"Touchstone," Mogget interrupted, hissing. "Shut up. You're to be useful, remember?"

"Yes," replied Touchstone, visibly calming his breathing, composing his face. "I'm sorry, Mogget. Milady."

"Please, please, just Sabriel," Sabriel said tiredly. "I've only just left school – I'm only eighteen! Calling me milady seems ridiculous."

"Sabriel," Touchstone said tentatively. "I will try to remember. 'Milady' is a habit... it reminds me of my place in the world. It's easier for me—"

"I don't care what's easier for you!" Sabriel snapped. "Don't call me milady and stop acting like a halfwit! Just be yourself. Behave normally. I don't need a valet, I need a useful... friend!"

"Very well, Sabriel," Touchstone said, with careful emphasis. He was angry now, but at least that was an improvement over servile, Sabriel thought.

"Now," she said to the smirking Mogget. "Have you got any ideas about this door?"

"Just one," replied Mogget, sliding between her legs and over to the thin line that marked the division between the two leaves of the door. "Push. One on each side."

"Push?"

"Why not?" said Touchstone, shrugging. He took up a position, braced against the left side of the door, palms flat on the metal-studded wood. Sabriel hesitated, then did the same against the right.

"One, two, three, push!" announced Mogget.

Sabriel pushed on "three" and Touchstone on "push," so their combined effort took several seconds to synchronise. Then the doors creaked slowly open, sunshine spilling through in a bright bar, climbing from floor to ceiling, dust motes dancing in its progress.

"It feels strange," said Touchstone, the wood humming beneath his hands like plucked lute strings.

"I can hear voices," exclaimed Sabriel at the same time, her ears full of half-caught words, laughter, distant singing.

"I can see time," whispered Mogget, so soft that his words were lost.

Then the doors were open. They walked through, shielding their eyes against the sun, feeling the cool breeze sharp on their skin, the fresh scent of pine trees clearing their nostrils of underground dust. Mogget sneezed quickly three times and ran about in a tight circle. The doors slid shut behind them, as silently and inexplicably as they'd opened.

They stood in a small clearing in the middle of a pine forest or plantation, for the trees were regularly spaced. The doors behind them stood in the side of a low hillock of turf and stunted bushes. Pine needles lay thick on the ground, pinecones peeking through every few paces, like skulls ploughed up on some ancient battleground.

"The Watchwood," said Touchstone. He took several deep breaths, looked at the sky, and sighed. "It is Winter, I think – or early Spring?"

"Winter," replied Sabriel. "It was snowing quite heavily, back near the Wall. It seems much milder here."

"Most of the Wall, the Long Cliffs and Abhorsen's House are on, or part of, the Southern Plateau," Mogget explained. "The plateau is between one and two thousand feet above the coastal plain. In fact, the area around Nestowe, where we are headed, is mostly below sea level and has been reclaimed."

"Yes," said Touchstone. "I remember. Long Dyke, the raised canals, the wind pumps to raise the water—"

"You're both very informative for a change," remarked Sabriel. "Would one of you care to tell me something I really want to know, like what are the Great Charters?"

"I can't," Mogget and Touchstone said together. Then

Touchstone continued, haltingly, "There is a spell... a binding on us. But someone who is not a Charter Mage, or otherwise closely bound to the Charter, might be able to speak. A child, perhaps, baptised with the Charter mark, but not grown into power."

"You're cleverer than I thought," commented Mogget. "Not that that's saying much."

"A child," said Sabriel. "Why would a child know?"

"If you'd had a proper education, you'd know too," said Mogget. "A waste of good silver, that school of yours."

"Perhaps," agreed Sabriel. "But now that I know more of the Old Kingdom, I suspect being at school in Ancelstierre saved my life. But enough of that. Which way do we go now?"

Touchstone looked at the sky, blue above the clearing, dark where the pines circled. The sun was just visible above the trees, perhaps an hour short of its noon-time zenith. Touchstone looked from it to the shadows of the trees, then pointed: "East. There should be a series of Charter Stones, leading from here to the eastern edge of the Watchwood. This place is heavily warded with magic. There are... there were, many stones."

The stones were still there, and after the first, some sort of animal track that meandered from one stone to the next. It was cool under the pines, but pleasant, the constant presence of the Charter Stones a reassuring sensation to Sabriel and Touchstone, who could sense them like lighthouses in a sea of trees.

There were seven stones in all and none of them broken, though Sabriel felt a stab of nervous tension every time they left the ambience of one and moved to another, a stark picture always flashing into her head – the bloodstained, riven stone of Cloven Crest.

The last stone stood on the very edge of the pine forest, atop a granite bluff thirty or forty yards high, marking the forest's eastern edge and the end of high ground.

They stood next to the stone and looked out, out towards the huge expanse of blue-grey sea, white-crested, restless, always rolling in to shore. Below them were the flat, sunken fields of Nestowe, maintained by a network of raised canals, pumps and dykes. The village itself lay three-quarters of a mile away, high on another granite bluff, the harbour out of sight on the other side.

"The fields are flooded," said Touchstone, in a puzzled tone, as if he couldn't believe what he was seeing.

Sabriel followed his gaze and saw that what she had taken for some crop was actually silt and water, sitting tepidly where food once grew. Windmills, power for the pumps, stood silent, trefoil-shaped vanes still atop scaffolding towers, even though a salt-laden breeze blew in from the sea.

"But the pumps were Charter-spelled," Touchstone exclaimed. "To follow the wind, to work without care..."

"There are no people in the fields – no one on this side of the village," Mogget added, his eyes keener than the telescope in Sabriel's pack.

"Nestowe's Charter Stone must be broken," Sabriel said, mouth tight, words cold. "And I can smell a certain stench on the breeze. There are Dead in the village."

"A boat would be the quickest way to Belisaere and I am reasonably confident of my sailing," Touchstone remarked. "But if the Dead are there, shouldn't we..."

"We'll go down and get a boat," Sabriel announced firmly. "While the sun is high."

chapter sixteen

There was a built-up path through the flooded fields, but it was submerged to ankle-depth, with occasional thigh-high slippages. Only the raised canal drains stood well above the brackish water and they all ran towards the east, not towards the village, so Sabriel and Touchstone were forced to wade along the path. Mogget, of course, rode, his lean form draped around Sabriel's neck like a white fox fur.

Water and mud, coupled with an uncertain path, made it slow going. It took an hour to cover less than a mile, so it was later in the afternoon than Sabriel would have wished when they finally climbed out of the water, up on to the beginnings of the village's rocky mount. At least the sky is clear, Sabriel thought, glancing up. The winter sun wasn't particularly hot and couldn't be described as glaring, but it would certainly deter most kindred of the Lesser Dead from venturing out.

Nevertheless, they walked carefully up to the village, swords loose, Sabriel with a hand to her bells. The path wound up in a series of steps carved from the rock, reinforced here and there with bricks and mortar. The village proper nestled on top of the bluff – about thirty cosy brick cottages, with wood-tile roofs, some painted bright colours, some dull, and some simply grey and weather-beaten.

It was completely silent, save for the odd gust of wind or the mournful cry of a gull, slipping down through the air above. Sabriel and Touchstone drew closer together, walking almost shoulder-to-shoulder up what passed for a main street, swords out now, eyes flickering across closed doors and shuttered windows. Both felt uneasy, nervous – a nasty, tingling, creeping sensation climbing up from spine, to nape of neck, to forehead Charter mark. Sabriel also felt the presence of Dead things. Lesser Dead, hiding from sunlight, lurking somewhere nearby, in house or cellar.

At the end of the main street, on the highest point of the bluff, a Charter Stone stood on a patch of carefully tended lawn. Half of the stone had been sheared away, pieces broken and tumbled, dark stone on green turf. A body lay in front of the stone, hands and feet bound, the gaping cut across the throat a clear sign of where the blood had come from – the blood for the sacrifice that broke the stone.

Sabriel knelt by the corpse, eyes averted from the broken stone. It was only recently ruined, she felt, but already the door to Death was creaking open. She could almost feel the cold of the currents beyond, leaking out around the stone, sucking warmth and life from the air. Things lurked there too, she knew, just beyond the border. She sensed their hunger for life, their impatience for night to fall.

As she expected, the corpse was of a Charter Mage, dead but three or four days. But she hadn't expected to find the dead person was a woman. Wide shoulders and a muscular build had deceived her for a moment, but there was a middle-aged woman before her, eyes shut, throat cut, short brown hair caked with sea-salt and blood.

"The village healer," said Mogget, indicating a bracelet on her wrist with his nose. Sabriel pushed the rope bindings aside for a better look. The bracelet was bronze with inlaid Charter marks of greenstone. Dead marks now, for blood dried upon the bronze, and no pulse beat in the skin under the metal.

"She was killed three or four days ago," Sabriel announced. "The stone was broken at the same time."

Touchstone looked back at her and nodded grimly, then resumed watching the houses opposite. His swords hung loosely in his hands, but Sabriel noticed that his entire body was tense, like a compressed jack-in-the-box, ready to spring.

"Whoever... whatever... killed her and broke the stone didn't enslave her spirit," Sabriel added quietly, as if thinking to herself. "I wonder why?"

Neither Mogget nor Touchstone answered. For a moment, Sabriel considered asking the woman herself, but her impetuous desire for journeys into Death had been soundly dampened by recent experience. Instead, she cut the woman's bonds and arranged her as best she could, ending up with a sort of curled-up sleeping position.

"I don't know your name, Healer," Sabriel whispered. "But I hope you go quickly beyond the Final Gate. Farewell."

She stood back and drew the Charter marks for the funeral pyre above the corpse, whispering the names of the marks as she did so – but her fingers fumbled and words went awry. The baleful influence of the broken stone pressed against her, like a wrestler gripping her wrists, clamping her jaw. Sweat beaded on her forehead and pain shot through her limbs, her hands shaking with effort, tongue clumsy, seeming swollen in her suddenly dry mouth.

Then she felt assistance come, strength flowing through her, reinforcing the marks, steadying her hands, clearing her voice. She completed the litany and a spark exploded above the woman, became a twisting flame, then grew to a fierce, white-hot blaze that spread the length of the woman's body, totally consuming it, to leave only ash, light cargo for the sea winds.

The extra strength came through Touchstone's hand, his open palm lightly resting on her shoulder. As she straightened up, the touch was lost. When Sabriel turned around, Touchstone was just drawing his right-hand sword, eyes fixed on the houses – as if he'd had nothing to do with helping her.

"Thank you," said Sabriel. Touchstone was a strong Charter Mage, perhaps as strong as she was. This surprised her, though she couldn't think why. He'd made no secret of being a Charter Mage – she'd just assumed he would only know a few of the more fighting-related marks and spells. Petty magics.

"We should move on," said Mogget, prowling backwards and forwards in agitation, carefully avoiding the fragments from the broken stone. "Find a boat and put to sea before nightfall."

"The harbour is that way," Touchstone added quickly, pointing with his sword. Both he and the cat seemed very keen to leave the area around the broken stone, thought Sabriel. But then so was she. Even in bright daylight, it seemed to dull the colour around it. The lawn was already more yellow than green, and even the shadows looked thicker and more abundant than they should. She shivered, remembering Cloven Crest and the thing called Thralk.

The harbour lay on the northern side of the bluff, reached by another series of steps in the rocky hill, or in the case of cargo, via one of the shear-legged hoists that lined the edge of the bluff. Long wooden jetties thrust out into the clear blue-green water, sheltered under the lee of a rocky island, a smaller sibling of the village bluff. A long breakwater of huge boulders joined island and shore, completing the harbour's protection from wind and wave.

There were no boats moored in the harbour, tied up to the jetties, or at the harbour wall. Not even a dinghy, hauled up for repair. Sabriel stood on the steps, looking down, mind temporarily devoid of further plans. She just watched the swirl of the sea around the barnacled piles of the jetties; the moving shadows in the blue, marking small fish schooling about their business. Mogget sat near her feet, sniffing the air, silent. Touchstone stood higher, behind her, guarding the rear.

"What now?" asked Sabriel, generally indicating the empty harbour below, her arm moving with the same rhythm as the swell, in its perpetual tilt against wood and stone.

"There are people on the island," Mogget said, eyes slitted

against the wind. "And boats tied up between the two outcrops of rock on the south-west."

Sabriel looked, but saw nothing, till she extracted the telescope from the pack on Touchstone's back. He stood completely still while she ferreted around, silent as the empty village. Playing wooden again, Sabriel thought, but she didn't really mind. He was being helpful, without metaphorically tugging his forelock every few minutes.

Through the telescope, she saw that Mogget was right. There were several boats partly hidden between two spurs of rock, and some slight signs of habitation: a glimpse of a washing line, blown around the corner of a tall rock; the momentary sight of movement between two of the six or seven ramshackle wooden buildings that nestled on the island's south-western side.

Shifting her gaze to the breakwater, Sabriel followed its length. As she'd half expected, there was a gap in the very middle of it, where the sea rushed through with considerable force. A pile of timber on the island side of the breakwater indicated that there had once been a bridge there, now removed.

"It looks like the villagers fled to the island," she said, shutting the telescope down. "There's a gap in the breakwater, to keep running water between the island and shore. An ideal defence against the Dead. I don't think even a Mordicant would risk crossing deep tidal water—"

"Let's go then," muttered Touchstone. He sounded nervous again, jumpy. Sabriel looked at him, then above his head, and saw why he was nervous. Clouds were rolling in from the south-east, behind the village – dark clouds, laden with rain. The air was calm, but now she saw the clouds, Sabriel recognised it was the calm before heavy rain. The sun would not be guarding them for very much longer and night would be an early guest.

Without further urging, she set off down the steps, down to the harbourside, then along to the breakwater. Touchstone followed more slowly, turning every few steps to watch the rear. Mogget did likewise, his small cat-face continually looking back, peering up at the houses.

Behind them, shutters inched open and fleshless eyes watched from the safety of shadows, watched the trio marching out to the breakwater, still washed in harsh sunlight, flanked by swift-moving waves of terrible water. Rotten, corroded teeth ground and gnashed in skeletal mouths. Farther back from the windows, shadows darker than ones ever cast by light whirled in frustration, anger – and fear. They all knew who had passed.

One such shadow, selected by lot and compelled by its peers, gave up its existence in Life with a silent scream, vanishing into Death. Their master was many, many leagues away and the quickest way to reach him lay in Death. Of course, message delivered, the messenger would fall through the Gates to a final demise. But the master didn't care about that.

The gap in the breakwater proved to be at least fifteen feet wide and the water was twice Sabriel's height, the sea surging through with a rough aggression. It was also covered by archers from the island, as they discovered when an arrow struck the stones in front of them and skittered off into the sea.

Instantly, Touchstone rushed in front of Sabriel and she felt the flow of Charter Magic from him, his swords sketching a great circle in the air in front of them both. Glowing lines followed the swords' path, till a shining circle hung in the air.

Four arrows curved through the air from the island. One, striking the circle, simply vanished. The other three missed completely, striking stones or sea.

"Arrow ward," gasped Touchstone. "Effective, but hard to keep going. Do we retreat?"

"Not yet," replied Sabriel. She could feel the Dead stirring in the village behind them and she could also see the archers now. There were four of them, two pairs, each behind one of the large, upthrust stones that marked where the breakwater joined the island. They looked young, nervous, and were already proven to be of little threat.

"Hold!" shouted Sabriel. "We are friends!"

There was no reply, but the archers didn't loose their nocked arrows.

"What's the village leader's title – usually, I mean? What are they called?" Sabriel whispered hurriedly to Touchstone, once again wishing she knew more about the Old Kingdom and its customs.

"In my day..." Touchstone replied slowly, his swords retracing the arrow ward, attention mostly on that, "in my day – Elder – for this size of village."

"We wish to speak with your Elder!" shouted Sabriel. She pointed at the cloud-front advancing behind her, and added, "Before darkness falls!"

"Wait!" came the answer and one of the archers scampered back from the rocks, up towards the buildings. Closer to, Sabriel realised they were probably boathouses or something like that.

The archer returned in a few minutes, an older man hobbling over the rocks behind him. The other three archers, seeing him, lowered their bows and returned shafts to quivers. Touchstone, seeing this, ceased to maintain the arrow ward. It hung in the air for a moment, then dissipated, leaving a momentary rainbow.

The Elder was named in fact, as well as title, they saw, as he limped along the breakwater. Long white hair blew like fragile cobwebs around his thin, wrinkled face and he moved with the deliberate intention of the very old. He seemed unafraid, perhaps possessed of the disinterested courage of one already close to death.

"Who are you?" he asked, when he reached the gap, standing above the swirling waters like some prophet of legend, his deep orange cloak flapping around him from the rising breeze. "What do you want?"

Sabriel opened her mouth to answer, but Touchstone had already started to speak. Loudly.

"I am Touchstone, sworn swordsman for the Abhorsen, who stands before you. Are arrows your welcome for such folk as we?"

The old man was silent for a moment, his deep-set eyes focused on Sabriel, as if he could strip away any falsity or illusion by sight alone. Sabriel met his gaze, but out of the corner of her mouth she whispered to Touchstone.

"What makes you think you can speak for me? Wouldn't a friendly approach be better? And since when are you my sworn—"

She stopped, as the old man cleared his throat to speak and spat into the water. For a moment, she thought that this was his response, but as neither the archers nor Touchstone reacted, it was obviously of no account.

"These are bad times," the Elder said. "We have been forced to leave our firesides for the smoking sheds, warmth and comfort for seawinds and the stench of fish. Many of the people of Nestowe are dead – or worse. Strangers and travellers are rare in such times and not always what they seem."

"I am the Abhorsen," Sabriel said reluctantly. "Enemy of the Dead."

"I remember," replied the old man slowly. "Abhorsen came here when I was a young man. He came to put down the haunts that the spice merchant brought, Charter curse him. Abhorsen. I remember that coat you're wearing, blue as a ten-fathom sea, with the silver keys. There was a sword also..."

He paused, expectantly. Sabriel stood silently, waiting for him to go on.

"He wants to see the sword," Touchstone said, voice flat, after the silence stretched too far.

"Oh," replied Sabriel, flushing.

It was quite obvious. Carefully, so as not to alarm the archers, she drew her sword, holding it up to the sun so the Charter marks could clearly be seen, silver dancers on the blade.

"Yes," sighed the Elder, old shoulders sagging with relief. "That is the sword. Charter-spelled. She is the Abhorsen."

He turned and tottered back towards the archers, worn voice increasing to the ghost of a fisherman's cross-water hail. "Come on, you four. Quick with the bridge. We have visitors! Help at last!"

Sabriel glanced at Touchstone, raising her eyebrows at the implication of the old man's last three words. Surprisingly, Touchstone met her gaze and held it.

"It is traditional for someone of high rank, such as yourself, to be announced by their sworn swordsman," he said quietly. "And the only acceptable way for me to travel with you is as your sworn swordsman. Otherwise, people will assume that we are, at best, illicit lovers. Having your name coupled to mine in such a guise would lower you in most eyes. You see?"

"Ah," replied Sabriel, gulping, feeling the flush of embarrassment come back and spread from her cheeks to her neck. It felt a lot like being on the receiving end of one of Miss Prionte's severest social put-downs. She hadn't even thought about how it would look, the two of them travelling together. Certainly, in Ancelstierre, it would be considered shameful, but this was the Old Kingdom, where things were different. But only some things, it seemed.

"Lesson two hundred and seven," muttered Mogget from somewhere near her feet. "Three out of ten. I wonder if they've got any fresh-caught whiting? I'd like a small one, still flopping—"

"Be quiet!" Sabriel interrupted. "You'd better pretend to be a normal cat for a while."

"Very well, milady. Abhorsen," Mogget replied, stalking away to sit on the other side of Touchstone.

Sabriel was about to reply scathingly when she saw the faintest curve at the corner of Touchstone's mouth. Touchstone? Grinning? Surprised, she misplaced the retort on her tongue, then forgot it altogether, as the four archers heaved a plank across the gap, the end smacking down on to stone with a startling bang.

"Please cross quickly," the Elder said, as the men steadied the plank. "There are many fell creatures in the village now and I fear the day is almost done."

True to his words, cloud-shadow fell across them as he spoke, and the fresh scent of closing rain mingled with the wet and salty smell of the sea. Without further urging, Sabriel ran quickly across the plank, Mogget behind her, Touchstone bringing up the rear.

chapter seventeen

All the survivors of Nestowe were gathered in the largest of the fish-smoking sheds, save for the current shift of archers who watched the breakwater. There had been one hundred and twenty-six villagers the week before – now there were thirty-one.

"There were thirty-two until this morning," the Elder said to Sabriel, as he passed her a cup of passable wine and a piece of dried fish atop a piece of very hard, very stale bread. "We thought we were safe when we got to the island, but Monjer Stowart's boy was found just after dawn today, sucked dry like a husk. When we touched him, it was like... burnt paper, that still holds its shape... we touched him and he crumbled into flakes of... something like ash."

Sabriel looked around as the old man spoke, noting the many lanterns, candles and rush tapers that added both to the light and the smoky, fishy atmosphere of the shed. The survivors were a very mixed group – men, women and children, from very young to the Elder himself. Their only common characteristic was the fear pinching their faces, the fear showing in their nervous, staccato movement.

"We think one of them's here," said a woman, her voice long gone beyond fear to fatalism. She stood alone, accompanied by the clear space of tragedy. Sabriel guessed she had lost her family. Husband, children – perhaps parents and siblings too, for she wasn't over forty.

"It'll take us, one by one," the woman continued, matter-of-fact, her voice filling the shed with dire certainty. Around her, people shuffled, twitchily, not looking at her, as if to meet her gaze would be to accept her words. Most looked at Sabriel and she saw hope in their eyes. Not blind faith or complete confidence, but a gambler's hope that a new horse might change a run of losses.

"The Abhorsen who came when I was young," the Elder continued – and Sabriel saw that at his age, this would be his memory alone, of all the villagers – "this Abhorsen told me that it was his purpose to slay the Dead. He saved us from the haunts that came in the merchant's caravan. Is it still the same, lady? Will Abhorsen save us from the Dead?"

Sabriel thought for a moment, her mind mentally flicking through the pages of *The Book of the Dead*, feeling it stir in the backpack that sat by her feet. Her thoughts strayed to her father; the forthcoming journey to Belisaere; the way in which Dead enemies seemed to be arrayed against her by some controlling mind.

"I will ensure this island is free of the Dead," she said at last, speaking clearly so all could hear her. "But I cannot free the mainland village. There is a greater evil at work in the Kingdom – that same evil that has broken your Charter Stone – and I must find and defeat it as soon as I can. When that is done, I will return – I hope with other help – and both village and Charter Stone will be restored."

"We understand," replied the Elder. He seemed saddened, but philosophic. He continued, speaking more to his people than to Sabriel. "We can survive here. There is the spring and the fish. We have boats. If Callibe has not fallen to the Dead, we can trade, for vegetables and other stuffs."

"You will have to keep watching the breakwater," Touchstone said. He stood behind Sabriel's chair, the very image of a stern bodyguard. "The Dead – or their living slaves – may try to fill it in with stones or push across a bridge. They can cross running water by building bridges of boxed grave dirt."

"So, we are besieged," said a man to the front of the mass of villagers. "But what of this Dead thing already here on the island, already preying upon us? How will you find it?"

Silence fell as the questioner spoke, for this was the one answer everyone wanted to hear. Rain sounded loud on the roof in the absence of human speech, steady rain, as had been falling since late afternoon. The Dead disliked the rain, Sabriel thought inconsequentially, as she considered this question. Rain didn't destroy, but it hurt and irritated the Dead. Wherever the Dead thing was on the island, it would be out of the rain.

She stood up with that thought. Thirty-one pairs of eyes watched her, hardly blinking, despite the cloying smoke from too many lanterns, candles and tapers. Touchstone watched the villagers; Mogget watched a piece of fish; Sabriel closed her eyes, questing outward with other senses, trying to feel the presence of the Dead.

It was there – a faint, concealed emanation, like an untraceable whiff of something rotten. Sabriel concentrated on it, followed it, and found it, right there in the shed. The Dead was somehow hiding among the villagers.

She opened her eyes slowly, looking straight at the point where her senses told her the Dead creature lurked. She saw a fisherman, middle-aged, his salt-etched face red under sun-bleached hair. He seemed no different than the others around him, listening intently for her reply, but there was definitely something Dead in him or very close by. He was wearing a boat cloak, which seemed odd, since the smoking shed was hot from massed humanity and the many lights.

"Tell me," Sabriel said. "Did anyone bring a large box with them out to the island? Something say an arm-span square a side, or larger? It would be heavy – with grave dirt."

Murmurs and enquiries met this question, neighbours turning to each other, with little flowerings of fear and suspicion. As they talked, Sabriel walked out through them, surreptitiously loosening her sword, signalling Touchstone to stay close by her. He followed her, eyes flickering across the little groups of villagers. Mogget, glancing up from his fish, stretched and lazily stalked behind Touchstone's heels, after a warning glare at the two cats who were eyeing the half-consumed head and tail of his fishy repast.

Careful not to alarm her quarry, Sabriel took a zigzag path

through the shed, listening to the villagers with studied attention, though the blond fisherman never left the corner of her eye. He was deep in discussion with another man, who seemed to be growing more suspicious by the second.

Closer now, Sabriel was sure that the fisherman was a vassal of the Dead. Technically, he was still alive, but a Dead spirit had suppressed his will, riding on his flesh like some shadowy string-puller, using his body as a puppet. Something highly unpleasant would be half-submerged in his back, under the boat cloak. Mordaut, they were called, Sabriel remembered. A whole page was devoted to these parasitical spirits in *The Book of the Dead*. They liked to keep a primary host alive, slipping off at night to sate their hunger from other living prey – like children.

"I'm sure I saw you with a box like that, Patar," the suspicious fisherman was saying. "Jall Stowart helped you get it ashore. Hey, Jall!"

He shouted that last, turning to look at someone else across the room. In that instant, the Dead-ridden Patar exploded into action, clubbing his questioner with both forearms, knocking him aside, running to the door with the silent ferocity of a battering ram.

But Sabriel had expected that. She stood before him, sword at the ready, her left hand drawing Ranna, the sweet sleeper, from the bandoleer. She still hoped to save the man, by quelling the Mordaut.

Patar slid to a halt and half-turned, but Touchstone was there behind him, twin swords glowing eerily with shifting

Charter marks and silver flames. Sabriel eyed the blades in surprise, she hadn't known they were spelled. Past time she asked, she realised.

Then Ranna was free in her hand – but the Mordaut didn't wait for the unavoidable lullaby. Patar suddenly screamed and stood rigid, the redness draining from his face, to be replaced by grey. Then his flesh crumpled and fell apart, even his bones flaking away to soggy ash as the Mordaut sucked all the life out of him in one voracious instant. Newly-fed and strengthened, the Dead slid out from the falling cloak, a pool of squelching darkness. It took shape as it moved, becoming a large, disgustingly elongated sort of rat. Quicker than any natural rat, it scuttled towards a hole in the wall and escape!

Sabriel lunged, her blade striking chips from the floor planks, missing the shadowy form by a scant instant.

Touchstone didn't miss. His right-hand sword sheared through the creature just behind the head, the left-wielded blade impaling its sinuous mid-section. Pinned to the floor, the creature writhed and arched, its shadow-stuff working away from the blades. It was remaking its body, escaping the trap.

Quickly, Sabriel stood over it, Ranna sounding in her hand, sweet, lazy tone echoing out into the shed.

Before the echoes died, the Mordaut ceased to writhe. Form half-lost by its shifting from the swords, it lay like a lump of charred liver, quivering on the floor, still impaled.

Sabriel replaced Ranna and drew the eager Saraneth. Its forceful voice snapped out, sound weaving a net of domination over the foul creature. The Mordaut made no effort to resist, even to make a mouth to whine its cause. Sabriel felt it succumb to her will, via the medium of Saraneth.

She put the bell back, but hesitated as her hand fell on Kibeth. Sleeper and Master had spoken well, but Walker sometimes had its own ideas, and it was stirring suspiciously under her hand. Best to wait a moment, to calm herself, Sabriel thought, taking her hand away from the bandoleer. She sheathed her sword and looked around the shed. To her surprise, everyone except Touchstone and Mogget was asleep. They had only caught the echoes of Ranna, which shouldn't have been enough. Of course, Ranna could be tricksome too, but its trickery was far less troublesome.

"This is a Mordaut," she said to Touchstone, who was stifling a half-born yawn. "A weak spirit, catalogued as one of the Lesser Dead. They like to ride with the Living – cohabiting the body to some extent, directing it, and slowly sipping the spirit away. It makes them hard to find."

"What do we do with it now?" asked Touchstone, eyeing the quivering lump of shadow with distaste. It clearly couldn't be cut up, consumed by fire, or anything else he could think of.

"I will banish it, send it back to die a true death," replied Sabriel. Slowly, she drew Kibeth, using both hands. She still felt uneasy, for the bell was twisting in her grasp, trying to sound of its own accord, a sound that would make her walk in Death.

She gripped it harder and rang the orthodox backwards, forwards and figure-eight her father had taught her. Kibeth's voice rang out, singing a merry tune, a capering jig that almost had Sabriel's feet jumping too, till she forced herself to be absolutely still.

The Mordaut had no such free will. For a moment, Touchstone thought it was getting away, the shadow form suddenly leaping upwards, unreal flesh slipping up his blades almost to the cross-hilts. Then, it slid back down again – and vanished. Back into Death, to bob and spin in the current, howling and screaming with whatever voice it had there, all the way through to the Final Gate.

"Thanks," Sabriel said to Touchstone. She looked down at his two swords, still deeply embedded in the wooden floor. They were no longer burning with silver flames, but she could see the Charter marks moving on the blades.

"I didn't realise your swords were ensorcelled," she continued. "Though I'm glad they are."

Surprise crossed Touchstone's face and confusion.

"I thought you knew," he said. "I took them from the Queen's ship. They were a Royal Champion's swords. I didn't want to take them, but Mogget said you—"

He stopped in mid-sentence, as Sabriel let out a heartfelt sigh.

"Well, anyway," he continued. "Legend has it that the Wallmaker made them, at the same time he – or she, I suppose – made your sword."

"Mine?" asked Sabriel, her hand lightly touching the worn bronze of the guard. She'd never thought about who'd made the sword – it just was. "I was made for Abhorsen, to slay those already Dead," the inscription said, when it said anything lucid at all. So it probably was forged long ago, back in the distant past when the Wall was made. Mogget would know, she thought. Mogget probably wouldn't, or couldn't, tell her – but he would know.

"I suppose we'd better wake everybody up," she said, dismissing speculation about swords for the immediate present.

"Are there more Dead?" asked Touchstone, grunting as he pulled his swords free of the floor.

"I don't think so," replied Sabriel. "That Mordaut was very clever, for it had hardly sapped the spirit of poor... Patar... so its presence was masked by his life. It would have come to the island in that box of grave dirt, having impressed the poor man with instructions before they left the mainland. I doubt whether any others would have done the same. I can't sense any here, at least. I guess I should check the other buildings and walk around the island, just to be sure."

"Now?" asked Touchstone.

"Now," confirmed Sabriel. "But let's wake everyone up first and organise some people to carry lights for us. We'd also better talk to the Elder about a boat for the morning."

"And a good supply of fish," added Mogget, who'd slunk back to the half-eaten whiting, his voice sharp above the heavy drone of snoring fisher-folk.

There were no Dead on the island, though the archers reported seeing strange lights moving in the village, during brief lulls in the rain. They'd heard movement on the breakwater too, and shot fire arrows on to the stones, but saw nothing before the crude, oily rag–wrapped shafts guttered out.

Sabriel advanced out on the breakwater and stood near the sea gap, her oilskin coat loosely draped over her shoulders, shedding rain to the ground and down her neck. She couldn't see anything through the rain and dark, but she could feel the Dead. There were more than she had sensed earlier, or they had grown much stronger. Then, with a sickening feeling, she realised that this strength belonged to a single creature, only now emerging from Death, using the broken stone as a portal. An instant later, she recognised its particular presence.

The Mordicant had found her.

"Touchstone," she asked, fighting to keep the shivers from her voice. "Can you sail a boat by night?"

"Yes," replied Touchstone, his voice impersonal again, face dark in the rainy night, the lantern-light from the villagers behind him lighting only his back and feet. He hesitated, as if he shouldn't be offering an opinion, then added, "But it would be much more dangerous. I don't know this coast and the night is very dark."

"Mogget can see in the dark," Sabriel said quietly, moving closer to Touchstone so the villagers couldn't hear her.

"We have to leave immediately," she whispered, while pretending to adjust her oilskin. "A Mordicant has come. The same one that pursued me before."

"What about the people here?" asked Touchstone, so softly the sound of the rain almost washed his words away – but there was the faint sound of reproof under his business-like tone.

"The Mordicant is after me," muttered Sabriel. She could

sense it moving away from the stone, questing about, using its otherworldly senses to find her. "It can feel my presence, as I feel it. When I go, it will follow."

"If we stay till morning," Touchstone whispered back, "won't we be safe? You said even a Mordicant couldn't cross this gap."

"I said, 'I think'," faltered Sabriel. "It has grown stronger. I can't be sure—"

"That thing back in the shed, the Mordaut, it wasn't very difficult to destroy," Touchstone whispered, the confidence of ignorance in his voice. "Is this Mordicant much worse?"

"Much," replied Sabriel shortly.

The Mordicant had stopped moving. The rain seemed to be dampening both its senses and its desire to find her and slay. Sabriel stared vainly out into the darkness, trying to peer past the sheets of rain, to gain the evidence provided by sight, as well as her necromantic senses.

"Riemer," she said, loudly now, calling to the villager who was in charge of their lantern-holders. He came forward quickly, gingery hair plastered flat on his rounded head, rainwater dripping down from a high forehead to catapult itself off the end of his pudgy nose.

"Riemer, have the archers keep very careful watch. Tell them to shoot anything that comes on to the breakwater – there is nothing living out there now. Only the Dead. We need to go back and talk to your Elder."

They walked back in silence, save for the sloshing of boots in puddles and the steady finger-applause of the rain. At least half of Sabriel's attention stayed with the Mordicant; a malign, stomach-ache inducing presence across the dark water. She wondered why it was waiting. Waiting for the rain to stop or perhaps for the now-banished Mordaut to attack from within. Whatever its reasons, it gave them a little time to get to a boat and lead it away. And perhaps, there was always the chance that it couldn't cross the breakwater gap.

"What time is low tide?" she asked Riemer, as a new thought struck.

"Ah, just about an hour before dawn," replied the fisherman. "About six hours, if I'm any judge."

The Elder awoke crankily from his second sleep. He was loath for them to go in the night, though Sabriel felt that at least half of his reluctance was due to their need for a boat. The villagers only had five left. The others had been sunk in the harbour, drowned and broken by the stones hurled down by the Dead, eager to stop the escape of their living prey.

"I'm sorry," Sabriel said again. "But we must have a boat and we need it now. There is a terrible Dead creature in the village – it tracks like a hunting dog and the trail it follows is mine. If I stay, it will try and come here – and, at the ebb, it may be able to cross the gap in the breakwater. If I go, it will follow."

"Very well," the Elder agreed mulishly. "You have cleansed this island for us; a boat is a little thing. Riemer will prepare it with food and water. Riemer! The Abhorsen will have Landalin's boat – make sure it is stocked and seaworthy. Take sails from Jaled, if Landalin's is short or rotten."

"Thank you," said Sabriel. Tiredness weighed down on her, tiredness and the weight of awareness. Awareness of her enemies, like a darkness always clouding the edge of her vision. "We will go now. My good wishes stay with you and my hopes for your safety."

"May the Charter preserve us all," added Touchstone, bowing to the old man. The Elder bowed back, a bent, solemn figure, so much smaller than his shadow, looming tall on the wall behind.

Sabriel turned to go, but a long line of villagers was forming on the way to the door. All of them wanted to bow or curtsey before her, to mutter shy thank yous and farewells. Sabriel accepted them with embarrassment and guilt, remembering Patar. True, she had banished the Dead, but another life had been lost in the doing. Her father would not have been so clumsy...

The second-to-last person in the line was a little girl, her black hair tied in two plaits, one on either side of her head. Seeing her made Sabriel remember something Touchstone had said. She stopped and took the girl's hands in her own.

"What is your name, little one?" she asked, smiling. A feeling of déjà vu swept over her as the small fingers met hers – the memory of a frightened first-grader hesitantly reaching out to the older pupil who would be her guide for the first day at Wyverley College. Sabriel had experienced both sides, in her time.

"Aline," said the girl, smiling back. Her eyes were bright and lively, too young to be dimmed by the frightened despair that clouded the adults' gaze. A good choice, Sabriel thought.

"Now, tell me what you have learned in your lessons about the Great Charter," Sabriel said, adopting the familiar, motherly and generally irrelevant questioning tone of the School Inspector who'd descended on every class in Wyverley twice a year.

"I know the rhyme..." replied Aline a little doubtfully, her small forehead crinkling. "Shall I sing it, like we do in class?"

Sabriel nodded.

"We dance around the stone, too," Aline added confidingly. She stood up straighter, put one foot forward, and took her hands away to clasp them behind her back.

> *Five Great Charters knit the land*
> *together linked, hand in hand*
> *One in the people who wear the crown*
> *Two in the folk who keep the Dead down*
> *Three and Five became stone and mortar*
> *Four sees all in frozen water.*

"Thank you, Aline," Sabriel said. "That was very nice."

She ruffled the child's hair and hastened through the final farewells, suddenly keen to get out of the smoke and the fish-smell, out into the clean, rainy air where she could think.

"So now you know," whispered Mogget, jumping up into her arms to escape the puddles. "I still can't tell you, but you know one's in your blood."

"Two," replied Sabriel distantly. "'Two in the folk who keep the Dead down'. So what is the... ah... I can't talk about it either!"

But she thought about the questions she'd like to ask, as Touchstone helped her aboard the small fishing vessel that lay just off the tiny, shell-laden beach that served the island as a harbour.

One of the Great Charters lay in the royal blood. The second lay in Abhorsen's. What were three and five, and four that saw all in frozen water? She felt certain that many answers could be found in Belisaere. Her father could probably answer more, for many things that were bound in Life were unravelled in Death. And there was her mother-sending, for that third and final questioning in this seven years.

Touchstone pushed off, clambered aboard and took the oars. Mogget leapt out of Sabriel's arms and assumed a figurehead position near the prow, serving as a night-sighted lookout, while mocking Touchstone at the same time.

Back on shore, the Mordicant suddenly howled, a long, piercing cry that echoed far across the water, chilling hearts on both boat and island.

"Bear a bit more to starboard," said Mogget, in the silence after the howl faded. "We need more sea-room."

Touchstone was quick to comply.

chapter eighteen

By the morning of the sixth day out of Nestowe, Sabriel was heartily tired of nautical life. They'd sailed virtually non-stop all that time, only putting into shore at noon for fresh water and only then when it was sunny. Nights were spent under sail or, when exhaustion claimed Touchstone, hove-to with a sea anchor, the unsleeping Mogget standing watch. Fortunately, the weather had been kind.

It had been a relatively uneventful five days. Two days from Nestowe to Beardy Point, an unprepossessing peninsula whose only interesting features were a sandy-bottomed beach and a clear stream. Devoid of life, it was also devoid of the Dead. Here, for the first time, Sabriel could no longer sense the pursuing Mordicant. A good, strong, south-easterly had propelled them, reaching northwards at too fast a pace for it to follow.

Three days from Beardy Point to the island of Ilgard, its rocky cliffs climbing sheer from the sea, a grey and pockmarked tenement, home to tens of thousands of seabirds. They passed it late in the afternoon, their single sail stretched to bursting, clinker-built hull heeling well over, bow slicing up a column of spray that salted mouths, eyes and bodies.

It was half a day from Ilgard to the Belis Mouth, that narrow strait that led to the Sea of Saere. But that was tricky sailing, so they spent the night hove-to just out of sight of Ilgard, to wait for the light of day.

"There is a boom-chain across the Belis Mouth," Touchstone explained, as he raised the sail and Sabriel hauled the sea anchor in over the bow. The sun was rising behind him, but had not yet pulled itself out of the sea, so he was no more than a dim shadow in the stern. "It was built to keep pirates and suchlike out of the Sea of Saere. You won't believe the size of it – I can't imagine how it was forged, or strung across."

"Will it still be there?" Sabriel asked cautiously, not wanting to prevent Touchstone's strangely talkative mood.

"I'm sure of it," replied Touchstone. "We'll see the towers on the opposite shores first. Winding Post, to the south, and Boom Hook to the north."

"Not very imaginative names," commented Sabriel, unable to help herself from interrupting. It was just such a pleasure to talk! Touchstone had lapsed back into non-communication for most of the voyage, though he did have a good excuse – handling the fishing boat for eighteen hours a day, even in good weather, didn't leave much energy for conversation.

"They're named after their purpose," replied Touchstone. "Which makes sense."

"Who decides whether to let vessels past the chain?" asked Sabriel. Already she was thinking ahead, wondering about

Belisaere. Could it be like Nestowe – the city abandoned, riddled with the Dead?

"Ah," said Touchstone. "I hadn't thought about that. In my time, there was a Royal Boom Master, with a force of guards and a squadron of small picket ships. If, as Mogget says, the city has fallen into anarchy..."

"There may also be people working for, or in alliance with, the Dead," Sabriel added thoughtfully. "So even if we cross the boom in daylight, there could be trouble. I think I'd better reverse my surcoat and hide my helmet wrapping."

"What about the bells?" asked Touchstone. He leaned past her, to draw the main sheet tighter, right hand slightly nudging the tiller to take advantage of a shift in the wind. "They're fairly obvious, to say the least."

"I'll just look like a necromancer," Sabriel replied. "A salty, unwashed necromancer."

"I don't know," said Touchstone, who couldn't see that Sabriel was joking. "No necromancer would be let into the city, or would stay alive, in—"

"In your day," interrupted Mogget, from his favourite post on the bow. "But this is now and I am sure that necromancers and worse are not uncommon sights in Belisaere."

"I'll wear a cloak—" Sabriel started to say.

"If you say so," Touchstone said, at the same time. Clearly, he didn't believe the cat. Belisaere was the royal capital, a huge city, home to at least fifty thousand people. Touchstone couldn't imagine it fallen, decayed and in the hands of the Dead. Despite his own inner fears and secret knowledge, he couldn't help but be confident that the Belisaere they were sailing towards would be little different from the two-hundred-year-old images locked in his memory.

That confidence took a blow as the Belis Mouth towers became visible above the blue line of the horizon, on opposite shores of the strait. At first, the towers were no more than dark smudges that grew taller as wind and wave carried the boat towards them. Through her telescope, Sabriel saw that they were made from a beautiful, rosy-pink stone that once must have been magnificent. Now, they were largely blackened by fire; their majesty vanished. Winding Post had lost the top three storeys, from seven; Boom Hook stood as tall as ever, but sunlight shone through gaping holes, showing the interior to be a gutted ruin. There was no sign of any garrison, toll-collector, windlass mules, or anything alive.

The great boom-chain still stretched across the strait. Huge iron links, each as wide and long as the fishing boat, rose green and barnacle-befouled out of the water and up into each of the towers. Glimpses of it could be seen in the middle of the Mouth, when the swell dipped and a length of chain shone slick and green in the wave trough, like some lurking monster of the deep.

"We'll have to go in close to the Winding Post tower, unstep the mast and row under the chain where it rises," Touchstone declared, after studying the chain for several minutes through the telescope, trying to gauge whether it had sunk enough to allow them passage. But even with their relatively shallow-draught boat, it would be too risky and they daren't wait for high tide, late in the afternoon. At some time in the past, perhaps when the towers were abandoned, the chain had been winched up to its maximum tension. The engineers who'd made it would have been pleased, for there seemed to be no noticeable slippage.

"Mogget, go to the bow and keep a lookout for anything in the water. Sabriel, could you please watch the shore and the tower, to guard against attack."

Sabriel nodded, pleased that Touchstone's stint as captain of their small vessel had done a lot to remove the servant nonsense out of him and make him more like a normal person. Mogget, for his part, jumped up to the bow without protest, despite the spray that occasionally burst over his head as they cut diagonally across the swell – towards the small triangle of opportunity between shore, sea and chain.

They came in as close as they dared before unstepping the mast. The swell had diminished, for the Belis Mouth was well-sheltered by the two arms of land, but the tide had turned and a tidal race was beginning to run from the ocean to the Saere Sea. So, even without mast and sail, they were borne rapidly towards the chain, Touchstone rowing with all his strength just to keep steerageway. After a moment, this clearly became impossible, so Sabriel took one of the oars and they rowed together, with Mogget yowling directions.

Every few seconds, at the end of a full stroke, her back nearly level with the thwarts, Sabriel snatched a glimpse over her shoulder. They were headed for the narrow passage, between the high but crumbling sea wall of Winding Post, and the enormous chain rising out of the swift-flowing sea in a swathe of white froth. She could hear the melancholy groaning of the links, like a chorus of pained walruses. Even that gargantuan chain moved at the sea's whim.

"Port a little," yowled Mogget. Touchstone backed his oar for a moment, then the cat jumped down, yelling, "Ship oars and duck!"

The oars came rattling, splashing in, both Sabriel and Touchstone simply lying down on their backs, with Mogget somewhere between them. The boat rocked and plunged, and the groan of the chain sounded close and terrible. Sabriel, one moment looking up at the clear, blue sky, in the next saw nothing but green, weed-strewn iron above her. When the swell lifted the boat up, she could have reached out and touched the great boom-chain of Belis Mouth.

Then they were past and Touchstone was already pushing out his oar, Mogget moving to the bow. Sabriel wanted to lie there, just looking up at the sky, but the collapsed sea wall of Winding Post was no more than an oar-length away. She sat up and resumed her duty as a rower.

The water changed colour in the Sea of Saere. Sabriel trailed her hand in it, marvelling at its clear, turquoise sheen. For all its colour, it was incredibly transparent. The water was very deep, but she could see down the first three or four fathoms, watching small fish dance under the bubbles of their boat's wake.

She felt relaxed, momentarily carefree, all the troubles that lay ahead and behind her temporarily lost in single-minded contemplation of the clear, blue-green water. There was no

Dead presence here, no constant awareness of the many doors to Death. Even Charter Magic was dissipated at sea. For a few minutes, she forgot about Touchstone and Mogget. Even her father faded from her mind. There was only the sea's colour, and its coolness on her hand.

"We'll be able to see the city soon," Touchstone said, interrupting her mental holiday. "If the towers are still standing."

Sabriel nodded thoughtfully and slowly took her hand from the sea, as if she were parting from a dear friend.

"It must be difficult for you," she said, almost to herself, not really expecting him to answer. "Two hundred years gone, the Kingdom slowly falling into ruin while you slept."

"I didn't really believe it till I saw Nestowe and then the Belis Mouth towers," replied Touchstone. "Now, I am afraid – even for a great city that I never believed could really change."

"No imagination," said Mogget sternly. "No thinking ahead. A flaw in your character. A fatal flaw."

"Mogget," Sabriel said indignantly, angry at the cat for crushing yet another possible conversation. "Why are you so rude to Touchstone?"

Mogget hissed and the fur bristled on his back.

"I am accurate, not rude," he snapped, turning his back to them with studied scorn. "And he deserves it."

"I'm sick of this!" announced Sabriel. "Touchstone, what does Mogget know that I don't?"

Touchstone was silent, knuckles white on the tiller, eyes focused on the distant horizon, as if he could already see the towers of Belisaere.

"You'll have to tell me eventually," said Sabriel, a touch of the prefect entering her voice. "It can't be that bad, surely?"

Touchstone wet his lips, hesitated, then spoke.

"It was stupidity on my part, not evil, milady. Two hundred years ago, when the last Queen reigned... I think... I know that I am partly responsible for the failing of the Kingdom, the end of the royal line."

"What!" exclaimed Sabriel. "How could you be?"

"I am," continued Touchstone miserably, his hands shaking so much the tiller moved, giving the boat a crazy zigzag wake. "There was a... that is..."

He paused, took a deep breath, sat up a little straighter, and continued, as if reporting to a senior officer.

"I don't know how much I can tell you, because it involves the Great Charters. Where do I start? With the Queen, I suppose. She had four children. Her oldest son, Rogir, was a childhood playmate of mine. He was always the leader, in all our games. He had the ideas — we followed them. Later, when we were growing up, his ideas became stranger, less nice. We grew apart. I went into the Guard, he pursued his own interests. Now I know that those interests must have included Free Magic and necromancy — I never suspected it then. I should have, I know, but he was secretive and often away.

"Towards the end... I mean a few months before it happened... well, Rogir had been away for several years. He came back, just before the Midwinter Festival. I was glad to see him, for he seemed to be more like he was as a child. He'd lost interest in the bizarrities that had attracted him. We spent more time together again; hawking, riding, drinking, dancing.

"Then, late one afternoon – one cold, crisp afternoon, near sunset – I was on duty, guarding the Queen and her ladies. They were playing Cranaque. Rogir came to her and asked her to come with him down to the place where the Great Stones are... hey, I can say it!"

"Yes," interrupted Mogget. He looked tired, like an alley cat that has suffered one kick too many. "The sea washes all things clear, for a time. We can speak of the Great Charters, at least for a little while. I had forgotten it was so."

"Go on," said Sabriel excitedly. "Let's take advantage of it while we can. The Great Stones would be the stones and mortar of the rhyme – the Third and Fifth Great Charter?"

"Yes," replied Touchstone remotely, as if reciting a lesson, "with the Wall. The people, or whatever they were who made the Great Charters, put three in bloodlines and two in physical constructions: the Wall and the Great Stones. All the lesser stones draw their power from one or the other.

"The Great Stones... Rogir came and said there was something amiss there, something the Queen must look into. He was her son, but she did not take great account of his wisdom or believe him when he spoke of trouble with the Stones. She was a Charter Mage and felt nothing wrong. Besides, she was winning at Cranaque, so she told him to wait till morning. Rogir turned to me, asked me to intercede, and, Charter help me, I did. I believed Rogir. I trusted him and my belief convinced the Queen. Finally, she agreed. By that time, the sun had set. With Rogir, myself, three guards and two ladies-in-waiting, we went down, down into the reservoir where the Great Stones are."

Touchstone's voice faded to a whisper as he continued, and grew hoarse.

"There was terrible wrong down there, but it was Rogir's doing, not his discovery. There are six Great Stones and two were just being broken, broken with the blood of his own sisters, sacrificed by his Free Magic minions as we approached. I saw their last seconds, the faint hope in their clouding eyes, as the Queen's barge came floating across the water. I felt the shock of the Stones breaking and I remember Rogir, stepping up behind the Queen, a saw-edged dagger striking so swiftly across her throat. He had a cup, a golden cup, one of the Queen's own, to catch the blood, but I was too slow, too slow..."

"So the story you told me at Holehallow wasn't true," Sabriel whispered, as Touchstone's voice cracked and faded, and the tears rolled down his face. "The Queen didn't survive..."

"No," mumbled Touchstone. "But I didn't mean to lie. It was all jumbled up in my head."

"What did happen?"

"The other two guards were Rogir's men," Touchstone continued, his voice wet with tears, muffled with sorrow. "They attacked me, but Vlare – one of the ladies-in-waiting – threw herself across them. I went mad, battle-mad, berserk. I killed both guards. Rogir had jumped from the barge and was wading to the Stones, holding the cup. His four sorcerers were waiting, dark-cowled, around the third stone, the next to be broken. I couldn't reach him in time, I knew. I threw my sword. It flew straight and true, taking him just above the heart. He screamed, the echo going on and on and he turned back towards me! Transfixed by my sword, but still walking, holding that vile cup of blood up, as if offering me a drink.

"'You may tear this body,' he said, as he walked. 'Rip it, like some poor-made costume. But I cannot die.'

"He came within an arm's length of me and I could only look into his face, look at the evil that lay so close behind those familiar features... then there was blinding white light, the sound of bells – bells like yours, Sabriel – and voices, harsh voices... Rogir flinching back, the cup dropped, blood floating on the water like oil. I turned, saw guardsmen on the stairs; a burning, twisting column of white fire; a man with sword and bells... then I fainted or was knocked unconscious. When I came to, I was in Holehallow, seeing your face. I don't know how I got there, who put me there... I still only remember in shreds and patches."

"You should have told me," Sabriel said, trying to put as much compassion in her voice as she could. "But perhaps it had to wait for the sea's freeing of that binding spell. Tell me, the man with the sword and bells, was it the Abhorsen?"

"I don't know," replied Touchstone. "Probably."

"Almost definitely, I would say," added Sabriel. She looked at Mogget, thinking of that column of twisting fire. "You were there too, weren't you, Mogget? Unbound, in your other form."

"Yes, I was there," said the cat. "With the Abhorsen of that time. A very powerful Charter Mage and a master of the bells, but a little too good-hearted to deal with treachery. I had terrible trouble getting him to Belisaere and, in the end, we were not timely enough to save the Queen or her daughters."

"What happened?" whispered Touchstone. "What happened?"

"Rogir was already one of the Dead when he came back to Belisaere," Mogget said wearily, as if he were telling a cynical yarn to a crew of hard-bitten cronies. "But only an Abhorsen would have known it and he wasn't there. Rogir's real body was hidden somewhere... is hidden somewhere... and he wore a Free Magic construct for his physical form.

"Somewhere along the path of his studies, he'd swapped real Life for power and, like all the Dead, he needed to take Life all the time to stay out of Death. But the Charter made it very difficult for him to do that, anywhere in the Kingdom. So he decided to break the Charter. He could have confined himself to breaking a few of the lesser stones, somewhere far away, but that would only give him a tiny area to prey on, and the Abhorsen would soon hunt him down. So he decided to break the Great Stones and for that he needed royal blood – his own family's blood. Or Abhorsen's, or the Clayr's, of course, but that would be much harder to get.

"Because he was the Queen's son, clever and very powerful, he almost achieved his aims. Two of the six Great Stones were broken. The Queen and her daughters were killed. Abhorsen intervened a little too late. True, he did manage to drive him deep into Death – but since his true body has never been found, Rogir has continued to exist. Even from Death, he has overseen the dissolution of the Kingdom – a Kingdom without a royal family, with one of the Great Charters crippled, corrupting and weakening all the others. He wasn't really beaten that night, in the reservoir. Just delayed and for two hundred years he's been trying to come back, trying to re-enter Life—"

"He's succeeded, hasn't he?" interrupted Sabriel. "He's the thing called Kerrigor, the one Abhorsens have been fighting for generations, trying to keep in Death. He is the one who came back, the Greater Dead who murdered the patrol near Cloven Crest, the master of the Mordicant."

"I do not know," replied Mogget. "Your father thought so."

"It is him," Touchstone said, distantly. "Kerrigor was Rogir's childhood nickname. I made it up, on the day we had the mud fight. His full ceremonial name was Rogirek."

"He – or his servants – must have lured my father to Belisaere just before he emerged from Death," Sabriel thought aloud. "I wonder why he came out into Life so near the Wall?"

"His body must be near the Wall. He would need to be close to it," Mogget said. "You should know that. To renew the master spell that prevents him from ever passing beyond the Final Gate."

"Yes," replied Sabriel, remembering the passages from *The Book of the Dead*. She shivered, but suppressed it before it became a racking sob. Inside, she felt like screaming, crying. She wanted to flee back to Ancelstierre, cross the Wall, leave the Dead and magic behind, go as far south as possible. But she quelled these feelings and said, "An Abhorsen defeated him once. I can do so again. But first, we must find my father's body."

There was silence for a moment, save for the wind in the canvas and the quiet hum of the rigging. Touchstone wiped his hand across his eyes and looked at Mogget.

"There is one thing I would like to ask. Who put my spirit in Death and made my body the figurehead?"

"I never knew what happened to you," replied Mogget. His green eyes met Touchstone's gaze and it wasn't the cat who blinked. "But it must have been Abhorsen. You were insane when we got you out of the reservoir. Driven mad, probably by the breaking of the Great Stones. No memory, nothing. It seems two hundred years is not too long for a rest cure. He must have seen something in you – or the Clayr saw something in the ice... ah, that was hard to say. We must be nearing the city and the sea's influence lessens. The binding resumes..."

"No, Mogget!" exclaimed Sabriel. "I want to know, I need to know, who you are. What's your connection with the Great..."

Her voice locked up in her throat and a startled gargle was the only thing that came out.

"Too late," said Mogget. He started cleaning his fur, pink tongue darting out, bright colour against white fur.

Sabriel sighed and looked out at the turquoise sea, then up at the sun, yellow disc on a field of white-streaked blue. A light breeze filled the sail above her, ruffling her hair in passing. Gulls rode it on ahead, to join a squawking mass of their brethren, feeding from a school of fish, sharp silver bursting near the surface.

Everything was alive, colourful, full of the joy of living. Even the salt tang on her skin, the stink of fish and her own unwashed body, was somehow rich and lively. Far, far removed from Touchstone's grim past, the threat of Rogir/Kerrigor and the chilling greyness of Death.

"We shall have to be very careful," Sabriel said at last, "and hope that... what was it you said to the Elder of Nestowe, Touchstone?"

He knew immediately what she meant.

"Hope that the Charter preserves us all."

chapter nineteen

Sabriel had expected Belisaere to be a ruined city, devoid of life, but it was not so. By the time they saw its towers and the truly impressive walls that ringed the peninsula on which the city stood, they also saw fishing boats, of a size with their own. People were fishing from them – normal, friendly people, who waved and shouted as they passed. Only their greeting was telling of how things might be in Belisaere. "Good sun and swift water" was not the typical greeting in Touchstone's time.

The city's main harbour was reached from the west. A wide, buoyed channel ran between two hulking defensive outworks, leading into a vast pool, easily as big as twenty or thirty playing fields. Wharves lined three sides of the pool, but most were deserted. To the north and south, warehouses rotted behind the empty wharves, broken walls and holed roofs testimony to long abandonment.

Only the eastern dock looked lively. There were none of the big trading vessels of bygone days, but many small coastal craft, loading and unloading. Derricks swung in and out; longshoremen humped packages along gangplanks; small children dived and swam in between the boats. No warehouses stood behind these wharves – instead, there were hundreds of open-topped booths, little more than brightly-decorated frameworks delineating a patch of space, with tables for the wares, and stools for the vendors and favoured customers. There seemed to be no shortage of customers in general, Sabriel noted, as Touchstone steered for a vacant berth. People were swarming everywhere, hurrying about as if their time was sadly limited.

Touchstone let the mainsheet go slack and brought the boat into the wind just in time for them to lose way and glide at an oblique angle into the fenders that lined the wharf. Sabriel threw up a line, but before she could leap ashore and secure it to a bollard, a street urchin did it for her.

"Penny for the knot," he cried, shrill voice piercing through the hubbub from the crowd. "Penny for the knot, lady?"

Sabriel smiled, with effort, and flicked a silver penny at the boy. He caught it, grinned and disappeared into the stream of people moving along the dock. Sabriel's smile faded. She could feel many, many Dead here... or not precisely here, but further up in the city. Belisaere was built upon four low hills, surrounding a central valley, which lay open to the sea at this harbour. As far as Sabriel's senses could tell, only the valley was free of the Dead – why, she didn't know. The hills, which made up at least two-thirds of the city's area, were infested with them.

This part of the city, on the other hand, could truly be said to be infested with life. Sabriel had forgotten how noisy a city could be. Even in Ancelstierre, she had rarely visited anything larger than Bain, a town of no more than ten thousand people. Of course, Belisaere wasn't a big city by Ancelstierran standards and it didn't have the noisy omnibuses and private cars that had been significantly adding to Ancelstierran noise for the last ten years, but Belisaere made up for it with the people. People hurrying, arguing, shouting, selling, buying, singing...

"Was it like this before?" she shouted at Touchstone, as they climbed up on to the wharf, making sure they had all their possessions with them.

"Not really," answered Touchstone. "The Pool was normally full, with bigger ships – and there were warehouses here, not a market. It was quieter, too, and people were in less of a rush."

They stood on the edge of the dock, watching the stream of humanity and goods, hearing the tumult and smelling all the new odours of the city replacing the freshness of the sea breeze. Cooking food, wood smoke, incense, oil, the occasional disgusting whiff of what could only be sewage...

"It was also a lot cleaner," added Touchstone. "Look, I think we'd best find an inn or hostelry. Somewhere to stay for the night."

"Yes," replied Sabriel. She was reluctant to enter the human tide. There were no Dead among them, as far as she could sense, but they must have some kind of accommodation or agreement with the Dead and that stank to her far more than sewage.

Touchstone snagged a passing boy by the shoulder as Sabriel continued to eye the crowd, nose wrinkling. They spoke together for a moment, a silver penny changed hands, then the boy slid into the rush, Touchstone following. He looked back, saw Sabriel staring absently and grabbed her by the hand, dragging both her and the lazy, fox-fur-positioned Mogget after him.

It was the first time Sabriel had touched him since he'd been revived and she was surprised by the shock it gave her. Certainly, her mind had been wandering and it was a sudden grab... his hand felt larger than it should and interestingly calloused and textured. Quickly, she slipped her hand out of his and concentrated on following both him and the boy, weaving across the main direction of the crowd.

They went through the middle of the open-topped market, along one street of little booths – obviously the street of fish and fowl. The harbour end was alive with boxes and boxes of fresh-caught fish, clear-eyed and wriggling. Vendors yelled their prices, or their best buy, and buyers shouted offers or amazement at the price. Baskets, bags and boxes changed hands, empty ones to be filled with fish or lobster, squid or shellfish. Coins went from palm to palm or, occasionally, whole purses disgorged their shining contents into the belt-pouches of the stallholders.

Towards the other end it grew a little quieter. The stalls here had cages upon cages of chickens, but their trade was slower and many of the chickens looked old and stunted. Sabriel, seeing an expert knife-man beheading row after row of chickens and dropping them to flop headless in a box, concentrated on shutting out their bewildered featherbrained experience of death.

Beyond the market there was a wide swathe of empty ground. It had obviously been intentionally cleared, first with fire, then with mattock, shovel and bar. Sabriel wondered why, till she saw the aqueduct that ran beyond and parallel to this strip of wasteland. The city folk who lived in the valley didn't have an agreement with the Dead – their part of the city was bounded by aqueducts, and the Dead could no more walk under running water than over it.

The cleared ground was a precaution, allowing the aqueducts to be guarded – and sure enough, Sabriel saw a patrol of archers marching atop it, their regularly moving shapes silhouetted, shadow puppets against the sky. The boy was leading them to a central arch, which rose up through two of the aqueduct's four tiers, and there were more archers there. Smaller arches continued on each side, supporting the aqueduct's main channel, but these were heavily overgrown with thorn bushes, to prevent unauthorised entry by the living, while the swift water overhead held back the Dead.

Sabriel drew her boat cloak tight as they passed under the arch, but the guards paid them no more attention than was required to extort a silver penny from Touchstone. They seemed very third-rate – even fourth-rate – soldiers, who were probably more constables and watchkeepers than anything else. None bore the Charter mark or had any trace of Free Magic.

Beyond the aqueduct, streets wound chaotically from an unevenly paved square, complete with an eccentrically-spouting fountain – the water jetted from the ears of a statue, a statue of an impressively crowned man.

"King Anstyr the Third," said Touchstone, pointing at the fountain. "He had a strange sense of humour, by all accounts. I'm glad it's still there."

"Where are we going?" asked Sabriel. She felt better now that she knew the citizenry weren't in league with the Dead.

"This boy says he knows a good inn," replied Touchstone, indicating the ragged urchin who was grinning just out of reach of the always-expected blow.

"Sign of Three Lemons," said the boy. "Best in the city, Lord, Lady."

He had just turned back from them to go on, when a loud, badly-cast bell sounded from somewhere towards the harbour. It rang three times, the sound sending pigeons racketing into flight from the square.

"What's that?" asked Sabriel. The boy looked at her, open-mouthed. "The bell."

"Sunfall," replied the boy, once he knew what she was asking. He said it as if stating the blindingly obvious. "Early, I reckon. Must be cloud coming or somefing."

"Everyone comes in when the sunfall bell sounds?" asked Sabriel.

"Course!" snorted the boy. "Otherwise the haunts or the ghlims get you."

"I see," replied Sabriel. "Lead on."

Surprisingly, the Sign of Three Lemons was quite a pleasant inn. A whitewashed building of four storeys, it fronted on to a smaller square some two hundred yards from King Anstyr's

Fountain Square. There were three enormous lemon trees in the middle of the square, somehow thick with pleasant-smelling leaves and copious amounts of fruit, despite the season. Charter Magic, thought Sabriel, and sure enough, there was a Charter Stone hidden among the trees, and a number of ancient spells of fertility, warmth and bountitude. Sabriel sniffed the lemon-scented air gratefully, thankful that her room had a window fronting the square.

Behind her, a maid was filling a tin bath with hot water. Several large buckets had already gone in – this would be the last. Sabriel closed the window and came over to look at the still-steaming water in anticipation.

"Will that be all, miss?" asked the maid, half-curtseying.

"Yes, thank you," replied Sabriel. The maid edged out the door and Sabriel slid the bar across, before divesting herself of her cloak, and then the stinking, sweat and salt-encrusted armour and garments that had virtually stuck to her after almost a week at sea. Naked, she rested her sword against the bath's rim – in easy reach – then sank gratefully into the water, taking up the lump of lemon-scented soap to begin removing the caked grime and sweat.

Through the wall, she could hear a man's – Touchstone's – voice. Then water gurgling, that maid giggling. Sabriel stopped soaping and concentrated on the sound. It was hard to hear, but there was more giggling, a deep, indistinct male voice, then a loud splash. Like two bodies in a bath rather than one.

There was silence for a while, then more splashing, gasps, giggles – was that Touchstone laughing? Then a series of short, sharp moans. Womanly ones. Sabriel flushed and gritted her teeth at the same time, then quickly lowered her head into the water so she couldn't hear, leaving only her nose and mouth exposed. Underwater, all was silent, save for the dull booming of her heart, echoing in her flooded ears.

What did it matter? She didn't think of Touchstone in that way. Sex was the last thing on her mind. Just another complication – contraception – messiness – emotions. There were enough problems. Concentrate on planning. Think ahead. It was just because Touchstone was the first young man she'd met out of school, that was all. It was none of her business. She didn't even know his real name...

A dull tapping noise on the side of the bath made her raise her head out of the water, just in time to hear a very self-satisfied, masculine and drawn-out moan from the other side of the wall. She was about to stick her head back under, when Mogget's pink nose appeared on the rim. So she sat up, water cascading down her face, hiding the tears she told herself weren't there. Angrily, she crossed her arms across her breasts and said, "What do you want?"

"I just thought that you might like to know that Touchstone's room is that way," said Mogget, indicating the silent room opposite the one with the noisy couple. "It hasn't got a bathtub, so he'd like to know if he can use yours when you're finished. He's waiting downstairs in the mean time, getting the local news."

"Oh," replied Sabriel. She looked across at the far, silent wall, then back to the close wall, where the human noises were now largely lost in the groaning of bedsprings. "Well, tell him I won't be long."

Twenty minutes later, a clean Sabriel, garbed in a borrowed dress made incongruous by her sword-belt (the bell-bandoleer lay under her bed, with Mogget asleep on top of it), crept on slippered feet through the largely empty common room and tapped the salty, begrimed Touchstone on the back, making him spill his beer.

"Your turn for the bath," Sabriel said cheerily. "My evil-smelling swordsman. I've just had it refilled. Mogget's in the room, by the way. I hope you don't mind."

"Why would I mind?" asked Touchstone, as much puzzled by her manner as the question. "I just want to get clean, that's all."

"Good," replied Sabriel, obscurely. "I'll organise for dinner to be served in your room, so we can plan as we eat."

In the event, the planning didn't take long, nor was it slow in dampening what was otherwise a relatively festive occasion. They were safe for the moment, clean, well-fed – and able to forget past troubles and future fears for a little while.

But, as soon as the last dish – a squid stew, with garlic, barley, yellow squash and tarragon vinegar – was cleared, the present reasserted itself, complete with cares and woe.

"I think the most likely place to find my father's body will be at... that place, where the Queen was slain," Sabriel said slowly. "The reservoir. Where is it, by the way?"

"Under the Palace Hill," replied Touchstone. "There are several different ways to enter. All lie beyond this aqueduct-guarded valley."

"You are probably right about your father," Mogget commented from his nest of blankets in the middle of Touchstone's bed. "But that is also the most dangerous place for us to go. Charter Magic will be greatly warped, including various bindings – and there is a chance that our enemy..."

"Kerrigor," interrupted Sabriel. "But he may not be there. Even if he is, we may be able to sneak in—"

"We might be able to sneak around the edges," said Touchstone. "The reservoir is enormous and there are hundreds of columns. But wading is noisy and the water is very still – sound carries. And the six... you know... they are in the very centre."

"If I can find my father and bring his spirit back to his body," Sabriel said stubbornly, "then we can deal with whatever confronts us. That is the first thing. My father. Everything else is just a complication that's followed on."

"Or preceded it," said Mogget. "So, I take it your master plan is to sneak in, as far as we can, find your father's body, which will hopefully be tucked away in some safe corner, and then see what happens?"

"We'll go in the middle of a clear, sunny day..." Sabriel began.

"It's underground," interrupted Mogget.

"So we have sunlight to retreat to," Sabriel continued in a quelling tone.

"And there are light shafts," added Touchstone. "At noon, it's a sort of dim twilight down there, with patches of faint sun on the water."

"So, we'll find Father's body, bring it back to safety, here," said Sabriel. "And... and take things from there."

"It sounds like a terribly brilliant plan to me," muttered Mogget. "The genius of simplicity..."

"Can you think of anything else?" snapped Sabriel. "I've tried and I can't. I wish I could go home to Ancelstierre and forget the whole thing – but then I'd never see Father again and the Dead would just eat up everything living in this whole rotten Kingdom. Maybe it won't work, but at least I'll be trying something, like the Abhorsen I'm supposed to be and you're always telling me I'm not!"

Silence greeted this sally. Touchstone looked away, embarrassed. Mogget looked at her, yawned and shrugged.

"As it happens, I can't think of anything else. I've grown stupid over the millennia – even stupider than the Abhorsens I serve."

"I think it's as good a plan as any," Touchstone said unexpectedly. He hesitated, then added, "Though I am afraid."

"So am I," whispered Sabriel. "But if it's a sunny day tomorrow, we will go there."

"Yes," said Touchstone. "Before we grow too afraid."

chapter twenty

eaving the safe, aqueduct-bounded quarter of Belisaere proved to be a more difficult business than entering it, particularly through the northern archway, which led out to a long-abandoned street of derelict houses, winding their way up towards the northern hills of the city.

There were six guards at the archway and they looked considerably more alert and efficient than the ones who guarded the passage from the docks. There was also a group of other people ahead of Sabriel and Touchstone waiting to be let through. Nine men, all with the marks of violence written in their expressions, in the way they spoke and moved. Every one was armed, with weapons ranging from daggers to a broad-bladed axe. Most of them also carried bows – short, deeply-curved bows, slung on their backs.

"Who are these people?" Sabriel asked Touchstone. "Why are they going out into the Dead part of the city?"

"Scavengers," replied Touchstone. "Some of the people I spoke to last night mentioned them. Parts of the city were abandoned to the Dead very quickly, so there is still plenty of loot to be found. A risky business, I think..."

Sabriel nodded thoughtfully and looked back at the men, most of whom were sitting or squatting by the aqueduct wall. Some of them looked back at her, rather suspiciously. For a moment, she thought they'd seen the bells under her cloak and recognised her as a necromancer, then she realised that she and Touchstone probably looked like rival scavengers. After all, who else would want to leave the protection of swift water? She felt a bit like a hard-bitten scavenger. Even freshly cleaned and scrubbed, her clothes and armour were not the sweetest items of wear. They were also still slightly damp, and the boat cloak that covered her up was on the borderline between damp and wet, because it hadn't been hung up properly after washing. On the positive side, everything had the scent of lemon, for the Sign of Three Lemons washerfolk used lemon-scented soap.

Sabriel thought the scavengers had been waiting for the guards, but clearly they had been waiting for something else, which they'd suddenly sighted behind her. The sitting or squatting men picked themselves up, grumbling and cursing, and shuffled together into something resembling a line.

Sabriel looked over her shoulder to see what they saw – and froze. For coming towards the arch were two men and about twenty children: children of all ages between six and sixteen. The men had the same look as the other scavengers and carried long, four-tongued whips. The children were manacled at the ankles, the manacles fastened to a long central chain. One man held the chain, leading the children down the middle of the road. The other followed behind, plying the air above the small bodies idly with his whip, the four tongues occasionally licking against an ear or the top of a small head.

"I heard of this too," muttered Touchstone, moving up closer to Sabriel, his hands falling on his sword hilts. "But I thought it was a beer story. The scavengers use children – slaves – as decoys, or bait, for the Dead. They leave them in one area, to draw the Dead away from where they intend to search."

"This is... disgusting!" raged Sabriel. "Immoral! They're slavers, not scavengers! We have to stop it!"

She started forward, mind already forming a Charter-spell to blind and confuse the scavengers, but a sharp pain in her neck halted her. Mogget, riding on her shoulders, had dug his claws in just under her chin. Blood trickled down in hairline traces, as he hissed close to her ear.

"Wait! There are nine scavengers and six guards, with more close by. What will it profit these children, and all the others who may come, if you are slain? It is the Dead who are at the root of this evil and Abhorsen's business is with the Dead!"

Sabriel stood still, shuddering, tears of rage and anger welling up in the corners of her eyes. But she didn't attack. Just stood, watching the children. They seemed resigned to their fate, silent, without hope. They didn't even fidget in their chains, standing still, heads bowed, till the scavengers whipped them up again and they broke into a dispirited shuffle towards the archway.

Soon, they were beyond the arch, heading up the ruined street, the scavenging team walking slowly behind them.

Sunshine shone bright on the cobbled street and reflected from armour and weapons – and briefly, from a little boy's blond head. Then they were gone, turning right, taking the way towards Coiner's Hill.

Sabriel, Touchstone and Mogget followed after ten minutes spent negotiating with the guards. At first, the leader, a large man in a gravy-stained leather cuirass, wanted to see an "official scavenger's licence," but this was soon translated as a request for bribes. Then it was merely a matter of bargaining, down to the final price of three silver pennies each for Sabriel and Touchstone, and one for the cat. Strange accounting, Sabriel thought, but she was glad Mogget stayed silent, not voicing the opinion that he was being undervalued.

Past the aqueduct and the soothing barrier of running water, Sabriel felt the immediate presence of the Dead. They were all around, in the ruined houses, in cellars and drains, lurking anywhere the light didn't reach. Dormant, while the sun shone, waiting for the night.

In many ways, the Dead of Belisaere were direct counterparts of the scavengers. Hiding by day, they took what they could by night. There were many, many Dead in Belisaere, but they were weak, cowardly and jealous. Their combined appetite was enormous, but the supply of victims sadly limited. Every morning saw scores of them lose their hold on Life, to fall back into Death. But more always came...

"There are thousands of Dead here," Sabriel said, eyes darting from side to side. "They're weak, for the most part – but so many!"

"Do we go straight on to the reservoir?" Touchstone asked. There was an unspoken question there, Sabriel knew. Should they – could they – save the children first?

She looked at the sky and the sun before answering. They had about four hours of strong sunlight, if no clouds intervened. Little enough time, anyway. Assuming that they could defeat the scavengers, could they leave finding her father till tomorrow? Every day made it less likely his spirit and body could be brought back together. Without him, they couldn't defeat Kerrigor – and Kerrigor had to be defeated for them to have any hope of repairing the stones of the Great Charter – banishing the Dead across the Kingdom...

"We'll go straight to the reservoir," Sabriel said, heavily, trying to blank out a sudden fragment of visual memory: sunlight on that little boy's head, the trudging feet...

"Perhaps we... perhaps we will be able to rescue the children on the way back."

Touchstone led the way with confidence, keeping to the middle of the streets, where the sun was bright. For almost an hour, they strode up empty, deserted streets, the only sound the clacking of their boot-nails on the cobbles. There were no birds or animals. Not even insects. Just ruin and decay.

Finally, they reached an iron-fenced park that ran around the base of Palace Hill. Atop the hill, blackened, burnt-out shells of tumbled stone and timber were all that remained of the Royal Palace.

"The last Regent burned it," said Mogget, as all three stopped to look up. "About twenty years ago. It was becoming infested with the Dead, despite all the guards and wards that various visiting Abhorsens put up. They say the Regent went mad and tried to burn them out."

"What happened to him?" asked Sabriel.

"Her, actually," replied Mogget. "She died in the fire – or the Dead took her. And that marked the end of any attempt at governing the Kingdom."

"It was a beautiful building," Touchstone reminisced. "You could see out over the Saere. It had high ceilings, and a clever system of vents and shafts to catch the light and the sea breeze. There was always music and dancing somewhere in the Palace, and Midsummer dinner on the garden roof, with a thousand scented candles burning..."

He sighed and pointed at a hole in the park fence.

"We might as well go through here. There's an entrance to the reservoir in one of the ornamental caves in the park. Only fifty steps down to the water, rather than the hundred and fifty from the Palace proper."

"One hundred and fifty-six," said Mogget. "As I recall."

Touchstone shrugged and climbed through the hole, on to the springy turf of the park. There was no one – and no thing – in sight, but he drew his swords anyway. There were large trees nearby and, accordingly, shadows.

Sabriel followed, Mogget jumping down from her shoulders to saunter forward and sniff the air. Sabriel drew her sword too, but left the bells. There were Dead about, but none close. The park was too open in daylight.

The ornamental caves were only five minutes' walk away,

past a fetid pond that had once boasted seven water-spouting statues of bearded tritons. Now their mouths were clogged with rotten leaves and the pond almost solid with yellow-green slime.

There were three cave entrances, side-by-side. Touchstone led them to the largest, central entrance. Marble steps led down the first three or four feet and marble pillars supported the entrance ceiling.

"It only goes back about forty paces into the hill," Touchstone explained, as they lit their candles by the entrance, sulphur matches adding their own noisome stench to the dank air of the cave. "They were built for picnics in high summer. There is a door at the back of this one. It may be locked, but should yield to a Charter-spell. The steps are directly behind, and pretty straight, but there are no light shafts. And it's narrow."

"I'll go first then," said Sabriel, with a firmness that belied the weakness in her legs and the fluttering in her stomach. "I can't sense any Dead, but they could be there..."

"Very well," said Touchstone, after a moment's hesitation.

"You don't have to come, you know," Sabriel suddenly burst out, as they stood in front of the cave, candles flickering foolishly in the sunshine. She suddenly felt awfully responsible for him. He looked scared, much whiter than he should, almost as pale as a Death-leeched necromancer. He'd seen terrible things in the reservoir, things that had once driven him mad, and despite his self-accusation, Sabriel didn't believe it was his fault. It wasn't his father down there. He wasn't an Abhorsen.

"I do have to," Touchstone replied. He bit his lower lip nervously. "I have to. I'll never be free of my memories, otherwise. I have to do something, make new memories, better ones. I need to... seek redemption. Besides, I am still a member of the Royal Guard. It is my duty."

"So be it," said Sabriel. "Anyway, I'm glad you're here."

"I am too – in a strange sort of way," said Touchstone and he almost, but not quite, smiled.

"I'm not," interrupted Mogget decidedly. "Let's get on with it. We're wasting sunlight."

The door was locked, but opened easily to Sabriel's spell, the simple Charter symbols of unlocking and opening flowing from her mind through to her index finger, which lay against the keyhole. But though the spell was successful, it had been difficult to cast. Even up here, the broken stones of the Great Charter exerted an influence that disrupted Charter Magic.

The faint candlelight showed damp, crumbly steps, leading straight down. No curves or turns, just a straight stair leading into darkness.

Sabriel trod gingerly, feeling the soft stone crumble under her heavy boots, so she had to keep her heels well back on each step. This made for slow progress, with Touchstone close behind her, the light from his candle casting Sabriel's shadow down the steps in front, so she saw herself elongated and distorted, sliding into the dark beyond the light.

She smelled the reservoir before she saw it, somewhere around the thirty-ninth step. A chill, damp smell that cut into her nose and lungs and filled her with the impression of a cold expanse.

Then the steps ended in a doorway on the edge of a vast, rectangular hall – a giant chamber where stone columns rose up like a forest to support a roof sixty feet above her head, and the floor before her wasn't stone, but water as cold and still as stone. Around the walls, pallid shafts of sunlight thrust down in counterpoint to the supporting columns, leaving discs of light on the water. These made the rim of the reservoir a complex study of light and shade, but the centre remained unknown, cloaked in heavy darkness.

Sabriel felt Touchstone touch her shoulder, then she heard his whisper.

"It's about waist-deep. Try and slip in as quietly as possible. Here – I'll take your candle."

Sabriel nodded, passed the candle back, sheathed her sword, and sat down on the last step, before slowly easing herself into the water.

It was cold, but not unbearable. Despite Sabriel's care, ripples spread out from her, silver on the dark water, and there had been the tiniest splash. Her feet touched the bottom and she only half stifled a gasp. Not from the cold, but from the sudden awareness of the two broken stones of the Great Charter. It hit her like the savage onset of gastric flu, bringing stomach cramps, sudden sweat and dizziness. Bent over, she clutched at the step, till the first pains subsided to a dull ache. It was much worse than the lesser stones, broken at Cloven Crest and Nestowe.

"What is it?" whispered Touchstone.

"Ah… the broken stones," Sabriel muttered. She took a deep breath, willing the pain and discomfort away. "I can stand it. Be careful when you get in."

She drew her sword and took her candle back from Touchstone, who prepared to enter the water. Even forewarned, she saw him flinch as his feet touched the bottom and sweat broke out in lines on his forehead, mirroring the ripples that spread from his entry.

Sabriel expected Mogget to jump up on her shoulder, given his apparent dislike for Touchstone, but he surprised her, leaping to the man. Touchstone was clearly startled too, but recovered well. Mogget draped himself around the back of Touchstone's neck and mewed softly.

"Keep to the edges, if you can. The corruption – the break – will have even more unpleasant effects near the centre."

Sabriel raised her sword in assent and led off, following the left wall, trying to break the surface tension of the water as little as possible. But the quiet slosh-slosh of their wading seemed very loud, echoing and spreading up and out through the cistern, adding to the only other noise – the regular dripping of water, plopping loudly from the roof, or more sedately sliding down the columns.

She couldn't sense any Dead, but she wasn't sure how much that was due to the broken stones. They made her head hurt, like a constant, too-loud noise; her stomach cramped; her mouth was full of the acrid taste of bile.

They had just reached the north-western corner, directly under one of the light shafts, when the light suddenly dimmed and the reservoir grew dark in an instant, save for the tiny, soft glow of the candles.

"A cloud," whispered Touchstone. "It will pass."

They held their breath, looking up, up to the tiny outline of light above, and were rewarded when sunlight came pouring back down. Relieved, they began to wade again, following the long west-east wall. But it was short-lived relief. Another cloud crossed the sun, somewhere in that fresh air so high above them, and darkness returned. More clouds followed, till there were only brief moments of light interspersed by long stretches of total dark.

The reservoir seemed colder without the sun, even a sun diluted by passage down long shafts through the earth. Sabriel felt the cold now, accompanied by the sudden, irrational fear that they had stayed too long and would emerge to a night full of waiting, life-hungry Dead. Touchstone felt the chill too, made more bitter by his memories of two hundred years past, when he'd waded in this same water, and seen the Queen and her two daughters sacrificed and the Great Stones broken. There had been blood on the water then and he still saw it – a single frozen moment of time that would not get out of his head.

Despite these fears, it was the darkness that helped them. Sabriel saw a glow, a faint luminescence off to her right, somewhere towards the centre. Shielding her eyes from the candle's glare, she pointed it out to Touchstone.

"There's something there," he agreed, his voice so low Sabriel barely heard it. "But it's at least forty paces towards the centre."

Sabriel didn't answer. She'd felt something from that faint light, something like the slight sensation across the back of her neck that came when her father's sending visited her at school. Leaving the wall, she pushed out through the water, a V-line of ripples behind her. Touchstone looked again, then followed, fighting the nausea that rose in him, coming in waves like repeated doses of an emetic. He was dizzy too, and could no longer properly feel his feet.

They went about thirty paces out, the pain and the nausea growing steadily worse. Then Sabriel suddenly stopped, Touchstone lifting his sword and candle, eyes searching for an attack. But there was no enemy present. The luminous light came from a diamond of protection, the four cardinal marks glowing under the water, lines of force sparkling between them.

In the middle of the diamond, a man-shaped figure stood, empty hands outstretched, as if he had once held weapons. Frost rimed his clothes and face, obscuring his features, and ice girdled the water around his middle. But Sabriel had no doubt about who it was.

"Father," she whispered, the whisper echoing across the dark water, to join the faint sounds of the ever-present dripping.

chapter twenty-one

"The diamond is complete," said Touchstone. "We won't be able to move him."

"Yes. I know," replied Sabriel. The relief that had soared inside her at the sight of her father was ebbing, giving way to the sickness caused by the broken stones. "I think... I think I'll have to go into Death from here and fetch his spirit back."

"What!" exclaimed Touchstone. Then, quieter, as the echoes rang, "Here?"

"If we cast our own diamond of protection..." Sabriel continued, thinking aloud. "A large one, around both of us and father's diamond – that will keep most danger at bay."

"Most danger," Touchstone said grimly, looking around, trying to peer past the tight confines of their candle's little globe of light. "It will also trap us here – even if we can cast it, so close to the broken stones. I know that I couldn't do it alone, at this point."

"We should be able to combine our strengths. Then, if you and Mogget keep watch while I am in Death, we should manage."

"What do you think, Mogget?" asked Touchstone, turning his head, so his cheek brushed against the little animal on his shoulder.

"I have my own troubles," grumbled Mogget. "And I think this is probably a trap. But since we're here and the – Abhorsen Emeritus, shall we say – does seem to be alive, I suppose there's nothing else to be done."

"I don't like it," whispered Touchstone. Just standing this close to the broken stones took most of his strength. For Sabriel to enter Death seemed madness, tempting fate. Who knew what might be lurking in Death, close by the easy portal made by the broken stones? For that matter, who knew what was lurking in or around the reservoir?

Sabriel didn't answer. She moved closer to her father's diamond of protection, studying the cardinal marks under the water. Touchstone followed reluctantly, forcing his legs to move in short steps, minimising the splash and ripple of his wake.

Sabriel snuffed out her candle, thrust it through her belt, then held out her open palm.

"Put your sword away and give me your hand," she said, in a tone that did not invite conversation or argument. Touchstone hesitated – his left hand held only a candle and he didn't want both his swords scabbarded – then, he complied. Her hand was cold, colder than the water. Instinctively, he gripped a little tighter, to give her some of his warmth.

"Mogget – keep watch," Sabriel instructed.

She closed her eyes and began to visualise the Eastmark, the first of the four cardinal wards. Touchstone took a quick look around, then closed his eyes too, drawn in by the force of Sabriel's conjuration.

Pain shot through his hand and arm, as he added his will to Sabriel's. The mark seemed blurry in his head and impossible to focus. The pins and needles that had already plagued his feet spread up above his knees, shooting them through with rheumatic pains. But he blocked off the pain, narrowing his consciousness to just one thing: the creation of a diamond of protection.

Finally, the Eastmark flowed down Sabriel's blade and took root in the reservoir floor. Without opening their eyes, the duo shuffled around to face the south and the next mark.

This was harder still and both of them were sweating and shaking when it finally began its glowing existence. Sabriel's hand was hot and feverish now, and Touchstone's flesh ricocheted violently between sweating heat and shivering cold. A terrible wave of nausea hit him and he would have been sick, but Sabriel gripped his hand, like a falcon its prey, and lent him strength. He gagged, dry-retched once, then recovered.

The Westmark was simply a trial of endurance. Sabriel lost concentration for a moment, so Touchstone had to hold the mark alone for a few seconds, the effort making him feel drunk in the most unpleasant way, the world spinning inside his head, totally out of control. Then Sabriel forced herself back and the Westmark flowered under the water. Desperation gave them the Northmark. They struggled with it for what seemed like hours, but was only seconds, till it almost squirmed from them uncast. But at that moment, Sabriel spent all the force of her desire to free her father and Touchstone pushed with the weight of two hundred years of guilt and sorrow.

The Northmark rolled brightly down the sword and grew to brilliance, brilliance dulled by the water. Lines of Charter-fire ran from it to the Eastmark, from Eastmark to Southmark to Westmark and back again. The diamond was complete.

Immediately, they felt a lessening of the terrible presence of the broken stones. The high-pitched pain in Sabriel's head dimmed; normal feeling returned to Touchstone's legs and feet. Mogget stirred and stretched, the first significant movement he'd made since taking up position around Touchstone's neck.

"A good casting," Sabriel said quietly, looking at the marks through eyes half-lidded in weariness. "Better than the last one I cast."

"I don't know how we did it," muttered Touchstone, staring down at the lines of Charter-fire. He suddenly became aware that he was still holding Sabriel's hand and slumping like an aged wood collector under a heavy burden. He straightened up suddenly, dropping her hand as if it were the fanged end of a snake.

She looked at him, rather startled, and he found himself staring at the reflection of his candle-flame in her dark eyes. Almost for the first time, he really looked at her. He saw the weariness there, and the incipient lines of care, and the way her mouth looked a little sad around the edges. Her nose was still swollen and there were yellowing bruises on her cheekbones. She was also beautiful and Touchstone realised that he had thought of her only in terms of her office, as Abhorsen. Not as a woman at all...

"I'd better be going," said Sabriel, suddenly embarrassed by Touchstone's stare. Her left hand went to the bell bandoleer, fingers feeling for the straps that held Saraneth.

"Let me help," said Touchstone. He stood close, fumbling with the stiff leather, hands weakened by the effort spent on the diamond of protection, his head bowed over the bells. Sabriel looked down on his hair and was strangely tempted to kiss the exact centre, a tiny part marking the epicentre where his tight brown curls radiated outwards. But she didn't.

The strap came undone and Touchstone stepped back. Sabriel drew Saraneth, carefully stilling the bell.

"It probably won't be a long wait for you," she said. "Time moves strangely in Death. If... if I'm not back in two hours, then I probably... I'll probably be trapped too, so you and Mogget should leave..."

"I'll be waiting," replied Touchstone firmly. "Who knows what time it is down here anyway?"

"And I'll wait, it seems," added Mogget. "Unless I want to swim out of here. Which I don't. May the Charter be with you, Sabriel."

"And with you," said Sabriel. She looked around the dark expanse of the reservoir. She still couldn't sense any of the Dead out there – and yet...

"We'll need it to be with us," Mogget replied sourly. "One way or another."

"I hope not," whispered Sabriel. She checked the pouch at her belt for the small things she'd prepared back at the Sign of

Three Lemons, then turned to face the Northmark and started to raise her sword, beginning her preparations to enter Death.

Suddenly, Touchstone sloshed forward and quickly kissed her on the cheek – a clumsy, dry-lipped peck that almost hit the rim of her helmet rather than her cheek.

"For luck," Touchstone said nervously. "Sabriel."

She smiled and nodded twice, then looked back to the north. Her eyes focused on something not there and waves of cold air billowed from her motionless form. A second later, ice crystals began to crack out of her hair and frost ran in lines down the sword and bell.

Touchstone watched, close by, till it grew too cold, then he retreated to the far southern vertex of the diamond. Drawing one sword, he turned outwards, holding his candle high, and started to wade around inside the lines of Charter-fire as if he were patrolling the battlements of a castle. Mogget watched too, from his shoulder, his green eyes lit with their own internal luminescence. Both of them often turned to gaze at Sabriel.

The crossing into Death was made easy – far too easy – by the presence of the broken stones. Sabriel felt them near her, like two yawning gates, proclaiming easy entry to Life for any Dead nearby. Fortunately, the other effect of the stones – the sickening illness – disappeared in Death. There was only the chill and tug of the river.

Sabriel started forward immediately, carefully scanning the grey expanse before her. Things moved at the edge of her vision; she heard movement in the cold waters. But nothing came towards her, nothing attacked, save the constant twining and gripping of the current.

She came to the First Gate, halting just beyond the wall of mist that stretched out as far as she could see to either side. The river roared beyond that mist, turbulent rapids going through to the Second Precinct, and on to the Second Gate.

Remembering pages from *The Book of the Dead*, Sabriel spoke words of power. Free Magic, that shook her mouth as she spoke, jarring her teeth, burning her tongue with raw power.

The veil of mist parted, revealing a series of waterfalls that appeared to drop into an unending blackness. Sabriel spoke some more words and gestured to the right and left with her sword. A path appeared, parting the waterfall like a finger drawn through butter. Sabriel stepped out on to it and walked down, the waters crashing harmlessly on either side. Behind her, the mist closed up and, as her rearmost heel lifted to make her next step, the path disappeared.

The Second Precinct was more dangerous than the First. There were deep holes, as well as the ever-present current. The light was worse too. Not the total darkness promised at the end of the waterfalls, but there was a different quality in its greyness. A blurring effect, that made it difficult to see further than you could touch.

Sabriel continued carefully, using her sword to probe the ground ahead. There was an easy way through, she knew, a course mapped and plotted by many necromancers and not a few Abhorsens, but she didn't trust her memory to tread confidently ahead at speed.

Always, her senses quested for her father's spirit. He was somewhere in Death, she was positive of that. There was always the faintest trace of him, a lingering memory. But it was not this close to Life. She would have to go on.

The Second Gate was essentially an enormous hole, at least two hundred yards across, into which the river sank like sinkwater down a drain. Unlike a normal drain, it was eerily silent, and with the difficult light, easy for the unwary to walk up to its rim. Sabriel was always particularly careful with this Gate – she had learned to sense the feel of its tug against her shins at an early age. She stopped well back when the tug came and tried to focus on the silently raging whirlpool.

A faint squelching sound behind her made her turn, sword scything around at full arm-stretch, a great circle of Charter-spelled steel. It struck Dead spirit-flesh, sparks flying, a scream of rage and pain filling the silence. Sabriel almost jumped back, at that scream, but she held her ground. The Second Gate was too close.

The thing she'd hit stepped back, its head hanging from a mostly-severed neck. It was humanoid in shape, at least to begin with, but had arms that trailed down below its knees, into the river. Its head, now flopping on one shoulder, was longer than it was wide or tall and possessed a mouth with several rows of teeth. It had flaming coals in its eyepits, a characteristic of the deep Dead from beyond the Fifth Gate.

It snarled and brought its long, skewer-thin fingers up out of the water to try and straighten its head, attempting to rest it back atop the cleanly-hewn neck.

Sabriel struck again and the head and one hand flew off, splashing into the river. They bobbed on the surface for a moment, the head howling, eyes flaming with hate across the water. Then it was sucked down, down into the hurly-burly of the Second Gate.

The headless body stood where it was for a second, then started to cautiously step sideways, its remaining hand groping around in front of it. Sabriel watched it cautiously, debating whether to use Saraneth to bind it to her will, and then Kibeth to send it on its way to final death. But using the bells would alert everything Dead between here and the First and Third Gates at least – and she didn't want that.

The headless thing took another step and fell sideways into a deep hole. It scrabbled there, long arms thrashing the water, but couldn't pull itself up and out. It only succeeded in getting across into the full force of the current, which snatched it up and threw it into the whirlpool of the Gate.

Once again, Sabriel recited words of Free Magic power, words impressed into her mind long ago from *The Book of the Dead*. The words flowed out of her, blistering her lips, strange heat in this place of leeching cold.

With the words, the waters of the Second Gate slowed and stilled. The whirling vortex separated out into a long spiral path, winding downwards. Sabriel, checking for a few last holes near the edge, gingerly strode out to this path and started down. Behind and above her, the waters began to swirl again.

The spiral path looked long, but to Sabriel it seemed only a matter of minutes before she was passing through the very base of the whirlpool and out into the Third Precinct.

This was a tricksome place. The water was shallow here, only ankle-deep, and somewhat warmer. The light was better too – still grey, but you could see farther out. Even the ubiquitous current was no more than a bit of a tickle around the feet.

But the Third Precinct had waves. For the first time, Sabriel broke into a run, sprinting as fast as she could towards the Third Gate, just visible in the distance. It was like the First Gate – a waterfall concealed in a wall of mist.

Behind her, Sabriel heard the thunderous crashing that announced the wave, which had been held back by the same spell that gave her passage through the whirlpool. With the wave came shrill cries, shrieks and screams. There were clearly many Dead around, but Sabriel didn't spare them a thought. Nothing and no one could withstand the waves of the Third Precinct. You simply ran as fast as possible, hoping to reach the next Gate – whichever way you were going.

The thunder and crashing grew louder and one by one the various screams and shouts were submerged in the greater sound. Sabriel didn't look, but only ran faster. Looking over her shoulder would lose a fraction of a second, and that might be enough for the wave to reach her, pick her up and hurl her through the Third Gate, stunned flotsam for the current beyond...

Touchstone stared out past the southern vertex, listening. He had heard something, he was sure, something besides the constant dripping. Something louder, something slow, attempting to be surreptitious. He knew Mogget had heard it too, from the sudden tensing of cat paws on his shoulder.

"Can you see anything?" he whispered, peering out into the darkness. The clouds were still blocking the light from the sun-shafts, though he thought the intervals of sunlight were growing longer. But, in any case, they were too far away from the edge to benefit from a sudden return of sun.

"Yes," whispered Mogget. "The Dead. Many of them, filing out of the main southern stair. They're lining up each side of the door, along the reservoir walls."

Touchstone looked at Sabriel, now covered in frost, like a wintering statue. He felt like shaking her shoulder, screaming for help...

"What kind of Dead are they?" he asked. He didn't know much about the Dead, except that Shadow Hands were the worst of the normal variety, and Mordicants, like the one that had followed Sabriel, were the worst of them all. Except for what Rogir had become. Kerrigor, the Dead adept...

"Hands," muttered Mogget. "All Hands, and pretty putrescent ones too. They're falling apart just walking."

Touchstone stared again, trying by sheer force of will to see — but there was nothing, save darkness. He could hear them, though, wading, squelching through the still water. Too still for his liking — suddenly he wondered if the reservoir had a drainhole and a plug. Then he dismissed it as a foolish notion. Any such plug or drain cover would have long since rusted shut.

"What are they doing?" he whispered anxiously, fingering his sword, tilting the blade this way and that. His left hand seemed to hold the candle steady, but the little flame flickered, clear evidence of the tiny shakes that ran down his arm.

"Just lining up along the walls, in ranks," Mogget whispered back. "Strange – almost like an honour guard..."

"Charter preserve us," Touchstone croaked, with a weight in his throat of absolute dread and terrible foreboding. "Rogir... Kerrigor. He must be here... and he's coming..."

chapter twenty-two

Sabriel reached the Third Gate just ahead of the wave, gabbling a Free Magic spell as she ran, feeling it fume up and out of her mouth, filling her nostrils with acrid fumes. The spell parted the mists and Sabriel stepped within, the wave breaking harmlessly around her, dumping its cargo of Dead down into the waterfall beyond. Sabriel waited a moment more, for the path to appear, then passed on – on to the Fourth Precinct.

This was a relatively easy area to traverse. The current was strong again, but predictable. There were few Dead, because most were stunned and rushed through by the Third Precinct's wave. Sabriel walked quickly, using the strength of her will to suppress the leeching cold and the plucking hands of the current. She could feel her father's spirit now, close by, as if he were in one room of a large house and she in another – tracking him down by the slight sounds of habitation. He was either here in the Fourth Precinct, or past the Fourth Gate in the Fifth Precinct.

She increased her pace a little again, eager to find him, talk with him, free him. She knew everything would be all right once Father was freed...

But he wasn't in the Fourth Precinct. Sabriel reached the Fourth Gate without feeling any intensification of his presence. This Gate was another waterfall, of sorts, but it wasn't cloaked in mist. It looked like the easy drop of water from a small weir, a matter of only two or three feet down. But Sabriel knew that if you approached the edge there was more than enough force to drag the strongest spirit down.

She halted well back and was about to launch into the spell that would conjure her path, when a niggling sensation at the back of her head made her stop and look around.

The waterfall stretched as far as she could see to either side and Sabriel knew that if she was foolish enough to try and walk its length, it would be an unending journey. Perhaps it eventually looped back on itself, but as there were no landmarks, stars or anything else to fix one's position, you'd never know. No one ever walked the breadth of an inner Precinct or Gate. What would be the point? Everyone went into Death or out of it. Not sideways, save at the border with Life, where walking along altered where you came out – but that was only useful for spirit-forms or rare beings like the Mordicant, who took their physical shape with them.

Nevertheless, Sabriel felt an urge to walk along next to the Gate, to turn on her heel and follow the line of the waterfall. It was an unidentifiable urge and that made her uneasy. There were other things in Death than the Dead – inexplicable beings of Free Magic, strange constructs and incomprehensible forces. This urge – this calling – might come from one of them.

She hesitated, thinking about it, then pushed out into the water, heading out parallel to the waterfall. It might be some Free Magic summoning or it might be some connection with her father's spirit.

"They're coming down the east and west stairs too," said Mogget. "More Hands."

"What about the south – where we came in?" asked Touchstone, looking nervously from side to side, ears straining to hear every sound, listening to the Dead wading out into the reservoir to form up in their strange, regimented lines.

"Not yet," replied Mogget. "That stair ends in sunlight, remember? They'd have to go through the park."

"There can't be much sunlight," muttered Touchstone, looking at the light-shafts. Some sunshine was coming through, heavily filtered by clouds, but it wasn't enough to cause the Dead in the reservoir any distress or lift Touchstone's spirits.

"When... when do you think he will come?" asked Touchstone. Mogget didn't need to ask who "he" was.

"Soon," replied the cat, in a matter-of-fact tone. "I always said it was a trap."

"So how do we get out of it?" asked Touchstone, trying to keep his voice steady. He was inwardly fighting a strong desire to leave the diamond of protection and run for the southern stair, splashing through the reservoir like a runaway horse, careless of the noise – but there was Sabriel, frosted over, immobile...

"I'm not sure we can," said Mogget, with a sideways glance at the two ice-rimmed statues nearby. "It depends on Sabriel and her father."

"What can we do?"

"Defend ourselves if we're attacked, I suppose," drawled Mogget, as if stating the obvious to a tiresome child. "Hope. Pray to the Charter that Kerrigor doesn't come before Sabriel returns."

"What if he does?" asked Touchstone, staring white-eyed out into the darkness. "What if he does?"

But Mogget was silent. All Touchstone heard was the shuffling, wading, splashing of the Dead as they slowly drew closer, like starving rats creeping up to a sleeping drunk's dinner.

Sabriel had no idea of how far she'd gone before she found him. That same niggling sensation prompted her to stop, to look out into the waterfall itself, and there he was. Abhorsen. Father. Somehow imprisoned within the Gate itself, so only his head was visible above the rush of the water.

"Father!" cried Sabriel, but she resisted the urge to rush forward. At first, she thought he was unaware of her, then a slight wink of one eye showed conscious perception. He winked again and moved his eyeballs to the right, several times.

Sabriel followed his gaze and saw something tall and shadowy thrust up through the waterfall, arms reaching up to pull itself out of the Gate. She stepped forward, sword and bell at the ready, then hesitated. It was a Dead humanoid, very similar in shape and size to the one who had brought the bells and sword to Wyverley College. She looked back at her father and he winked again, the corner of his mouth curving up ever so slightly – almost a smile.

She stepped back, still cautious. There was always the chance that the spirit chained in the waterfall was merely the mimic of her father or, even if it was him, that he was under the sway of some power.

The Dead creature finally hauled itself out, muscles differently arranged to a human's visibly straining along the forearms. It stood on the rim for a moment, bulky head questing from side to side, then lumbered towards Sabriel with that familiar rolling gait. Several paces away from her – out of sword's reach – it stopped and pointed at its mouth. Its jaw worked up and down, but no sound issued from its red and fleshy mouth. A black thread ran from its back, down into the rushing waters of the Gate.

Sabriel thought for a moment, then replaced Saraneth, one-handed, and drew Dyrim. She cocked her wrist to ring the bell, hesitated – for to sound Dyrim would alert the Dead all around – then let it fall. Dyrim rang, sweet and clear, several notes sounding from that one peal, mixing together like many conversations overheard in a crowd.

Sabriel rang the bell again before the echoes died, in a series of slight wrist-twitches, moving the sound out towards the Dead creature, weaving into the echoes of the first peal. Sound seemed to envelop the monster, circling around its head and muted mouth.

The echoes faded. Sabriel replaced Dyrim quickly, before it could try and sound of its own accord, and drew Ranna. The Sleeper could quell a large number of Dead at once and she feared many would come to the sound of the bells. They would probably expect to find a foolish, half-trained necromancer, but even so, they would be dangerous. Ranna twitched in her hand, expectantly, like a child waking at her touch.

The creature's mouth moved again and now it had a tongue, a horrid, pulpy mess of white flesh that writhed like a slug. But it worked. The thing made several gurgling, swallowing sounds, then it spoke with the voice of Abhorsen.

"Sabriel! I both hoped and feared you would come."

"Father..." Sabriel began, looking at his trapped spirit rather than the creature. "Father..."

She broke down and started to cry. She had come all this way, through so many troubles, only to find him trapped, trapped beyond her ability to free him. She hadn't even known that it was possible to imprison someone within a Gate!

"Sabriel! Hush, daughter! We have no time for tears. Where is your physical body?"

"In the reservoir," sniffed Sabriel. "Next to yours. Inside a diamond of protection."

"And the Dead? Kerrigor?"

"There was no sign of them there, but Kerrigor is somewhere in Life. I don't know where."

"Yes, I knew he had emerged," muttered Abhorsen, via the

thing's mouth. "He will be near the reservoir, I fear. We must move quickly. Sabriel, do you remember how to ring two bells simultaneously? Mosrael and Kibeth?"

"Two bells?" asked Sabriel, puzzled. Waker and walker? At the same time? She had never even heard it was possible – or had she?

"Think," said Abhorsen's mouthpiece. "Remember. *The Book of the Dead.*"

Slowly, it came back, pages floating down into conscious memory, like leaves from a shaken tree. The bells could be rung in pairs, or even greater combinations, if enough necromancers were gathered to wield the bells. But the risks were much greater...

"Yes," said Sabriel, slowly. "I remember. Mosrael and Kibeth. Will they free you?"

The answer was slow in coming.

"Yes. For a time. Enough, I hope, to do what must be done. Quickly, now."

Sabriel nodded, trying not to think about what he had just said. Subconsciously, she had always been aware that Abhorsen's spirit had been too long from his body, and too deep in the realm of Death. He could never truly live again. Consciously, she chose to barricade this knowledge from her mind.

She sheathed her sword, replaced Ranna, and drew Mosrael and Kibeth. Dangerous bells, both, and more so in combination than alone. She stilled her mind, emptying herself of all thought and emotion, concentrating solely on the bells. Then, she rang them.

Mosrael she swung in a three-quarter circle above her head; Kibeth she swung in a reverse figure-eight. Harsh alarm joined with dancing jig, merging into a discordant, grating, but energetic tone. Sabriel found herself walking towards the waterfall, despite all her efforts to keep still. A force like the grip of a demented giant moved her legs, bent her knees, made her step forward.

At the same time, her father was emerging from the waterfall of the Fourth Gate. His head was freed first and he flexed his neck, then rolled his shoulders, raised his arms over his head and stretched. But still Sabriel stepped on, till she was only two paces from the rim and could look down into the swirling waters, the sound of the bells filling her ears, forcing her onwards.

Then Abhorsen was free and he leapt forward, thrusting his hands into the bell-mouths, gripping the clappers with his pallid hands, making them suddenly quiet. There was silence, and father and daughter embraced on the very brink of the Fourth Gate.

"Well done," said Abhorsen, his voice deep and familiar, lending comfort and warmth like a favourite childhood toy. "Once trapped, it was all I could do to send the bells and sword. Now, I am afraid we must hurry, back to Life, before Kerrigor can complete his plan. Give me Saraneth, for now... no, you keep the sword and Ranna, I think. Come on!"

He led the way back, walking swiftly. Sabriel followed at his heels, questions bursting up in her. She kept looking at him, looking at the familiar features, the way his hair was ragged at the back, the silver stubble just showing on his chin and sideburns. He wore the same sort of clothes as she did, complete with the surcoat of silver keys. He wasn't quite as tall as she remembered.

"Father!" she exclaimed, trying to talk, keep up with him and keep watch, all at the same time. "What is happening? What is Kerrigor's plan? I don't understand. Why wasn't I brought up here, so I would know things?"

"Here?" asked Abhorsen, without slowing. "In Death?"

"You know what I mean," protested Sabriel. "The Old Kingdom! Why did... I mean, I must be the only Abhorsen ever who doesn't have a clue about how everything works! Why! Why?"

"There's no simple answer," replied Abhorsen over his shoulder. "But I sent you to Ancelstierre for two main reasons. One was to keep you safe. I had already lost your mother and the only way to keep you safe in the Old Kingdom was to keep you either with me or always at our House – practically a prisoner. I couldn't keep you with me, because things were getting worse and worse since the death of the Regent, two years before you were born. The second reason was because the Clayr advised me to do so. They said we needed someone – or will need someone – they're not good with time – who knows Ancelstierre. I didn't know why then, but I suspect I do now."

"Why?" asked Sabriel.

"Kerrigor's body," replied Abhorsen. "Or Rogir's, to give him his original name. He could never be made truly dead because his body is preserved by Free Magic, somewhere in Life. It's like an anchor that always brings him back. Every Abhorsen since the breaking of the Great Stones has been looking for that body – but none of us ever found it, including me, because we never suspected it is in Ancelstierre. Obviously, somewhere close to the Wall. The Clayr will have located it by now, because Kerrigor must have gone to it when he emerged into Life. Right, do you want to do the spell or shall I?"

They had reached the Third Gate. He didn't wait for her answer, but immediately spoke the words. Sabriel felt strange hearing them, rather than speaking them – curiously distant, like a far-off observer.

Steps rose before them, cutting through the waterfall and the mist. Abhorsen took them two at a time, showing surprising energy. Sabriel followed as best she could. She felt tiredness in her bones now, a weariness beyond exhausted muscles.

"Ready to run?" asked Abhorsen. He took her elbow as they left the steps and went into the parted mists, a curiously formal gesture that reminded her of when she was a little girl, demanding to be properly escorted when they took a picnic basket out on one of her father's corporeal school visitations.

They ran before the wave, with hands inside the bells, faster and faster, till Sabriel thought her legs would seize up and she'd tumble head over heels, around and around and around, finally clattering to a halt in a tangle of sword and bells.

But she made it somehow, Abhorsen chanting the spell that would open the base of the Second Gate, so they could ascend through the whirlpool.

"As I was saying," Abhorsen continued, taking these steps two at a time as well, speaking as swiftly as he climbed. "Kerrigor could never be properly dealt with till an Abhorsen found the body. All of us pushed him back at various times, as far back as the Seventh Gate, but that was merely postponing the problem. He grew stronger all the time, as lesser Charter Stones were broken and the Kingdom deteriorated – and we grew weaker."

"Who's we?" asked Sabriel. All this information was coming too quickly, particularly when given at the run.

"The Great Charter bloodlines," replied Abhorsen. "Which to all intents and purposes, means Abhorsens and the Clayr, since the royal line is all but extinct. And there is, of course, the relict of the Wallmakers, a sort of construct left over after they put their powers in the Wall and the Great Stones."

He left the rim of the whirlpool and strode confidently out into the Second Precinct, Sabriel close at his heels. Unlike her earlier halting, probing advance, Abhorsen practically jogged along, obviously following a familiar route. How he could tell, without landmarks or any obvious signs, Sabriel had no idea. Perhaps, when she had spent thirty-odd years traversing Death, she would find it as easy.

"So," continued Abhorsen. "We finally have the chance to finish Kerrigor once and for all. The Clayr will direct you to his body, you will destroy it, and then banish Kerrigor's spirit form – which will be severely weakened. After that, you can get the surviving royal Prince out of his suspended state, and with the aid of the Wallmaker relict, repair the Great Charter Stones..."

"The surviving royal Prince," asked Sabriel, with a feeling of unlooked-for knowledge rising in her. "He wasn't... ah... suspended as a figurehead in Holehallow was he... and his spirit in Death?"

"A bastard son, actually, and possibly crazy," Abhorsen said, without really listening. "But he has the blood. What? Oh, yes, yes he is... you said was... you mean—"

"Yes," said Sabriel unhappily. "He calls himself Touchstone. And he's waiting in the reservoir. Near the Stones. With Mogget."

Abhorsen paused for the first time, clearly taken aback.

"All our plans go astray, it seems," he said sombrely, sighing. "Kerrigor lured me to the reservoir to use my blood to break a Great Stone, but I managed to protect myself, so he contented himself with trapping me in Death. He thought you would be lured to my body and he could use your blood – but I was not trapped as securely as he thought and planned a reverse. But now, if the Prince is there, he has another source of blood to break the Great Charter—"

"He's in the diamond of protection," Sabriel said, suddenly feeling afraid for Touchstone.

"That may not suffice," replied Abhorsen grimly. "Kerrigor grows stronger every day he spends in Life, taking the strength from living folk, and feeding off the broken Stones. He will soon be able to break even the strongest Charter Magic defences. He may be strong enough now. But tell me of the Prince's companion. Who is Mogget?"

"Mogget?" repeated Sabriel, surprised again. "But I met him at our House! He's a Free Magic – something – wearing the shape of a white cat, with a red collar that carries a miniature Saraneth."

"Mogget," said Abhorsen, as if trying to get his mouth around an unpalatable morsel. "That is the Wallmaker relict, or their last creation, or their child – no one knows, possibly not even him. I wonder why he took the shape of a cat? He was always a sort of albino dwarf-boy to me, and he practically never left the House. I suppose he may be some sort of protection for the Prince. We must hurry."

"I thought we were!" snapped Sabriel, as he started off again. She didn't mean to be bad-tempered, but this was not her idea of a heartfelt reunion between father and daughter. He hardly seemed to notice her, except as a repository for numerous revelations and as an agent to deal with Kerrigor.

Abhorsen suddenly stopped and gathered her into a quick, one-armed embrace. His grip felt strong, but Sabriel felt another reality there, as if his arm was a shadow, temporarily born of light, but doomed to fade at nightfall.

"I have not been an ideal parent, I know," Abhorsen said quietly. "None of us ever is. When we become the Abhorsen, we lose much else. Responsibility to many people rides roughshod over personal responsibilities; difficulties and enemies crush out softness; our horizons narrow. You are my daughter and I have always loved you. But now, I live again for only a short time – a hundred hundred heartbeats, no more – and I must win a battle against a terrible enemy. Our parts now, which perforce we must play – are not father and daughter, but one old Abhorsen, making way for the new. But behind this, there is always my love."

"A hundred hundred heartbeats..." whispered Sabriel, tears falling down her face. She gently pushed herself out of his embrace and they started forward together, towards the First Gate, the First Precinct, Life – and then, the reservoir.

chapter twenty-three

Touchstone could see the Dead now and had no difficulty hearing them. They were chanting and clapping, decayed hands meeting together in a steady, slow rhythm that put all the hair on the back of his head on edge. A ghastly noise, hard sounds of bone on bone, or the liquid thumpings of decomposed, jellying flesh. The chanting was even worse, for very few of them had functioning mouths. Touchstone had never seen or heard a shipwreck – now he knew the sound of a thousand sailors drowning, all at once, in a quiet sea.

The lines of the Dead had marched out close to where Touchstone stood, forming a great mass of shifting shadow, spread like a choking fungus around the columns. Touchstone couldn't make out what they were doing, till Mogget, with his night-sight, explained.

"They're forming up into two lines, to make a corridor," the little cat whispered, though the need for silence was long gone. "A corridor of Dead Hands, reaching from the Northern Stair to us."

"Can you see the doorway of the stair?" Touchstone asked. He was no longer afraid, now he could see and smell the putrescent, stinking corpses lined up in mockery of a parade. I should have died in this reservoir long ago, he thought. There has just been a delay of two hundred years...

"Yes, I can," continued Mogget, his eyes green with sparkling fire. "A tall beast has come, its flesh boiling with dirty flames. A Mordicant. It's crouching in the water, looking back and up like a dog to its master. Fog is rolling down the stairs behind it – a Free Magic trick, that one. I wonder why he has such an urge to impress?"

"Rogir always was flamboyant," Touchstone stated, as if he might be commenting on someone at a dinner party. "He liked everyone to be looking at him. He's no different as Kerrigor, no different Dead."

"Oh, but he is," said Mogget. "Very different. He knows you're here and the fog's for vanity. He must have been terribly rushed making the body he wears now. A vain man – even a Dead one – would not like this body looked at."

Touchstone swallowed, trying not to think about that. He wondered if he could charge out of the diamond, flèche with his swords into that fog, a mad attack – but even if he got there, would his swords, Charter-spelled though they were, have any effect on the magical flesh Kerrigor now wore?

Something moved in the water, at the limits of his vision, and the Hands increased the tempo of their drumming, the frenzied gurgle-chanting rising in volume.

Touchstone squinted, confirming what he thought he'd seen – tendrils of fog, lazily drifting across the water between the lines of the Dead, keeping to the corridor they'd made.

"He's playing with us," gasped Touchstone, surprised by his own lack of breath for speech. He felt like he'd already sprinted a mile, his heart going thump-thump-thump-thump...

A terrible howl suddenly rose above the Dead drumming and Touchstone leapt back, nearly dislodging Mogget. The howl rose and rose, becoming unbearable, and then a huge shape broke out of the fog and darkness, stampeding towards them with fearful power, great swathes of spray exploding around it as it ran.

Touchstone shouted or screamed – he wasn't sure – threw away his candle, drew his left-sword and thrust both blades out, crouching to receive the charge, knees so bent he was chest-deep in the water.

"The Mordicant!" yelled Mogget, then he was gone, leaping from Touchstone to the still-frosted Sabriel.

Touchstone barely had time to absorb this information and a split-second image of something like an enormous, flame-shrouded bear, howling like the final scream of a sacrifice – then the Mordicant collided with the diamond of protection and Touchstone's out-thrust swords.

Silver sparks exploded with a bang that drowned the howling, throwing both Touchstone and the Mordicant back several yards. Touchstone lost his footing and went under, water bubbling into his nose and still-screaming mouth. He panicked, thinking the Mordicant would be on him in a second, and flipped himself back up with unnecessary force, savagely ripping his stomach muscles.

He almost flew out of the water, swords at guard again, but the diamond was intact and the Mordicant retreating, backing away along the corridor of Hands. They'd stopped their noise, but there was something else – something Touchstone didn't recognise, till the water drained out of his ears.

It was laughter, laughter echoing out of the fog, which now billowed across the water, coming closer and closer, till the retreating Mordicant was enveloped in it and lost to sight.

"Did my hound scare you, little brother?" said a voice from within the fog.

"Ow!" exclaimed Sabriel, feeling Mogget's claws on her physical body. Abhorsen looked at her, raising one silvery eyebrow questioningly.

"Something touched my body in Life," she explained. "Mogget, I think. I wonder what's happening?"

They stood at the very edge of Death, on the border with Life. No Dead had tried to stop them and they'd passed easily through the First Gate. Perhaps any Dead would quail from the sight of two Abhorsens...

Now, they waited. Sabriel didn't know why. Somehow, Abhorsen seemed to be able to see into Life or to work out what was happening. He stood like an eavesdropper, body slightly bent, ear cocked to a non-existent door.

Sabriel, on the other hand, stood like a soldier, keeping watch for the Dead. The broken stones made this part of Death an attractive high road into Life and she had expected to find many Dead here, trying to take advantage of the "hole." But it was not so. They seemed to be alone in the grey, featureless river, their only neighbours the swells and eddies of the water.

Abhorsen closed his eyes, concentrating even harder, then opened them to a wide-eyed stare and touched Sabriel lightly on the arm.

"It is almost time," he said gently. "When we emerge, I want you to take... Touchstone... and run for the Southern Stairs. Do not stop for anything, anything at all. Once outside, climb up to the top of the Palace Hill, to the West Yard. It's just an empty field now – Touchstone will know how to get there. If the Clayr are watching properly, and haven't got their whens mixed up, there'll be a Paperwing there—"

"A Paperwing!" interrupted Sabriel. "But I crashed it."

"There are several around," replied Abhorsen. "The Abhorsen who made it – the forty-sixth, I think – taught several others how to construct them. Anyway, it should be there. The Clayr will also be there, or a messenger, to tell you where to find Kerrigor's body in Ancelstierre. Fly as close to the Wall as possible, cross, find the body – and destroy it!"

"What will you be doing?" whispered Sabriel.

"Here is Saraneth," replied Abhorsen, not meeting her gaze. "Give me your sword and... Astarael."

The seventh bell. Astarael the sorrowful. Weeper.

Sabriel didn't move, made no motion to hand over bell or blade. Abhorsen pushed Saraneth into its pouch and did up the strap. He started to undo the strap that held Astarael, but Sabriel's hand closed on his, gripping it tightly.

"There must be another way," she cried. "We can all escape together—"

"No," said Abhorsen firmly. He gently pushed her hand away. Sabriel let go and he took Astarael carefully from the bandoleer, making sure it couldn't sound. "Does the walker choose the path, or the path the walker?"

Numbly, Sabriel handed him her sword... his sword. Her empty hands hung open by her sides.

"I have walked in Death to the very precipice of the Ninth Gate," Abhorsen said quietly. "I know the secrets and horrors of the Nine Precincts. I do not know what lies beyond, but everything that lives must go there, in the proper time. That is the rule that governs our work as the Abhorsen, but it also governs us. You are the fifty-third Abhorsen, Sabriel. I have not taught you as well as I should – let this be my final lesson. Everyone and everything has a time to die."

He bent forward and kissed her forehead, just under the rim of her helmet. For a moment, she stood like a stringed puppet at rest, then she flung herself against his chest, feeling the soft fabric of his surcoat. She seemed to diminish in size, till once again she was a little girl, running to his embrace at the school gates. As she could then, she heard the slow beating of his heart. Only now, she heard the beats as grains in a timepiece, counting his hard-won hundred hundreds, counting till it was time for him to die.

She hugged him tightly, her arms meeting around his back, his arms outstretched like a cross, sword in one hand, bell in the other. Then, she let go.

They turned together and plunged out into Life.

Kerrigor laughed again, an obscene cackle that rose to a manic crescendo, before suddenly cutting to an ominous silence. The

Dead resumed their drumming, softer now, and the fog drifted forward with horrible certainty. Touchstone, drenched and partly-drowned, watched it with the taut nerves of a mouse captivated by a gliding snake. Somewhere in the back of his mind, he noted that it was easier to see the whiteness of the fog. Up above, the clouds had gone and the edges of the reservoir were once again lit by filtered sunlight. But they were forty paces or more from the edge...

A cracking noise behind him made him start and turn, a jolt of fear suddenly overlaid with relief. Sabriel, and her father, were returning to Life! Ice flakes fell from them in miniature flurries and the layer of ice around Abhorsen's middle broke into several small floes and drifted away.

Touchstone blinked as the frost fell away from their hands and faces. Now, Sabriel was empty-handed and Abhorsen wielded the sword and bell.

"Thank the Charter!" exclaimed Touchstone, as they opened their eyes and moved.

But no one heard him, for in that instant a terrible scream of rage and fury burst out of the fog, so loud the columns shivered and ripples burst out across the water.

Touchstone turned again and the fog was flying away in shreds, revealing the Mordicant crouched low, only its eyes and long mouth, bubbling with oily flames, visible above the water. Behind it, with one elongated hand upon its bog-clay head, stood something that might be thought of as a man.

Staring, Touchstone saw that Kerrigor had tried to make the body he currently inhabited look like the Rogir of old, but either his skills, memory or taste were sadly lacking. Kerrigor stood at least seven feet tall, his body impossibly deep-chested and narrow-waisted. His head was too thin and too long, and his mouth spread from ear to ear. His eyes did not bear looking at, for they were thin slits burning with Free Magic fires – not eyes at all.

But somehow, even so warped, he did have a little of the look of Rogir. Take a man, make him malleable, stretch and twist...

The hideous mouth opened, yawning wider and wider, then Kerrigor laughed, a short laugh, punctuated by the snap of his closing jaws. Then he spoke and his voice was as warped and twisted as his body.

"I am fortunate. Three bearers of blood – blood for the breaking! Three!"

Touchstone kept staring, hearing Kerrigor's voice, still somewhat like Rogir's, rich but rotten, wet like worm-ridden fruit. He saw both the new, twisted Kerrigor and the other, better-fashioned body he'd known as Rogir. He saw the dagger again, slashing across the Queen's throat, the blood cascading out, the golden cup...

A hand grabbed him, turned him around, took his left sword from his grasp. He suddenly refocused, gasping for air again, and saw Sabriel. She had his left sword in her right hand and now took his open palm in her left, dragging him towards the south. He let her pull, following in a splashing, loose-limbed run. Everything seemed to close in then, his vision narrowing, like a half-remembered dream.

He saw Sabriel's father – the Abhorsen – for the first time devoid of frost. He looked hard, determined, but he smiled, and bowed his head a fraction as they passed. Touchstone wondered why he was going the wrong way... towards Kerrigor, towards the dagger and the catching cup. Mogget was on his shoulder too, and that was unlike Mogget, going into danger... there was something else peculiar about Mogget too... yes, his collar was gone... maybe he should turn and go back, put Mogget's collar back on, try and fight Kerrigor...

"Run! Damn you! Run!" screamed Sabriel as he half-turned. Her voice snapped him out of whatever trance he'd been in. Nausea hit, for they'd left the diamond of protection. Unwarned, he threw up immediately, turning his head as they ran. He realised he was dragging on Sabriel's hand and forced himself to run faster, though his legs felt dead, numbed by savage pins and needles. He could hear the Dead again now, chanting and drumming, drumming fast. There were voices too, raised loud, echoing in the vast cavern. The howl of the Mordicant and a strange, buzzing, crackling sound that he felt rather than heard.

They reached the Southern Stair, but Sabriel didn't slacken her pace, jumping up and off, out of the twilight of the reservoir into total darkness. Touchstone lost her hand, then found it again, and they stumbled up the steps together, swords held dangerously ahead and behind, striking sparks from the stone. Still they heard the tumult from behind, the howling, drumming, shouting, all magnified by the water and the vastness of the reservoir. Then another sound began, cutting through the noise with the clarity of perfection.

It started softly, like a tuning fork lightly struck, but grew, a pure note, blown by a trumpeter of inexhaustible breath, till there was nothing but the sound. The sound of Astarael.

Sabriel and Touchstone both stopped, almost in mid-stride. They felt a terrible urge to leave their bodies, to shuck them off as so much worn-out baggage. Their spirits – their essential self – wanted to go, to go into Death and plunge joyfully into the strongest current, to be carried to the very end.

"Think of Life!" screamed Sabriel, her voice only just audible through the pure note. She could feel Touchstone dying, his will insufficient to hold him in Life. He seemed almost to expect this sudden summons into Death.

"Fight it!" she screamed again, dropping her sword to slap him across the face. "Live!"

Still he slipped away. Desperate, she grabbed him by the ears and kissed him savagely, biting his lip, the salty blood filling both their mouths. His eyes cleared and she felt him concentrate again, concentrate on Life, on living. His sword fell and he brought his arms up around her and returned her kiss. Then he put his head on her shoulder, and she on his, and they held each other tightly till the single note of Astarael slowly died.

Silence came at last. Gingerly, they let each other go. Touchstone shakily groped around for his sword, but Sabriel lit a candle before he could cut his fingers in the dark. They looked at each other in the flickering light. Sabriel's eyes were wet, Touchstone's mouth bloody.

"What was that?" Touchstone asked huskily.

"Astarael," replied Sabriel. "The final bell. It calls everyone who hears it into Death."

"Kerrigor..."

"He'll come back," whispered Sabriel. "He'll always come back, till his real body's destroyed."

"Your father?" Touchstone mumbled. "Mogget?"

"Dad's dead," said Sabriel. Her face was composed, but her eyes overflowed into tears. "He'll go quickly beyond the Final Gate. Mogget – I don't know."

She fingered the silver ring on her hand, frowned, and bent to pick up the sword she'd taken from Touchstone.

"Come on," she ordered. "We have to get up to the West Yard. Quickly."

"The West Yard?" asked Touchstone, retrieving his own sword. He was confused and sick, but he forced himself up. "Of the Palace?"

"Yes," replied Sabriel. "Let's go."

chapter twenty-four

The sunshine was harsh to their eyes, for it was surprisingly only a little past noon. They stumbled out on to the marble steps of the cave, blinking like nocturnal animals prematurely flushed out of an underground warren.

Sabriel looked around at the quiet, sunlit trees, the placid expanse of grass, the clogged fountain. Everything seemed so normal, so far removed from the crazed and twisted chamber of horrors that was the reservoir, deep beneath their feet.

She looked at the sky too, losing focus in the blue, retreating lines of clouds just edging about the fuzzy periphery of her vision. My father is dead, she thought. Gone for ever...

"The road winds around the south-western part of Palace Hill," a voice said, somewhere near her, beyond the blueness.

"What?"

"The road. Up to the West Yard."

It was Touchstone talking. Sabriel closed her eyes, told herself to concentrate, to get a grip on the here and now. She opened her eyes and looked at Touchstone.

He was a mess. Face blood-streaked from his bleeding lip, hair wet, plastered flat, armour and clothes darkly sodden. Water dripped down the sword he still held out, angled to the ground.

"You didn't tell me you were a Prince," Sabriel said, in a conversational tone. She might have been commenting on the weather. Her voice sounded strange in her own ears, but she didn't have the energy to do anything about it.

"I'm not," Touchstone replied, shrugging. He looked up at the sky while he spoke. "The Queen was my mother, but my father was an obscure northern noble, who 'took up with her' a few years after her consort's death. He was killed in a hunting accident before I was born... look, shouldn't we be going? To the West Yard?"

"I suppose so," Sabriel said dully. "Father said there will be a Paperwing waiting for us there, and the Clayr, to tell us where to go."

"I see," said Touchstone. He came closer and peered at Sabriel's vacant eyes, then took her unresisting and oddly floppy arm and steered her towards the line of beech trees that marked a path to the western end of the park. Sabriel walked obediently, increasing her pace as Touchstone sped up, till they were practically jogging. Touchstone was pushing on her arm, with many backward glances; Sabriel moving with a sleepwalker's jerky animation.

A few hundred yards from the ornamental caves, the beeches gave way to more lawn and a road started up the side of Palace Hill, switchbacking twice to the top.

The road was well-paved, but the flagstones had pushed up, or sunk down, over two decades without maintenance, and there were some quite deep ruts and holes. Sabriel caught her foot in one and she almost fell, Touchstone just catching her. But this small shock seemed to break her from the effects of the larger shock and she found a new alertness cutting through her dumb despair.

"Why are we running?"

"Those scavengers are following us," Touchstone replied shortly, pointing back through the park. "The ones who had the children at the gate."

Sabriel looked where he pointed and, sure enough, there were figures slowly moving through the beech-lined path. All nine were there, close together, laughing and talking. They seemed confident Sabriel and Touchstone could not escape them and their mood looked to be that of casual beaters, easily driving their stupid prey to a definite end. One of them saw Sabriel and Touchstone watching and used a gesture that distance made unclear, but was probably obscene. Laughter carried to them, borne by the breeze. The men's intentions were clear. Hostile.

"I wonder if they deal with the Dead," Sabriel said bleakly, revulsion in those words. "To do their deeds when sunlight lends its aid to the living..."

"They mean no good, anyway," said Touchstone, as they set off again, building up from a fast walk to a jog. "They have bows and I bet they can shoot, unlike the villagers of Nestowe."

"Yes," replied Sabriel. "I hope there is a Paperwing up there..."

She didn't need to expand upon what would happen if it wasn't. Neither of them were in any shape for fighting, or much Charter Magic, and nine bowmen could easily finish them off – or capture them. If the men were working for Kerrigor, it would be capture and the knife, down in the dark of the reservoir...

The road grew steeper and they jogged in silence, breath coming fast and ragged, with none to spare for words. Touchstone coughed and Sabriel looked at him with concern, till she realised she was coughing too. The shape they were in, it might not take an arrow to finish matters. The hill would do it anyway.

"Not... much... further," Touchstone gasped as they turned at the switchback, tired legs gaining a few seconds of relief on the flat, before starting the next incline.

Sabriel started to laugh, a bitter, coughing laugh, because it was still a lot further. The laugh became a shocked cry as something struck her in the ribs like a sucker punch. She fell sideways, into Touchstone, carrying both of them down on to the hard flagstones. A long-shot arrow had found its mark.

"Sabriel!" Touchstone shouted, voice high with fear and anger. He shouted her name again and then Sabriel suddenly felt Charter Magic explode into life within him. As it grew, he leapt up and thrust his arms out and down towards the enemy, towards that over-gifted marksman. Eight small suns flowered at his fingertips, grew to the size of his clenched fists and shot out, leaving white trails of after-image in the air. A split second later, a scream from below testified to their finding at least one target.

296

Numbly, Sabriel wondered how Touchstone could possibly still have the strength for such a spell. Wonder became surprise as he suddenly bent and lifted her up, pack and all, cradling her in his arms – all in one easy motion. She screamed a little as the arrow shifted in her side, but Touchstone didn't seem to notice. He threw his head back, roared out an animal-like challenge, and started to run up the road, gathering speed from an ungainly lurch to an inhuman sprint. Froth burst from his lips, blowing out over his chin and on to Sabriel. Every vein and muscle in his neck and face corded out, and his eyes went wild with unseeing energy.

He was berserk and nothing could stop him now, save total dismemberment. Sabriel shivered in his grasp and turned her face into his chest, too disturbed to look on the savage, snorting face that bore so little resemblance to the Touchstone she knew. But at least he was running away from the enemy...

On he ran, leaving the road, climbing over the tumbled stones of what had once been a gateway, hardly pausing, jumping from one rock to another with goat-like precision. His face was as bright red as a fire engine now, the pulse in his neck beating as fast as a hummingbird's wings. Sabriel, forgetting her own wound in sudden fear that his heart would burst, started shouting at him, begging him to come out of the rage.

"Touchstone! We're safe! Put me down! Stop! Please, stop!"

He didn't hear her, his whole concentration bent on their path. Through the ruined gateway he ran, on along a walled path, nostrils wide, head darting from side to side like a scent-following hound.

"Touchstone! Touchstone!" Sabriel sobbed, beating on his chest with her hands. "We've got away! I'm all right! Stop! Stop!"

Still he ran, through another arch; along a raised way, the stones falling away under his feet; down a short stair, jumping gaping holes. A closed door halted him for a moment and Sabriel breathed a sigh of relief, but he kicked at it viciously, till the rotten wood collapsed and he could back through, carefully shielding Sabriel from splinters.

Beyond the door was a large, open field, bordered by tumbledown walls. Tall weeds covered the expanse, with the occasional stunted, self-sown tree rising above them. Right at the western edge, perched where a wall had long since crumbled down the hill, there were two Paperwings, one facing south and the other north – and two people, indistinct silhouettes bordered with the flaming orange of the afternoon sun that was sinking down behind them.

Touchstone broke into a gait that could only be described as a gallop, parting the weeds like a ship ploughing a sargasso sea. He ran right up to the two standing figures, gently placed Sabriel on the ground before them – and fell over, eyes rolling back to whiteness, limbs twitching.

Sabriel tried to crawl over to him, but the pain in her side suddenly bit sharp and deadly, so it was all she could do to sit up and look at the two people, and beyond them, the Paperwings.

"Hello," they said, in unison. "We are, for the moment, the Clayr. You must be the Abhorsen and the King."

Sabriel stared, dry-mouthed. The sun was in her eyes, making it hard for her to see them clearly. Young women, both, with long blonde hair and bright, piercing blue eyes. They wore white linen dresses, with long, open sleeves. Freshly-pressed dresses that made Sabriel feel extremely dirty and uncivilised, in her reservoir-soaked breeches and sweaty armour. Like their voices, their faces were identical. Very pretty. Twins.

They smiled and knelt down, one by Sabriel's side, the other by Touchstone's. Sabriel felt Charter Magic slowly welling up in them, like water rising in a spring – then it flowed into her, taking away the hurt and pain of the arrow. Next to her, Touchstone's breath became less laboured and he sank into the easy quiet of sleep.

"Thank you," croaked Sabriel. She tried to smile, but seemed to have lost the knack of it. "There are slavers... human allies of the Dead... behind us."

"We know," said the duo. "But they are ten minutes behind. Your friend – the King – ran very, very fast. We saw him run yesterday. Or tomorrow."

"Ah," said Sabriel, laboriously pushing herself up on to her feet, thinking of her father and what he had said about the Clayr confusing their whens. Best to find out what she needed to know before things got really confusing.

"Thank you," she said again, for the arrow fell on the ground as she fully straightened up. It was a hunting arrow, narrow-headed, not an armour-punching bodkin. They had only meant to slow her down. She shivered and felt the hole between the armour plates. The wound didn't feel healed exactly – just older, as if it had struck a week ago, instead of minutes.

"Father said you would be here... that you have been watching for us, and watching for where Kerrigor has his body."

"Yes," replied the Clayr. "Well, not us exactly. We've only been allowed to be the Clayr today, because we're the best Paperwing pilots..."

"Or actually, Ryelle is..." one of the twins said, pointing at the other. "But since she would need a Paperwing to fly home in, two Paperwings were needed, so..."

"Sanar came too," Ryelle continued, pointing back at her sister.

"Both of us," they chorused. "Now, there isn't much time. You can take the red and gold Paperwing... we painted it in the royal colours when we knew last week. But first, there's Kerrigor's body."

"Yes," said Sabriel. Her father's – her family's – the Kingdom's enemy. For her to deal with. Her burden, no matter how heavy and how feeble her shoulders currently felt, she had to bear it.

"His body is in Ancelstierre," said the twins. "But our vision is weak across the Wall, so we don't have a map or know the place names. We'll have to show you – and you'll have to remember."

"Yes," agreed Sabriel, feeling like a dull student promising to deal with a question quite beyond her. "Yes."

The Clayr nodded and smiled again. Their teeth were very white and even. One, possibly Ryelle – Sabriel had already got them confused – brought a bottle made of clear green glass out from the flowing sleeve of her robe, the telltale flash of Charter Magic showing it hadn't been there before. The other woman – Sanar – produced a long ivory wand out of her sleeve.

"Ready?" they asked each other simultaneously and, "Yes," before their question had even penetrated Sabriel's tired brain.

Ryelle unstoppered the bottle with a resonant 'pop' and in one quick motion, poured out the contents along a horizontal line. Sanar, equally quickly, drew the wand across the falling water – and it froze in mid-air, to form a pane of transparent ice. A frozen window, suspended in front of Sabriel.

"Watch," commanded the women and Sanar tapped the ice-window with her wand. It clouded over at that touch, briefly showed a scene of whirling snow, a glimpse of the Wall, then steadied into a moving vision – much like a film shot from a travelling car. Wyverley College had frowned on films, but Sabriel had been to see quite a few in Bain. This was much the same, but in colour, and she could hear natural sounds as clearly as if she were there.

The window showed typical Ancelstierran farmland – a long field of wheat, ripe for the harvest, with a tractor stopped in the distance, its driver chatting with another man perched atop a cart, his two draught-horses standing stolidly, peering out through their blinkers.

The view raced closer towards these two men, veered around them with a snatch of caught conversation, and continued – following a road, up and over a hill, through a small wood and up to a crossroads, where the gravel intersected with a macadamised route of greater importance. There was a sign there and the "eye," or whatever it was, zoomed up to it, till the signpost filled the whole of the ice-window. "Wyverley 2½ miles," it read, directing travellers along the major road, and they were off again, shooting down towards Wyverley village.

A few seconds later, the moving image slowed, to show the familiar houses of Wyverley village: the blacksmith-come-mechanic's shop; the Wyvern public house; the constable's trim house with the blue lantern. All landmarks known to Sabriel. She concentrated even more carefully, for surely the vision, having shown her a fixed point of reference, would now race off to parts of Ancelstierre which were unknown to her.

But the picture still moved slowly. At a walking pace, it went through the village and turned off the road, following a bridle-path up the forested hill known as Docky Point. A nice enough hill, to be sure, covered by a cork tree plantation, with some quite old trees. Its only point of interest was the rectangular cairn upon the hilltop... the cairn... The image changed, closing in on the huge, grey-green stones, square-cut and tightly packed together. A relatively recent folly, Sabriel remembered from their local history lessons. A little less than two hundred years old. She'd almost visited it once, but something had changed her mind...

The image changed again, somehow sinking through the stone, down between the lines of mortar, zigzagging around the blocks, to the dark chamber at its heart. For an instant the ice-window went completely dark, then light came. A bronze sarcophagus lay under the cairn, metal crawling with Free Magic perversions of Charter marks. The vision dodged these shifting marks, penetrated the bronze. A body lay inside, a living body, wreathed in Free Magic.

The scene shifted, moving with jagged difficulty to the face of the body. A handsome face that swam closer and closer into focus, a face that showed what Kerrigor once had been. The human face of Rogir, his features clearly showing that he had shared a mother with Touchstone.

Sabriel stared, sickened and fascinated by the similarities between the half-brothers – then the vision suddenly blurred, spinning into greyness, greyness accompanied by rushing water. Death. Something huge and monstrous was wading against the current, a jagged cutting of darkness, formless and featureless, save for two eyes that burned with unnatural flame. It seemed to see her beyond the ice-window and lurched forward, two arms like blown storm clouds reaching forward.

"Abhorsen's Get!" screamed Kerrigor. "Your blood will gush upon the Stones..."

His arms seemed about to come through the window, but suddenly, the ice cracked, the pieces collapsing into a pile of swift-melting slush.

"You saw," the Clayr said together. It wasn't a question. Sabriel nodded, shaking, her thoughts still on the likeness between Kerrigor's original human body and Touchstone. Where was the fork in their paths? What had put Rogir's feet on the long road that led to the abomination known as Kerrigor?

"We have four minutes," announced Sanar. "Till the slavers come. We'll help you get the King to your Paperwing, shall we?"

"Yes, please," replied Sabriel. Despite the fearsome sight of Kerrigor's raw spirit form, the vision had imbued her with a new and definite sense of purpose. Kerrigor's body was in Ancelstierre. She would find it and destroy it, and then deal with his spirit. But they had to get to the body first...

The two women lifted Touchstone up, grunting with the effort. He was no lightweight at any time, and now was even heavier, still sodden with water from his ducking in the reservoir. But the Clayr, despite their rather ethereal appearance, seemed to manage well enough.

"We wish you luck, cousin," they said, as they walked slowly to the red and gold Paperwing, balanced so close to the edge of the broken wall, the Saere glistening white and blue below.

"Cousin?" Sabriel murmured. "I suppose we are cousins – of a sort, aren't we?"

"Blood relatives, all the children of the Great Charters," the Clayr agreed. "Though the clan dwindles…"

"Do you always – know what is going to happen?" Sabriel asked, as they gently lowered Touchstone into the back of the cockpit, and strapped him in with the belts normally used for securing luggage.

Both the Clayr laughed. "No, thank the Charter! Our family is the most numerous of the bloodlines and the gift is spread among many. Our visions come in snatches and splinters, glimpses and shadows. When we must, the whole family can spend its strength to narrow our sight – as it has done through us today. Tomorrow, we will be back to dreams and confusion, not knowing where, when or what we see. Now, we have only two minutes…"

Suddenly, they hugged Sabriel, surprising her with the obvious warmth of the gesture. She hugged them back, gladly, grateful for their care. With her father gone, she had no family left – but perhaps she would find sisters in the Clayr and perhaps Touchstone would be…

"Two minutes," repeated both the women, one in each ear. Sabriel let them go and hurriedly took *The Book of the Dead* and the two Charter Magic books from her pack, wedging them down next to Touchstone's slightly snoring form. After a second's thought, she also stuffed in the fleece-lined oilskin and the boat cloak. Touchstone's swords went into the special holders next, but the pack and the rest of its contents had to be abandoned.

"Next stop, the Wall," Sabriel muttered as she climbed into the craft, trying not to think about what would happen if they had to land somewhere uncivilised in between.

The Clayr were already in their green and silver craft and, as Sabriel did up her straps, she heard them begin to whistle, Charter Magic streaming out into the air. Sabriel licked her lips, summoned her breath and strength, and joined in. Wind rose behind both the craft, tossing black hair and blonde, lifting the Paperwings' tails and jostling their wings.

Sabriel took a breath after the wind-whistling and stroked the smooth, laminated paper of the hull. A brief image of the first Paperwing came to mind, broken and burning in the depths of Holehallow.

"I hope we fare better together," she whispered, before joining with the Clayr to whistle the last note, the pure clear sound that would wake the Charter Magic in their craft.

A second later, two bright-eyed Paperwings leapt out from the ruined palace of Belisaere, glided down almost to the swell in the Sea of Saere, then rose to circle higher and higher above the hill. One craft, of green and silver, turned to the north-west. The other, of red and gold, turned south.

Touchstone, waking to the rush of cold air on his face and the unfamiliar sensation of flying, groggily muttered, "What happened?"

"We're going to Ancelstierre," Sabriel shouted. "Across the Wall, to find Kerrigor's body – and destroy it!"

"Oh," said Touchstone, who only heard "across the Wall." "Good."

chapter twenty-five

"Beg pardon, sir," said the soldier, saluting at the doorway to the officer's bathroom. "Duty officer's compliments and can you come straightaway?"

Colonel Horyse sighed, put down his razor and used the flannel to wipe off the remains of the shaving soap. He had been interrupted shaving that morning and had tried several times during the day to finish the job. Perhaps it was a sign he should grow a moustache.

"What's happening?" he asked, resignedly. Whatever was happening, it was unlikely to be good.

"An aircraft, sir," replied the private, stolidly.

"From Army HQ? Dropping a message cylinder?"

"I don't know, sir. It's on the other side of the Wall."

"What!" exclaimed Horyse, dropping all his shaving gear, picking up his helmet and sword, and attempting to rush out, all at the same time. "Impossible!"

But, when he eventually sorted himself out and got down to the Forward Observation Post — an octagonal strongpoint that

307

thrust out through the Perimeter to within fifty yards of the Wall – it quite clearly was possible. The light was fading as the afternoon waned – it was probably close to setting on the other side – but the visibility was good enough to make out the distant airborne shape that was descending in a series of long, gradual loops... on the other side of the Wall. In the Old Kingdom.

The Duty Officer was watching through big artillery spotter's binoculars, his elbows perched on the sandbagged parapet of the position. Horyse paused for a moment to think of the fellow's name – he was new to the Perimeter Garrison – then tapped him on the shoulder.

"Jorbert. Mind if I have a look?"

The young officer lowered the binoculars reluctantly and handed them across like a boy deprived of a half-eaten lollipop.

"It's definitely an aircraft, sir," he said, brightening up as he spoke. "Totally silent, like a glider, but it's clearly powered somehow. Very manoeuvrable and beautifully painted, too. There's two... people in it, sir."

Horyse didn't answer, but took up the binoculars and the same elbow-propping stance. For a moment, he couldn't see the aircraft and he hastily panned left and right, then zigzagged up and down – and there it was, lower than he expected, almost in a landing approach.

"Sound stand-to," he ordered harshly, as the realisation struck him that the craft would land very close to the Crossing Point – perhaps only a hundred yards from the gate.

He heard his command being repeated by Jorbert to a sergeant and then bellowed out, to be taken up by sentries, duty NCOs and eventually, to hand-cranked klaxons and the old bell that hung in the front of the Officer's Mess.

It was hard to see exactly who or what was in the craft, till he twiddled with the focus and Sabriel's face leapt towards him, magnified up to a recognisable form, even at the current distance. Sabriel, the daughter of Abhorsen, accompanied by an unknown man – or something wearing the shape of a man. For a moment, Horyse considered ordering the men to stand-down, but he could already hear hobnailed boots clattering on the duckboards, sergeants and corporals shouting – and it might not really be Sabriel. The sun was weakening and the coming night would be the first of the full moon...

"Jorbert!" he snapped, handing the binoculars back to the surprised and unready subaltern. "Go and give the Regimental Sergeant-Major my compliments, and ask him to personally organise a section of the Scouts – we'll go out and take a closer look at that aircraft."

"Oh, thank you, sir!" gushed Lieutenant Jorbert, obviously taking the "we" to include himself. His enthusiasm surprised Horyse, at least for a moment.

"Tell me, Mr Jorbert," he asked. "Have you by any chance sought a transfer to the Flying Corps?"

"Well, yes, sir," replied Jorbert. "Eight times..."

"Just remember," Horyse said, interrupting him. "That whatever is out there may be a flying creature, not a flying machine – and its pilots may be half-rotted things that should be properly dead, or Free Magic beings that have never really lived at all. Not fellow aviators, knights of the sky, or anything like that."

Jorbert nodded unmilitarily, saluted, and turned on his heel.

"And don't forget your sword next time you're duty officer," Horyse called after him. "Hasn't anyone told you your revolver might not work?"

Jorbert nodded again, flushed, almost saluted, then scuttled off down the communication trench. One of the soldiers in the Forward Observation Post, a corporal with a full sleeve of chevrons denoting twenty years' service, and a Charter mark on his forehead to show his Perimeter pedigree, shook his head at the departing back of the young officer.

"Why are you shaking your head, Corporal Anshy?" snapped Horyse, irked by his many interrupted shaves and this new and potentially dangerous appearance of an aircraft.

"Water on the brain," replied the corporal cheerfully – and rather ambiguously. Horyse opened his mouth to issue a sharp reprimand, then closed it as the corners of his mouth involuntarily inched up into a smile. Before he could actually laugh, he left the post, heading back to the trench junction where his section and the RSM would meet him to go beyond the Wall.

Within five paces, he'd lost his smile.

The Paperwing slid to a perfect landing in a flurry of snow. Sabriel and Touchstone sat in it, shivering under oilskin and boat cloak, respectively, then slowly levered themselves out to stand knee-deep in the tightly-packed snow. Touchstone smiled at Sabriel, his nose bright red and eyebrows frosted.

"We made it."

"So far," replied Sabriel, warily looking around. She could see the long grey bulk of the Wall, with the deep honey-coloured sun of Autumn on the Ancelstierran side. Here, the snow lay banked against the grey stone and it was overcast, with the sun almost gone. Dark enough for the Dead to be wandering around.

Touchstone's smile faded as he caught her mood and he took his swords from the Paperwing, giving the left sword to Sabriel. She sheathed it, but it was a bad fit – another reminder of loss.

"I'd better get the books, too," she said, bending in to retrieve them from the cockpit. The two Charter Magic books were fine, untouched by snow, but *The Book of the Dead* seemed wet. When Sabriel pulled it out, she found it wasn't snow-wet. Beads of dark, thick blood were welling up out of its cover. Silently, Sabriel wiped it on the hard crust of the snow, leaving a livid mark. Then she tucked the books away in the pockets of her coat.

"Why... why was the book like that?" asked Touchstone, trying, and almost succeeding, to sound curious rather than afraid.

"I think it's reacting to the presence of many deaths," Sabriel replied. "There is great potential here for the Dead to rise. This is a very weak point—"

"Ssshhh!" Touchstone interrupted her, pointing towards the Wall. Shapes, dark against the snow, were moving in an extended line towards them, at a deliberate, steady pace. They carried bows and spears, and Sabriel at least, recognised the rifles slung across their backs.

"It's all right," Sabriel said, though a faint stab of nervousness touched her stomach. "They're soldiers from the Ancelstierran side – still, I might send the Paperwing on its way..."

Quickly, she checked that they'd taken everything from the cockpit, then laid her hand on the nose of the Paperwing, just above its twinkling eye. It seemed to look up at her as she spoke.

"Go now, friend. I don't want to risk you being dragged into Ancelstierre and taken apart. Fly where you will – to the Clayr's glacier or, if you care to, to Abhorsen's House, where the water falls."

She stepped back and formed the Charter marks that would imbue the Paperwing with choice, and the winds to lift it there. The marks went into her whistle and the Paperwing moved with the rising pitch, accelerating along till it leapt into the sky at the peak of the highest note.

"I say!" exclaimed a voice. "How did you do that?"

Sabriel turned to see a young, out-of-breath Ancelstierran officer, the single gold pip of a second lieutenant looking lonely on his shoulder-straps. He was easily fifty yards in front of the rest of the line, but he didn't seem frightened. He was clutching a sword and a revolver, though, and he raised both of them as Sabriel stepped forward.

"Halt! You are my prisoners!"

"Actually, we're travellers," replied Sabriel, though she did stand still. "Is that Colonel Horyse I can see behind you?"

Jorbert turned half around to have a look, realised his mistake, and turned back just in time to see Sabriel and Touchstone smiling, then chuckling, then out-and-out laughing, clutching at each other's arms.

"What's so funny?" demanded Lieutenant Jorbert, as the two of them laughed and laughed, till the tears ran down their cheeks.

"Nothing," said Horyse, gesturing to his men to encircle Sabriel and Touchstone, while he went up and carefully placed two fingers on their foreheads – testing the Charter they bore within. Satisfied, he lightly shook them, till they stopped their shuddering, gasping laughter. Then, to the surprise of some of his men, he put an arm around each of them and led them back to the Crossing Point, towards Ancelstierre and sunshine.

Jorbert, left to cover the withdrawal, indignantly asked the air, "What was so funny?"

"You heard the Colonel," replied Regimental Sergeant-Major Tawklish. "Nothing. That was a hysterical reaction, that was. They've been through a lot, those two, mark my words."

Then, in the way that only RSMs have with junior officers, he paused, crushing Jorbert completely with a judicious, and long delayed, "Sir."

The warmth wrapped Sabriel like a soft blanket as they stepped out of the shadow of the Wall, into the relative heat of an Ancelstierran Autumn. She felt Touchstone falter at her side, and stumble, his face staring blindly upwards to the sun.

"You both look done in," said Horyse, speaking in the kindly, slow tone he used on shell-shocked soldiers. "How about something to eat, or would you rather get some sleep first?"

"Something to eat, certainly," Sabriel replied, trying to give him a grateful smile. "But not sleep. There's no time for that. Tell me – when was the full moon? Two days ago?"

Horyse looked at her, thinking that she no longer reminded him of his own daughter. She had become Abhorsen, a person beyond his ken, in such a short time...

"It's tonight," he said.

"But I've been in the Old Kingdom at least sixteen days..."

"Time is strange between the kingdoms," Horyse said. "We've had patrols swear they were out for two weeks, coming back in after eight days. A headache for the paymaster..."

"That voice, coming from the box on the pole," Touchstone interrupted, as they left the zigzag path through the wire defences and climbed down into a narrow communication trench. "There is no Charter Magic in the box or the voice..."

"Ah," replied Horyse, looking ahead to where a loudspeaker was announcing stand-down. "I'm surprised it's working. Electricity runs that, Mr Touchstone. Science, not magic."

"It won't be working tonight," Sabriel said quietly. "No technology will be."

"Yes, it is rather loud," Horyse said, in a strong voice. More softly, he added, "Please don't say anything more till we get to my dugout. The men have already picked something up about tonight and the full moon..."

"Of course," replied Sabriel wearily. "I'm sorry."

They walked the rest of the way in silence, slogging along the zigzagging communication trench, passing soldiers in the fighting trenches, ready at their stand-to positions. The soldiers' conversations stopped as they passed, but resumed as soon as they turned the next zig or zag and were out of sight.

At last, they descended a series of steps into Colonel Horyse's dugout. Two sergeants stood guard outside – this time, Charter Mages from the Crossing Point Scouts, not the regular garrison infantry. Another soldier doubled off to the cookhouse, to fetch some food. Horyse busied himself with a small spirit-burner and made tea.

Sabriel drank it without feeling much relief. Ancelstierre and the universal comforter of its society – tea – no longer seemed as solid and dependable as she had once thought.

"Now," said Horyse. "Tell me why you don't have time to sleep."

"My father died yesterday," Sabriel said, stony-faced. "The wind flutes will fail tonight. At moonrise. The Dead here will rise with the moon."

"I'm sorry to hear about your father. Very sorry," Horyse said. He hesitated, then added, "But as you are here now, can't you bind the Dead anew?"

"If that were all, yes, I could," Sabriel continued. "But there is worse to come. Have you ever heard the name Kerrigor, Colonel?"

Horyse put his tea down.

"Your father spoke of him once. One of the Greater Dead, I think, imprisoned beyond the Seventh Gate?"

"More than Greater, possibly the Great," Sabriel said bleakly. "As far as I know, he is the only Dead spirit to also be a Free Magic adept."

"And a renegade member of the royal family," added Touchstone, his voice still harsh and dry from the cold winds of their flight, unquenched by tea. "And he is no longer imprisoned. He walks in Life."

"All these things give him power," Sabriel continued. "But there is a weakness there too. Kerrigor's mastery of Free Magic, and much of his power in both Life and Death, is dependent on the continual existence of his original body. He hid it, long ago, when he first chose to become a Dead spirit – and he hid it in Ancelstierre. Near the village of Wyverley, to be exact."

"And now he's coming to fetch it..." said Horyse, with terrible prescience. Outwardly, he looked calm, all those long years of Army service forming a hard carapace, containing his feelings. Inwardly, he felt a trembling that he hoped wasn't being transmitted to the mug in his hand.

"When will he come?"

"With the night," replied Sabriel. "With an army of the Dead. If he can emerge out of Death close to the Wall, he may come earlier."

"The sun—" Horyse began.

"Kerrigor can work the weather, bring fog or dense cloud."

"So what can we do?" asked Horyse, turning his palms outwards, towards Sabriel, his eyes questioning. "Abhorsen."

Sabriel felt a weight placed upon her, a burden adding to the weariness that already pressed upon her, but she forced herself to answer.

"Kerrigor's body is in a spelled sarcophagus under a cairn, a cairn atop a little hill called Docky Point, less than forty miles away. We need to get there quickly – and destroy the body."

"And that will destroy Kerrigor?"

''No," said Sabriel, shaking her head wistfully. "But it will weaken him... so there may be a chance..."

"Right," said Horyse. "We've still got three or four hours of daylight, but we'll need to move quickly. I take it that Kerrigor and his... forces... will have to cross the Wall here? They can't just pop out at Docky Point?"

"No," agreed Sabriel. "They'll have to emerge in Life in the Old Kingdom and physically cross the Wall. It would probably be best not to try and stop him."

"I'm afraid we can't do that," replied Horyse. "That's what the Perimeter Garrison is here for."

"A lot of your soldiers will die to no purpose then," said Touchstone. "Simply because they'll be in the way. Anything, and anybody, that gets in Kerrigor's way will be destroyed."

"So you want us to just let this... this thing and a horde of Dead descend on Ancelstierre?"

"Not exactly," replied Sabriel. "I would like to fight him at a time and a place more of our choosing. If you lend me all the soldiers here who have the Charter mark and a little Charter Magic, we may have enough time to destroy Kerrigor's body. Also, we will be almost thirty-five miles from the Wall. Kerrigor's power may only be slightly lessened, but many of his minions will be weaker. Perhaps so weak, that destroying or damaging their physical forms will be sufficient to send them back into Death."

317

"And the rest of the garrison? We'll just stand aside and let Kerrigor and his army through the Perimeter?"

"You probably won't have a choice."

"I see," muttered Horyse. He got up and paced backwards and forwards, six steps, all the dugout would allow. "Fortunately, or unfortunately perhaps – I am currently acting as the General Officer commanding the whole Perimeter. General Ashenber has returned south, due to... ah... ill health. A temporary situation only – Army HQ is loath to give any sort of higher command to those of us who wear the Charter mark. So the decision is mine..."

He stopped pacing and stared back at Sabriel and Touchstone – but his eyes seemed to see something well beyond them and the rusty corrugated iron that walled the dugout. Finally, he spoke.

"Very well. I will give you twelve Charter Mages – half of the full complement of the Scouts – but I will also add some more mundane force. A detachment to escort you to... what was it? Docky Point. But I can't promise we won't fight on the Perimeter."

"We need you too, Colonel," Sabriel said, in the silence that followed his decision. "You're the strongest Charter Mage the garrison has."

"Impossible!" Horyse exclaimed emphatically. "I'm in command of the Perimeter. My responsibilities lie here."

"You'll never be able to explain tonight, anyway," Sabriel said. "Not to any general down south, or to anyone who hasn't crossed the Wall."

"I'll... I'll think about it while you have something to eat," Horyse declared, the rattle of a tray and plates tactfully announcing the arrival of a mess orderly on the steps. "Come in!"

The orderly entered, steam rising around the edges of the silver dishes. As he put the tray down, Horyse strode out past him, bellowing.

"Messenger! I want the Adjutant, Major Tindall and the CSM from 'A' Company, Lieutenant Aire from the Scouts, the RSM and the Quartermaster. In the Operations Room in ten minutes. Oh... call in the Transport Officer too. And warn the Signals staff to stand by for coding."

chapter twenty-six

Everything moved rapidly after the tea was drunk. Almost too rapidly for the exhausted Sabriel and Touchstone. Judging from the noises outside, soldiers were rushing about in all directions, while they ate their belated lunch. Then, before they could even begin to digest, Horyse was back, telling them to get moving.

It was somewhat like being a bit player in the school play, Sabriel thought, as she stumbled out of the communication trench and on to the parade ground. There was an awful lot happening around her, but she didn't really feel part of it. She felt Touchstone lightly brush her arm and smiled at him reassuringly – it had to be even worse for him.

Within minutes, they were hustled across the parade ground, towards a waiting line of trucks, an open staff car and two strange steel-plated contraptions. Lozenge-shaped, with gun turrets on either side and caterpillar tracks. Tanks, Sabriel realised. A relatively recent invention. Like the trucks, they were roaring, engines belching blue-grey smoke. No problem now, Sabriel thought, but the engines would stop when the wind blew in from the Old Kingdom. Or when Kerrigor came...

Horyse led them to the staff car, opened the back door and gestured for them to get in.

"Are you coming with us?" Sabriel asked hesitantly, as she settled back in the heavily-padded leather seats, fighting a wave of tiredness that threatened immediate sleep.

"Yes," replied Horyse, slowly. He seemed surprised at his own answer and suddenly far away. "Yes, I am."

"You have the Sight," said Touchstone, looking up from where he was adjusting his scabbard before sitting down. "What did you see?"

"The usual thing," replied Horyse. He got in the front seat and nodded to the driver – a thin-faced veteran of the Scouts, whose Charter mark was almost invisible on his weather-beaten forehead.

"What do you mean?" asked Sabriel, but her question was lost as the driver pressed the starter switch, and the car coughed and spluttered into life, a tenor accompaniment to the bass cacophony of the trucks and tanks.

Touchstone jumped at the sudden noise and vibration, then smiled sheepishly at Sabriel, who'd lightly rested her fingers on his arm, as if calming a child.

"What did he mean 'the usual thing'?" asked Sabriel.

Touchstone looked at her, sadness and exhaustion vying for first place in his gaze. He took her hand in his own and traced a line across her palm – a definite, ending sort of line.

"Oh," muttered Sabriel. She sniffed and looked at the back of

Horyse's head, eyes blurring, seeing only the line of his cropped silver hair extending just past his helmet rim.

"He has a daughter the same age as me, back at... somewhere south," she whispered, shivering, clutching Touchstone's hand till his fingers were as white as her own. "Why, oh why, does everything... everyone..."

The car started forward with a lurch, preceded by two motorcycle outriders and followed by each of the nine trucks in turn, carefully spaced out every hundred yards. The tanks, with tracks screeching and clanking, took a side road up to the railway siding where they would be loaded up and sent on to Wyverley Halt. It was unlikely they would arrive before nightfall. The road convoy would be at Docky Point before six in the afternoon.

Sabriel was silent for the first ten miles, her head bowed, hand still clutching tightly on Touchstone's. He sat silently too, but watching, looking out as they left the military zone, looking at the prosperous farms of Ancelstierre, the sealed roads, the brick houses, the private cars and horse-drawn vehicles that pulled off the road in front of them, cleared aside by the two red-capped military policemen on motorcycles.

"I'm all right now," Sabriel said quietly, as they slowed to pass through the town of Bain. Touchstone nodded, still watching, staring at the shop windows in the High Street. The townspeople stared back, for it was rare to see soldiers in full Perimeter battle equipment, with sword-bayonets and shields – and Sabriel and Touchstone were clearly from the Old Kingdom.

"We have to stop by the Police Station and warn the Superintendent," Horyse announced as their car pulled in next to an imposing white-walled edifice with two large, blue electric lanterns hanging out the front, and a sturdy sign proclaiming it to be the headquarters of the Bainshire Constabulary.

Horyse stood up, waved the rest of the convoy on, then vaulted out and dashed up the steps, a curiously incongruous figure in mail and khaki. A constable descending the steps looked ready to stop him, but stopped himself instead and saluted.

"I'm all right," Sabriel repeated. "You can let go my hand."

Touchstone smiled and flexed his hand a little in her grip. She looked a bit puzzled, then smiled too, her fingers slowly relaxing till their hands lay flat on the seat, little fingers just touching.

In any other town, a crowd would certainly have formed around an Army staff car with two such unusual passengers. But this was Bain, and Bain was close to the Wall. People took one look, saw Charter marks, swords and armour, and went the other way. Those with natural caution, or a touch of the Sight, went home and locked their doors and shutters, not merely with steel and iron, but also with sprigs of broom and rowan. Others, even more cautious, took to the river and its sandy islets, without even pretending to be fishing.

Horyse came out five minutes later, accompanied by a tall, serious-looking man whose large build and hawk-like visage were made slightly ridiculous by a pair of too-small pince-nez clinging to the end of his nose. He shook hands with the

Colonel, Horyse returned to the car, and they were off again, the driver crashing through the gears with considerable skill.

A few minutes later, before they'd left the last buildings of the town, a bell began to ring behind them, deep and slow. Only moments later, another followed from somewhere to the left, then another, from up ahead. Soon, there were bells ringing all around.

"Quick work," Horyse shouted into the back of the car. "The Superintendent must have made them practise in the past."

"The bells are a warning?" asked Touchstone. This was something he was familiar with and he began to feel more at home, even with this sound, warning of dire trouble. He felt no fear from it – but then, after facing the reservoir for a second time, he felt that he could cope with any fear.

"Yes," replied Horyse. "Be inside by nightfall. Lock all doors and windows. Deny entry to strangers. Shed light inside and out. Prepare candles and lanterns for when the electricity fails. Wear silver. If caught outdoors, find running water."

"We used to recite that in the junior classes," Sabriel said. "But I don't think too many people remember it, even the people around here."

"You'd be surprised, ma'am," interrupted the driver, speaking out of the corner of his mouth, eyes never leaving the road. "The bells haven't rung like this in twenty years, but plenty of folk remember. They'll tell anyone who doesn't know – don't fret about that."

"I hope so," replied Sabriel, a momentary flash of remembrance passing through her mind. The people of

Nestowe, two-thirds of their number lost to the Dead, the survivors huddled in fish-drying sheds on a rocky island. "I hope so."

"How long till we reach Docky Point?" asked Touchstone. He was remembering too, but his memories were of Rogir. Soon he would look on Rogir's face again but it would only be a husk, a tool for what Rogir had become...

"About an hour at the most, I should think," replied Horyse. "Around six o'clock. We can average almost thirty miles an hour in this contraption – quite remarkable. To me, anyway. I'm so used to the Perimeter and the Old Kingdom – the small part we saw on patrol, anyway. I'd have liked to have seen more of it... gone further north..."

"You will," said Sabriel, but her voice lacked conviction, even to her own ears. Touchstone didn't say anything and Horyse didn't reply, so they drove on in silence after that, soon catching the truck convoy, overtaking each vehicle till they were in front again. But wherever they drove, the bells preceded them, every village bell-tower taking up the warning.

As Horyse had predicted, they arrived at Wyverley village just before six. The trucks stopped in a line all through the village, from policeman's cottage to the Wyvern pub, the men debussing almost before the vehicles stopped, quickly forming up into ranks on the road. The signals truck parked under a telephone pole and two men swarmed up to connect their wires. The military policemen went to each end of the village, to redirect traffic. Sabriel and Touchstone got out of the car and waited.

"It's not much different from the Royal Guard," Touchstone said, watching the men hurry into their parade positions, the sergeants shouting, the officers gathering around Horyse, who was speaking on the newly-connected phone. "Hurry up and wait."

"I'd have liked to see you in the Royal Guard," Sabriel said, "And the Old Kingdom, in... I mean before the Stones were broken."

"In my day, you mean," said Touchstone. "I would have liked that too. It was more like here, then. Here normally, I mean. Peaceful and sort of slow. Sometimes I thought life was too slow, too predictable. I'd prefer that now..."

"I used to think like that at school," Sabriel answered. "Dreaming about the Old Kingdom. Proper Charter Magic. Dead to bind. Princes to be—"

"Rescued?"

"Married," replied Sabriel absently. She seemed intent on watching Horyse. He looked like he was getting bad news over the telephone.

Touchstone didn't speak. Everything seemed to sharpen in focus for him, centring on Sabriel, her black hair gleaming like a raven's wing in the afternoon sun. I love her, he thought. But if I say the wrong thing now, I may never...

Horyse handed the telephone back to a signaller and turned towards them. Touchstone watched him, suddenly conscious that he probably only had five seconds to be alone with Sabriel, to say something, to say anything. Perhaps the last five seconds they would ever have alone together...

I am not afraid, he said to himself.

"I love you," he whispered. "I hope you don't mind."

Sabriel looked back at him and smiled, almost despite herself. Her sadness at her father's death was still there, and her fears for the future – but seeing Touchstone staring apprehensively at her somehow gave her hope.

"I don't mind," she whispered back, leaning towards him. She frowned, "I think... I think I might love you too, Charter help me, but now is—"

"The telephone line to the Perimeter Crossing Point just went out," Horyse announced grimly, shouting above the village bell even before he was close enough to talk. "A fog started rolling across the Wall over an hour ago. It reached the forward trenches at four forty-six. After that, none of the advance companies could be reached by phone or runner. I was just speaking to the Duty Officer then – that young chap who was so interested in your aircraft. He said the fog was just about to reach his position. Then the line went silent."

"So," said Sabriel. "Kerrigor didn't wait till sundown. He's working the weather."

"From the timings given by the Perimeter," Horyse said, "this fog – and whatever's in it – is moving southwards at around twenty miles an hour. As the crow flies, it'll reach us around half past seven. Dark, with the moonrise yet to come."

"Let's go then," snapped Sabriel. "The bridle-path to Docky Point starts from behind the pub. Shall I lead?"

"Best not," replied Horyse. He turned and shouted some orders, accompanied by considerable waving and pointing.

Within a few seconds, men were moving off around the pub, taking the path to Docky Point. First, the Crossing Point Scouts, archers and Charter Mages all. Then, the first platoon of infantry, bayonets fixed, rifles at the ready. Past the pub, they shook out into an arrowhead formation. Horyse, Sabriel, Touchstone and their driver followed. Behind them came the other two platoons and the signallers, unreeling field telephone wire from a large and cumbersome drum.

It was quiet among the cork trees, the soldiers moving as silently as they could, communicating by hand signals rather than shouts, only their heavy tread and the occasional rattle of armour or equipment disturbing the quiet.

Sunshine poured down between the trees, rich and golden, but already losing its warmth, like a butter-coloured wine that was all taste and no potency.

Towards the top of the hill, only the Crossing Point Scouts went on up. The lead platoon of infantry followed a lower contour around to the northern side; the other two platoons moved to the south-west and south-east, forming a defensive triangle around the hill. Horyse, Sabriel, Touchstone and the driver continued on.

The trees fell away about twenty yards from the top of the hill, thick weeds and thistles taking their place. Then, at the highest point, there was the cairn: a solid, hut-sized square of grey-green stones. The twelve Scouts were grouped loosely around it, four of them already levering one of the corner stones out with a long crowbar, obviously carried up for this purpose.

As Sabriel and Touchstone came up, the stone fell with a thud, revealing more blocks underneath. At the same time, every Charter Mage present felt a slight buzzing in their ears and a wave of dizziness.

"Did you feel that?" asked Horyse unnecessarily, as it was clear from everyone's expressions and the hands that had gone to ears that they all had.

"Yes," replied Sabriel. To a lesser extent, it was the same sort of feeling the Broken Stones caused in the reservoir. "It will get worse, I'm afraid, as we get closer to the sarcophagus."

"How far in is it?"

"Four blocks deep, I think," said Sabriel. "Or five. I... saw it... from an odd perspective."

Horyse nodded and indicated to the men to keep prying away the stones. They went to it with a will, but Sabriel noticed they kept looking at the position of the sun. All the Scouts were Charter Mages, of various power – all knew what sundown would bring.

In fifteen minutes, they'd made a hole two blocks wide and two deep in one end, and the sickness was growing worse. Two of the younger Scouts, men in their early twenties, had become violently sick and were recuperating further down the hill. The others were working more slowly, their energies directed to keeping lunches down and quelling shaking limbs.

Surprisingly, given their lack of sleep and generally rundown state, Sabriel and Touchstone found it relatively easy to resist the waves of nausea emanating from the cairn. It didn't compare with the cold, dark fear of the reservoir, there on the hill, with the sunshine and the fresh breeze, warming and cooling at the same time.

When the third blocks came out, Horyse called a brief rest break, and they all retreated down the hill to the tree line, where the cairn's sickening aura dissipated. The signallers had a telephone there, the handset sitting on the upturned drum. Horyse took it, but turned to Sabriel before the signaller wound the charging handle.

"Are there any preparations to be made before we remove the last blocks? Magical ones, I mean."

Sabriel thought for a moment, willing her tiredness away, then shook her head. "I don't think so. Once we have access to the sarcophagus, we may have to spell it open – I'll need everyone's help for that. Then, the final rites on the body – the usual cremation spell. There will be resistance then, too. Have your men often cast Charter Magic in concert?"

"Unfortunately, no," replied Horyse, frowning. "Because the Army doesn't officially admit the existence of Charter Magic, everyone here is basically self-taught."

"Never mind," Sabriel said, trying to sound confident, aware that everyone around her was listening. "We'll manage."

"Good," replied Horyse, smiling. That made him look very confident, thought Sabriel. She tried to smile too, but was uncertain about the result. It felt too much like a grimace of pain.

"Well, let's see where our uninvited guest has got to," Horyse continued, still smiling. "Where does this phone connect to, Sergeant?"

"Bain Police," replied the Signals Sergeant, winding the charging handle vigorously. "And Army HQ North, sir. You'll have to ask Corporal Synge to switch you. He's on the board at the village."

"Good," replied Horyse. "Hello. Oh, Synge? Put me through to Bain. No, tell North you can't get through to me. Yes, that's right, Corporal. Thank you... ah... Bainshire Constabulary? It's Colonel Horyse. I want to speak to Chief Superintendent Dingley... yes. Hello, Superintendent. Have you had any reports of a strange, dense fog... what! Already! No, on no account investigate. Get everyone in. Shutter the windows... yes, the usual drill. Yes, whatever is in... Yes, extraordinarily dangerous... hello! Hello!"

He put the handset down slowly and pointed back up the hill.

"The fog is already moving through the northern part of Bain. It must be going much faster. Is it possible that this Kerrigor could know what we're up to?"

"Yes," replied Sabriel and Touchstone, together.

"We'd better get a move on then," Horyse announced, looking at his watch. "I'd say we now have less than forty minutes."

chapter twenty-seven

The last blocks came away slowly, pulled out by sweating, white-faced men, their hands and legs shivering, breath ragged. As soon as the way was clear, they staggered back, away from the cairn, seeking patches of sunlight to combat the dreadful chill that seemed to eat at their bones. One soldier, a dapper man with a white-blond moustache, fell down the hill and lay retching, till stretcher-bearers ran up to take him away.

Sabriel looked at the dark hole in the cairn and saw the faint, unsettling sheen from the bronze sarcophagus within. She felt sick too, with the hair on the back of her neck frizzing up, skin crawling. The air seemed thick with the reek of Free Magic, a hard, metallic taste in her mouth.

"We will have to spell it open," she announced, with a sinking heart. "The sarcophagus is very strongly protected. I think... the best thing would be if I go in with Touchstone taking my hand, Horyse his, and so on, to form a line reinforcement of the Charter Magic. Does everyone know the Charter marks for the opening spell?"

The soldiers nodded or said, "Yes, ma'am." One said, "Yes, Abhorsen."

Sabriel looked at him. A middle-aged corporal, with the chevrons of long service on his sleeve. He seemed one of the least-affected by the Free Magic.

"You can call me Sabriel, if you want," she said, strangely unsettled by what he had called her.

The corporal shook his head. "No, Miss. I knew your dad. You're just like him. The Abhorsen, now. You'll make this Dead bugger – begging your pardon – wish he'd stayed properly bloody dead."

"Thank you," Sabriel replied, uncertainly. She knew the corporal didn't have the Sight – you could always tell – but his belief in her was so concrete...

"He's right," said Touchstone. He gestured for her to go in front of him, making a courtly bow. "Let's finish what we came to do, Abhorsen."

Sabriel bowed back, in a motion that had almost the feel of ritual about it. The Abhorsen bowing to the King. Then she took a deep breath, her face settling into a determined mould. Beginning to form the Charter marks of opening in her mind, she took Touchstone's hand and advanced towards the open cairn, its dark, shadowy interior in stark contrast with the sunlit thistles and the tumbled stones. Behind her, Touchstone half-turned to take Horyse's callused hand as well, the Colonel's other hand already gripping Lieutenant Aire's, Aire gripping a Sergeant's, the Sergeant the long-service Corporal's, and so on down the hillside. Fourteen Charter Mages in all, if only two of the first rank.

Sabriel felt the Charter Magic welling up the line, the marks glowing brighter and brighter in her mind, till she almost lost her normal vision in their brilliance. She shuffled forwards into the cairn, each step bringing that all-too familiar nausea, the pins and needles, uncontrollable shaking. But the marks were strong in her mind, stronger than the sickness.

She reached the bronze sarcophagus, slapped her hand down and let the Charter Magic go. Instantly, there was an explosion of light and a terrible scream echoed all through the cairn. The bronze grew hot and Sabriel snatched back her hand, the palm red and blistered. A second later, steam billowed out all around the sarcophagus, great gouts of scalding steam, forcing Sabriel out, the whole line going down like dominoes, tumbling out of the cairn and down the hill.

Sabriel and Touchstone were thrown together, about five yards down from the entrance to the cairn. Somehow, Sabriel's head had landed on Touchstone's stomach. His head was on a thistle, but both of them lay still for a moment, drained by the magic and the strength of the Free Magic defences. They looked up at the blue sky, already tinged with the red of the impending sunset. Around them there was much swearing and cursing, as the soldiers picked themselves up.

"It didn't open," Sabriel said, in a quiet, matter-of-fact voice. "We don't have the power or the skill—"

She paused and then added, "I wish Mogget wasn't... I wish he was here. He'd think of something..."

Touchstone was silent, then he said, "We need more Charter Mages – it would work if the marks were reinforced enough."

"More Charter Mages," Sabriel said tiredly. "We're on the wrong side of the Wall..."

"What about your school?" asked Touchstone and then "Ow!" as Sabriel suddenly shot up, disrupting his balance, then "Ow!" again as she bent down and kissed him, pushing his head further into the thistle.

"Touchstone! I should have thought... the Senior magic classes. There must be thirty-five girls with the Charter mark and the basic skills."

"Good," muttered Touchstone, from the depths of the thistle. Sabriel put out her hands and helped him up, smelling the sweat on him, and the fresh, pungent odour of crushed thistles. He was halfway up when she suddenly seemed to lose her enthusiasm and he almost fell back down again.

"The girls are there," said Sabriel slowly, as if thinking aloud. "But have I any right to involve them in something that..."

"They're involved anyway," interrupted Touchstone. "The only reason that Ancelstierre isn't like the Old Kingdom is the Wall, and it won't last once Kerrigor breaks the remaining Stones."

"They're only schoolchildren," Sabriel said sadly. "For all we always thought we were grown women."

"We need them," said Touchstone again.

"Yes," said Sabriel, turning back towards the knot of men gathered as close as they dared to the cairn. Horyse, and some of the stronger Charter Mages, peering back towards the entrance and the shimmering bronze within.

"The spell failed," Sabriel said. "But Touchstone has just reminded me where we can get more Charter Mages."

Horyse looked at her, urgency in his face. "Where?"

"Wyverley College. My old school. The Fifth and Sixth Form Magic classes, and their teacher, Magistrix Greenwood. It's less than a mile away."

"I don't think we've got time to get a message there and get them over here," Horyse began, looking up at the setting sun, then at his watch – which was now going backwards. He looked puzzled for a moment, then ignored it. "But... do you think it would be possible to move the sarcophagus?"

Sabriel thought about the protective spell that she'd encountered, then answered. "Yes. Most of the wards were on the cairn, for concealment. There's nothing to stop us moving the sarcophagus, save the side-effects of the Free Magic. If we can stand the sickness, we can shift it—"

"And Wyverley College – it's an old, solid building?"

"More like a castle than anything," replied Sabriel, seeing the way he was thinking. "Easier to defend than this hill."

"Running water... No? That would be too much to hope for. Right! Private Macking, run down to Major Tindall and tell him that I want his company ready to move in two minutes. We're going back to the trucks, then on to Wyverley College – it's on the map, about a mile..."

"South-west," Sabriel provided.

"South-west. Repeat that back."

Private Macking repeated the message in a slow drawl, then ran off, clearly keen to get away from the cairn. Horyse turned to the long-service corporal and said, "Corporal Anshey. You look pretty fit. Do you think you could get a rope around that coffin?"

"Reckon so, sir," replied Corporal Anshey. He detached a coil of rope from his webbing as he spoke and gestured with his hand to the other soldiers. "Come on, you blokes, get yer ropes out."

Twenty minutes later, the sarcophagus was being lifted by shear-legs and rope aboard a horse-drawn wagon, appropriated from a local farmer. As Sabriel had expected, dragging it within twenty yards of the trucks stopped their engines, put out electric lights and disrupted the telephone.

Curiously, the horse, a placid old mare, didn't seem overly frightened by the gleaming sarcophagus, despite its bronze surface sluggishly crawling with stomach-churning perversions of Charter marks. She wasn't a happy horse, but not a panicked one either.

"We'll have to drive the wagon," Sabriel said to Touchstone, as the soldiers pushed the suspended coffin aboard with long poles and collapsed the shear-legs. "I don't think the Scouts can withstand the sickness much longer."

Touchstone shuddered. Like everyone else, he was pale, eyes red-rimmed, his nose dripping and teeth chattering. "I'm not sure I can, either."

Nevertheless, when the last rope was twitched off, and the soldiers hurried away, Touchstone climbed up to the driver's seat and picked up the reins. Sabriel climbed up next to him, suppressing the feeling that her stomach was about to rise into her mouth. She didn't look back at the sarcophagus.

Touchstone said "tch-tch" to the horse and flicked the reins. The mare's ears went up and she took up the load, pacing forward. It was not a quick pace.

"Is this as fast as..." Sabriel said anxiously. They had a mile to cover and the sun was already bloody, a red disc balanced on the line of the horizon.

"It's a heavy load," Touchstone answered slowly, quick breaths coming between his words, as if he found it difficult to speak. "We'll be there before the light goes."

The sarcophagus seemed to buzz and chuckle behind them. Neither of them mentioned that Kerrigor might arrive, fog-wreathed, before the night did. Sabriel found herself looking behind every few seconds, back along the road. This meant catching glimpses of the vilely shifting surface of the coffin, but she couldn't help it. The shadows were lengthening and every time she caught a glimpse of some tree's pale bark, or a whitewashed mile marker, fear twitched in her gut. Was that fog curling down the road?

Wyverley College seemed much further than a mile. The sun was only a three-quarter disc by the time they saw the trucks turn off the road, turning up the bricked drive that led to the wrought-iron gates of Wyverley College. Home, thought Sabriel for a moment. But that was no longer true. It had been home for the better part of her life, but that was past. It was the home of her childhood, when she was only Sabriel. Now, she was also Abhorsen. Now, her home lay in the Old Kingdom, as did her responsibilities. But like her, these travelled.

Electric lights burned brightly in the two antique glass

lanterns on either side of the gate, but they dimmed to mere sparks as the wagon and its strange cargo drove through. One of the gates was off its hinges and Sabriel realised the soldiers must have forced their way through. It was unusual for the gates to be locked before full dark. They must have closed them when they heard the bells, Sabriel realised, and that alerted her to something else...

"The bell in the village," she exclaimed, as the wagon passed several parked trucks and wheeled around to stop near the huge, gate-like doors to the main building of the school. "The bell – it's stopped."

Touchstone brought the wagon to a halt and listened, cocking an ear towards the darkening sky. True enough, they could no longer hear the Wyverley village bell.

"It is a mile," he said hesitantly. "Perhaps we're too far, the wind..."

"No," said Sabriel. She felt the air, cool with evening, still on her face. There was no wind. "You could always hear it here. Kerrigor has reached the village. We need to get the sarcophagus inside, quickly!"

She jumped down from the wagon and ran over to Horyse, who was standing on the steps outside the partially-open door, talking to an obscured figure within. As Sabriel got closer, edging through groups of waiting soldiers, she recognised the voice. It was Mrs Umbrade, the headmistress.

"How dare you barge in here!" she was pronouncing very pompously. "I am a very close personal friend of Lieutenant-General Farnsley, I'll have you know – Sabriel!"

The sight of Sabriel in such strange garb and circumstance seemed to momentarily stun Mrs Umbrade. In that second of fish-mouthed silence, Horyse motioned to his men. Before Mrs Umbrade could protest, they'd pushed the door wide open and streams of armed men rushed in, pouring around her startled figure like a flood around an island.

"Mrs Umbrade!" Sabriel shouted. "I need to talk to Mrs Greenwood urgently, and the girls from the Senior Magic classes. You'd better get the rest of the girls and the staff up to the top floors of the North Tower."

Mrs Umbrade stood, gulping like a goldfish, till Horyse suddenly loomed over her and snapped, "Move, woman!"

Almost before his mouth closed, she was gone. Sabriel looked back to check that Touchstone was organising the shifting of the sarcophagus, then followed her in.

The entrance hall was already blocked by a conga line of soldiers, passing boxes in from the trucks outside, stacking them up all along the walls. Khaki-coloured boxes marked ".303 Ball" or "B2E2 WP Grenade," piled up beneath pictures of prize-winning hockey teams or gilt-lettered boards of merit and scholastic brilliance. The soldiers had also thrown open the doors to the Great Hall and were busy in there, closing shutters and piling pews up on their ends against the shuttered windows.

Mrs Umbrade was still in motion at the other end of the entrance hall, bustling along towards a knot of obviously nervous staff. Behind them, peering down from the main stair, was a solid rank of prefects. Behind them, higher up the stair, and just able to see, were several gaggles of non-prefectorial fifth and sixth formers. Sabriel didn't doubt that the rest of the school would be lining the corridors behind them, all agog to hear what the commotion was all about.

Just as Mrs Umbrade reached her staff, all the lights went out. For a moment, there was total, shocked quiet, then the noise redoubled. Girls screaming, soldiers shouting, crashes and bangs as people ran into things and each other.

Sabriel stood where she was and conjured the Charter marks for light. They came easily, flowing down to her fingertips like cool water from a shower. She let them hang there for a moment, then cast them at the ceiling, drops of light that grew to the size of dinner plates and cast a steady yellow light all down the hall. Someone else was also casting similar lights down by Mrs Umbrade and Sabriel recognised the work of Magistrix Greenwood. She smiled at that recognition, a slight upturning of just one side of her mouth. She knew the lights had gone out because Kerrigor had passed the electric sub-station, and that was halfway between the school and the village.

As expected, Mrs Umbrade wasn't telling her teachers anything useful – just going on about rudeness and some General. Sabriel saw the Magistrix behind the tall but bent figure of the Senior Science Mistress, and waved.

"And I was never more shocked to see one of our—" Mrs Umbrade was saying, when Sabriel stepped up next to her and gently laid the marks of silence and immobility on the back of her neck.

"I'm sorry to interrupt," Sabriel said, standing next to the temporarily frozen form of the Headmistress. "But this is an emergency. As you can see, the Army is temporarily taking over. I am assisting Colonel Horyse, who is in charge. Now, we need all the girls in the two Senior Magic classes to come down to the Great Hall – with you, Magistrix Greenwood, please. Everyone else – students, staff, gardeners, everyone – must go to the top floors of the North Tower and barricade yourselves in. Till dawn tomorrow."

"Why?" demanded Mrs Pearch, the Mathematics Mistress. "What's all this about?"

"Something has come from the Old Kingdom," Sabriel replied shortly, watching their faces change as she spoke. "We will shortly be attacked by the Dead."

"So there will be danger to my students?" Mistress Greenwood spoke, pushing her way forward, between two frightened English teachers. She looked Sabriel in the face, as if in recognition, and then added, "Abhorsen."

"There will be danger to everyone," Sabriel said bleakly. "But without the aid of the Charter Mages here, there isn't even a chance..."

"Well," replied Mrs Greenwood with some decision. "We'd better get organised then. I'll go and fetch Sulyn and Ellimere. I think they're the only two Charter Mages among the Prefects – they can organise the others. Mrs Pearch, you'd better take charge of the... ah... evacuation to the North Tower, as I imagine Mrs Umbrade will be... err... deep in thought. Mrs Swann, you'd best round up cook and the maids – get some fresh water, food and candles, too. Mr Arkler, if you would be so kind as to fetch the swords from the gymnasium..."

Seeing that all was under control, Sabriel sighed and quickly walked back outside, past soldiers stringing oil lamps up in the corridor. Despite them, it was still lighter outside, the sky washed red and orange with the last sunlight of the day.

Touchstone and the Scouts had the sarcophagus down and roped up. It now seemed to glow with its own ugly inner light, the flickering Free Magic marks floating on the surface like scum or clots in blood. Apart from the Scouts pulling the ropes, no one went close to it. Soldiers were everywhere, coiling out barbed wire, filling sandbags from the rose gardens, preparing firing positions on the second floor, tying trip flares. But in all this commotion, there was an empty circle around the glistening coffin of Rogir.

Sabriel walked towards Touchstone, feeling the reluctance in her legs, her body revolting at the thought of going any closer to the bloody luminescence of the sarcophagus. It seemed to radiate stronger waves of nausea now, now that the sun had almost fled. In the twilight, it looked larger, stronger, its magic more forceful and malign.

"Pull!" shouted Touchstone, heaving on the ropes with the soldiers. "Pull!"

Slowly, the sarcophagus slid across the old paving stones, inching towards the front steps, where other soldiers were hastily hammering a wooden ramp together, fitting it over the steps.

Sabriel decided to leave Touchstone to it and walked a little way down the drive, to where she could see out of the iron gates.

343

She stood there, watching, her hands nervously running over the handles of the bells. Six bells now – all probably ineffective against the awful might of Kerrigor. And an unfamiliar sword, strange to her touch, even if it was forged by the Wallmaker.

The Wallmaker. That reminded her of Mogget. Who knew what he had been, that strange combination of irascible companion to the Abhorsens and blazing Free Magic construct sworn to kill them. Gone now, swept away by the mournful call of Astarael...

I left this place knowing almost nothing about the Old Kingdom and I've come back with not much more, Sabriel thought. I am the most ignorant Abhorsen in centuries and perhaps one of the most sorely tried...

A clatter of shots interrupted her thoughts, followed by the zing of a rocket arcing up into the sky, its yellow trail reaching down towards the road. More shots followed. A rapid volley – then sudden silence. The rocket burst into a white parachute flare, that slowly descended. In its harsh, magnesium brilliance, Sabriel saw fog rolling up the road, thick and wet, stretching back into the dark as far as she could see.

chapter twenty-eight

Sabriel forced herself to walk back to the main doors, rather than break into a screaming run. Lots of soldiers could see her – they were still placing lanterns out in lines, radiating out from the steps, and several soldiers were holding a coil of concertina wire, waiting to bounce it out. They looked anxiously at her as she passed.

The sarcophagus was just slipping off the ramp into the corridor ahead of her. Sabriel could easily have pushed past it, but she waited outside, looking out. After a moment, she became aware that Horyse was standing next to her, his face half-lit by the lanterns, half in shadow.

"The fog... the fog is almost at the gates," she said, too quickly to be calm.

"I know," replied Horyse steadily. "That firing was a picket. Six men and a corporal."

Sabriel nodded. She had felt their deaths, like slight punches in her stomach. Already she was hardening herself not to notice, to wilfully dull her senses. There would be many more deaths that night.

Suddenly, she felt something that wasn't a death, but things already dead. She stood bolt upright and exclaimed, "Colonel! The sun is truly down – and something's coming, coming ahead of the fog!"

She drew her sword as she spoke, the Colonel's blade flickering out a second later. The wiring party looked around, startled, then bolted for the steps and the corridor. On either side of the door, two-man teams cocked the heavy, tripod-mounted machine-guns and laid their swords across the newly-made sandbag walls.

"Second floor, stand ready!" Horyse shouted, and above her head, Sabriel heard the bolts of fifty rifles working. Out of the corner of her eye, she saw two of the Scouts step back outside and take up position behind her, arrows nocked, bows ready. She knew they were ready to snatch her inside, if it came to that...

In the expectant quiet, there were only the usual sounds of the night. Wind in the big trees out past the school wall, starting to rise as the sky darkened. Crickets beginning to chirp. Then Sabriel heard it – the massed grinding of Dead joints, no longer joined by gristle; the padding of Dead feet, bones like hobnails clicking through necrotic flesh.

"Hands," she said, nervously. "Hundreds of Hands."

Even as she spoke, a solid wall of Dead flesh hit the iron gates, throwing them over in a split second's crash. Then vaguely human forms were everywhere, rushing towards them, Dead mouths gulping and hissing in a ghastly parody of a war cry.

"Fire!"

In the instant's delay after this command, Sabriel felt the terrible fear that the guns wouldn't work. Then rifles cracked and the machine-guns beat out a terrible, barking roar, red tracer rounds flinging out, ricocheting from the paving in a crazy embroidery of terrible violence. Bullets tore Dead flesh, splintered bone, knocked the Hands down and over – but still they came, till they were literally torn apart, broken into pieces, hung up on the wire.

The firing slowed, but before it could entirely cease, another wave of Hands came stumbling, crawling, running through the gateway, slipping, tumbling over the wall. Hundreds of them, so densely packed they crushed the wire and came on, till the last of them were mown down by the guns at the very foot of the front steps. Some, still with a slight vestige of human intelligence, retreated, only to be caught in great gouts of flame from white phosphorus grenades thrown out from the second floor.

"Sabriel – get inside!" Horyse ordered, as the last of the Hands flopped and crawled in crazy circles, till more bullets thudded into them and made them still.

"Yes," replied Sabriel, looking out at the carpet of bodies, the flickering fires from the lanterns and lumps of phosphorus burning like candles in some ghastly charnel house. The stench of cordite was in her nose, through her hair, on her clothes, the machine-guns' barrels glowing an evil red to either side of her. The Hands were already dead, but even so, this mass destruction made her sicker than any Free Magic...

347

She went inside, sheathing her sword. Only then did she remember the bells. Possibly, she could have quelled that vast mob of Hands, sent them peaceably back into Death, without – but it was too late. And what if she had been overmastered?

Shadow Hands would be next, she knew, and they could not be stopped by physical force, or her bells, unless they came in small numbers... and that was as likely as an early dawn...

There were more soldiers in the corridor, but these were mailed and helmed, with large shields and broad-headed spears streaked with silver and the simplest Charter marks, drawn in chalk and spit. They were smoking and drinking tea from the school's second-best china. Sabriel realised they were there to fight when the guns failed. There was an air of controlled nervousness about them – not bravado exactly – just a strange mixture of competence and cynicism. Whatever it was, it made Sabriel walk casually between them, as if she were in no hurry at all.

"Evening, miss."

"Good to hear the guns, hey? Practically never work up north!"

"Won't need us at this rate."

"Not like the Perimeter, is it, ma'am?"

"Good luck with the bloke in the metal cigar case, miss."

"Good luck to all of you," replied Sabriel, trying to smile in answer to their grins. Then the firing started again and she winced, losing the smile – but their attention was off her, focused back outside. They weren't nearly as casual as they pretended, Sabriel thought, as she edged through the side doors leading from the corridor into the Great Hall.

Here, the mood was much more frightened. The sarcophagus was up the far end of the Hall, resting across the speaker's dais. Everyone else was as far away as possible up at the other end. The Scouts were on one side, also drinking tea. Magistrix Greenwood was talking to Touchstone in the middle, and the thirty or so girls – young women, really – were lined up on the opposite wall to the soldiers. It was all rather like a bizarre parody of a school dance.

Behind the thick stone walls and shuttered windows of the Great Hall, the gunfire could almost be mistaken for extremely heavy hail, with grenades for thunderclaps, but not if you knew what it was. Sabriel walked in to the centre of the Hall and shouted.

"Charter Mages! Please come here."

They came, the young women quicker than the soldiers, who were showing the weariness of the day's work and proximity to the sarcophagus. Sabriel looked at the students, their faces bright and open, a thin layer of fear laid over excitement at the spice of the unknown. Two of her best schoolfriends, Sulyn and Ellimere were among the crowd, but she felt far distant from them now. She probably looked it too, she thought, seeing respect and something like wonder in their eyes. Even the Charter marks on their foreheads looked like fragile cosmetic replicas, though she knew they were real. It was so unfair that they had to be caught up in this...

Sabriel opened her mouth to speak and the noise of gunfire suddenly ceased, almost on cue. In the silence, one of the girls giggled nervously. Sabriel, however, suddenly felt many deaths come at once and a familiar dread touched her spine with cold fingers. Kerrigor was closing in. It was his power that had stilled the guns, not a lessening of the assault. Faintly, she could hear shouts and even... screams... from outside. They would be fighting with older weapons now.

"Quickly," she said, walking towards the sarcophagus as she spoke. "We must make a handfast ring around the sarcophagus. Magistrix, if you would place everyone – Lieutenant, please put your men in among the girls..."

Anywhere else, at any other time, there would have been ribald jokes and giggles about that. Here, with the Dead about the building, and the sarcophagus brooding in their midst, it was simply an instruction. Men moved quickly to their places, the young women took their hands purposefully. In a few seconds, the sarcophagus was ringed by Charter Mages.

Linked by touch now, Sabriel didn't need to speak. She could feel everyone in the ring. Touchstone to her right, a familiar and powerful warmth. Mrs Greenwood to her left, less powerful, but not without skill – and so on, right around the ring.

Slowly, Sabriel brought the Charter marks of opening to the forefront of her mind. The marks grew, power flowing round and round the ring, growing in force till it started to project inwards, like the narrowing vortex of a whirlpool. Golden light began to stream about the sarcophagus, visible streaks rotating clockwise around it, with greater and greater speed.

Still Sabriel kept the power of the Charter Magic flowing in to the centre, drawing on everything the Charter Mages could produce. Soldiers and schoolgirls wavered, and some fell to their knees, but the hands stayed linked, the circle complete.

Slowly, the sarcophagus itself began turning on the platform, with a hideous shrieking noise, like an enormous unoiled hinge. Steam jetted forth from under its lid, but the golden light whisked it away. Still shrieking, the sarcophagus began to spin faster and faster, till it was a blur of bronze, white steam and yolk-yellow light. Then, with a scream more piercing than any before, it suddenly stopped, the lid flying off to hurtle over the Charter Mages' heads, smashing into the floor a good thirty paces away.

The Charter Magic went too, as if earthed by its success, and the ring collapsed with fewer than half the participants still on their feet.

Wavering, her hands still tightly gripped by Touchstone and the Magistrix, Sabriel tottered over to the sarcophagus and looked in.

"Why," said Mrs Greenwood, with a startled glance back up at Touchstone. "He looks just like you!"

Before Touchstone could answer, steel clashed outside in the corridor and the shouting grew louder. Those Scouts still standing drew their swords and rushed to the doors – but before they could reach them, other soldiers were pouring in, bloodied, terrified soldiers, who ran to the corners, or threw themselves down, and sobbed, or laughed, or shook in silence.

Behind this rush came some of the heavily-armoured soldiery of the corridor. These men still had some semblance of control. Instead of running on, they hurled themselves back against the doors and dropped the bar in place.

"He's inside the main doors!" one of them shouted back towards Sabriel, his face white with terror. There was no doubt about who "he" was.

"Quick, the final rites!" Sabriel snapped. She drew her hands from the others' grasp and held them out over the body, forming the marks for fire, cleansing and peace in her mind. She didn't look too closely at the body. Rogir did look very much like a sleeping, defenceless Touchstone.

She was tired and there were still Free Magic protections around the body, but the first mark soon lingered in the air. Touchstone had transferred his hand to her shoulder, pouring power into her. Others of the circle had crept up and linked hands again – and suddenly Sabriel felt a stirring of relief. They were going to make it – Kerrigor's human body would be destroyed and the greater part of his power with it...

Then the whole of the northern wall exploded, bricks cascading out, red dust blowing in like a solid wave, knocking everyone down in blinding, choking ruin.

Sabriel lay on the floor, coughing, hands pushing feebly on the floor, knees scrabbling as she tried to get up. There was dust and grit in her eyes, and the lanterns had all gone out. Blind, she felt around her, but there was only the still-scalding bronze of the sarcophagus.

"The blood price must be paid," said a crackling, inhuman voice. A familiar voice, though not the liquid, ruined tones of Kerrigor... but the terrible speech of the night in Holehallow, when the Paperwing burned.

Blinking furiously, Sabriel crawled away from the sound,

around the sarcophagus. It didn't speak again immediately, but she could hear it closing in, the air crackling and buzzing at its passage.

"I must deliver my last burden," the creature said. "Then the bargain is done and I may turn to retribution."

Sabriel blinked again, tears streaming down her face. Vision slowly came back, a picture woven with tears and the first rays of moonlight streaming through the shattered wall, a picture blurred with the red dust of pulverised bricks.

All Sabriel's senses were screaming inside her. Free Magic, the Dead, danger all around...

The creature that had once been Mogget blazed a little more than five yards away. It was squatter than it had appeared previously, but equally misshapen, a lumpy body slowly drifting towards her atop a column of twisting, whirling energies.

A soldier suddenly leapt up behind it, driving a sword deep into its back. It hardly noticed, but the man screamed and burst into white flames. Within a second, he was consumed, his sword a molten lump of metal, scorching the thick oak planks of the floor.

"I bring you Abhorsen's sword," the creature said, dropping a long, dimly-seen object to one side. "And the bell called Astarael."

That, it laid carefully down, the silver glinting momentarily before it was lowered into the sea of dust.

"Come forward, Abhorsen. It is long since time that we begun."

The thing laughed then, a sound like a match igniting, and it started to move around the sarcophagus. Sabriel loosened the ring on her finger and edged away, keeping the sarcophagus between them, her thoughts racing. Kerrigor was very near, but there still might be time to turn this creature back into Mogget and complete the final rites...

"Stop!"

The word was like a foul lick across the face by a reptilian tongue, but there was power behind it. Sabriel stood still, against her own desire, as did the blazing thing. Sabriel tried looking past it, lidding her eyes against the light, trying to puzzle out what was happening at the other end of the Hall. Not that she really needed to see.

It was Kerrigor. The soldiers who'd barred the door lay dead around him, pale flesh islands about a sea of darkness. He had no shape now, but there were semi-human features in the great ink-splash of his presence. Eyes of white fire and a yawning mouth that was lined with flickering coals of a red as dark as drying blood.

"Abhorsen is mine," croaked Kerrigor, his voice deep and somehow liquid, as if his words came bubbling out like lava mixed with spittle. "You will leave her to me."

The Mogget-thing crackled and moved again, white sparks falling like tiny stars in its wake.

"I have waited too long to allow my revenge to be taken by another!" it hissed, ending on a high-pitched yowl that still had something of the cat. Then it flew at Kerrigor, a shining electric comet hurtling into the darkness of his body, smashing into his shadowy substance like a hammer tenderising meat.

For a moment, no one moved, shocked by the suddenness of the attack. Then, Kerrigor's dark shape slowly recongealed, long tendrils of bitter night wrapping around his brilliant attacker, choking and absorbing it with the implacable voracity of an octopus strangling a bright-shelled turtle.

Desperately, Sabriel looked around for Touchstone and Magistrix Greenwood. Brick dust was still falling slowly through the moonlit air, like some deadly rust-coloured gas, the bodies lying around seemingly victims of its choking poison. But they had been struck by bricks or wooden splinters from the smashing of the pews.

Sabriel saw the Magistrix first, lying a little away, curled up on her side. Anyone else might have thought her merely unconscious, but Sabriel knew she was dead. Struck by a long, stiletto-like splinter from a shattered pew, the iron-hard wood had driven right through her.

She knew Touchstone was alive – and there he was, propped up against a pile of broken masonry. His eyes reflected the moonlight.

Sabriel walked over to him, stepping between the bodies and the rubble, the patches of freshly-spilled blood and the silent, hopeless wounded.

"My leg is broken," Touchstone said, his mouth showing the pain of it. He tilted his head towards the gaping hole in the wall. "Run, Sabriel. While he's busy. Run south. Live a normal life..."

"I can't," replied Sabriel softly. "I am the Abhorsen. Besides, how could you run with me, you with your broken leg?"

"Sabriel…"

But Sabriel had already turned away. She picked up Astarael, practised hands keeping it still. But there was no need, for the bell was choked with brick dust, its voice silent. It would not ring true until cleaned, with patience, magic and steady nerves. Sabriel stared at it for a second, then gently placed it back down on the floor.

Her father's sword was only a few paces further away. She picked it up and watched the Charter marks flow along the blade. This time, they didn't run through the normal inscription, but said: "The Clayr saw me, the Wallmaker made me, the King quenched me, the Abhorsen wields me so that no Dead shall walk in Life. For this is not their path."

"This is not their path," whispered Sabriel. She took up the guard position and looked down the Hall to the writhing hulk of darkness that was Kerrigor.

chapter twenty-nine

Kerrigor seemed to have finished with the Free Magic thing that had once been Mogget. His great cloud of darkness was complete again, with no sign of white fire, no dazzling brilliance fighting away within.

He was remarkably still and Sabriel had a moment's brief hope that he was somehow wounded. Then the awful realisation came. Kerrigor was digesting, like a glutton after an overly ambitious meal.

Sabriel shuddered at the thought, bile tainting her mouth. Not that her end was likely to be better. Both she and Touchstone would be taken alive, and kept that way, till they pumped out their life's blood, throats yawning, down in the dark of the reservoir...

She shook her head, dispelling that image. There had to be something... Kerrigor had to be weaker, so far from the Old Kingdom... perhaps weakened more than her Charter Magic. She doubted that a single bell could sway him, but two, in concert?

It was dark in the Hall, save for the moonlight falling through the shattered wall behind her. And quiet. Even the wounded were slipping away in silence, their cries muted, last wishes whispered. They kept their agony close, as if a scream might attract the wrong attention. There were things worse than death in the Hall...

Even in darkness, the form of Kerrigor was darker still. Sabriel watched him carefully, undoing the straps that held Saraneth and Kibeth with her left hand. She sensed other Dead all around, but none entered the Hall. There were still men to fight or feast upon. What went on in the Hall was their Master's business.

The straps came undone. Kerrigor didn't move, his burning eyes closed, his fiery mouth shut.

In one quick motion, Sabriel sheathed her sword and drew the bells.

Kerrigor did move then. Swiftly, his dark bulk bounding forward, halving the gap between them. He grew taller too, stretching upwards till he almost reached the vaulted ceiling. His eyes opened to full, raging, flaming fury, and he spoke.

"Toys, Abhorsen. And too late. Much too late."

It was not just words he spoke, but power, Free Magic power that froze Sabriel's nerves, caught at her muscles. Desperately, she struggled to ring the bells, but her wrists were locked in place...

Tantalisingly slowly, Kerrigor glided forward, till he was a mere arm's length away, towering over her like some colossal statue of rough-hewn night, his breath rolling down on her with the stench of a thousand abattoirs.

Someone – a girl quietly coughing out her last breath on the floor – touched Sabriel's ankle with a light caress. A small spark of golden Charter Magic came from that dying touch, slowly swelling into Sabriel's veins, travelling upwards, warming joints, freeing muscles. At last it reached her wrists and hands – and the bells rang out.

It was not the clear, true sound it should be, for somehow the bulk of Kerrigor took the sound in and warped it – but it had an effect. Kerrigor slid back and was diminished, till he was little more than twice Sabriel's height.

But he was not subject to Sabriel's will. Saraneth had not bound him and Kibeth had only forced him back.

Sabriel rang the bells again, concentrating on the difficult counterpoint between them, forcing all her will into their magic. Kerrigor would fall under her domination, he would walk where she willed...

And for a second, he did. Not into Death, for she lacked the power, but into his original body, inside the broken sarcophagus. Even as the chime of the bells faded, Kerrigor changed. Fiery eyes and mouth ran into each other like molten wax and his shadow-stuff folded into a narrow column of smoke, roaring up into the ceiling. It hovered among the rafters for a moment, then descended with a hideous scream, straight into the Rogir-body's open mouth.

With that scream, Saraneth and Kibeth cracked, shards of silver falling like broken stars, crashing to the earth. Mahogany handles turned to dust, drifting through Sabriel's fingers like smoke.

Sabriel stared at her empty hands for a second, still feeling the harsh imprint of bell-handles... then, without any conscious thought, there was a sword hilt in her hand as she advanced upon the sarcophagus. But before she could see into it, Rogir stood up and looked at her – looked with the burning fire-pit eyes of Kerrigor.

"An inconvenience," he said, with a voice that was only marginally more human. "I should have remembered you were a troublesome brat."

Sabriel lunged at him, sword blowing white sparks as it struck, punching through his chest to project out the other side. But Kerrigor only laughed and reached down till he held the blade with both hands, knuckles pallid against the silver-sparking steel. Sabriel tugged at the sword, but it would not come free.

"No sword can harm me," Kerrigor said, with a giggle like a dying man's cough. "Not even one made by the Wallmakers. Especially not now, when I have finally assumed the last of their powers. Power that ruled before the Charter, power that made the Wall. I have it now. I have that broken puppet, my half-brother – and I have you, my Abhorsen. Power and blood – blood for the breaking!"

He reached out and pulled the sword further into his chest, till the hilt was lodged against his skin. Sabriel tried to let go, but he was too quick, one chill hand clutching her forearm. Irresistibly, Kerrigor drew her towards him.

"Will you sleep, unknowing, till the Great Stones are ready for your blood?" whispered Kerrigor, his breath still reeking of carrion. "Or will you go waking, every step of the way?"

Sabriel stared back, meeting his gaze for the first time. Surely, there in the hellfire of his eyes, she could see the faintest spark of blazing white? She unclenched her left fist and felt the silver ring slip down her finger. Was it expanding?

"What would you have, Abhorsen?" continued Kerrigor, his mouth peeling back, skin already breaking at the corners, the spirit within corroding even this magically-preserved flesh. "Your lover crawls towards us – a pathetic sight – but I shall have the next kiss..."

The ring was hanging in Sabriel's hand, hidden behind her back. It had grown larger – but she could still feel the metal expanding...

Kerrigor's blistered lips moved towards hers and still the ring moved in her hand. His breath was overpowering, reeking of blood, but she had long gone beyond throwing up. She turned her head aside at the last second and felt dry, corpse-like flesh slide across her cheek.

"A sisterly kiss," chuckled Kerrigor. "A kiss for an uncle who has known you since birth – or slightly before – but it is not enough..."

Again, his words were not just words. Sabriel felt a force grip her head and move it back to face him, while her mouth was wedged apart, as if in passionate expectation.

But her left arm was free.

Kerrigor's head bent forward, his face looming larger and larger – then silver flashed between them and the ring was around his neck.

Sabriel felt the compulsion snap off and she leant back, trying to hurl herself away. But Kerrigor didn't let go of her arm.

He seemed surprised, but not anxious. His right hand went up to touch the band, fingernails falling as he did so, bone already pushing through at the fingertips.

"What is this? Some relic of..."

The ring constricted, cutting through the pulpy flesh of his neck, revealing the solid darkness within. That too was compressed, forced inwards, pulsating as it tried to escape. Two flaming eyes looked down in disbelief.

"Impossible," croaked Kerrigor. Snarling, he pushed Sabriel away, throwing her to the floor. In the same motion he drew the sword from his chest, the blade slowly coming free with a sound like a rasp on hardwood.

Swiftly as a snake, arm and sword went out, striking through Sabriel, through armour and flesh and deep into the wooden floor beyond. Pain exploded and Sabriel screamed, body convulsing around the blade in one awful reflexive curve.

Kerrigor left her there, impaled like a bug in a collection, and advanced upon Touchstone. Sabriel, through eyes fogged with pain, saw Kerrigor look down and rip a long, jagged splinter from one of the pews.

"Rogir," Touchstone said. "Rogir..."

The splinter came down with a strangled shriek of rage. Sabriel closed her eyes and looked away, slipping into a world of her own, a world of pain. She knew she should do something about the blood pouring out of her stomach, but now – with Touchstone dead – she just lay where she was and let it bleed.

Then Sabriel realised she hadn't felt Touchstone die.

She looked again. The splinter had broken on his armoured

coat. Kerrigor was reaching out for another splinter – but the silver ring had slipped down to his shoulders now, shredding the flesh away as it fell, like an apple corer punching the Dead spirit out of the rotting corpse.

Kerrigor struggled and shrieked, but the ring bound his arms. Capering madly, he threw himself from side to side, seeking to cast off the silver band that held him – only causing yet more flesh to fall away, till no flesh remained, nothing but a raging column of darkness, constrained by a silver ring.

Then the column collapsed upon itself like a demolished building, to become a mound of rippling shadow, the silver ring shining like a ribbon. A gleaming red eye shone amid the silver – but that was only the ruby, grown to match the metal.

There were Charter marks on the ring again, but Sabriel couldn't read them. Her eyes wouldn't focus and it was too dark. The moonlight seemed to have gone. Still, she knew what must be done. Saraneth – her hand crept to the bandoleer, but the sixth bell wasn't there – or the seventh, or the third. Careless of me, thought Sabriel, careless – but I must complete the binding. Her hand fell on Belgaer for a moment and almost drew it – but no, that would be release... Finally, she drew Ranna, whimpering with the pain of even that small movement.

Ranna was unusually heavy, for so slight a bell. Sabriel rested it against her chest for a moment, gathering strength. Then, lying on her back, transfixed with her own sword, she rang the bell.

Ranna sounded sweet and felt comforting, like a long-expected bed. The sound echoed through the Hall and out, to where a few men still battled with the Dead. All who heard it ceased their struggles and lay themselves down. The badly wounded slipped easily into Death, joining the Dead who had followed Kerrigor; those less hurt fell into a healing sleep.

The mound of darkness that had been Kerrigor split into two distinct hemispheres, bounded by an equatorial ring of silver. One hemisphere was as black as coal; the other a gleaming white. Gradually, they melted into two distinct forms – two cats, joined at the throat like Siamese twins. Then the silver ring split in two, a ring around each neck, and the cats separated. The rings lost their brilliance, slowly changing colour and texture till they were red leather bands, each supporting a miniature bell, a miniature Ranna.

Two small cats sat side by side. One black, one white. Both leaned forward, throats moving, and each spat up a silver ring. The cats yawned as the rings rolled towards Sabriel, then curled up and went to sleep.

Touchstone watched the rings roll through the dust, silver flashing in the moonlight. They hit Sabriel's side, but she didn't pick them up. Both her hands still clutched Ranna, but it was silent, resting below her breasts. Her sword loomed above her, blade and hilt casting the moonshadow of a cross upon her face.

Something from his childhood memory flashed through Touchstone's mind. A voice, a messenger's voice, speaking to his mother.

"Highness, we bring sorrowful tidings. The Abhorsen is dead."

epilogue

Death seemed colder than ever before, Sabriel thought, and wondered why, till she realised she was still lying down. In the water, being carried along by the current. For a moment, she started to struggle, then she relaxed.

"Everyone and everything has a time to die..." she whispered. The living world and its cares seemed far away. Touchstone lived and that made her glad, inasmuch as she could feel anything. Kerrigor was defeated, imprisoned if not made truly dead. Her work was done. Soon she would pass beyond the Ninth Gate and rest for ever...

Something grabbed her arms and legs, picked her up out of the water and set her down on her feet.

"This is not your time," said a voice, a voice echoed by half a hundred others.

Sabriel blinked, for there were many shining human shapes around her, hovering above the water. More than she could count. Not Dead spirits, but something else, like the mother-sending called by the paper boat. Their shapes were vague, but instantly recognisable, for all wore the deep blue with the silver keys. Every one was an Abhorsen.

"Go back," they chorused. "Go back."

"I can't," sobbed Sabriel. "I'm dead! I haven't the strength..."

"You are the last Abhorsen," the voices whispered, the shining shapes closing in. "You cannot pass this way until there is another. You do have the strength within you. Live, Abhorsen, live..."

Suddenly, she did have the strength. Enough to crawl, wade and fall back up the river, and gingerly edge back into Life, her shining escort dropping back at the very last. One of them – perhaps her father – lightly touched her hand in the instant before she left the realm of Death behind.

A face swam into view – Touchstone's, staring down at her. Sound hit her ears, distant, raucous bells that seemed out of place, till she realised they were ambulance bells, ambulances racing in from the town. She could sense no Dead at all, nor feel any great magic, Free or Charter. But then, Kerrigor was gone and they were nearly forty miles from the Wall...

"Live, Sabriel, live," Touchstone was muttering, holding her icy hands, his own eyes so clouded with tears he hadn't noticed hers opening. Sabriel smiled, then grimaced as the pain came back. She looked from side to side, wondering how long it would take Touchstone to realise.

The electric lights had come back on in parts of the Hall and soldiers were placing lanterns out again. There were more survivors than she'd expected, tending to the wounded, propping up dangerous brickwork, even sweeping up the brick-dust and grave-mould.

There were also many dead and Sabriel sighed as she let her senses roam. Colonel Horyse, killed outside on the steps; Magistrix Greenwood; her innocent schoolfriend Ellimere; six other girls; at least half the soldiers...

Her eyes wandered to closer regions, to the two sleeping cats, the two silver rings next to her on the floor.

"Sabriel!"

Touchstone had finally noticed. Sabriel turned her gaze back to him and lifted her head cautiously. He'd removed her sword, she saw, and several of her schoolfriends had cast a healing spell, good enough for the moment. Typically, Touchstone had done nothing for his own leg.

"Sabriel," he said again. "You're alive!"

"Yes," said Sabriel, with some surprise. "I am."

coming in 2003

Lirael

GARTH NIX

The sequel to the critically acclaimed Sabriel.

Venture further into the magical landscape of the Old
Kingdom for a spellbinding tale of discovery, destiny
and danger...

 Collins

An imprint of HarperCollinsPublishers